STAR CROSSED

MARILYNN BYERLY

Hard Shell Word Factory

ISBN: 0-7599-0100-7
Ebook ISBN: 1-58200-567-2
Published March 2001
Electronic edition published February 2000

Hard Shell Word Factory
PO Box 161
Amherst Jct. WI 54407
books@hardshell.com
http://www.hardshell.com

Chapter 1

"Picking the right star to wish on?"

Tristan Mallory jolted in his chair at Kellen's voice. He blinked, seeing again the moving starfield on the forward viewing screen. Kellen Votrain sauntered through the hatch onto the tiny bridge and plopped down in the chair beside him at the ship's command console.

"Or is it star intoxication?" Kellen handed him his beer.

"A bit of both." Tristan pulled the tab and waited a moment for the can to cool its contents then sipped.

Kellen grinned and leaned back, propping his heels on the top of the console. He raised his beer can. "To both."

"To both." Tristan sipped again.

"Picked out your star? Must have the perfect one if you want your wish to come true."

"Not the binaries. Fickle wishing stars binaries. How about that one?" He pointed at the luminous yellow star at the left bottom corner of the screen.

"Good choice. Trigellan. Like Poppa Sol himself. Earth colony on the third planet."

"Arden."

"Beautiful diseased Arden." Kellen's green eyes glimmered with seriousness as he examined Tristan's face, then he turned back to the starfield. "And your wish?"

Tristan shrugged.

Kellen rephrased his question. "What's wrong, Tris?"

"I'm not sure. Boredom. Emptiness when I should feel complete."

"Life as a megamind scientist isn't to your liking then?"

"Yes, and..."

"No. Remember how it was with us after graduate school. Let's do that again. I'll plot a course away from that bloody dull conference, and you and I will sneak out of the known galaxy. We'll find the planets, you can figure out what makes them tick, and I'll figure out how to communicate with the local version of people. It's not as much fun playing Columbus without you along. And we haven't named a system after you yet."

"And probably never will."

"Is it my fault women have a weakness for me?"

Tristan mimicked, "Oh my dear, you're so beautiful. I'll name a star system after you." He snorted. "God, what a line."

"It works." Kellen jerked upright. "What the..."

Warning strobes flashed on the control console. Kellen fingered the controls with the skill of a concert pianist.

Tristan leaned forward in disbelief. "Another ship on collision course out in the middle of nowhere?"

Their ship bucked. Kellen's can sailed off the console, a tail of beer following it. Kellen swore and also stated the obvious. "They're shooting at us." He punched the communication switch. "This is *The Helen of Troy, The Helen of Troy.* We're not hostile. Repeat, not hostile. Hold your fire."

The ship shuddered as another force bolt hit.

Their eyes met, all questions and answers settled in a moment. Tristan grabbed the controls as Kellen charged toward the weapons bubble beneath the bridge. Tristan began evasive action, intending to get the hell away from the larger ship, a heavily armed fighter by the size of it.

A force bolt shimmered across their hull; the ship's structure groaned.

Swearing through his teeth, he dodged the next bolt. The ship's laser buzzed as Kellen shot back.

The Helen reared and bucked with a direct hit. Fire exploded behind him. His fingers touched suddenly stiff controls. All power gone, the ship wallowed then floated sideways like a dead whale caught in a current. Even the ship's weapons were gone.

He glanced back at the holocaust and the automatic fire sprinkler fighting the flames then hit the communications button. "We surrender. This is *The Helen of Troy.* We surrender. Acknowledge."

Not even static answered. Either they weren't replying or couldn't hear him. He shrugged and considered the identity of their enemy. *The Helen* was in a peaceful trading zone in human space. Pirates rather than aliens.

The weapons system screamed with disintegrating metal and buckled.

"Kellen!" He ran toward the weapons bubble and peered down. Acrid smoke flared upward. Flames around him, Kellen sprawled at the base of the ladder.

Some tiny, reasonable part of Tristan's brain told him it was suicide, but he shimmied down the ladder and knelt by his friend. He sought a pulse.

At his touch, Kellen swore violently. "Get the hell back up, you idiot."

Returning the compliment, Tristan threw the other man across his shoulder and began to drag them both up the ladder. That tiny voice told him his hand was scorching on the ladder, but he paid no attention.

The journey up was ten times longer than the journey down. He dumped Kellen onto the floor of the bridge and crawled up beside him.

The ship shuddered again, the wall behind them beginning to bulge. The tiny voice told him to run, but he threw himself over Kellen's body as the propulsion system exploded.

Darkness.

Pain and darkness. He swam up through miles of darkness and pain then opened his eyes. Tears streaming down his smoke-blackened face, Kellen leaned over him. Eerie red emergency lights shimmered in the smoke. He forced his voice up through the darkness between them. "You okay?"

"Nothing major." Kellen blinked tears. "Oh, Tris. You damn fool."

He didn't ask how he was. The terrible pain and his friend's eyes, sea green with grief, told him. He smiled. "Guess I made the wish on the wrong star." His body shuddered.

Kellen's hand found his and held. "You damn fool."

"Love you too, Kell. Only brother my parents didn't have."

"Me too."

"God watch over you." Tristan closed his eyes and stopped fighting the darkness' pull. Images drifted past. His parents, brothers, his sister, and little Peter. He'd never hear his nephew pronounce his name correctly. He smiled at them. They'd be all right. They had each other. Then he saw beautiful, loving Dorian. He pleaded to her image, "Please forgive me for leaving you, too."

Kellen was calling his name, but he drifted deeper in darkness until his friend's voice faded away. Finally, he settled so deep even his tiny voice couldn't be heard.

PATTA stamped her foot with anger then stalked up and down in front of Mara's couch. "You have as little sense as a man."

Mara's eyebrows rose at the childish insult, but she said nothing. She leaned back on the couch and watched her rab-cat dancing and playing with the sunlight motes from the living room oriel window. His long ears waved and fluttered in intricate patterns of thought and emotion.

"Are you listening to me, Mara?"

"Yes, I am." She forced her eyes back to her friend.

Patta plopped down beside her and smoothed her long fashionably curly black hair. "I only want what's best for you."

"I know. I don't feel a male is what's best for me. Artificial insemination is the perfect way to have my child. Jorel always—"

"The Goddess take your mother's soul." Patta sighed. "I didn't mean to say that. Your mother has been dead three years, and yet you still try to please her."

"She was eminently sensible, and I agree with her thoughts on this point. I want a healthy child. With a man I risk having a boy, and I don't think I could bear..." She lowered her eyes.

"Having a boy and losing him in a few hours is a terrible possibility we all must accept, but...It's not just the child we're talking about. You've won a chance to own a man. A man in your bed for a year. Don't you want that?"

"Not particularly."

Patta howled with frustration. "You are strange, Mara d'Jorel. Bizarre. We all dream of the chance, and you refuse it. Don't you like it when you buy a night at the Common?"

Mara reddened. "I've never gone."

"You've never..." Patta closed her gaping mouth. "You can afford the outrageous price. Why?"

"It seems wrong to me. Plus, I've researched breeding, and it sounds unpleasant."

"It's not unpleasant. At first it's painful, but it becomes pleasant."

"The harem is a filthy system. I won't have any part of it, or the poor men within it."

"I hear Jorel's voice coming from your mouth. Crackpot Jorel and her manhating words. Men aren't hurt by it. They go willingly into the harem for the sake of Arden. They enjoy breeding, and you know they don't have the ability to do anything else."

"That's untrue. They're not allowed to do anything else because of the harem."

"Do you want humans to die out here?"

"No, but I believe we can find better options than the harem and places like the Common."

"Get up and make a speech about it."

Mara winced at her friend's contempt.

Patta squeezed her hand in apology. "Can't you at least look at the selection of men. It would be good for you to have a man. There is more to life than your scientific studies, and maybe a man's a good place to start. Live a little, Mara. You aren't a computer terminal."

"I'll look at them to please you, but nothing more. I've already determined the proper genetic pattern to complement mine for my child, and I won't risk less because of some pretty face and body."

Her friend crowed with triumph. "You admit finding men pretty."

"Some pictures have aesthetic appeal."

"You sound like a vocabulary test sometimes, but I like you anyway." Patta rubbed her hands together. "Let's look at the pictures and drool."

Mara strode into the study section of her bedroom suite and sat down at her computer. She entered the government computer and began to type access codes. With the final secret code she'd gained through the lottery win, she opened the harem catalog available at present.

Staring discreetly out at the pink lufta tree in the walled garden, Patta stood at the French doors. Mara flourished her hand in offering. "Help yourself."

Patta pulled a lattice chair up against her and sat down at its edge, but insisted, "No, we're looking for you."

Sighing, Mara studied the first file. "Roger." She glanced at Roger's naked full body holograph then carefully read the physical statistics.

"He's huge! Right where it counts, too. Wouldn't he be interesting in bed." Patta squawked when Mara flipped away from the picture to the intelligence and genetic statistics.

"He won't do at all. Look at that intelligence quotient. I wouldn't have a dog that foolish. And he'll give a child heart problems."

"Oooh, look at that one. What wonderful lips and the cute little nose, and his p—"

"Statistics even worse than the first." She flipped to the next male file.

"Let me do this. You're not in the spirit of this thing at all."

Smiling to herself, Mara let Patta take over. Soon her friend was engrossed in the holographs.

After a dozen files, Patta groaned. "They're right. The prettiest ones are in the lottery, not in the Common. Oh, Mara, look. Green eyes.

I've never even heard of green eyes before. He's the prettiest man I've ever seen. I'm in needing of breeding with that one."

Mara's rab-cat tapped her pants leg with his ears. Bending, she brought Floppy into her lap. He curled up and purred as she stroked his black fur. She glanced toward the computer screen as Patta flipped to the next file. The green-eyed man had a two-word name, and the second name wasn't in Arden matriarchal form. She almost asked Patta to flip back so she could look at the name and the file, but she bit her tongue to avoid more of Patta's goading. Later, she'd go back and examine that file.

Leaning back in her chair, she watched her friend drool over the files. Patta was right. Many were quite pretty.

Finally, Patta reached Roger again. "So many to choose from. I can't make up my mind. Probably the green-eyed one with the incredible build. How about you?"

Mara shrugged and caressed Floppy's ears.

"You weren't even looking at all those pretty men. You weren't even looking. You are a computer terminal."

"I was enjoying your pleasure. I won't pick with the same regard as I choose the color of a tunic."

"You can say that." Before Patta could begin her standard Mara you ought to pay attention to your appearance speech, Floppy thumped Mara's wrist with his paw to get her attention then wiggled his ears toward the data card on the console table.

"An excellent idea, Floppy. Patta, would you please insert the data card and request a search on the harem file."

"You don't listen to me, but you do that stupid creature."

"Rab-cats may be as intelligent as we are."

"Don't give me another lecture on the native animals." Patta inserted the data card and punched buttons. "What's this?"

"The male genetic profile I'm searching for."

"The perfect baby. Let's see if any of these beauties fit your exacting standards."

Not expecting to find a perfect match in the harem, Mara turned her attention to Floppy. The sperm banks sent from other worlds were a much better possibility.

"By the Goddess, he's blond! And blue eyes. I thought blond and blue exotics were extinct here."

"They're rare because there weren't enough recessive blond and blues on the colony ship, and..." She gazed up at the holograph and lost her train of thought and her mind.

Patta giggled. "You can close your mouth now. Aesthetically pleasing, isn't he?"

"He's beautiful!" Curly blond hair, eyes that blazed blue with intense intelligence and strength, oval face, strong, well-proportioned features. Unlike the other holographs, he was dressed and only his face and part of his chest was shown. An official picture for identity. Refusing to be swayed by appearance, she cleared her throat. "Flip to his intelligence and genetic profiles please."

She read them, read them again, then shook her head. "Incredible. I can't believe he could be in the harem."

"He wasn't in the regular catalog. I'd have remembered him. Does he fit what you want?"

"Better. I'd never dreamed I could..."

Patta smirked. "Ready to order him, manhater?"

"Flip back to his picture." Mara examined the holograph. "Where is the identification?"

Patta shrugged.

"Here let me." Mara typed commands until she dredged out identification. "Tristan Mallory." She gasped with recognition. "I knew it. We've gotten into the off-world sperm bank. He's a respected Earth astrophysicist. Young, brilliant..."

"Your rival." Patta tapped the screen. "Then why does he have a harem catalog number?"

Mara dug further into the file for his location. "Rosalind Hospital, room 736. Ten miles away. Mother died at Rosalind. I was born there." She stared at the information, trying to assimilate it into her understanding of her world.

"Are you ill? You're green." Patta rested her hand on Mara's shoulder.

"I think Arden's shaking apart under my feet."

"What do you mean?"

"Why is an Earth scientist in our lottery?"

"His ship crashed here? It's happened before. The asteroid belt damages them, and we're the nearest habitable planet. Better the plague on Arden than death in space. What does it matter. He's here. Do you want him, or don't you?"

"You don't understand. He shouldn't be in the lottery."

"Why not? He's a man."

"He's not a man, he's a scientist!"

MARA COULDN'T stop the irrational pounding of her heart as she strode down the hospital corridor, but she smoothed her face into calmness. She might have been on a mad rush to reach this hospital since she'd found out Tristan Mallory was here, but she mustn't let it show.

Shoulders back, head erect, eyes guarded. Her best casual yet elegant city clothes to match that impression. She smiled, remembering how Patta had dragged her to the computer and forced her to buy these fine clothes when she wouldn't have bothered. She suppressed the smile. Cool importance to face the local bureaucratic dragons.

Stopping at the nurse's station on the seventh floor, she nodded to the nurse flanked by dozens of computer screens and terminals. "I've come to visit room 736." She turned as if it were beyond possibility that *she* would be refused and strode toward her goal.

His room was dully functional—a bath, one chair for visitors, empty white walls, and a bedstand by the bed. He floated on his back in an antigravity bed, a sheet draped over him up to his shoulders.

She whispered, "Hello?" When he didn't reply, she tiptoed up to him and stared down. He slept so deeply only the flutter of his throat and pulse told he lived. His strong features were softer without open eyes and intense awareness. His lashes and short curls were honey shining with sunlight, his skin honey several shades darker.

His shoulders were broad, the chest wide, the waist not so narrow as a woman's, the hips narrower than his chest, large thighs, long legs....

The holograph had shown his beauty, but it hadn't expressed his massiveness. The heavier bones, the denser weight. Natural male massiveness her studies had said. The male is larger than the female in humans. Simple facts known in the mind but not the gut until this first man. A man.

Her hand settled almost without volition in the bare hollow of his shoulder. Skin warm, smooth, not so delicate as a woman's yet pleasing, the muscle texture harder. She flushed, heat seeping up her arm, and jerked away in confusion.

He moaned, the sound deeper than any woman's, and thrashed.

Her heart aching from his obvious pain, she cooed as she would to a frightened infant and stroked his forehead and curls. He stilled under her touch.

His silk curls twined around her fingers. Before she could analyze the peculiar sensations creeping up her arm from his hair, she glanced down at his bare chest. His sheet had slid to his waist.

She gasped in horror. A mass of recent surgical incisions covered his chest, extending downward. Tubes and devices draped from his far side like tentacles.

The room fluttered before her. She closed her eyes and forced herself into calmness. It wouldn't come, tears came instead. She blinked them away and eased the sheet back up.

Sniffing, she swiped away her tears. The dark hollows under his eyes and the paleness of his honey skin finally registered on her overloaded senses.

"What are you doing here?" One of the bureaucratic dragons had finally found her.

Mara turned toward the nurse, a short stocky woman with gray brown hair and wrinkles of bitterness around her eyes and mouth. Mara smiled politely. "I'm visiting this patient."

"This isn't the Common. Move your rich, self-important little ass out of here. This is my territory."

"If I sought breeding, I'd pick a more lively subject than this, nor would I have sought him here. I came to visit. What happened to him?"

"Ship crash. The best surgeons spent hours on him for all the good it did. He won't even wake to full sense again. This pretty one will never see the harem."

The room fluttered again, but Mara refused to give in to the weakness or the grief. "May the Goddess watch over him."

"And I will too. Get out."

He groaned, the sound ripped out of him.

Mara spun and bent over him. He stared with wide unfocused eyes the smoky blue of the larra flower. She beamed at him. "Dr. Mallory?"

The nurse patted her shoulder. "Don't bother. He doesn't see or hear you."

"Dr. Mallory?" His eyes brightened as if the smoke was dissipating. She gaped in awe as smoky blue became bright pure blue, as confusion became intelligence and kindness. Somewhere inside her, a silver bell pealed, its song echoing to her soul.

His answering smile had the bell's song within it, too. His nearest hand lifted as if draped by huge weights. She caught it and held it within her hands.

Relaxing as if she'd given him what he sought, he mouthed, "Who?"

"I'm Mara d'Jorel."

"Quasars?"

Pride surged that he knew her work. "Yes, I wrote the article on quasars."

"Where?"

"Arden. A hospital on Arden."

Fear and sadness flickered across his face. He knew what Arden was. "My friend?"

Before she could say she didn't understand, the nurse replied, "Your companion is dead," then added more kindly, "He didn't survive the ship crash onto Arden. It was a very quick and merciful death."

His hand tightened around Mara's, and he closed his eyes, tears streaming down his face.

Helpless against his pain and the tumult inside her she didn't understand, Mara blinked tears.

After several minutes his hand relaxed, and his breathing slowed as if he'd drifted back into sleep. She eased his hand back onto the bed.

His hand clutched hers, and his eyes snapped open. "Don't..."

"I won't leave you alone in this. I promise you. We quasar experts stick together like binary stars."

He smiled, a brief quirk of lips at her feeble joke, and released her hand, trusting her words. Soon, he drifted into genuine sleep.

She stood for a long time watching him, his hand in hers. One of his hands engulfed two of hers. She wasn't a small woman, but he made her feel tiny.

The nurse patted her shoulder. She jumped, having forgotten the other woman's existence. "You'd better leave now."

"I'll be back."

The nurse sighed. "I can see that. Poor broken creature shouldn't die alone."

"Dr. Mallory isn't a creature. He's as human as we are."

"Why do you call him that? Him a doctor?"

Mara stiffened at the contempt. "He's a physicist and astronomer from Earth. He has at least two doctorates. Probably more that I don't know about. He's a respected scientist. He probably would have been...He will be one of the greatest when he becomes older."

"Don't you go planning his future. You've seen one miracle more than I expected when he woke up. He has no chance of recovery." The nurse shook her head. "Between his injuries and the stress of our higher gravity, he just doesn't have the strength to survive."

Mara recalled young Floppy the day she'd found him, ripped and broken by a large predator, his mother dead nearby. "Sometimes, you don't have the strength to go on alone by yourself, but if someone's there who cares, who can share strength, you can make it. Dr. Mallory has no sister or mother here so I'll give him my strength."

She leaned over and brushed Tristan's curls off his forehead. "He'll not die. I'll not let him die," then she added silently, "And he'll not go into that filthy harem either. Even if I have to take this planet and my life apart to do it."

Chapter 2

Kellen leaned back in his wheelchair and studied the huge walled hospital garden. Tended paths, flowers, shrubs, and trees were scattered about in informal formal style much like any other human-tended landscape he'd ever seen. When he closed his eyes, he could swear he was on Earth—chlorophyll plants, moisture, oxygen, humus soil. Arden's air and plants smelled more like Earth than any other human habitable planet he'd ever been on. The gravity was wrong, though, too heavy. He felt as if draped with weights.

The sky was Earth blue with great white fluffy clouds and yellow sun, the ground brown and fertile, the grass and most of the Earth-like plants green, but a nearby tree's lacy leaves were flamingo pink, its natural color, apparently, rather than its fall color. The season was warm, like temperate spring. A few small shrubs had varying shades of pink in them. Evidently a local variety of chlorophyll. Wouldn't his friend Jack the berserk botanist love those pink plants. Presently, Kellen didn't give a damn about pink plants or anything else.

"Kellen Votrain?" The woman's deep voice was polite greeting, not a questioning of his identity.

He looked up. Tall and slender with tiny breasts and well-formed muscles, her black hair unfemininely short, she wore severe black pants and a black tunic with gold insignia bars of rank on the shoulders. Her features and huge brown eyes, however, had Madonna beauty and sadness although her face was devoid of emotions. Cops and professional soldiers had the same look on whatever human planet he'd ever been on. "I wondered when the local government would show up. Have a seat." He motioned to the lawn chair across from his wheelchair.

Nodding, she settled in the chair. "Cadaran d'Hasta. I'm head of Arden's Internal Security."

He offered his hand, but she stared blankly at it. He lowered the hand. "Never mind, an Earth custom of greeting. What can I do for you?"

"I've come to welcome you to and indoctrinate you about Arden."

"I'm honored to be welcomed by such a high ranking official."

She laughed. “We have few newcomers who require this visit.”

“So I would imagine.”

“I wished to inquire about your ship. Why were you under attack?”

“Unprovoked attack in open trade lanes. We were on the way to a major science conference on Omikron Five.”

“You don’t know who?”

“A large ship, an armed fighter of a model I’m unfamiliar with, but derivative enough in design to probably be human. It attacked without warning and fired on us until we were dead in space. My friend...Tristan Mallory was mortally wounded saving my life. Smoke filled the ship...That’s all I remember until I woke here. How did I get to Arden?”

“A ship we trade with, we are allowed trade if no human contact is necessary, saw the attack. The pirate ship fled from the bigger ship. You and your companion were found. The trader didn’t have the medical facilities to save you so they put you aboard the robot ship that brought our goods.”

For a fierce moment, Kellen wished he hadn’t been sent here. “And my friend’s body?”

Cadaran’s face shone with the proper amount of official sympathy. “He was buried with all the dignity of our belief.”

“Thank you.” Kellen closed his eyes a moment to control his grief. “I’d like to contact his family.”

“They have been told of his death.”

“I assumed so. Still I wish to speak with them. They’re a very close family, and I’ve known them for years. It would help them to hear from me.”

“And your own family?”

“Orphan. No close kin. Tris was the only name on forms that asked for next of kin.” Kellen sighed. “Didn’t think he’d be the first to go with my line of work and his.”

“Arden is your home now and your family.”

Forever, if the plague didn’t get him first. He sagged back in his wheelchair.

“Should I call a nurse?”

“Just gravity exhaustion. I won’t even have any romantic scars soon.”

“Romantic?”

“An Earth joke regarding male aggression and ego.”

Her "oh" lacked understanding but disinterest in learning more. She folded her fingers together on her lap. "I'm certain you've heard of Arden before the Blockade."

He nodded.

"Very well then, I'll only touch on that time briefly. One hundred and fifty years after Arden was settled, a plague hit our people. Many died, particularly the men. Men seem to have little immunity. Our scientists could find no cure, and we called for help." Cadaran's face twisted with old bitterness. "The only help sent was a threat. If anyone tried to leave the planet, the Confederation fleet would blow the ship out of the sky. Anyone."

"They feared spreading the plague to other colonies."

She raised an elegant black eyebrow. "You approve?"

"Emotionally, no. I lost my parents to the starsus plague on Vega Two. I was six. They may have escaped death if we could have left. Logically, I have to approve. Many more worlds could have been decimated before the cure was found."

"No cure was found here. The plague killed all those susceptible to it. Our ancestors who had natural resistance remained, but the Confederation wouldn't lift the ban because they still feared the plague. No one came in, and no one came out. Our Council made decisions then. Hard decisions. We decided that since Earth and other humans didn't care about us, we wouldn't care about them. We would begin fresh. We deleted Earth history and cultural artifacts from our books and the lessons of our children. Even now we only allow scientific and trading information to enter our world, or leave it."

Kellen leaned forward with interest. He'd never heard anything about this. "But you speak Earth Basic."

"We'd lost most of our population, and many of our experts. We had no time to invent or learn a new language."

"Reasonable."

"Our greatest challenge was surviving as a race on this planet. Only five percent of our men had survived, and not all of them were capable of breeding. We realized we must drastically change our society. Men became protected, no work or risk allowed in their lives, and they became a collective possession of the women."

"You outlawed monogamous marriage?"

"All forms of marriage, if I understand the word correctly. By lottery, each woman capable of childbearing was given a chance to breed. She would choose what man she wanted from the harem for a short time."

Dismay shivered down his spine at the word "harem." "And the man's choice?"

"What choice? He was only a man, after all. He bred as he was told to."

Kellen's useless leg muscles tensed with a desire to flee. "That was two hundred years ago. What about today?"

"There have been changes."

He whispered fervently, "Thank God for that."

"Only certain women are allowed to enter the harem lottery to win and buy a breeder. Women of power and ability. The others worthy of having children may choose from the sperm banks we purchase from off planet."

"Certainly you've rebuilt your male population."

"Alas, no. Male children often die of the plague within hours of birth. It is our great tragedy."

"That's very sad."

"We have a strong society. We are still here."

"I'll be happy to help any way I can. I have a doctorate in xeno-anthropology, and I'm trained in first contact with alien races. I understand from reading an article by one of your scientists, Mara d'Jorel, that you have a native race of aliens—rab-cats. She seems to believe they're as intelligent as humans although they have no technology. Rather like the dolphins on Earth."

"She believes so." Cadaran shrugged. "They are only animals to me. She is no expert."

"Well, I am. I can answer that question." He fought down a surge of panic at her disinterest. "I'm also trained as an explorer. With all your problems, I'm certain you've had little chance to learn your world as well as you should."

"Men have only one role on Arden." Cadaran caught his chin and lifted it, studying his face. "You are quite beautiful. The black curls and strong features. And the green eyes are fetching. Unique, I believe, in the harem." She glanced downward, stripping him with a look. "Quite beautiful and well-built. You'll bring a fine price in the lottery."

He refused to flinch away from her. He met her eyes with equal arrogance. "I am a citizen of Earth, and I demand my freedom. I won't be a slave on this world, or any other."

"I like spirit. I'm tempted to bid on you myself when you are well enough for breeding." Her smile was feral. "I haven't had a man to play with in a long time." Her hand settled between his legs and caressed, her nails scraping his pajamas. "Very well-built."

He flinched this time. "I choose the women I bed, and they choose me. That is the civilized method."

Her laugh was like church bells, but her eyes were devil cold. "Not here, my pretty green eyes. Not here. Earth citizenship has no power on Arden, and a man has even less. And if you refuse to cooperate, we have ways around that too. Some quite unpleasant."

With the sick panic from the trap closing around him, Kellen felt enormous relief Tristan hadn't lived to face this hellish place.

TRISTAN fought his way up through the darkness, his terrible journey slightly easier than the last time, and opened his eyes. He stared at sky and moving clouds then glanced around, seeing meadow landscape and pieces of hospital wall.

Video projections were on the walls and ceiling. Disappointed the meadow scene was only an illusion, he would have closed his eyes again, but real beauty leaned over him and smiled. "Do you like it? I thought it would make this dull box more cheerful."

Mara's hazel eyes glimmered with the afterglow of the projected sunlight. Her cropped chestnut hair a polished copper helmet, she beamed at him, light shading and highlighting her high cheekbones and elegant nose.

He whispered, "Beautiful."

So unselfconscious she didn't even recognize the compliment, she nodded. "It is. I have acquired others, too. A seashore, mountains, and...I mustn't tell you everything. I want to leave some surprises." Her lips twisted with mischief like a pixie's, humor and intelligence dancing in gold-flecked eyes.

He sighed, his lids fluttering with weakness.

The pixie became a Madonna. Understanding and grieving for his pain, she stroked his curls then left him to rest. His eyes followed her fluid and graceful body as she moved across the room to the dresser. Reflected video colors and images danced over her white tunic and pants, painting long slender legs with golden flowers, firm young buttocks with the improbable pinks of shrubs, round full breasts with sun-sparkled creek. She bent toward a potted plant she'd brought, its pink leaves quivering in perpetual motion, and tested the soil for dampness with her finger tips.

Loneliness and fear stabbed like a dagger as he remembered his mother often doing the same thing. He'd chafed his whole life at the claustrophobia of a close loving family, even as he'd recognized his great luck in having them. He'd give anything to be home again. Home to his mother, sister, and Dorian fussing over him and tyrannizing the hospital staff for the best care. Home to the loving strength of his father and brothers. Home to die.

He fought the panic. He hadn't been afraid on that burning broken bridge with Kellen leaning over him, but he was now. Afraid and homesick. A man his age homesick even if it was for a world and family he'd never see again.

Drawn by his pain, Mara leaned toward him. "Dr. Mallory?"

"Tristan." He spoke his name clearly. His eyes flickered over to the bottle on the bedstand and back to her. "Would you?"

With the intuition of great kindness, she read his request in his eyes. "Certainly." She squeezed skin lotion onto her fingers and began to massage it onto his forehead.

Sighing happily, he closed his eyes. He felt like a conniving adolescent who'd create any ploy to be touched. His skin, dry from the treatments on his wounds, had been tended by the nurse a few hours before, but she'd squirted it on and smeared it with gloves as if despising touching him. He wanted to be touched, caressed, and fussed over, especially by a beautiful woman with warm hands and a gentle touch.

Her fingertips probed in circles down his temples, then settled under his ears, his pulse throbbing against them. Her fingers traced his neck and up his jaw line with hesitant curiosity as if she'd never touched anyone like that before then stroked his cheek. She announced as if it were a scientific discovery, "Your face skin has prickles."

His leaden hand rubbed his cheek. "Beard starting again."

"Oh, of course." She nodded wisely as if he'd mentioned some obscure scientific fact she'd momentarily forgotten.

He laughed, the deep sound surprising him as much as it did her. "Oh, Mara."

She caught the hand he'd been too weak to return to his side and held it between hers. "Yes, Tristan?"

He stared transfixed at the soft beauty and tenderness effusing her face, and deep inside him something strengthened and wakened. He decided he had no intention of dying.

DORIAN Dalia shifted in the driver's seat of her land flitter and glanced down at the passing scenery—blurs of oak tops, grass, and an occasional route marker—the usual pretty landscape from her Shenandoah farm to central North Carolina. No discernible hazards ahead, and the control panel was all green, the automatic pilot functioning correctly.

She hadn't gotten over her distrust of automatic pilots since David had died, spattered over an Appalachian mountainside when his on-board computer had malfunctioned. She didn't think she ever would completely trust one again. Not that she gave a damn about dying, little in life mattered since her husband had died, but she refused to be another victim to a flitter computer glitch.

Tristan always laughed about her computer paranoia.

Tristan. He must be the reason Elaine had called and asked her to come to the Mallorys immediately. Maybe Tristan had come home early from the science conference on Omikron Five!

No, that was hardly likely. Dorian's face twisted with dismay when she thought of the probable reason Tristan's sister had called. Tristan's family had said nothing when she started spending so much time with Tristan after David had died, but the silences had been eloquent. The silences were about to disappear. The Mallorys were waiting to speak with her.

She smiled, remembering her first days on Earth, her first days at the Mallorys who'd opened their home to her so she could attend Earth high school and college. A frontier planet kid with a hick education but great potential, she'd come to Mother Earth to spread her wings.

The two oldest boys, Gareth and Geoffrey, were already breezing through college, but Tristan and Elaine were still at home, Tristan a year older than she and Elaine a few years younger. What great and kind friends they'd been when they could have made her new life hell.

Dorian's gaze flicked back toward the control panel's lights. Just a few more minutes, and she'd be at the Mallorys. She could script what they'd say to her.

Ariadne Mallory, more a mother to her than her true mother, would smile kindly. "We understand your grief at David's death. Really, we do, Dory, but..."

Dignified, brilliant Justin Mallory would nod at his wife's words. "Yes, we do."

Elaine, the most sensible and outspoken child, especially when it came to Dorian, would not be so polite. "You're using Tristan's sympathy to push him into something that's not right for him."

"Or you," Ariadne would add kindly.

Elaine's blue eyes would glimmer with annoyance at her mother's interruption. "You're pushing him into unhappiness through your own unhappiness. I understand your emptiness since David died, but it gives you no right to trap him."

Dorian considered her own defense to such words. "I love Tristan. I didn't realize how until David died. Can't you understand that?"

Elaine would reply with a rude noise. "He's only been dead a year. You're so screwed up inside, how could you know what you feel about Tristan or anyone else."

"I believe Tristan loves me."

Ariadne would nod. "Yes, but not the way you want him to."

"If he loves you so much, why did he leap at this chance to go to the conference with Kellen? You've pushed him into flight."

Dorian blinked at Elaine's unexpected words. Her subconscious had just spoken using Elaine's mouth. Had she pushed him away?

The autopilot beeped politely. She switched it off.

Her hands settling on the controls, she glanced down at the Mallory home, an ancient white stone mansion surrounded by rolling lawn and forest. In the near distance, the afternoon sun glittered on the lake where Tristan had taught her how to swim.

She landed beside Gareth's blue sports flitter. Her door folded open, and she stepped out, stretching stiff muscles. She examined the other flitters. Everyone was here, even Geoffrey who lived in Florida. Tristan's wasn't here, he wasn't home from the conference yet.

She strolled into the house and stopped in the hall. Sunlight from the front windows painted the wood floor and wall paneling the honey gold of Mallory hair.

Hushed voices in the den.

As she walked through the open den door, the room stilled, everyone in tableau. Somewhere inside, she felt her normal admiring reaction to the family's physical presence, all these astonishingly beautiful blonds with their brilliant blue eyes. Ariadne sat with Geoffrey near the fireplace, his arm around her shoulders. Even more self-contained than usual, Elaine sat by the door, her hands folded in her lap. Gareth and Justin had been talking by the glass door to the patio. Geoffrey's wife and two-year-old Peter weren't present although Peter's favorite stuffed bear sprawled abandoned under his grand-mother's feet.

The grief in the room hit her like a blow to the stomach.

The room swayed, the ground and her existence teetering under her.

She clutched her hand to her mouth. "Not Tris. Not Tris, too." She found herself in Justin's arms.

Justin whispered, "He didn't arrive at the conference. They found pieces of *The Helen*. Her propulsion system had exploded. He and Kellen...Both gone. Gone in an instant."

A long time after she'd cried herself out in Justin's arms, she began to wonder. She'd known her husband had died before the state trooper came to her door; David's presence had been ripped out of her soul like a piece of her body the moment he'd died. She'd known, but she hadn't felt anything with Tristan.

Perhaps Tristan had....

No, all possibilities had been checked. Tristan was too important for a cursory search. He must be dead.

But inside her, he didn't feel dead, not like her husband had. Perhaps....

TRISTAN watched Mara's curious face as she unscrewed the depilatory stick she'd finally won after a week of bureaucratic hassle with the hospital. She lifted it to her nose and sniffed then examined the smooth white surface. He said, "You rub it on the skin. Lasts a week."

Nodding absently, she twisted the stick up a little higher over the rim then back down.

She reminded him of a child with her fascination for small mysteries, she reminded him of a fine scientist who should never lose that fascination.

Bending over him, she trailed a finger across his cheek stubble as if testing height. He must look scrubby with seven days' growth of beard. Hell, he looked like death warmed over, or more accurately death held at bay by sheer force of will.

Her lips puckered with thought.

His puckered with wishful thinking at the extremely unscientific curiosity about what those soft lips would taste like. Death warmed over, yet his libido was still working.

Her tongue touched her lips. His pulse picked up. He'd have to be completely dead to be immune to her. She rubbed the stick experimentally under his throat then back up. "Hmmm." The stick began to move with precision and authority across his throat.

"Don't you ever use this stuff?" He lifted his chin to give her working room.

She studied him as if concerned for his mental condition. "Women don't have beards."

"You don't remove your leg and underarm hair?"

"No, why should I?"

"It's a custom on Earth to do that."

"What purpose does it serve?"

"The skin is pleasantly smooth and pleasing to a man's touch."

"Oh, breeding."

Not wanting to continue a scientific discussion on the social customs of Earth lovemaking and a personal approach being impossible, he changed the subject. "Didn't you ever watch your dad do this when you were a kid?"

Her hazel eyes fogged a moment like someone conversing in a foreign language who had to pause to remember vocabulary.

He forgot his question. "Is Earth Basic your native language?"

"Yes, don't I speak it well?"

"Yes."

"Things you say confuse me. In all likelihood caused by cultural variation exaggerated by two hundred years of separation from Earth culture. What is a dad?"

"Your father."

Her eyes fogged again. "Oh, you mean my mother's breeder. No, I never saw him remove his beard. I never saw him at all."

"Oh, Mara, I'm sorry. I'm sorry he's dead." He squeezed her wrist in sympathy.

"Whether he's dead is unknown. Perhaps he was dead even before I was conceived."

"What!"

"Sperm are frozen in banks until use. One hundred years is the present frozen life, I believe."

"More or less. Don't forget my upper lip." He stilled until she'd finished his lip. He wriggled his nose, the stuff stank. "Why did she choose to have you that way?"

Mara's expression closed a moment as if he'd hit a tender or taboo subject then cleared. "She wanted an intelligent child. No man on Arden was adequate genetic material."

His hackles rose at such a cold-blooded way of having children. "You missed a great deal not having a father. Your mother?"

"She died three years ago of an illness. Would you like me to do your legs and under your arms too?"

He inhaled hard then relaxed. "Only women use it there."

Her brows rose, and she eyed him as if he were an unpredictable lab specimen. "Why not? Smooth skin is pleasing to a woman's touch, too."

"I guess it is, but it's not our custom. We only remove the hair on our faces. Some men grow beards or moustaches... hair on the upper lip, but I've never cared for it. Most women don't like it on men either."

She twisted her head in question.

"It tickles and itches their tender skin. Men's head hair is usually worn short although fashions change from time to time. Women's hair can be worn long or short, but men like longer hair on women." He added before the inevitable question, "Its texture and beauty are very sensual...pleasing to the touch."

Her eyes strayed up to his curls, and her fingers clenched as if tempted to test her own response to male hair, but politeness won over scientific curiosity. She closed and put the depilatory stick on the bed stand then picked up a towel and began to rub at his whiskers.

He mumbled into the towel, "Tell me about your life."

"I live in the home that was my mother's and my mother's mother's. We have all been scientists. Mother's light energy converter helped us achieve a certain wealth. I receive a small percent of its galactic profits from the government."

"Your mother was Jorel d'Nissa!"

"Of course, doesn't my name say so. I live with Novia. She was my mother's housekeeper, then my nanny, and later my housekeeper. I have a chubby elderly black collie, and a tabby cat who thinks she sits on the Arden council. And of course, Floppy. He's..."

Tristan flinched at the male pronoun. A husband or lover?

She jerked the towel from his throat. "I didn't mean to hurt you."

"Floppy is?"

Bending toward him until her nose brushed his cheek, she peered at his skin then rubbed his cheek with hers experimentally. "As smooth as mine. Quite efficient and pleasing. I can understand why an Earth woman would wish beard gone."

Her action had been straightforward curiosity rather than sexual teasing, but he felt her cheek caress down to his toes. He turned his face toward hers, their noses bumping. Their eyes locked. "Who's Floppy?"

Her eyes sparkled with the sexual attraction flaring between them. "My rab-cat."

Why had he been jealous of a Floppy? Maybe his brain had been damaged during the ship crash. His hand weighed thirty pounds, but it obeyed his command by raising. He caressed her cheek but couldn't quite lift his head to reach her lips a few tantalizing inches above his. "Do you kiss on Arden?"

"Of course." She smiled with that maddening unselfconsciousness.

How could such a brilliant woman be so stupid? "Kiss me please."

She bussed the tip of his nose with her lips and straightened away from him with the air of a kiss well done.

He sighed. This was going to be a very long and frustrating convalescence.

Chapter 3

Mara swiped her wet palms on her pants and took a deep breath for courage. She hadn't been this frightened when she'd taken her oral exams for her doctorate. Then, she'd only risked destroying her career and making a fool of herself and her mother in front of the greatest scientists on Arden. Now, much more was at stake.

She straightened, throwing her shoulders back, and strode through the archway into the walled garden. Thea d'Louisa sat in a high-back wicker chair in the shade of the veranda of her house. Thea studied her with imperial arrogance and nodded slightly as their eyes met.

Knelling by the elderly woman, Mara accepted the ritual kiss on the cheek. Thea was over eighty, but with her stiff-backed grace and brown hair—gray wouldn't dare appear without permission—she appeared younger. Only the wrinkles around the eyes, and the slight tick of the head from a nerve disease escaped Thea's stubborn refusal to age.

"Heavens, Mara, how you've matured. You must be..."

"Twenty-five, Thea."

"That old. I haven't seen you since your mother's funeral."

"Yes." A familiar stab of grief shot through her.

"I've heard good things about you, very good things about your work. You're doing Arden proud." Thea motioned to the chair across from her. "Take a seat, girl. Take a seat. How I miss Jorel. What conversations we had."

Mara settled into the chair and allowed herself a slight smile. "Conversation is too bland a term."

"Heavens, yes. We'd divide the universe between us and sort out its problems. We did not always agree."

"Only on the things of greatest importance to Arden and science."

"Ah, The Jorel Foundation. Is that what brings you, child?"

"Partially."

"Certainly not in need of a Foundation grant. Jorel left you well settled."

"No, I lack nothing. I live well with more than enough for my own research and the computer and lab equipment I must buy off planet."

"Frightfully expensive these new machines, but far better than the pre-Blockade antiques I spent my early days with."

"The Foundation has made us even with the rest of the galaxy."

Thea motioned her onward to the reason for her visit.

"I came to seek your help. You are the most respected scientist on Arden as well as being head of the Foundation."

Thea threw her head back and laughed. "Merely the oldest living fossil, child."

"An Earth scientist, Tristan Mallory, has crash landed on Arden. He's in Rosalind Hospital now struggling for his life."

"And?"

"He's brilliant, Thea. An astrophysicist as I am. Several of his papers are remarkable for such a young scientist."

"His age?"

"Thirty-one. If he survives, and I feel strongly that he will, I fear for him."

"We don't kill people for landing on Arden, only those who try to get off."

"The man we might not kill, but our society will destroy the scientist. He'll be thrown into the lottery."

"Ah. You've acquired Jorel's mania about the lottery."

Mara controlled her face. "I share my mother's feelings about the lottery, but I don't seek to destroy it, only keep Tristan out of it."

Thea's expression hardened. "You wish to keep a man out of it. That's not the way of Arden."

"Not a man, a scientist! A great scientist. He can do so much for knowledge. He's written seminal papers on black holes and quasars. He may be the one to tap the power of the black hole for travel or energy. Can you imagine the great good that would bring? Why should that genius be wasted in a few women's beds? They would be as well served with the sperm we now buy off planet."

"Such fire, Mara! Is it the man or the scientist you fight for?"

Mara took a deep breath. "Jorel taught me that my greatest allegiances were to my world and to science—the advancement of knowledge for the good of both Arden and humans everywhere. She spoke of the sisterhood of scientists. All scientists, not just those of us on Arden. I speak for a scientist."

"And very well too. She and I wanted to make Arden known to all those humans who'd forgotten us, not just known, respected. So they couldn't turn their backs on Arden again."

Mara nodded. "So they would renew their efforts to cure the plague. So we could have the stars again as we deserve as humans."

"It's a dream we may never see. Even our own government has given up the fight for the cure."

"But the Foundation is funding research."

Thea's nervous tick became more pronounced. "We are stymied. The government fears biological research may reintroduce the plague."

"But it's never left. Adults rarely die, but the infant boys! A few months ago, my neighbor Jane lost her child a few hours after birth. She'd been so thrilled, a freak conception from the Common, and to lose the child. Tell Jane the plague isn't here."

"Bureaucratic, contemptible fools. I have tried, Mara. I've tried so hard."

For a moment, Mara saw the age Thea hadn't been able to hold completely at bay. "I know, Thea. I know. Jorel had enormous respect for you, and what you've done for Arden and science. Without your vision, she could never have turned the light converter's profits to such splendid use in the Foundation."

Thea patted her hand with powder dry fingers.

"Can you help Tristan? The doctors believe that if he survives he'll be an invalid, useless for the lottery. I don't know what would happen to him then. And if he becomes well.... The lottery is such a terrible waste of a great mind."

"What do you wish for him?"

"Full citizenship as a sister of Arden so he can't be put into the harem. I promise sponsorship, and I'll pay his medical bills and for his care. If I can't get full citizenship, I'll accept guardianship of him for life."

"And if you get none of these things?"

"I have lottery right. I'll claim him that way."

"And lose him in a year's time without even a child to show for the effort if he's so ill."

"I'll have gained a year's reprieve for him, and more time for myself to get him out of the lottery. And perhaps a year more for his great mind to soar before it's shackled to some woman's bed."

"If you use the lottery, others will remember your mother's beliefs and laugh at her when her daughter shows so little respect for those beliefs."

Mara paled. "I know. But Jorel would understand that I honor the spirit if not the letter of her beliefs in choosing Tristan. Will you help me?"

"Perhaps, child. Perhaps. With such failing power as I have with the government, even my full-hearted support may not be enough. You ask personal repeal of one of few great unchangeable laws that govern our world."

MARA'S pixie smile of greeting didn't hide the worry that had deepened in her eyes ever since she'd first visited Tristan. He returned her smile as she bent over him in bed. Desperation had joined the worry. What was wrong?

He struggled to keep his own face and expression bland when she kissed his forehead with warm lips. In the last month she'd kissed every damn inch of his face but the inches he wanted kissed. His lips tingled and puckered with kiss deprivation. Always the masochist, he bit them rather than complain.

A sea bird sailed over her head. He requested, "Would you?"

She nodded and clicked off the video projection of the seashore.

His smile genuine now, he devoured her with starving eyes. He hadn't seen her in over twelve hours. "Pink suits you. That's a pretty new outfit."

Like a tongue-tied child, her eyes went down, and she blushed, smoothing the elegantly flared tunic over her hips.

Shaking his head, he added that reaction to his long mental list—"Mara, the child-woman" which was so opposite from the other list—"Dr. d'Jorel, the brilliant scientist." He pushed the remote control at his fingertips, and the bed's head lifted, elevating him into a sitting position.

Sitting down in the chair by his bed, she took his offered hand in hers. "How are you this morning?"

Refusing to add the slightest bit of worry to those eyes, he lied. "Fine. Happy to have graduated to a real bed. One I can see and feel."

She glanced down at his hospital waterbed. "An anti-gravity bed must be quite disconcerting."

"Quite. It's also pleasant not to have the nurses and doctors expecting to find me dead every time they walk in. Their disappointment is so depressing."

"Tristan!" Mara's hazel eyes widened with distress. "That's not true. They're pleased you've proven them wrong."

"Sure, that's why they treat me like an Ard..." He colored and cursed his loose tongue.

"A what?"

"It's a cliche, an expression. A person one wants to avoid contact with at all costs. A person with a disease."

"You were going to say Arden, weren't you?"

He couldn't lie to such hurt, wise eyes, especially since they wouldn't believe it. "An Arden leper. That's the expression. I didn't even think.... The expression's so old people don't even consider its literal meaning. I didn't mean..."

"Arden's so forsaken we aren't even a fresh cliche anymore." She sighed.

He damned himself for wounding her so deeply. "I didn't..."

She squeezed his hand. "I know you didn't mean to insult me. You have too much kindness in you for that."

"Cowardice, not kindness. I wouldn't insult the only human in the universe who cares I exist." He bit his tongue again. "Forget I said that. It's the new pain killer. It makes me babble. Tell me how your big project is going."

"I'm not the only person who cares for you. You've spoken of a mother and sister. How could they not help but care for you."

"I thought they..." He fought the self-pity in his voice. "I've heard nothing from them. Not a damn thing. What am I supposed to think? Mom would send a card or flowers to a casual acquaintance, but me... I didn't expect her to come here, but she could..."

Mara's face clouded, her fingers tightening around his. "They have great concern for you."

"I want to think so, but the alternative to thinking they don't give a damn is they're all dead. I prefer..."

"I can't believe either answer. There must be another. A problem with mail to Arden, or...I'll find out."

"I've asked the nurses about that, but no answer. They won't even help me send a letter or video."

"You should have asked me."

He thought of her inexhaustible tenderness and patience, and her two visits a day, over six hours taken away from her work. "You give so much."

She glanced contemptuously around at the video projector, plants, and reading material she'd brought. "These things mean little. I would give much more to have you happy and well."

"You're the most unselfconscious...I was speaking of you. You've torn your life apart for a total stranger!"

Her face glowing with deep feeling, she stood. "You are not a stranger. At first it was for a fellow scientist, but after I knew you...I have great kinning for you."

His heart chugged against his ribs in hope. "What is kinning?"

"Deep family feeling. Like between a mother and child." She smiled with greater radiance. "You are like a sister to me."

He choked back an incredulous laugh and his inclination to point out her vocabulary mistake. Sometimes their words were so different they might as well be speaking different languages. He ignored the stab of disappointment and the hissing of his deflating male ego. "You are a very dear friend. I feel deep kinning for you, Mara."

"You do?" Surprise and shy pleasure made her voice tremble.

"I do. Why is that so hard to believe?"

She lowered her eyes.

He changed the subject to ease her embarrassment. "How is your mysterious project going?"

"Not well. Thea d'Louisa is ill. I had her support in it, and the others who were to aid me..."

"Bowed out when your most important supporter failed you."

"Yes, exactly. If she does not recover, I'm stymied. But I won't give up. Never!"

"I can see that. I'm sorry I can't help you, but I'm afraid the Mallory influence doesn't extend to Arden."

"I wish it did. Your family is powerful?"

"In science circles, yes. My dad is Chairman of the Science Foundation and has the Sagan Professorship at Triangle University. My *brother* Gareth runs Compco, the computer research firm. Geoffrey is a science advisor to the Earth Colony Congress."

Mara's eyes became huge with admiration.

"Mom is an important Arthurian scholar. And despite the rumors, she didn't marry Dad for his last name. Although she did name all of us. Elaine..." He stopped. Mara's eyes had fogged over as she searched for vocabulary.

"Arthurian?"

"King Arthur and the Knights of the Round Table. The famous classical literature regarding them. Writers like Geoffrey of Monmouth, Tennyson, Mallory, T.H. White, Marion Zimmer Bradley, Mary Stewart." Mara's eyes were still foggy. "The knights Tristan, Gareth, Lancelot."

"Why do nights have names? Do days have names on Earth?"

"K-n-i-g-h-t. I'll explain that some other time. You must have avoided the humanities in college."

"No, I did well." The fog left her eyes. "Oh. We don't study Earth history or literature here. We don't even have the records."

"Why the heck not? That's your history too."

She answered blandly, "Why did Earth turn her back on us when we needed help? Why should we remember her when all she remembers of us is an old cliché?"

"That's how your people think. Do you?"

"I feel maimed in my limited contact with off-world scientists. I have the Earth sciences and scientists, but no context for them. I regret the loss with you. I wish to understand your mother's discipline because she is your mother. And Elaine?"

"My sister is following my mother in literature. Her specialty remains to be seen. And of course Dorian, she's..." He faltered, painful and tender memories coming.

Mara examined his face as if it were an intricate and vital equation to be solved. "And Dorian?"

He didn't know how to describe his feelings, he didn't understand them to describe them. He shrugged. "A very dear friend. We grew from teenagers together. We are very close. She is a physician specializing in research, mainly in immunology. She's done some fine articles on the effects of space travel on the human body."

"You have kinning for her?"

"Kinning and much more."

Her flat "oh" tore him from poignant regrets. It had a distinctly jealous sound to it. Unsettled emotions fluttered across her face. "Have you examined those equations I gave you?"

Agreeing a change of subject was best for them both, he rested his hand on the remote control and hit a button. The reading screen flipped down from the ceiling to his eye level. He push-buttoned to the notes she'd give him on her next article. He bit his tongue to keep from complaining about the archaic screen's slowness. It wasn't her fault or Arden's he was so spoiled by living on Earth with its superlative technology, or theirs that as a distant and quarantined planet they were forced to live on antique technology. He reached her notes on the evolution of the quasar and studied the long series of elegant equations.

She asked, "What do you think?"

"Interesting."

Sharing the same polite fiction that he could understand the equations with his brain fried by pain killers, she began to explain her research and the ideas behind the equations. He nodded at the right places and offered comments and criticisms, some of whom surprised him with their validity.

After an hour of spirited give and take, she paused and clicked off the screen for him. "I've tired you out. I should let you rest."

She glowed with happiness and the burning passion of a true scientist in the presence of challenging science. Shop talk agreed with her. With her flushed skin and dewy eyes, she'd never looked lovelier. He ached with loneliness in response.

"See you this afternoon." She bent toward him to give him a parting kiss on his forehead.

"Why don't you kiss me on the lips?"

"Lips? You don't....That sounds unsanitary."

"It's not. Kissing on the lips is an Earth kinning custom."

"It is?" The devil and angel of scientists—curiosity—whispered in her ear as it had his. She shrugged and nudged his lips with hers.

His weak arms obeyed him, lifting and draping around her shoulders and neck, his fingers twining in silken chestnut hair. His fingers stroked her nape. He hadn't imagined it, she was letting her hair grow to please him. His lips nudged back.

She blinked, her lashes brushing his cheek.

His lips moved gently against hers. He closed his eyes, savoring their warmth and softness after a month of curiosity. Her lips slid experimentally against his as she returned the kiss.

He tasted the bow of her lips with his tongue, the salt and sweetness.

She quivered, the waterbed shivering with her reaction, and sagged against him. Her pulse throbbed beneath his fingers.

His heart pounded in response, and he wanted to draw her into the bed beside him, but his muscles betrayed him, his arms sliding to the mattress. He recalled why he'd sensibly avoided acting on their sexual attraction while he was so ill. His body recalled the joys of a woman's body and burned.

Her eyes misty with sensual awakening and confusion, Mara straightened from his stilled lips and stared at him. She touched her lips with trembling fingers.

Grinning as if the kiss hadn't smashed into him like a comet, too, he mentally dared her to call him her sister again.

THE nurse dumped clothes on the end of Kellen's hospital bed. "Put these on."

Kellen jolted up in bed and blinked sleep from his eyes as she left without looking back. The force lock hissed into place on the door. He sighed and stretched. He'd give a million credits for a friendly face, preferably a friendly male face on Earth. He slid out of bed and shook out the simple white linen tunic. His hackles rose. Street clothes, not pajamas. Hello, harem; good bye, hospital.

His hands shook as he stripped and dressed in the clothes. He calmed himself by thinking of every plan he'd concocted for escape when this moment came. He might not be able to escape this hospital prison cell, but....

The door hummed open. Two Amazons in black military tunics strode in. The one with red hair raked him with burning eyes. "Hello, pretty."

The brunette licked her lips knowingly and smiled.

His stomach rolled. He felt like a tavern whore on a sleazy frontier planet.

"Come to Garnet, pretty. Give Garnet a kiss." The redhead smacked her lips.

"Go to hell."

"Pretty doesn't want to play." Garnet pouted. "We're the best you'll see. Women, not the rich sows in the lottery."

The brunette glanced around and mouthed "monitors."

Garnet shrugged with a to-hell-with-them smirk.

The brunette grabbed his arm. "Let's get out of here before she gets my ass in the trap, too." She glanced down at his face. "By the Goddess, green eyes! As green as a tanra stone."

Garnet forced his face around to her. He fought his inclination to fight her. "What a price you'll bring. A one of a kind exotic."

"Green isn't the half of it. He's built."

Kellen stepped away from the brunette's groping hands into Garnet's. Her fingers bit into his shoulders at his neck.

"Out we go." Garnet shoved him toward the door.

Kellen tottered forward as if still struggling with the extra gravity and injuries. The soldiers grabbed each elbow and all put carried him through the door and down the hall. He sagged, letting them tire themselves. They passed the nurse he called Adolf as much for her personality as her resemblance to Hitler. He mimed a kiss of good bye.

Her lips turned down in reply, then they were out of the hospital. The air and temperature smelled of spring, the sky a fluffy white and blue.

Kellen sniffed his first open air in weeks.

Garnet glanced around the empty parking area. "You drive around aimlessly. I'll sit in the back with him, then you can have him."

"We're supposed..."

The other soldier winked. "You know how long these hospital transfers take. We waited forever to get him." They stopped in front of an antique-style land flitter. The door accordioned open, and Kellen was shoved into the back before he could make any move to escape. Garnet leapt into the back with him.

He scrunched to the far side with his back to the wall.

"He's shy. Maybe he's never done this before." Brunette closed the driver's door. "Save some for me, and remember no bruises on the merchandise." The flitter lifted and took off.

As he made a mental note about direction, Garnet grabbed his wrist with steel claw fingers and jerked him toward her. "Come to Garnet, pretty."

Glancing at the driver's rearview mirror, he didn't fight as Garnet wrapped her arms around him. Her hard nipples daggers against his chest, she slammed her lips into his, her tongue seeking entrance.

As she invaded his mouth, he heaved with nausea. For the first time, he understood the violation of rape. He fell backwards onto the floorboard with her on top of him. She weighed more than he did. Her hand slid into his pants.

He hit her then, a killing blow to the throat. She gurgled and arced like a woman in orgasm and went limp.

Brunette swore in envy.

Moaning, he pulled Garnet's hand away from him, and thrashed himself out from under her body as if in the grip of sexual union. He eased upward over the front seat.

Brunette's eyes were glued to the mirror, and she saw him coming.

He smiled seductively. "Ready for your turn, soldier?" He smashed his fist into her face. She ducked, and it skidded off her cheek. Rolling over the top of the seat, he attacked.

As the other soldier had reached into his pants, he'd realized that it would be die or escape, no middle ground of surviving in the harem was acceptable to him. He went for the kill.

Brunette fought back, her training in self-defense obvious, her lack of battle experience even more obvious. He'd grown up street fighting on a brutal planet and taken graduate work on planets so uncivilized they didn't yet have human names. He smashed toward the woman's most tender defensive area, her breasts. A woman's natural instincts winning over training, she lifted her arms to shield them, and he chopped into her throat.

She dodged, but he hit her anyway. She careened into the door and slumped. He dragged her body away from the controls and dumped her into the passenger seat. Sliding into the driver's seat, he examined the archaic computer controls then flicked off the automatic pilot and took the wheel in his hands.

Below him were suburban houses, behind him the towers and larger buildings of Galina, the largest city on Arden. To the west were the mountains he intended to hide in. He turned northeast into the open meadows so he could dump the bodies where they wouldn't be found any time soon.

When he'd researched the planet's environment in the hospital, he'd decided to escape into the wilderness. He'd lived off the land before, and that life's harshness and loneliness beat being some rich cow's sex slave. Even facing the tyrlin—the huge local version of the Bengal tiger—was preferable to that.

After twenty minutes he eased the flitter down beside a dense growth of green bushes. He opened the door, dragged Garnet's body into the bushes, and dumped it where it couldn't be seen from the air. He studied her face a moment. He'd never killed a woman before, but he felt no regret. This scum couldn't even be defined as human, let alone a woman, and he was now at war with the whole damn planet anyway. He went for the other soldier.

Grabbing her under the armpits, he dragged her out of the flitter. Her foot caught in the seat. As he reached for the foot, she twisted and smashed something into his leg.

Numbness spread through him as he saw the medical sprayer in her hand. He kicked toward her face but fell instead.

Hatred and blood lust clouding dark eyes, she bent over him. "By the Goddess, I should kill you for Garnet."

"You're too cowardly to kill and too stupid." He added, "You fight like a Luntaran lizard." On any other world a soldier would kill him for those words, but she studied him blankly. He struggled frantically for an Arden insult. "You fight like a man."

That insult caused results. She reached toward him, clutched his tunic, and tossed him into the back seat.

Sprawled on the seat, he tried to make his muscles work, but the drug already had him in complete paralysis. He could only watch her retrieve the body and put it gently into the passenger seat. She buckled it in and got in herself. They were soon on their original heading.

He thought wistfully of execution for murder but didn't believe it possible. He was too profitable on the government meat market. Well maybe he'd get an owner with the beauty of a Tenly sunset, a huge kind heart, and abolitionist sympathies. He sighed. Not damn likely.

The flitter landed, and he was heaved over Brunette's shoulder. Dangling, he had an excellent view of a house of magnificent proportions then an interior of equal splendor. His new owner wasn't poor.

Brunette dumped him on a bed, pinned his left arm to the bed, and encircled his wrist with a porcelain bracelet. It closed tightly with the permanent sound of a manacle. "Filthy man." Brunette spat on him and bolted as if fighting her inclination to kill him.

Gradually, the paralysis left him. He crawled out of the bed and swayed onto his feet, clutching the bed stand to remain upright. He examined his new prison.

The large bedroom was wood-paneled with functional yet stylish furnishings—an intricately carved wooden bed, a dresser, and a chair shaped like a throne. The bedspread was a long-haired black animal's skin. The paintings were of fine artistry and dark prime colors. The overall impression was of wealth and barbaric colonialism.

Stumbling toward the high-set oriel widow, he stepped up on the chair. Woods in the distance, lawn, trees, and shrubs near the house. He tried the seal of the window, but his hands were wooden. He let them fall.

"Damn." Staggering into the small bathroom, he cut on the cold water, stuck his head in the wash basin, and let the water wash away some of his mental fog.

Water still dripping down his face, he strode back into the bedroom. He glanced at the closed bedroom door but didn't even try it. The oriel window was his best chance.

His fingers traced the window's edge until he found the hidden latch. The window swung open. Its opening was small but with a little wiggling and will he could make it.

He boosted himself up and was blasted backward to the floor in a wave of pain. Blinking, he tried to force back the black haze and confusion. What the hell had happened?

"A forcefield, Green Eyes. Triggered by your detention bracelet." Cadaran swaggered across the room to him and smirked down at him with her Madonna eyes and feral smile. "The bracelet won't come off, and neither will the field. Next time it will be electrified. Someone without the bracelet can walk in and out of the room with no trouble, but you never. The field is a full sphere around the room. You can't even dig your way out or go through the ceiling."

He didn't say anything. He should have known the window had been too easy.

"I should slit your throat for Garnet." Kneeling down beside him, Cadaran shrugged. "But she disobeyed orders and couldn't believe my warning that a man can be dangerous. I'll consider her an object lesson for the rest of my troops and call it even. Besides, you're so pretty, and I like spirit." She corrected herself, "I like breaking spirit."

She caressed his throat with her nails. "Welcome to my home and bed, Green Eyes."

Chapter 4

"And he has *two* living brothers!" To see how her friend took that amazing news, Mara glanced toward Patta, who slouched in the passenger seat of her flitter.

Patta stared back blankly. "What's a brother?"

"Like a sister but a boy."

"If Jenny'd been a boy who survived, she'd be my brother instead of my sister?"

"Yes, and Tristan has two brothers. Both are as brilliant as Tristan and their sister."

"His mother has three living boys." Patta shook black curls. "What would you do with all those men on Earth? It's mindboggling."

"You wouldn't put them in a harem." Mara bit her lip to hold back criticism. She needed Patta's help in the coming confrontation, not her animosity. "Four children. Wouldn't it be lovely to be allowed so many children, and not to fear losing them to the plague? And the most incredible thing is Tristan's mother kept the same breeder for all of them. He's called a father. They live together."

Patta wriggled her nose. "A man under foot all the time! I don't think I'd like that. They're such silly creatures."

"Tristan isn't silly, and neither is his father. His father is Justin Mallory."

"Should I be impressed?"

"If you were an astronomer, you would be. He's brilliant."

"A family of freak male geniuses, who would have thought it."

"They are extremely intelligent, but..." Mara glanced around the little flitter for listeners then berated herself for being foolish. "I wouldn't repeat this to others if I were you."

Grinning, Patta crossed her lips with her fingers. "Out with it."

"In reading all the articles and research from other planets....Half of all scientists and scholars, at least in the scientific fields I'm familiar with, are men."

"I wouldn't dare repeat that. I'd be laughed off the planet. Really?"

"Yes."

"The Goddess works in mysterious ways."

"Her wonders to show. The same breeder for all those children. And even though Tristan's mother must be past childbearing age, she and her breeder stay together because of marriage. That must be some form of long term breeding contract."

"Like the year or conception contract the lottery winners sign for their lottery choice?"

"Evidently."

"Have you decided to choose Tristan?"

"As my lottery choice? Only if I can't get him out of the lottery any other way." Mara sighed and leaned her cheek on her hand against the window.

"You aren't weak with exhaustion and crying your eyes out after every visit like you were, but something's still wrong. Tell Patta all about it."

Hoping Patta wouldn't insist she stop visiting Tristan as Novia had from the first, Mara told the truth, "He's so hurt, and his pain makes me ache. In those first weeks when he was fighting to stay alive, I couldn't let him see how it ripped me inside for him to be hurting. How I had to fight to act cheerful and..." She blinked tears.

"You're too tenderhearted. You adopt every wounded stray. You were a basket case over that rab-cat when you found him dying and brought him home. Now you're doing the same thing over this man. You and your pets! You should put all that maternal energy into a real baby and a healthy man who'd give you one."

"I always sensed Floppy was more than an animal. It was like finding a human baby who'd been hurt. And you can't call Tristan a pet. He's just like us."

"Only male. Sure, if you want to believe that. So he's no longer in critical condition. Why the long face?"

"His nerves here," Mara touched the small of her back, "aren't healing as they should. He has very limited movement of his legs."

"He sure won't be much fun in bed like that! Even if he is a gorgeous blue and blond exotic."

Biting her tongue to hold back a sarcastic remark, Mara reminded herself Patta wasn't as shallow and cold-hearted as she sounded sometimes. "That is the least important thing about him."

"It's the only thing important about him, Mara. A man has no value on Arden except to breed children. Don't you let his tall tales about Earth make you forget that."

Mara outlined her lips with her finger. She could still feel his lips against hers that morning and the absurd rush of sensations through her body. "I don't ever forget I'm on Arden. Sometimes, may the Goddess forgive me, I wish he won't regain the use of his legs so they can't take him away from me."

"Private ownership of men died with the start of the plague." Patta examined her like a stern mother.

"I don't want to own him, only keep him safe and happy. Like Floppy. I want to adopt him."

"You are the stupidest genius around. What you need is a few nights in the Common to learn what men are for. Wrap your legs around a man's waist and let him use what he's got for the best pleasuring, and you'll forget all about your crippled pet scientist and adoption."

Blushing, Mara looked away.

"Well, at least he's made you pay attention to your appearance for the first time in your life. You might want to adopt him, but that doesn't keep you from displaying your feathers to the best advantage like a female Tessel bird in breeding heat."

"I have been dressing up to impress the hospital bureaucracy when I visit. They must continue to believe I'm important so they won't stop me from seeing him."

Patta made a rude noise in reply. The flitter's automatic pilot beeped, saving Mara from a half-hearted attempt to refute the charges against her. Flipping it off, she landed the flitter in one of the parking areas of the planetary government's massive main complex. She stepped through the accordioned door and straightened her pink tunic and her hair. "Is my appearance suitable?"

Beside her, Patta stretched and tugged her own tunic smooth. "You look very important and wealthy. You've shown excellent taste ever since you decided to pay attention to your appearance."

"One must identify and concentrate on the important in life." Mara closed her eyes and whispered a brief prayer for courage to the Goddess. "I hate doing these things. My stomach is in knots."

"I shouldn't speak so hard of your pet scientist. He's given you a fashion sense and a reason to flex all that important muscle you inherited from Jorel. In defense of that man and his welfare, you go after bureaucrats like a brave little rab-cat protecting her kitten from a giant tyrlin."

"Many of the public dragons are as stupidly malicious as a tyrlin. I don't know how we survive on this planet at the hands of such incompetents."

"Luck and a few good dragons like my cousin Nedra."

"I didn't mean to insult Nedra."

Patta laughed. "I know, little mother rab-cat. Let's go."

Mara followed her through the labyrinthine impersonal halls of the complex. They took an elevator to a lower level and wound through more halls until they reached an office door in what must be the most remote section of the building.

The door swung open in Patta's hands.

Mara peeked in expecting cobwebs but found a neat cubicle office glowing with computer screen light, bright holograph seascapes on the walls, and potted plants.

"Patta!" The woman sitting at the computer stood and hugged Patta enthusiastically then studied Mara.

Studying her back, Mara saw her resemblance to Patta in the black curls and oval face. "Mara d'Jorel."

Nedra's eyes flickered in recognition of the important name. "Nedra d'Enid."

Patta laughed. "You've lost weight, Nedra. You look good."

Chuckling, Nedra motioned they be seating. She and Patta exchanged family information for several minutes before she turned her attention back to Mara. "How can I help you?"

Mara explained about who Tristan was and how he'd become trapped on Arden. "He hasn't received any mail from his family, and he's been unable to send any out. I want to rectify the situation."

"You know the rules." Nedra frowned. "No personal communication between the citizens of Arden and outworlders. I recall vetting your scientific communications with outworlders so you must understand the restrictions."

"I understand them very well, and I abide by them. I only have scientific communications with fellow scientists, but this is different. Tristan Mallory is from Earth, he's critically ill and separated from his family. Certainly letters exchanged would cause no harm, and it would cause great good for Tristan. Hearing from his mother would help the healing process, and you know what she must be going through with a child critically injured on a planet closed to her and she can't communicate. According to the mercy taught by the Goddess, we should help them both."

"I didn't expect a Sunday lesson today." Nedra chuckled.

Patta echoed the laugh. "At least it wasn't a science lesson, then she really gets preachy."

Mara straightened her head with dignity. "We are discussing matters involving the kinning between mother and child, the most sacred of all human relationships. I don't find that funny."

"Nor do I." Nedra settled back in her chair and crossed her hands on her lap. "Very well, you're intelligent so I'll tell you the truth rather than putting the bureaucratic stall on you. It is impossible to open communications between them. Totally against the rules made specifically for this situation."

"But why?"

"In the early days after the plague, situations like this arose. Families would communicate. Offworlders were torn when they learned of death and illness in their kin here on Arden, ripped apart by the knowledge of young orphan kin who begged for aid. Some got past the blockade and landed. They wanted to take off again, but couldn't. They were trapped, and many died of the plague. We learned from that experience that personal communications is harder on both parties than cold government statements. It seems cruel now, but it's far kinder to both the man and his mother not to let them communicate."

Mara considered her words then shook her head. "I can't agree. Tristan and his mother are both intelligent, sensible people. They would handle the situation properly. He accepts being trapped on Arden and knows she can't come because of her other children, and she must accept that also."

"No exceptions. Absolutely no exceptions. I'm sorry Mara d'Jorel, but I can't help you. If this man can be as sensible as you say, he should understand the prohibitions. He belongs to Arden now, not to Earth. Earth and her people are dead to him as they are dead to us all. Dead as they chose to be when they refused us aid in the plague."

Mara shivered at the ritual words of separation. She stood and met Nedra's eyes. "I lost my mother a few years ago. We were very close. I have discovered that even death doesn't separate us, not really. I don't think I'll ever really lose my mother, and I don't think Arden will ever really lose Earth either. They're too much in our bones and blood to ever lose no matter how much we pretend they're not. I think it's past time Arden discovered that."

"I'll say that was personal recall." Nedra studied her coldly. "But someone not a cousin to Patta would call it treason. Watch your tongue, daughter of Jorel, for she's not alive to protect you from such deadly charges."

THE ceiling fans swirled lazily, stirring the spring desert air drifting through the open door of the sleazy bar. The fan's blades reflected the late afternoon light across empty tables and chairs that littered the room. The bartender sprawled on the bar, fast asleep, his snores the only sound except for the soft whir of the fans.

Kellen leaned back in his chair and propped his feet on the table. He sipped his beer then eyed Tristan over the glass rim. "Well, this is your fantasy, what do you want to do?"

Tristan squirmed in his chair. Damn, even in daydreams his logical brain had to add its own two credits to the proceedings. He focused on the cold beer, remembering its texture and taste. He stretched his own legs under the table and balanced them with his heels. He had several desperately important things he wanted to talk about but didn't have the words to start any of them. "This was a great place. I love the planet Egan."

"Great place, great times. Remember the night we rescued that girl from the drunk borilium miner, and we had to take on a bar full of his huge friends? Or the time on Bevan we stopped a war between the locals and the human colonists?" Kellen grinned happily from the memory. "You should have stayed with me instead of going back to dull old Earth."

"Maybe I should have."

"Should haves, would haves. They can rule your life if you let 'em. You couldn't have ignored that internal Mallory imperative to do the sensible thing any more than I could have resisted the call of the stars." Kellen cocked his head. "I can hear those Sirens singing still."

Tristan laughed. "I miss you, Kellen."

"I miss you, Tris. What's wrong?"

"What's right?" He rubbed his legs. "They won't tell me, but I can see it in the doctors' eyes. I don't think my legs are getting any better. I can barely move them. The rest of my life as a cripple..." He winced when his voice quivered at the last word.

"You've screwed up their diagnosis so far, don't let them win on this one. Keep fighting until you can dance Mara across this bar room floor."

Tristan grinned. "I'd like that."

"You sure do luck out with women. Kind, intelligent, and as pretty as a Tenly sunset. I'd like to name a solar system after her!"

"Watch your mouth."

Kellen smirked. "So it's like that, is it? You're smitten."

"No, she's only a friend, and she's not your type of casual fling."

"Hey, I keep my hands off friends' women and relations. I've never put the first finger on Elaine, or Dorian, or that redhead you were so taken with in graduate school."

"Not that she didn't ask. Why didn't you tell me she was after you?"

"She was after half the men on campus. I knew you'd realize it sooner or later. When you wanted to see it."

"There are none so blind."

"Etc., etc. Do you know who Mara reminds me of?"

"She's totally unique to me."

"She reminds me of you when we first met—studious, serious, and as naive as hell. All books and no experience."

Tristan flushed. "I was never that bad."

"I guess not, growing up on sophisticated Earth, but pretty damn close. A hundred to one she's a virgin."

"I wasn't a..."

"But pretty damn close." Kellen smiled smugly and sipped his beer. "Still not too good in comparison to me."

"That was choice, not opportunity. A one night stand has never been my way. You know that."

"Ol' love'm and never leave'm Mallory. I know."

"I don't think Mara is just wearing science blinkers against experience, all wrapped up in her work. There's something weird about Arden."

"In what sense?"

"A very strict society, perhaps. Especially about sex. She'd never been kissed, didn't even know about it. I don't even think she's been around men much before me."

"Sexually segregated. Interesting. Have you asked her about her world?"

"Not really."

"Why the hell not, great scientist?"

"Because that would be cheating."

Kellen roared with laughter, the last of his beer swaying in his glass.

"I'm so damn bored! This is as close to a puzzle as my poor fried brain can handle. She's such a wonderful puzzle herself, new facets of her personality appearing every day, and this world is even better. The vile-tempered nurses who act as if I'm filth, and the maternal ones who act like I can't understand anything but baby talk. The video shows only have two channels. One has educational shows mainly for children, and the other only comes on for local sports, women's sports. There's not the first drama or comedy or even news program."

"Maybe you're just not allowed to see them."

"Another act of segregation. Perhaps."

"So what are you going to do about Mara?"

"Do?" Tristan considered an answer. "Enjoy her while I have her. I've got this paranoid fear she'll disappear, and I'll be stuck in this hospital alone. I get panicky if she's a few minutes late for a visit."

His green eyes sparkling with mischief, Kellen rubbed his ear. "You could always marry her and raise baby astrophysicists."

Tristan choked on his beer. "But Dorian..."

"Is on Earth, and you're on Arden. Never the twain shall meet."

"Dorian will come. You know her."

"Barely. Remember."

"I guess you don't. She's the most loving, loyal person I've ever met. I expect her any day in a ship loaded with the most sophisticated lab equipment in the galaxy. She'll come, take up residence, and take up the fight against the plague. It won't stand a chance with her after it. She's a brilliant medical researcher, and one hell of a stubborn lady. I'll be off the planet in a few years."

"Pipe dreams, Tris. Why isn't she here now?"

"I don't know, but it's out of character for her not to be here when I need her. Maybe she's having trouble getting the equipment."

"Maybe she discovered she didn't love you enough to strand herself on a plague-ridden planet. Maybe you should settle for Mara who is here."

"Whatever happens with Dorian, Mara deserves better than to be settled for."

"She wants you and is so damn innocent she doesn't know it."

"What's to want? An invalid with nothing to offer her. I had nothing but the clothes on my back when I arrived here. If the government weren't paying for this room..."

"Well, golden boy, you got your wish. No one can call you that now."

Tristan groaned and covered his eyes.

"Born with wealth, looks, intelligence, and excellent family, the golden boy is graced by the gods with easy fortune. Isn't that the way the myth goes? You saw yourself like that. Everything you ever wanted came to your hands easily, too easily."

"I never had to sweat for anything."

Kellen chuckled. "Busting your butt in graduate school and after isn't sweating? The dangerous black hole research and equations weren't sweating?"

"Not really."

"With final results, genius looks easy. You forget the hard work and only remember the results."

"You've said that before."

"And you aren't buying it this time either. You're a bloody fool, Tris."

"Usually. You're one of the few people who sees it."

"You wanted a woman who wants you for the true man beneath all that gold. Well, it's stripped off now. You look like hell—skinny, tubes dripping out of you. No money. No family or influence. A brain fried on painkillers."

"No legs."

"Now's the time to show the rest of the universe and Mara what you're worth without the glitter. Especially Mara. Stop whining and get to work."

"I've stayed alive."

Kellen applauded. "Definite guts."

"More guts than I thought I had."

"Mara knew they were there."

"Half the guts were hers. I wouldn't have survived without her strength and tenderness."

"And as pretty as a Tenly sunset too. She deserves a hell of a lot more than a bunch of glitter or being settled for."

Tristan saluted his friend with his beer. "I know."

IT was a war of nerves, and Cadaran was winning.

Kellen clinched his fists and stalked the length of his prison bedroom again. It was past midnight. When would she get here? Maybe she wasn't coming tonight. She meant to let him stew and worry about all those veiled threats.

"Waiting up for me. How charming, Green Eyes." Cadaran swaggered into the room then stopped, hands on hips, in front of him.

He forced his hands open. "Go to hell, Cadaran."

Her Madonna eyes shimmering with mock dismay, she smiled as if killing prey. "I'm heart-broken. So you aren't going to co-operate."

"No."

"I hoped you'd say that. I love to show a man who's boss." She backhanded him, her knuckles clipping his jaw.

Too surprised to duck, he fell hard, stars bursting around him. He wiggled his throbbing jaw and scrambled to his feet. She had the whack of a bar bruiser.

He punched toward her breast.

She'd had battle experience. Countering the blow with a casual movement of hand, she clouted his temple with her other fist.

Another constellation twinkled overhead as he kicked at her knee.

Dancing back, she laughed with genuine pleasure and smashed into his chest with her foot.

He backed, avoiding the worst of the blow. "Karate. Very good."

"Arden attack moves," she corrected. "I was an advanced instructor before I rose to command."

Spinning, he gouged at her eyes. She ducked, and he hit her stomach with his elbow. She landed on her back. "Dirty fighting. I survived advanced instructors before I grew up." He smashed toward her face with his foot.

She scurried backwards on her hands and knees.

Before he could attack again, searing pain shot through his left arm. He screamed and pitched forward on his knees, clutching his arm to his chest.

Cadaran stood and brushed off her black uniform. "I would dearly love to rip you apart with my bare hands, but I promised to return your expensive body to the harem in decent shape. I fear I must restrain my enthusiasm."

Flame shot through his left hand. He gasped. "What causes this?"

"Your detention bracelet has a pain stimulator." She pulled out a gold-banded necklace from under her tunic collar. A green stone pendant surrounded by gold wire frame hung from it. "A mind trigger. I think a key word, and it tells your bracelet to fry you. Very simple and elegant." She chuckled. "And by the way, if you try to rip it off my neck, it will automatically stun you. Death would be more pleasant than that stun so I don't recommend it."

"As charming a weapon as your own sweet self." He staggered to his feet.

"Ready for bed, Green Eyes?" She smirked happily.

"Go to hell." Fire jolted through him and shorted out his skull.

He found himself, after a moment of blackness, curled in agony on the floor.

"Stubborn, stubborn. But such a nice change from all the local males raised from infants to indulge our every whim. Dull, unappealingly dull." She smiled in question.

He didn't bother rising. "Go to hell." An eternity of agony later, he sprawled on the floor in a pool of his own sweat. He rasped, "Go to hell," and flinched, awaiting the pain. It didn't come.

"Sorry to disappoint you, but as much as I'd like to, I'm not allowed to destroy your mind." She sighed unhappily. "I fear even I can't have everything I want."

Reaching down, she grabbed his wrist and dragged him easily to his feet. "Oh, by the way, Green Eyes. There is a side-effect to being born and raised on a planet heavier in gravity than Earth. We develop denser bones and greater strength."

She clutched his tunic's front, lifted him, and tossed him six feet. He rolled and sprang to his feet. "The average woman on Arden can crush your bones if she wants to, and I'm not average. I was being gentle in our earlier discussion. Don't push me."

"I tremble with fear." He sneered with a certainty he no longer felt. "Go to hell."

"How pretty you are with your eyes blazing with stupid courage." She snared his wrist, and her fingers probed inward.

He tried to break free, but she held him easily. When she found the tender nerve and gouged, a moan escaped before he could stop it.

"Kneel before me, Green Eyes. Acknowledge me your better."

Blinking pain tears, he returned her stare.

"Kneel." She gouged deeper, her fingers tightening around the bones of his wrist.

In his imagination, he could feel the bone giving way. He gasped, but his eyes didn't waver.

"Kneel, and I won't hurt you."

"Go to hell." The vice tightened, her finger jamming into the nerve.

Cadaran was surrounded by blackness and stars. "Kneel."

"Go to hell." He smiled at his small victory and passed out.

Chapter 5

The hammering of her heart woke Mara. Sprawled in sweaty disarray, she stared up at the dark ceiling above her bed then flipped over on her side and hugged her aching breasts. Clinching her thighs together, she tried to make the steady throbbing go away, but it intensified.

Moonlight shimmering through the French doors called her. Swearing under her breath, she slid out of bed.

She tiptoed past Sheba who opened one cat eye then closed it as if Mara weren't worth waking up for. His ears quivering with happy dreams, Floppy in his bed in the far corner curled more tightly in his sleep. She eased a French door open and walked out into the moonlight.

The air was warm and sweet with the cinnamon scent of lufta tree and garden flowers. She inhaled deeply and stretched, her damp gown tight against her taut nipples. Wriggling her nose at the tantalizing friction, she pulled the gown over her head. Confident of privacy because of the high walls around the garden, she tossed the gown on a chair and walked toward the pool. She stopped only to fasten a lifesaver ring snugly around her wrist in case she began to drown then slid into the pool, its surface mercury in the moonlight.

She sighed, the warm water caressing her, and began to swim languidly. Clearing her mind, she concentrated on the water, the stars above, and the night sounds of bird, wind, and rustling leaves.

The dream images which had awakened her floated back into consciousness like a leaf blown toward her on the water. Gold hair shining, Tristan hovering above her in bed, his eyes sky blue with warmth. The feathering of his hands up and down her arm and bare back. The scent and heat of him surrounding her. She'd clung to him, her arms around his shoulders, her legs around his waist....

They'd been breeding!

Mara blushed and tried to remember what it felt like, but the sensations were as vague as her personal knowledge of the event. Her research had explained the mechanics of breeding, but had been woefully inadequate on the sensations. Perhaps she should ask Patta.

No, absolutely not. Patta would drag her to the Common and dare her to find out for herself. The scientist in her was curious, but not curious enough to go against a life of contempt for the Common and all it stood for.

Closing her eyes, Mara floated in the water. Her breasts ached, the nipples full as they had when she'd dreamed of breeding. They'd ached like that when Tristan had kissed her that morning.

Tristan had kissed her in her dream!

She blanched with shame. Kissing was a special element of kinning, not of breeding. Tristan was like a sister... brother to her, not like a man from the harem. She must be an emotional deviant, unworthy of Tristan's friendship, to feel and dream like that. She should stay away from him so she wouldn't reveal her sickness or humiliate him with it.

Fighting her churning emotions, she began to swim hard from one end of the pool to the other in steady strokes until she could swim no further safely then she paddled to the ladder.

Floppy sat on the ground by the ladder, one of her towels in front of him. She crawled out of the pool and shook out the towel then wrapped it around her. She blinked away the water from her eyes and removed the lifesaver ring. "Thank you for the towel."

He wiggled his ears genially in reply and trotted back toward the bedroom door. The air cold now that she was wet, she hastened after him. She toweled herself dry in the bathroom then stood under the heat blower until her hair and body were completely dry then slipped into a fresh gown.

The bed made her flinch so she sat down in her favorite chair which faced the garden. Floppy jumped into her lap and curled up, his chin resting on her forearm, his ears along the side of his head.

Appreciating his diplomatic silence, she stroked his head and tried to reason out the questions she faced. The importance of protecting Tristan from her emotional problems clashed with her certainty that she couldn't desert him when he was truly alone and injured.

"I wish Mother were here. She'd explain these new feelings to me as she did when I was maturing. I miss her so much."

The rab-cat purred and rubbed his chin against her wrist in comfort.

"Don't you ever want a mate, Floppy? You're mature now."

His ears flicked a soft "yes."

Her heart landed in her stomach. "You can go home to your

people. I'll take you to the mountains tomorrow."

His ear flicked "no."

"Why not?"

He purred and twined his ears around her wrist as a kitten would around a mother rab-cat's neck. "I have great kinning for you, too. But a mother rab-cat would free you to a mate. Your inept human mother will do the same thing."

"Yes. Yes, no."

"You're not ready for a mate yet?" His nod confirmed her guess. "I understand. I think part of my problem is I'm past due a mate of my own, but I can't bear the Common. I envy you rab-cats who mate for life."

Floppy's green eyes glowed with confusion, and he twisted his head as if to ask, "Why can't you mate for life?"

"Because of our stupid government and the even stupider plague. If a person even attempts to change things around here, she's in dreadful trouble. I only said something against the system today, and someone accused me of treason. Government has far less respect for the truth then we scientists do. Prison or death for only speaking my mind!"

The rab-cat snarled as if facing an enemy.

She stroked his head. "I'm safe enough. She isn't going to turn me in. But she did give me a scare. I must control my tongue and be as devious as everyone in government if I want to keep Tristan out of the harem."

The rab-cat sneezed with disgust.

She chuckled. "Don't be so jealous of him. My kinning for him doesn't lessen my kinning for you. Before long, he may come to stay with us, and you'll care as deeply as I do. He's.... He's splendid!"

The unexpected image of Tristan lying in her bed made her blood surge. She faced a terrible ordeal when he came here. If she failed to control her breeding instincts, she would destroy their kinning and shame herself. Perhaps it would be better if he didn't come.

CADARAN sprawled back in her chair and examined Kellen's unconscious form on the floor. She yawned and straightened her black silk robe. She was all undressed and ready to go, and her pleasurer was still asleep. Certainly he should be waking by now. She was bored and itchy. Very itchy.

Why hadn't she commandeered a man lately? The creatures were so much fun. Actually, most were boring, as boring as a pleasuring machine and twice as mechanical.

Kellen stirred, his beautiful head lolling back. Exposed throat, long lashes, and black curls across his forehead made him appear vulnerable and sweet. Wouldn't the pampered wealthy ladies pay a fortune for that.

Cadaran yawned again.

He rolled to his side, but his left wrist remained glued to the floor. Waking completely, he jerked at the wrist but the detention bracelet remained stuck. His gaze swept the room as if he were a trained soldier in search of enemy.

In spite of herself, she leaned forward with interest. "Welcome back, Green Eyes."

His eyes narrowed when they met hers, and his face tightened with hatred.

Her loins throbbed in anticipation. "I fractured your wrist, but it's been attended to."

Examining the wrist collar, he wiggled the fingers of his right hand. "I've had worse."

"Are you a soldier?"

As if he weren't pinned to the floor, he pillowed his head with his free arm and crossed his legs at the ankles. "Are you?"

She laughed at the insult. "Are you?"

"No. I grew up alone on a tough planet, and my environment has rarely improved through the years. More by choice than necessity."

"Civilization is such a bore."

"Arden isn't civilization. Even the most primitive planets would look down their noses at Arden. Slavery's been outlawed by humans for over six hundred years."

"But it's so much fun, my pretty little pleasurer."

"Not to me it isn't."

She wriggled her nose. "Spoilsport."

He smiled with equal humor. "Bitch."

The word had the distinct sound of a vile insult. "I would ask for the definition of the word, but I don't wish to waste the rest of my night waiting for you to regain consciousness again."

"A female animal of particularly bad temperament."

She chuckled. "You have a strong death wish."

"I have an even stronger desire not to spend the rest of my life servicing bitches like you."

"As long as you're profitable, you will survive, and when you've lost your looks or your other valuable asset, you'll spend the rest of your life wishing you were still servicing women."

Fear and hopelessness flickered in his eyes before the courage returned.

Her own anticipation increased. "I've decided to give you two choices about your future. The first is you come willingly to my bed or any other woman's to pleasure her, or—"

"You know my feelings on that point."

"Or, the second choice. You have heard of lotus?" She twisted her head in inquiry.

He turned powder white, but his voice remained even. "Yes. Its twisted presence is known and loathed throughout the galaxy."

"Good. You understand its ultimate price—mind death or emasculation. Its powerful addictive qualities and the brutal pain of withdrawal. The mind control elements and its aphrodisiac qualities."

"I said I understood about it."

"Excellent, Green Eyes. Well, our scientists on Arden have refined it even further, giving us greater control of our unwilling men."

"I'm certain you enjoyed the research personally."

"Immensely." She beamed. "Two choices. Free will or lotus?"

He rolled until his back was to her.

She almost pitied him the terrible decision she gave him.

After several minutes he faced her, his face serene. "Admit your weakness. You don't have the guts to break me. I've bested you at every point so you're hiding now with this pathetic threat."

Only her greatest control kept her from kicking his face in. She laughed. "Nice move, Green Eyes. I'll give you points for trying but nothing else."

"Gutless. You can't beat me, a mere man. You have to hide behind drugs to defeat me."

Smiling, she smoothed her robe. "If I didn't get a share of your profit, I'd take you apart. But business before pleasure."

"Gutless woman."

"Who happens to hold your future in her hand. Free will or lotus?"

"I don't breed with animals of free will. Especially not with a tyrlin who'd eat her own young."

Cadaran flushed. "You have an excellent knowledge of the local invective for such a short visit."

"My profession."

"And this is mine." She knelt by him and caught his free arm before he hit her. He twisted against her grip. She took the medical sprayer from her robe and held it up. "Final choice, Green Eyes."

"Go to hell."

"Hell is here in my hand." She pressure-sprayed the contents into his shoulder.

He winced and closed his eyes.

After she brushed herself off, she strolled back to her chair and lolled back in regal serenity. His body began to twitch, a sheen of sweat covering his face, and he moaned with agony. After several minutes of internal chemical storm, his body relaxed.

She mentally released his detention bracelet from the floor. "Stand up, Green Eyes."

His eyes haggard but aware, he crawled upright then staggered to his feet.

"Undress."

His muscular arms crossed his chest, and the tunic went off over his head. He shook the curls out of his face. His proportions were excellent, the chest smooth, the flesh firm and shapely, the waist narrow.

"Very nice. Don't be shy."

He eased the pants down his hips and stepped out of them.

She groaned. Long hairy legs, well-muscled thighs for power thrusts in bed, and a manhood of splendid proportions set in a forest of black curls. "I'm going to enjoy you, Green Eyes. Turn around. Nice buns! Around again."

He faced her.

"Kneel and acknowledge me your better."

He bit his lips, his struggle to fight her command evident in his eyes and the sweat dripping down his face, but he dipped smoothly to his knees. "You are my better."

Dampness surged between her legs.

He opened his mouth to take the words back.

"Shut up."

The lips clamped closed.

She giggled. It was like watching a man trapped inside a robot, fully aware but unable to control the robot's actions. "Come to me on your knees."

He knelt at her feet. "The bitch queen on her throne."

"Words, very good, but don't be too pleased. It will become more and more difficult to fight as your system becomes used to it." She ruffled his curls. "You are so pretty and so built." Her fingers caressed down his chest and flat belly and circled his manhood. She stroked.

He flinched and quivered, the pain intensifying as his staff grew in her hand.

Straightening, she simpered playfully, "Does that hurt?"

His face twitched with agony.

"One of the side effects of the drug. Well, no matter." Coming to her feet, she tossed off her robe. "Come then."

She stretched out on the tyrlin skin on the bed. The black fur feathering her back and inner thighs intensified her desire. "I normally prefer a position where I don't have to see the man, only enjoy his gift, but I want to see your face." She opened her arms. "Come to me and pleasure me with all your knowledge and your wonderful gift."

His face and throat clinched with revulsion and the drug, he crawled up beside her.

"Don't you dare throw up on me." She smirked. "You have my permission to speak as you wish now."

He rubbed his hand across the fur. "What is this?"

"Tyrlin."

"How appropriate. It matches your hair. Your hair, all of it, disappears like you're part of it."

"And you said you wouldn't breed with an animal, and here I am." She opened her arms. "Don't be shy."

Another war was fought in his eyes. His hand stretched toward her as if fighting a force field. His hand covered her breast, his thumb feathering her nipple.

"Harder."

He pinched her between two fingers, his other hand trailing down her ribs to her thighs. It settled between her legs and probed. "You're ready and waiting. All this turns you on, doesn't it?"

She closed her eyes, her pelvis thrusting into his hand. "Oh yes."

"You aren't interested in sex. Rape is about power and hatred, and you're eating this up."

Watching his violated expression through half-closed lids, she smiled. "Of course. Tell me how handsome I am."

His hand massaged deeper. "Is the height of female physical attractiveness called handsome here?"

"What else?"

"In Earth basic, a woman is beautiful, a man handsome."

"A man is merely an ornament. He can only be beautiful. Harder."

Her pelvis danced against his hand. "Tell me."

"Even lotus doesn't teach you how to lie with pretty words." He closed his eyes. "Okay, how about your nipples are like sour cherries, purple and ripe." His free hand slid across her ribs. "You have very good skin tone. Your crew cut shows off pleasant ears. Your nose is fitted just right between your big brown eyes with their lying Madonna sadness. Your—"

She laughed. "Enough."

"I warned you."

"Show me where your real talent lies."

Rolling on to her, he stared into her eyes. "I hate you, Cadaran. I wish you in hell." He slammed into her, his magnificent gift filling her, and began to thrust as if they were still fighting and he'd found a new weapon.

Groaning, she met his painful thrusts, her arms clinging to his shoulders. "Just the way I like it."

After a long time, his fingers slid under her buttocks lifting, and he revved up, his powerful hips tensing and grinding.

Screaming with pleasure, her mind shorting out, she ripped his back with her fingers.

When she returned from the darkness, he still pounded into her. She met his thrusts and stared up into his face at the physical pain and humiliation, the hopelessness. Her mind exploded again.

His breath rasped with exertion, and he slowed his pace.

She writhed beneath him, the friction of his chest on her nipples like flame, and concentrated on the drilling fullness and heat. Blood and sweat from his back dribbled down his ribs onto his chest. Lifting, she licked blood off his nipple. Her mind detonated again.

His own movements had become desperate, his thrusts faster. The muscles of his neck and face strained upward as he sought his own darkness. She chuckled, and let him seek a peace within her which wasn't there.

Hours passing, she fed off his pain, her own many pleasures so intense and prolonged that even she was sated. As the last of the spasms of an orgasm ceased, she shoved at his shoulder. "No more. Get off me."

His eyes hollow with total exhaustion, he crawled off her then curled into a heaving ball. His shredded back had stopped bleeding, but sweat poured off him, his hair dripping with wetness. His muscles quivered.

"Poor Green Eyes. Have I worn you out?" She patted his butt. "You were very good. Best I've had in ages. I'm going to enjoy owning you."

He moaned and buried his face in the fur.

"Your gift will go down and stop hurting in a few hours. It's another new side effect of lotus. I keep coming with you inside, but you can't. To borrow a moldering cliché, you have a gift that keeps on giving."

Sliding off the bed, she stretched. "I feel wonderful. Now it's off to bed for me." Tossed her robe over her shoulder, she glanced back at the man, but he was too lost in exhaustion and pain to even curse her. She sighed, regretting the loss. "It would have been the perfect end of a very long but nice evening. Sleep well, Green Eyes. You'll need your strength for me tomorrow." Giggling, she exited the prison bedroom with the dignity of a queen.

MARA sleeping was as beautiful as he'd fantasied. Tristan held his breath and leaned a little closer. She was curled slightly in the extended recliner chair by his hospital bed, her breasts rising and falling in soft cadence, her long chestnut lashes quivering with dreams. He traced velvet skin along her high cheekbone with the tip of his finger.

Her lips parted slightly, beckoning.

His tongue touched his lips as he remembered her warm sweetness, the shy response of her first kiss, the quivering of her body as sensuality stirred. And he'd given no more than an innocent kiss. He would taste her fully this time. It was time for this beauty to wake completely for him.

He leaned over the edge of his bed, but brutal inches separated their lips, and his medical tether would allow him no further. He sighed.

Picking up the edge of his sheet, he stretched it through his fist to form a feather and planted a kiss on the feather's tip. "Give her this kiss for me."

The feather nodded agreement. He extended it toward her lips.

It bent, and the kiss fell off on the tip of her nose before it reached her lips.

Her nose twitched.

He retrieved the feather, straightened it, then reapplied the kiss. "Get it right this time."

The sheet feather caressed the line of her lips with exquisite slowness then wiggled the kiss on the bow of her lips.

She stirred.

Folding his hands and feather on his chest as if he hadn't been a naughty boy trying to wake her up, he sat back up, and beamed when her eyes fluttered open. "Good morning."

Blinking, she stared at him with giant hazel eyes.

Enjoying her confusion, he chuckled. "I'm the one who's usually asleep in here."

Her cheeks turned a charming bright pink. "You were asleep so I sat down to wait and...My sleep was limited last night." Her blush deepened.

"The quasar project. I know just how that is. I don't even realize the long hours until my body protests in the wee hours."

"Yes, the quasar project."

"I missed you yesterday afternoon. I missed you so much. I don't think I can ever express how much your visits mean to me, Mara."

Straightening, she smoothed perfectly smooth hair. "Being here gives me pleasure too, Tristan."

"You are the lifeline to a drowning man. The light buoy to a lost ship. The..." He stammered to a stop. "You know what I mean."

"I believe I do. I've been alone too ever since my mother died. I have few friends who understand my work, and almost no colleagues on Arden."

"Why not?"

She laughed with gentle irony. "A quarantined planet has little need for astronomers, and few scientists are stupid enough to go into a field where they can't do real research."

"I guess not."

"Plus, Arden stresses practical rather than theoretical sciences. The planet's interplanetary income comes from our scientists' inventions and research information."

"The local government gets the profit from your inventions?"

"Of course. We receive ten percent for exported inventions and forty percent of local profit."

"That's one hell of an income tax rate. On Earth, the inventor gets the majority of the money."

"Mother's inventions still give me a good income as well as support The Jorel Foundation."

"One of the major inventions of the last fifty years would. The less fortunate scientists must barely survive."

"We have grants."

"You must." He caught her hand and squeezed. "But I don't want to spend my morning discussing pay rates. What did you find out?"

"Your mail is held back by the government."

"What?" He listened with disbelief as she faltered through an explanation of the local ban on communication with other worlds. "You mean I can't contact my own family! They can't contact me!" Anger raged, fed by the last month's helplessness and aloneness. "Because of a stupid two-hundred year old law!" Red blazing inside, he slammed his fist on the bed.

When the flame flickered and died leaving only emptiness, he rediscovered the room around him. He sagged back in bed. "I'll never talk with my family again. Never know how they are. Never keep up with Peter's growing up. Elaine's future. They're as dead to me as if Earth didn't exist anymore." He shook his head. "No, I'm dead. Dead on this damn planet."

Covering his eyes with his hands, he shivered. "The warm friendly universe I was born into just disappeared."

Mara squeezed his forearm tentatively.

He fought for emotional control and found it with a faint hope, now stronger since it was his only hope. "Dorian will come."

"What?" Mara's hand jerked away from him.

"Dorian will come. Nothing will keep her away when I need her. She's a lot like you. Warm, caring, brave for others."

"Then she'll come." Mara stared blankly at the floor.

"What about setting up my Earth credit here? Certainly, more Earth credits to tax to death won't interfere with the government's noble ideals."

"No possibility. A colder refusal than the other. They won't even contact your Earth bank to transfer your credits."

"No family, no money, no job. How do they expect me to support myself?"

Mara examined the floor with greater interest. "I have already established a credit account for you here."

"I should have known. So you're the reason I can now get all the extras like a vid monitor."

Her gaze finally returning to him, she nodded.

A kept man, who'd ever guess it of him. "I can't accept..."

"Why not? I have enough for two."

"I'll find a way to pay you back."

"I owe you far more than you'll ever owe me."

"I owe you my life. I guess you don't consider that much."

"I didn't mean to insult...."

He struggled to keep his face angry. "You certainly cut deep with your insults, but I'll forgive you. Kiss and make-up?"

She twisted her head in question.

"An old Earth custom to end quarrels. We kiss to show no hard feelings remain." Congratulating himself for being a crafty fox, he opened his arms to her.

Curiosity about kissing after too brief a first sample shimmered in her hazel eyes followed by sensual desire. She bent toward him.

His arms circled her shoulders bringing her closer.

As their lips neared, she quivered, not with desire but sick panic. Her nostrils flared, and she pulled back against his arms.

Murmuring soft nonsense as if she were a frightened child, he stroked the back of her head. She closed her eyes and shuddered but didn't fight his embrace.

"Oh, Mara." He kissed her forehead and released her. She brushed his cheek with warm lips and sat down and away from him as if escaping deadly danger.

He wanted to ask what was wrong, but her fear answered where words could not. He'd made a terrible error kissing her and waking her sensuality. Until then, she'd innocently accepted their relationship as between equals, scientists and "sisters." Now she saw him as a man, and in such a strictured society, their sensual response must be taboo without marriage.

Closing his eyes, he fought to control total panic. He'd not only lost his family and his life on Earth; he'd also destroyed his relationship with Mara.

Chapter 6

Lt. Hallie d'Leda walked through Cadaran's front door expecting trouble. Her eyes swept over the living room and stopped at the full length painting of her commander in chief. She straightened Cadaran's formal portrait with careful hands then caressed the lufta wood frame. What a magnificent woman Cadaran was. If Hallie could only be a tenth as fine an officer, she'd be fortunate.

She glanced down at the smeared dust on her hands. As she'd suspected, Edrea was gold bricking. "While the commander's away, the sub-ordinates will play," she murmured and began to prowl around the room in search of other indications of neglect. The soil around the potted plants was bone dry, the furniture powdered with dust, and the carpeting filthy. It was amazing how dirty things could get in a few days. Edrea had been too lazy even to cut on the robot cleaners.

Hallie cursed and began to stalk through the other rooms. She kept avoiding the harem room, but, finally, she steeled herself to go in. If anything happened to Cadaran's expensive new bull, the manure would hit the afterburners. Cadaran had kept him for an unprecedented six weeks and usually bounced into headquarters around noon with a big smile on her face. Hallie would be happy to see him go and Cadaran return to her usual efficient self. Bulls! The Goddess take their balls!

Opening the door, she entered. The afternoon light barely penetrated the room through the tiny oriel window. She pushed on the overhead light. The bull stretched on his back in the rumpled bed, his arms wrapped around his ribs, a sheet draped carelessly over bare loins.

Just like a bull to sleep all day. Worthless.

His breakfast sat on the table by the door, the heated cereal untouched and unpleasantly congealed. She didn't blame him for that. She wouldn't eat that swill either. There was no sign of lunch although late afternoon.

"Bull." She bit her tongue for using her private slang. "Man. Man. Wake up." When he didn't wiggle, she prodded his shoulder with her fingers then wiped them off on her uniform.

Moaning, he clutched his ribs, his head falling sideways, his damp black curls covering his eyes.

Her hackles rising with apprehension, she examined him. The left side of his jaw was bruised as were his upper chest and rib area. If he were one of her troopers, she'd say he'd been in a brawl, but delicate little bulls didn't brawl.

Damn, his fragile Earther bones and body must have been injured. She'd called the medics in half a dozen times since he'd been here about various fractures and injuries from his pathetic attempts at pleasuring a powerful woman like Cadaran.

Staunching the images and the anger she always felt about this bull, she eased his arms away from his ribs and ran her fingers along his left side.

He opened bleary eyes as bright a green as a rab-cat's.

She gawked with fascination for a moment before dragging her gaze back to his ribs.

He flinched at her touch and slurred, "Who? Seen you before."

"I'm Cadaran's aide. Where do you hurt?"

"The usual. Fractured ribs, slight internal injuries, lotus withdrawal." He beamed, bitter irony shining only in his eyes.

"Fragile Earther." A terrible suspicion snarled for attention. "Did Edrea do this?"

"Your noble leader. A farewell present 'til she came back. Left her a few myself."

Snorting with disbelief, Hallie left.

By the time the medic had reglued his ribs with a medi-laser and repaired other minor damage, he was dead white despite the pain killers. Hallie helped the medic ease him from the diagnostic table onto his bed.

The medic's eyes swept over his nakedness, then she winked with sexual approval at Hallie, who glared and pulled clean sheets over him. The medic shrugged, packed her equipment, and left.

Hallie felt his rab-cat eyes on her. "Can you eat?"

"Vaguely remember how." He smiled beguilingly.

"When did you eat last?"

"Day the bitch left."

"What's a bitch?"

"A handsome woman on Earth."

"Oh. You haven't eaten in two days! I'm going to gut Edrea and leave her for the tyrlins."

Hallie settled for verbally gutting Edrea for the neglect of house and bull. If she hadn't come, the bull could have died. She prepared nutrient drink herself and brought it into the harem room.

He dozed, his head thrown back on the pillow, his throat exposed. Fragile, helpless little bull. She nudged his shoulder. "Bull, wake up."

His lids crept open.

"Food." She helped him sit up then tipped the drink to his lips. He sipped slowly then rested his head on her shoulder. She flinched and bit her lip but let him stay. The things she did for Cadaran.

He sipped again then snuggled against her shoulder. "You're very kind."

She snorted. "I grew up on a farm. I don't believe in abusing the livestock. It ruins profits."

"Grew up on a farm too. On Earth. Sure do miss it, and my mother." He gazed at her with huge liquid green eyes.

Her heart almost twisted in pity before she ordered it not to. "I sure don't miss my farm. Soldiering's a better life."

"My name is Kellen. I was an explorer. Xeno-anthropologist. Never missed the farm 'til this place. Haven't even seen the sky in weeks."

"Shut up and drink your meal." She shoved the glass to his lips.

He drank. "Don't like me, do you?"

"No, I don't."

Beaming, he rubbed his cheek against her shoulder. "Well, I like you, Lt. Hallie. You are a true bitch."

Hallie blinked with surprise. She'd never been called handsome before.

MARA put her finger to her lip for silence as she entered Tristan's hospital room and pointed vigorously at the cooler flask in her hand.

Tristan looked about wildly for spies in the empty room and mimicked her gestures.

She giggled in spite of her best attempt at keeping a serious face and came to his bed. "Good morning, Tristan." She kissed his forehead.

"Good morning, pixie." Beaming, he slid his left fingers through her shoulder length curls in a semi-caress. Because he hadn't tried to kiss her lips since the first time, she no longer flinched at his touch. He elevated his bed until he was sitting partially upright. "What's the secret?"

"A celebration in honor of our third anniversary."

"Three months in this hellish place with a heavenly angel

watching over me." He stretched lazily, the sheet drifting to his waist. The brutal scars zigzagging across his chest no longer brought tears to her eyes. Some were now new pink flesh on honey skin, the others pale reminders of their former ugliness. Muscle and meat had even partially filled in the bone thin hollows of his broad chest and arms. Her heart thudded in response.

She flushed, realizing she was staring at his chest, and stifled the breeding feelings which always threatened to erupt in his presence.

He beamed, his smile as sunny a gold as his hair. "I have a surprise for you on our anniversary, too."

"You do? What?" She leaned closer. "Tell me."

"A woman who obviously can't handle suspense. I'll tell you later. What have you brought me?" He leaned closer.

"Obviously a man who can't handle suspense. But *I* won't be cruel." She unscrewed the canister and presented it.

His nose twitched as he sniffed. "Smells fruity." He stuck in a finger. "Feels cold and creamy. Ice cream!"

"Ice cream. Homemade kista ice cream."

"What's kista?"

She pulled two spoons from her tunic pocket and gave him one. "Try it."

He scooped out pink ice cream with the red kista fruit swirled through it and sampled. Closing his eyes, he rolled it around his mouth then swallowed. "That's wonderful. Almost like strawberries from home. Bless you, Mara."

Beaming, she gave him the canister.

After several spoonfuls, he gazed at her through long lashes like a child who knows he's been naughty. "Share?"

She took a spoonful. "Go ahead. I had some before I came."

Sighing happily, he concentrated on the ice cream.

Watching him, she couldn't decide if his intense pleasure at small things was a natural element of his personality, or if his near death had made him more appreciative. He certainly had made her much more appreciative of the world since he'd entered it three months before. His sense of joy was as great as Floppy's. She'd always assumed that joy was the nature of a rab-cat, but perhaps Floppy had discovered it too after so nearly dying.

Tristan's spoon rattled around the bottom of the canister. He lifted the spoon and finished off the last of the ice cream with an ecstatic smile.

Her heart surged with a rush of kinning so intense the room spun dizzily around her. She closed her eyes and blinked away tears of emotion.

The canister clattered onto the bed stand.

Mara opened her eyes.

"I had a different doctor visit earlier."

She straightened worriedly. "I wasn't expecting a specialist. Who was she?"

"A Dr. Ilka d'Vida. She said she was with the government. She was quite pleasant."

The harem's chief medical examiner! "Did she examine you?"

"Yes, she poked and prodded then mumbled over my records."

"What did she say?"

"Not much. They never tell me anything. I'm only the patient."

Mara uttered a silent prayer her carefully prepared future for Tristan wasn't about to be destroyed. "I'll find her and beat or bribe the information out of her."

"Sic 'em, pixie. Get those dragons."

"I warned you I had a vicious, tenacious side."

"Like a snapping turtle. Once you take hold, you never let go." He chuckled. "Just so long as the snapping turtle's on my side I'm happy."

"Behave then."

"Yes, ma'am." He saluted.

"You had a surprise for me." She stared menacingly at him. "Out with it before I get mean again."

Throwing his arms up, he parodied horror. "Don't hurt me. Don't hurt me." His blue eyes sparkled like a sunny day after a week of rain. "Ready?"

"Yes!"

"Here it is." He tugged at his sheet until his bare feet were uncovered.

She studied them. Even his well-formed, elegant feet gave her an absurd wave of tenderness and breeding feelings. "You have very pretty toes. That was a nice surprise."

He chuckled. "Thank you, I think so too, but that's not the surprise. Watch this."

The feet swayed to the left, they swayed to the right, the toes wiggled, the feet swayed forward and back.

Tears of joy streamed down her cheeks. "Oh, Tristan. That's so wonderful." She hugged him burying her face on his chest.

He held her, stroking her head, and let her sob her happiness out. "I woke up this morning on my side, my legs curled under me."

Sniffing, she blinked tears onto his shoulder. Somehow she'd managed to get totally onto the bed. "Do you have complete movement?"

His arm tightened around her waist, and he rubbed his cheek against the top of her head. "Not yet, but they can't hold me down now. I'm going to dance you across that bar room yet."

"What?"

"I meant I'm not stopping until I'm back to the way I was before."

"May the Goddess watch over you."

"She has so far."

Mara's heart fell as she considered what this improvement might mean. "Did that new doctor see the movement?"

"Yes, of course."

Wincing, Mara prayed harder.

"What's wrong?" His fingers twined in her curls.

"I hadn't meant to tell you this yet, but.... Would you like to stay with me when you're strong enough?"

"Of course! That would be wonderful. Away from this medical box..." He paused. "What about you? Won't others talk?"

"My mother never cared. She did what she believed in despite what others thought. I can do no less. How could giving you a home be wrong?"

His voice caught. "A home, Mara?"

She gazed up into the sky blue sweetness of his eyes. "By the laws of Arden, as a...newcomer you need the protection of a citizen. Would you trust me with that protection?"

His heart pounded against her ear, and he smiled. "I'll trust you with anything I have, even my body, such as it is."

"Thank you." She returned the smile shyly, then dropped her gaze.

Curled together, they both remained silent for a long time, Tristan probably thinking of a future away from this room while she considered the obstacles of getting him out and keeping him once she got him out.

"You haven't told me how my wiggling toes can screw up your taking me out of this place."

"Timing. I've just gotten first approval to keep you, but you were considered a total invalid."

"And a less total invalid can't leave here?"

"Maybe not with me. The government might prefer a different

guardian."

"You make me sound like a child."

"Arden isn't Earth." She caressed the hand tucked at her stomach. "Our laws are very different because of the plague and the drastic shifts in our social structure because of it."

Fortunately, he didn't question her further because she didn't know how to explain her problems without explaining the harem, and that was one thing she preferred not to discuss. Especially not when his health was still precarious. She couldn't see proud, wise Tristan accepting life as a harem breeder, and with a future in the harem, he might stop fighting his injuries.

But if he did regain full use of his legs....

She winced again, hating herself for wanting both his complete cure and no cure at all.

"Mara?" He caressed her temple and cheek.

His eyes blazed blue with deep emotion as they met hers. She was suddenly intensely conscious of sensations she'd struggled to ignore—the heat and male essence of his body, his soft flesh against her cheek, the strong, firm muscles of the arm that circled her waist, his chest rubbing against her breast.

Desperately afraid he was going to kiss her and desperately eager that he would, she stared frozen by the heat of his eyes.

He leaned closer and brushed a kiss on her forehead. "Thank you, Mara. Whatever happens with the dragons, thank you for offering me a new home."

The warmth of his kiss filling her, she blinked tears. "I have such kinning for you."

"And I have such kinning for you, pixie." His arm slid away from her almost brusquely. "As much as I'm enjoying snuggling with you like a pair of kittens, I fear we may shock a nurse."

She wiggled hastily out of the bed and smoothed her tunic and hair. Both of them had always avoided physical displays of affection with others present. Tristan had understood the need instinctively without her warning. The nurses might think they were displaying breeding behavior and Mara would be barred from ever seeing Tristan again.

While Tristan uncharacteristically fussed with the sheets around his hips, she sat down in the chair by the bed.

"Your version of Basic confuses me sometimes, but it has strong points. We don't have an elegant word like kinning to express family affection. I'd like to add it to our vocabulary."

"You don't? What do you use?"

"Love. It's even more of a catch-all word on Earth. It expresses kinning, fondness for anything from ice cream to your planet, the feeling between a husband and wife—"

"What are a husband and wife?"

"My mother and father are wife and husband to each other."

"Oh, a breeding pair. Why did your mother choose your father to be her breeder, I mean her husband?"

Tristan chuckled and brushed back his curls with a thrust of his fingers. "She says Dad picked her, but I think the decision and attraction were mutual. Dad went to a reading by a famous Earth poet, the only empty chair was right beside him, and Mom took it. They were more interested in each other than the poet."

"That's all? Chance and breeding attraction brought marriage between them?"

"No, but it was the start. Their relationship developed from that. Mutual interests, friendship, then love."

Mara sighed with relief. For a moment, she'd feared their relationship had the same flimsy basis as the reason Patta would choose a breeder at the Common. Such a frivolous basis didn't jibe with the mental image she'd created of his family from the hours of wonderful stories he'd told about them. She wanted him to define "love" between husband and wife but didn't have the nerve to ask.

"If your mother had met a man who loved her like that, you'd have a father now. You'd have known about removing beards without meeting me."

Mara considered all the stories of Tristan's tender relationship with his father then replied fiercely, "I wish I had one."

THE image of a handsome, older physician with graying brown hair and shrewd, kind eyes, Ilka d'Vida smiled with acerbity and motioned to the empty chair in front of her desk. "I've been expecting you."

Mara nodded, smiling, and settled into the chair. She knotted her fingers on her lap and tried to concentrate all her fear and tension into them while keeping her face and eyes serene. "Tristan told me you visited."

"A charming man. Quite intelligent. I enjoyed talking to him."

"He's brilliant."

Ilka chuckled. "A trace of maternal pride there."

"I thought him brilliant before I met him. I've mentioned he's a professional colleague. I've known his articles and reputation for years."

"Indeed." Ilka tented her fingers on the top of her desk.

"His slight increase in movement. What does it mean?"

"He's stymied every prediction we've made of his condition so far. Normally I would say he may gain partial use of his legs but would remain in a wheelchair."

"He has strong will, but I fear he may have used up his miracles."

"Perhaps. I didn't expect such pessimism from you."

"I think you understand my reasoning."

The doctor nodded. "Fear of losing him."

"Do I still have permission to take him into my home?"

"I see no reason not to. The hospital environment isn't conducive to healing."

"No." Mara fought a surge of elation at that small victory. "And if he does regain use of his legs?"

"You know the answer to that."

"I'd like to change the answer." Mara bit her tongue.

Ilka's eyes twinkled with amusement.

"I've asked about you. You're a true scientist, a fine doctor. You didn't get your position through politics."

Ilka laughed. "I got this position through lack of politics. I'd prefer another."

"If Tristan had been a great medical researcher who could find the cure for the plague or some other terrible problem, would you want that genius to be thrown away so his body could breed with some fool who thinks only of breeding, shopping, and the latest ball scores?"

"I wouldn't be thrilled with the prospect."

"In his profession, he has the very real chance to improve human existence through his work. He has the ability and the background to tap black holes as an energy source. A few more years of work, and he'll have the theoretical equations."

Ilka whistled.

"Yes. Can you imagine the good that will bring?"

"And the profits and reputation to Arden for all the greedy little bureaucrats."

"Exactly." They shared the smile of fellow conspirators. "You'll help me?"

"How can I not. But frankly, I can't do you much good. Medical decisions are the only ones I make without interference. I'm tied up in stupid regulations and self-important superiors. I can't help the poor men I'm supposed to watch over. Even those in...less than perfect situations."

"But I've given you a sweet to tempt the bureaucrats with."

"A sweet which requires a mind to understand it. I fear most don't have one."

"Tell them Jorel's energy light converter was nothing in comparison to what Tristan's equations and the tapping of black holes can bring them. Planets have gone to war for less profit."

"That's a frightening idea."

"The plague is a marvelous military defense."

"And cheap. So you'd like me to spread the message of his value."

"If you would."

"He might not land in the harem, but you won't keep him."

Mara's stomach somersaulted. "I hope they'll realize I'm the only scientist on Arden capable of helping him with his research."

"That's sensible. Don't expect sensible from them."

"I'm praying for a miracle." Mara twisted her fingers. "If Tristan's declared healthy enough for the harem, would you make certain I have first choice. I have lottery right."

"You seek lottery right. Officially?"

"If he goes into the harem, yes."

"I'll prepare the papers to sign."

Mara paled. "Certainly my year with him doesn't start immediately!"

Ilka patted her shoulder. "If the papers are signed now, I'll have them on the day he's declared healthy so he won't be taken away from you."

"Thank you."

"He'll be very expensive to buy, and the cost of equipping a harem room is incredible."

"I expected that. I've been conserving funds and liquidating some property."

"He's in no shape to sire a child. He may never be. Do you intend to breed with him if you can?"

"His genetic profile compliments mine. That's how I became aware of his presence on Arden. I want him as sperm source for my child, but breeding isn't necessary."

Ilka studied her with wise family doctor eyes. "He's very

beautiful. There's no shame in wanting to breed with him."

"But he's a colleague and a friend. Breeding seems... wrong."

"He's certainly nothing like most of the men I see. If you don't conceive by the end of your year with him, I'll see what I can do about using artificial insemination for a child. Maybe several children if I can arrange it. A pity to waste his genetic material on most of the women who have lottery right."

The idea of having Tristan's children warming her and the inevitable image of some other woman taking him away chilling her, Mara thanked the doctor.

Chapter 7

Her chubby cheeks reddening with fury, Novia pounded the kitchen counter with her fist. "You're bringing a man into my house!"

Sighing, Mara straightened. "I told you over a month ago Tristan would come if I could get him."

Novia mangled her short steel gray hair with her fingers as if fighting a desire to mangle Mara. "A man in Jorel's house! Your mother should have let me spank you like I wanted when you were naughty. See what her soft heart has brought her—a daughter who spits on her memory."

Mara winced at the vicious dig. "Mother would understand about Tristan, but it is my decision."

"A daughter who thinks with her hormones, not her mind. Use your mind, little one. Use your mind."

"I am using my mind, and my heart. If I were using my hormones, I wouldn't be bringing in an invalid."

Novia's eyes burned with righteous zeal. "Men are dangerous creatures, spiteful and troublemaking. You're bringing down doom on your head, on all our heads."

"Certainly you don't believe that crackpot nonsense. Tristan is wonderful—kind, generous, brilliant. You won't even notice he's a man after you get used to him."

Snorting, Novia turned her back. "Jorel and I raised a rattle brain idiot. Publicly bringing in a man after your mother spoke so passionately against them. She accepted scorn for what she believed in, laughter from fools, and she never lowered her head or her proud voice, and now you! Everyone will laugh at my Jorel because of you." Novia sniffed and swiped at tears.

Mara rested her hand on Novia's shoulder. "Please believe me. I'm doing what I must. I'm certain Mother would understand. I'm doing what I believe in too. It may seem I'm going against her, but I'm following the spirit of her beliefs if not her direct words."

"Self-justification, that's what it is. Following your own way. I'm ashamed of you."

"I won't change my mind."

The doorbell buzzed.

"That will be the government workers." Mara trudged to the front door and let the two women in. She led them into her bedroom suite. "This will be the harem room area. Here are my perimeters." She showed them into the adjoining study area then out into the walled garden. "I want access into the garden. Put the forcefield generators on the walls."

The older worker whistled. "That will cost a fortune."

"I know. I won't have him locked away in a tiny room with no access outside."

"It's your money, ma'am."

"I'll be in the outer living area if you need me."

Her mouth twisted with disbelief, Novia waited at the bedroom door then followed her back into the kitchen.

Mara sagged into a chair at the breakfast table. "Go ahead and say it."

Novia stood behind another chair and rung its top with her big hands. "Your mother's suite a harem! That's desecration."

"Mother has been dead three years. It is my suite now, my house. I'm forced by law to have the damned forcefield generators."

"Hormones! You're worse than that brainless Patta and her chatter of the Common. Bringing your bedwarmer into your own room."

"When Tristan comes, I'll move into the spare bedroom."

"I knew I should have forbidden that girl visiting when she first showed her nose in here when you were kids."

"Patta has been a loyal friend. She doesn't agree with what I'm doing, but she's supported me and helped me."

"And I don't." Novia mimed holding a baby in her arms. "I was the first to hold you, helped name you. I held your mother first. As much kinning for you both as if you'd been my own blood." She sniffed loudly. "And you say I don't support you."

Mara blinked her own tears. "I have great kinning for you. You are the grandmother I didn't have."

"Then listen to me. Don't bring that man here. Forget him."

Mara thought of Tristan alone in that hospital room. "No."

Her chin held high, Novia stiffened. "Very well, I'm leaving if he comes. I'll go stay with my sister in Galina."

"I don't want you to leave, I need you, but leave if you must. He needs me as you don't. I hoped to give him a new family for the one he's lost, but if I can only offer myself, then so be it."

Novia blinked with disbelief. "You choose that man over me!"

"No, I choose one option over the other. I have deep kinning for you both." She stood. "No more of this. I won't change my mind. Please stay, but I understand if you have to leave." She trudged into the living room.

His long ears quivering with interest, Floppy sat on the sofa and watched the workers in the bedroom.

Plopping down beside him, she stroked the rab-cat's black head. "Oh, Floppy. Novia just doesn't understand."

His ears went back, and he glared at her, his version of the silent treatment about Tristan still in force. He leaped from the sofa and escaped toward the kitchen and Novia, his tail straight and quivering with fury.

Mara fought tears. All she'd wanted to do was give Tristan a home and family, and all she'd succeeded in doing was destroying the home and family she had.

HER back and legs stiffening instinctively into parade ground at ease, Hallie stood in front of Cadaran's desk as she waited for Cadaran's attention.

Cadaran pulled an information cube from her computer and stuffed it into her uniform pocket then faced Hallie with a warm smile. "So kind of you to come to my home at this hour of the night, Lieutenant."

"Happy to, sir. Problems?"

"Captain Rani who handles harem consignments. She's proven totally unreliable, much too trigger happy despite repeated warnings. I must replace her, and until I do, I must see to shipments. I want you to keep an eye on things for me until I get back in a few days."

"I'm unfamiliar with her."

Huge brown eyes framed by short-cropped black hair, Cadaran beamed. "As you should be. That aspect of my work is strictly for higher echelons."

"Yes, sir. How can I help you tonight?"

"Such loyalty is so refreshing." Cadaran studied her. "You've changed your hair color. The blonde streaks are very nice."

Hallie blushed. "Thank you, sir. My drab brown hair needed something."

Emotions shifted behind Cadaran's eyes although her smile never wavered. "I haven't thanked you for taking such good care of Green Eyes while I was gone several weeks ago. Feeding him meals and tending him. I appreciate such personal attention when my work keeps you so busy already."

"I didn't trust anyone else enough with such a valuable man, especially your personal property."

Cadaran's smile tightened. "It's so nice to have someone you can trust."

Hallie's hackles rose with apprehension. What had she done?

"I understand you talked together."

Edrea had been spying. "He babbled a great deal, nothing important. He missed you and was lonely."

"I'm certain he was. And you talked to him?"

Hallie searched her memory. "Very little. He did ask me about rab-cats. I told him of the colony which lives near my mother's farm. Was that all right, sir?"

"Nothing treasonous in that subject."

Hallie didn't feel particularly reassured. "No, sir."

Cadaran settled back into her desk chair. "According to your records, you've never visited the Common."

"No, sir."

"Why not?"

Hallie replied bluntly with part of the truth, "I can't afford it."

"Even a common soldier can afford it with military discounts, Lieutenant."

"Most of my pay goes to my mother to restock the farm. We lost most of our dairy herd to a tyrlin. Damn thing murdered them just to murder them."

"A good daughter. I thought you might enjoy learning what pleasuring's like with a man. For a change."

"Sir?"

"Green Eyes is primed for pleasuring. Enjoy him with my blessings since I have to leave."

Cold shivered down Hallie's spine. "I can't do that."

"I just said you could."

"I meant it's too generous, sir."

"I insist. Don't worry. He's a gentle creature. He won't harm you."

"He's just a man. Why should I be afraid of him?"

“Why, indeed?” Cadaran came to her feet. “I must be going. Enjoy him and my house while I’m gone.” She nodded briskly. “I believe in giving my soldiers what they deserve.”

Hallie watched Cadaran sashay out then slumped into a nearby chair. Bed that bull! Her skin crawled with dismay. To actually have him touch her, put his staff in her. She squirmed.

What if she got pregnant? Her military career would be ruined, and back to the farm for her and the baby. Well, she did adore children, but she’d never dreamed of having one herself. No, the military was better for blunt, tall, plain Hallie.

But he’d said she was handsome.

She smoothed her new hairdo. No woman had ever called her handsome. Just like a bull to have such bad taste.

She should just leave and forget Cadaran’s offer. But Cadaran would find out and be offended.

Hallie sighed. She had no choice. She must bed the bull.

But not immediately. She walked into the living room and helped herself to a glass of ballard at the bar. First, she was going to get drunk.

HALLIE swaggered into the harem room, a half empty bottle of ballard in her left hand. The bull sat on the edge of the bed, his back to her, his head and shoulders slumped.

She cleared her throat.

He jumped to his feet and spun, his knee-length green silk robe whirling against his form. His face shifted from sullen hatred to surprise. “Hello, Lt. Hallie.”

Words caught in her throat so she nodded.

“I was expecting Cadaran.”

“She’s gone, called away for a few days on business.” Hallie rewarded herself for a steady voice by taking another swig of ballard. It burned its way down her throat and further blunted her discretion. “She said I had to breed with you.”

He pushed back the long black curls on his forehead and eyed her. “Where I come from there are actions beyond the power of your commanding officer. Who you have sex with is one of them.”

“Can’t offend her.” She shrugged unhappily.

“I sure as hell would.”

“Stupid bull. Let’s get this over with. Come here.” She took another swig and put the bottle on the bed stand.

He moved toward her, a curious jerk to his walk as if he were a child's marionette, and stopped in front of her. He glanced down at the bottle. "May I?"

"Help yourself."

Picking up the bottle, he sipped, swirling the liquor around his mouth, then swallowed. "Pretty good. What's it called?"

"Ballard."

"I sure do miss beer. Haven't had one since I landed on this cursed planet."

"Didn't know bulls drank beer."

"This one does." He took another swallow.

She forced herself to sit down on the edge of the bed. She'd best get this over with before the warm buzz of the alcohol faded and panic returned. She yanked off her shoes then began to tug at her tunic with shaking hands.

He sat down beside her. "I don't have any choice, but you do. If you don't want to do this, you don't have to. You can tell her you did."

The surge of relief made her dizzier than the ballard. She dropped her hands. "Would you back me up?"

"I have trouble lying under lotus with a direct question, but I'll try."

"Then I'd better go through with it."

"Why don't you want to have sex with me? I thought this was a planet of sex-starved females. Is Cadaran's repulsiveness rubbing off on me?" He gulped down more ballard then handed her the bottle.

Hallie guzzled down the last of the liquor. "Most of us aren't sex-starved, and Cadaran is the handsomest woman around, handsomest woman I've ever seen."

"I see."

She blushed, realizing he did.

Dark emotions behind his eyes, he smiled. "So I'm not ugly. What a relief."

Trapped by the green magic of his eyes, she ignored his sardonic tone and studied his strong even features and long black curls. "You're beautiful."

"And for this I busted my butt for a doctorate."

A mere bull was making fun of her, but she didn't know how to respond. She slammed down the bottle onto the bed stand and fumbled her tunic upward. It tangled on her head.

"Let me." Big warm hands slid up her arms, and the tunic was tossed away. His eyes settled on her breasts. "Nice to see curves again."

Hallie squirmed defensively. "They're not much."

"Wine glass size. A favorite of many bulls." He sighed, pain twisting his features. "Let's both get it over with. How do you want it? You have to tell me. I'm literally yours to command."

She sought frantically for inspiration. "The way you do it with Cadaran."

He laughed, a cold sound that froze her. "As you wish." He nudged her backwards on the bed and leaned over her.

A quiver of fear and uncertainty shook through her. His hand settled on her breast and kneaded, fingers digging into her nipple.

Biting her lips, she closed her eyes. She'd expected a stupid, awkward bull to be painful, and she'd been right. His hands slid downward into her pants and panties. Both crept over her hips to her legs and settled on her feet on the floor. She kicked them away, her thighs clinching instinctively.

He eased off the bed.

She forced open her eyes. He stood up, unknotted his robe, and slipped it off his shoulders.

His nakedness powerful and magnetic, she stared at the harsh male muscles of his chest and thighs, the big bones, the angular strength so different from the subtle curves and softness of a woman. He was a bull, all male vitality and danger.

He knelt beside her on the bed. "You have to give the lotus a nudge. Here." He lifted her hand and pulled it to his staff.

Flushing, she forced herself not to yank her hand away. His fingers circled hers and guided the movement of her hands. She gasped, feeling his response and the raw power she was waking.

He moaned with pain, his whole body quivering as he grew. Her insides clinched with dread at his size.

Breeding must be painful to both, she decided dismally, and she wondered how humans had reproduced enough to colonize the stars.

"No more." He eased her hand away.

She was too frightened to bluff it out anymore. "What now?"

"Have you ever done this before?"

"No."

"Shit." His face twisted with dark emotions. "I can't do it. Even on this damn immoral slaver planet."

"Do what?"

"You don't want it the way Cadaran does. Order me not to."

"Why not?"

"Cadaran has sick sexual tastes." At her sound of disbelief, he added, "She's had a great deal of experience. What I do to her would hurt you."

Working with troops, Hallie had learned to recognize a lie easily, and she didn't recognize one now. "Very well, don't do it like you do with Cadaran. How should you do it?"

"Tell me to make love to you."

"What is making love?"

"Just tell me, and I'll show you."

She could always make him stop. "Make love to me."

He stretched out beside her and smiled down at her. "I won't hurt you. Don't be afraid."

"I'm not. Cadaran said you were gentle."

He chuckled. "That woman must have it in for you sending you to me. What did you do to make her angry?"

"Angry? This was a reward."

"It wouldn't have been if I acted as she expected me to. Trust me on that. She wanted you hurt."

Hallie shook away the thought.

"Suit yourself." He rubbed his face between her breasts, his nose feathering a nipple then the other. "You have beautiful breasts."

"Thank you." She gasped, her nipples rising. His lips and tongue followed the path of his nose, each paying lavish homage to her breasts.

Unexpected sensations flared through her. She hadn't expected this from a man's touch. She concentrated on the subtle skill of his lips and the flutter of his hand on her thigh.

His fingers settled in the curls at the base of her belly. His lips left her nipple, and he mumbled against her skin. "What do you call this on Arden?" His fingers wiggled on her belly.

Feeling like a girl again sharing naughty talk with another, she giggled. "The center of pleasure."

"And this?" He rubbed himself against her thigh, his heat branding her.

Moisture and excitement flooding, she jolted. "The gift or staff."

His hand and lips circled then began to pleasure once more. She relaxed, her thighs opening to the teasing probe of his fingers. His hand danced and seduced always drawing back before reaching its goal until she was mindless and eager for what she'd feared minutes before. Her pelvis thrust to meet his fingers. Her legs parted. The fingers danced within.

She moaned, and her hips joined the dance.

He nibbled downward. Rockets flared in her stomach. Sliding off the bed, he knelt between her legs, and his lips and tongue seduced as his fingers had.

His breath, ragged and hot, seared her tender flesh, then his tongue found her center and probed.

She began to writhe. She'd never, never expected this from a man.

He brought her to the edge of pleasure, then retreated, then to the edge again, then back, each time the precipice higher. Moaning, she arced, her head back, her throat tense and straining.

His finger replaced his tongue.

Lost in the struggle for ultimate pleasure, she wasn't conscious he'd mounted her until his staff eased into her, his chest rubbing her nipples.

Suddenly very still and aware, she gasped as the heat and fullness penetrated. He murmured soft nonsense words of assurance, stroking her ribs and hips, and began to move gently.

This wasn't intrusion as she'd expected, but completion and pleasure.

Wrapping her arms around his shoulders, her feet coming up, her legs circling his thighs, she followed the rhythm his hands showed her. He thrust now with growing power, the bull vitality still held in check.

The edge of pleasure was before her again. If she just reached out...Her hips thrust faster. If she just reached out....

He pulled her away from the edge then drew her there again with his staff and the caress of hands. If she just reached out....

He retreated from the edge.

"Please, bull."

His voice was hoarse. "Say my name."

"Please, Green Eyes."

"My name."

She struggled frantically to remember. "Kellen. Please, Kellen."

He dropped her over the edge, his own body following. He cried out in pain and pleasure, his hot seed filling her.

Much later, she found herself on solid ground again, the man draped on her, their skin wet, their bodies still joined. His head drooped on her shoulder as if he were asleep or unconscious. She nudged his shoulder worriedly. "Did I hurt you?"

Grunting a negative, he propelled them both completely onto the bed with a powerful thrust of hips, then rolled bringing them to their sides. "What do you think?"

"I never thought a man could do that to me."

"I had a few surprises myself." He sat up and picked up the bottle of ballard. He sipped the last few drops. "Who'd ever thought this would be an antidote for..."

She sat up. "What?"

"Never mind. Is there any more of this around here?"

"Bottles."

"Get some more, then we'll discover what else this man can do for you."

Blushing, she slid out of bed. Very sore between the legs, she walked into the living room and collected a bottle. Fortunately, Edrea was only here during the day so she was spared her snide comments. Somewhere in Hallie's mind, a little voice was saying she'd done as Cadaran wanted, and she could go home, but her body was too damn curious and surprisingly happy. She'd stay.

He sat up in bed, his back against the headboard, the sheet pulled up to his waist. Smiling, he lifted the sheet for her. Shyly returning the smile, she slid in and gave him the bottle. He opened it and sipped then passed it to her. She sipped and passed it to him.

"Did that rab-cat really save you from the tyrlin?" He wrapped his arm around her shoulder.

She recalled a story she hadn't completed when she'd visited him the last time Cadaran had left him in her care. "Yes."

"The tyrlin was sneaking toward you and the cows, and some of the rab-cats who lived near your farm came charging toward you to warn you. What happened next?"

Remembering, she shivered. "I didn't understand what was happening. We'd always lived peacefully with the little cats. I thought they'd gone mad or were trying to attack me. Then they stopped in front of me and formed a line, their backs to me, and snarled. I saw the tyrlin in the rocks then. I wasn't armed. I shouted warning to the cows and took off running toward the farm house."

He nuzzled her ear. "What happened then?"

"The cows scattered, feeling my fear, and so did the rab-cats. I glanced back, and the damn tyrlin was after me. Those things are devils, killing for sheer meanness. I saw its fangs and burning red eyes and expected to meet the Goddess immediately. I stumbled and fell." She shook her head. "Out of nowhere, one of those rab-cats came flying toward the charging tyrlin. It leaped at its throat, landed, then the tyrlin went down. It was dead, flat dead. The rab-cat landed on its feet, shook itself, then trotted over to see if I was okay, wiggled its ears at me, and trotted off with the others following."

Kellen whistled. "An animal a little larger than a house cat stops a Bengal tiger. How?"

Hallie shrugged. "The tyrlin didn't have a mark on it. We called the authorities, and they took the carcass, but if they found out how it was killed, they didn't tell us. The next growing season, we planted a huge field of cat plant rather than a small patch for the rab-cats. They deserved it."

"And then some. I wonder how it killed the tyrlin. Venom? Psionics? Pressure to some vital nerve? Whatever their method I wouldn't want one of them angry with me. Do you think the rab-cat has human level intelligence?"

She thought of all her years on the farm watching the charming little cats. "They aren't stupid, and they're not like other animals. Maybe."

"I sure would like to meet some and have a go at communicating. That's my profession, alien communications." He sighed heavily, and his shoulders sagged.

Pity filled her, but she didn't know how to offer comfort.

"Rab-cats remind me of dolphins. Before we learned to communicate with dolphins and found out their enormous intelligence, they'd occasionally save a human swimmer's life."

He told her stories of dolphins, Earth seas, and early attempts at communications, then he began to tell of his own six months during graduate school learning to communicate with them. He went on to tell of some of his adventures in space and the people of different races he'd met. The words and memories poured out as if they'd been stoppered inside him for months.

She listened, enraptured by other worlds and another life so totally different from and yet similar to her own. She laughed and blinked tears, some of his adventures reminding her so much of military life she felt as if he were just one of the girls having a drink with her.

When he sputtered to a stop, he leaned back wearily and sipped from the bottle of ballard then handed it to her. She sipped then put it on the bed stand. "I'm sorry you're on Arden, bull. Our own men grow up in the harem and accept it, but you can't."

"I'm sorry, too." His eyes twinkled suddenly. "Can't you say my name?"

Lifting her eyebrows provocatively, she smiled. "Make me."

He pounced. They scuffled playfully for a few moments before she let him pin her face down on the mattress, his body draped over her. He blew with his lips against the nape of her neck. "Say my name."

She refused to squirm against the tickling dampness. "Bull, bull, bull."

"This calls for torture." His hands slid under her at breasts and belly and began delicious torture. She did squirm then, her body waking.

After long minutes, she moaned, "You're so good."

"Who's so good?"

"You."

"More torture." He nipped her shoulders and neck, his full staff rubbing and nuzzling her thighs.

She buried her face and stifled her desire to beg for more breeding.

His arms encircled her, bringing her to her hands and knees. He pointed her head so she could see them both in the mirror behind the bed. He knelt directly behind her.

"What are you doing?"

"Watch." His hands caught her hips, and he entered her.

She groaned with pleasure, slight pain, and surprise as he filled her, his chest rubbing against her back.

He whispered in her ear, "On the farm, did you ever watch a bull mate with a cow? Did you wonder how it felt? All that maleness within you? Did you feel dampness between your legs as you watched?"

Blushing, she refused to answer.

"I thought so. Now you're going to find out." He began to move within her. His hands caressed her hips and buttocks then trailed upward, enclosing dangling breasts and rotating.

The subtle pressures different with this new position, she moaned and began to rock back against him.

His fingers settled between her legs and caressed. "You're so sweet here, Hallie. So sweet and tight."

Her head jerked back against his face, and she cried out.

His thighs tensed, and he began to thrust against her with all the male power he'd held in check.

Images of breeding bulls jumbled in mental white heat with the mirror images of their writhing bodies, she met him with her own intensity. "You are a bull."

"Say my name."

She squealed like a breeding heifer, her head drooping, and rotated her hips into his slower thrusts to reach complete pleasure.

"Say my name."

Unable to bear anymore, she began to moan his name over and over again like a chant for release.

He gave her that release, his staff and fingers driving her into white hot pleasure, held her upright through the conflagration, then drove her again into flame.

Her legs and arms swayed as the pleasure spasms shot through her. Kellen moaned her name and exploded within her.

Much later, she rediscovered herself on her belly in bed, Kellen still draped over her. He nuzzled her ear.

She sighed happily and didn't protest when he stretched her out against him, his arm intimately around her waist, his face in her hair. To her surprise, she drifted off to sleep in his arms as if more than simple breeding had passed between them.

Later, he began to ask her questions. She answered them, letting him believe alcohol, sleep, and sex had weakened her sense of duty. She explained how a central computer controlled his detention bracelet and only Cadaran controlled the code key to release him. She even gave him a rough idea how the forcefields worked. She didn't tell him he had no chance of escape even with this information, nor that he had nowhere to hide on this planet even if he did escape.

She let him make love to her in thanks for the information. She refused to tell him all she'd been able to give him in exchange for such tender pleasures had been false hope.

Chapter 8

This was the most important moment in her life, the moment when her actions would change her entire future, her entire definition of who and what Mara d'Jorel was. Mara stared down at the harem contract which offered her limited ownership of Tristan Mallory, protected male of Arden, for one year or conception of a child.

Ilka d'Vida leaned across her desk. "I admit his fee is enormous, but I felt I couldn't have it low enough to tempt some bureaucrat into auctioning his services off rather than letting you have him. With his exotic beauty, he'd bring a fortune."

Mara shook her head in confusion. "I hadn't even looked at the price." She looked and flinched. "I must be taking care of his medical expenses by myself."

Her shrewd eyes crinkling, Ilka chuckled. "Arden will come out better than even on the transaction. The harem is extremely profitable."

"Between the government profits on Jorel's light converter and Tristan, taxes won't be raised for many years." Mara sighed. "Just as well. I won't be able to afford them."

"They'll find some way to spend the money."

Nodding absently, Mara stared at the contract.

"What's wrong?"

"Are you familiar with Jorel's feelings about the harem?"

"I think most women are. Not many make such a public stand against the harem system, and she was one of the few the government didn't throw in jail for doing it."

"We know why I'm signing this, but everyone else..."

"Most are fools."

"I feel as if...From the moment I sign this I'm another person. No longer Jorel's obedient little girl."

"We all must face that moment when we step away from our mother's shadow. It's called growing up. Few of us want it, but most of us must accept it."

"Well, so be it. Mara grows up." She picked up the stylus and signed the computer contract with a steady hand then planted an imprint of her thumb beside it.

Ilka saved the contract in her computer for later use. "Maybe we'll never need that. Tristan may remain an invalid, or better yet, we'll take him out of the harem and put him back at work where he belongs, with you."

"With me. Any luck yet?"

"Just feelers among possible allies. I must tread softly. Cadaran d'Hasta, head of Internal Security, is a fanatic about the harem. She resists the slightest changes in policy and has gained enormous control over the harem process."

Mara winced. "I've heard she's tough and smart."

"And vicious. Well, she's as greedy as the rest. The credits his black hole equations can bring should bring her around with the others."

"I pray they will." Mara nodded. "Thank you again."

"For a good cause—science and Arden."

"Science and Arden." Mara left the government building and got into her flitter. All the way home, she stared blindly at the countryside as she tried to absorb the enormity of what she'd done today and the tremendous change in herself and her life from the moment she'd seen Tristan's holograph in the harem catalog. She couldn't find a moment or choice she regretted even with the emotional price she would now pay.

The flitter settled by her house. She wandered in, still in a daze. No one greeted her, even Sheba and Coalie now ignored her as much as Novia and Floppy did. In her study, the computer's red light for new mail and messages was on. She glanced at her morning's list of mail on the computer screen, but nothing seemed worth reading. Her new copy of *Astronomy Journal* was already printed and waiting to be read. She picked it up and leafed through it with growing excitement. Her professional journals were the only real contact she had with her colleagues on Earth and the other colonies.

Plopping down in her desk chair, she flipped forward toward the table of contents. A full page color holograph of Tristan leaped out at her.

She gawked. Exuding charm, health, and intelligence, he smiled out at her, his essence and beauty captured in one picture. Her heart twisted with kinning and desire. She would replace the framed dull holograph from the harem files with this one to keep by her bed with her pictures of her mother, Novia, and Floppy.

After she had gazed at the holograph like a besotted mother with a newborn for a long time, her brain whistled loudly for attention. What was his holograph doing in the journal? She spread out the magazine and studied the accompanying article rimmed in black. It was Tristan's obituary.

Horrified, she dropped the magazine. Fighting illogical panic, she fell to her knees, opened the magazine back to the article, and read. Earth thought Tristan had died in the ship crash, no, not a crash. They thought the ship had blown up in space over a day's journey from Arden.

His family believed he was dead!

Tears streamed down her cheeks as she imagined his grieving family who had become so real to her through Tristan's long stories. Her heart aching for them, she read the obituary carefully. Not just a bland statement of his achievements, it was deeply personal and true to Tristan. Kinning, respect, and the terrible loss of his warmth and genius filled the piece. Several paragraphs spoke of his friend Kellen's contributions to space exploration and xeno-anthropology. Mara blinked tears for the man Tristan still bitterly grieved for.

The author of the obituary was Dorian Dalia.

Ice encased Mara's heart. She flipped to the back of the magazine and scanned the biographical notes of the contributors. Dorian's biography highlights jumped out at her—Earth, brilliant medical researcher, spent her teenaged years with the Mallorys. Yes, that was Tristan's beloved Dorian.

So this was why Dorian hadn't come. She didn't know Tristan was here on Arden waiting for her.

A deeper cold than jealousy filled Mara as she realized what the obituary meant. Arden had deliberately kept silent about Tristan's presence on the planet. Her planet's government was more wicked than she'd imagined to allow such cruelty and lies. Tristan was indeed dead to Earth now. And if Arden had left him dead, they intended to keep him dead. They wouldn't want his name on the black hole equations or his reputation to help Arden.

Once more her carefully laid plans to save him from the harem had been blown to hell.

DEEPLY intrigued, Mara bent closer to see the computer screen on Tristan's lap.

He shifted in his hospital bed and angled the screen for her. The animated figure on the screen looked like two tornadoes joined at their narrow stems. He tapped the top tornado which was black. "This is the black hole. Notice the swirling matter being sucked into its center at the stem. That swirling matter is what I'll tap for power. Like water is used to push an ancient water wheel, the matter being drawn into the maw of the black hole will push my energy collectors."

She shook her head. "Incredible if you can do it."

"It won't be easy. The pull of a black hole is one of the greatest forces in the universe. Stabilizing a power plant will be difficult. But that's another worry and another diagram." He tapped the white tornado. "The quasar I theorize on the other side of the black hole. I believe the energy sucked into the black hole comes out somewhere else in a quasar."

"Which spits out matter with the same abandon a black hole sucks it in."

"Exactly."

"Do you believe our black holes spit out through quasars in parallel universes or are they connected in this universe."

"Connected. That's why the Oz tunnel will work."

Mara's finger traced from the black tornado into the white. "Go into the black hole and come out somewhere else through a quasar. Instant transportation through enormous distances if we can build a ship to withstand the black hole's gravity. It's been theorized before but never proven."

"I was preparing to prove it when..." Pain flickered across his face, and he sighed. "Some other scientist who can leave their planet will do it for me. Dorian knew of my research notes, we've discussed the idea. She and Dad won't let my research be wasted. Someone else will send my probe through."

Mara struggled to keep her voice even. "What does Dorian have to do with this research? I thought she was a medical researcher."

"She is. I've been concerned with the effects of the black hole on humans."

"You weren't going through the hole yourself! That's suicide!"

He chuckled. "Of course not. We're hundreds of years away from that. I was concerned with the effects on those of us sending out a robot probe."

"Thank the Goddess! For a moment I was grateful your crash trapped you here in safety." She blushed. "Not that I'm ungrateful for your presence for myself."

"I understand. I'm not quite crazy enough to kill myself in the name of science, especially when a robot probe will work just as well."

"You!" She punched his arm.

Sunlight sparkling in his eyes, he chuckled. "Besides, who wants to travel an Oz tunnel without Dorothy. You'd make an excellent Dorothy."

She laughed, remembering his wonderful rendition of the Earth children's story to her and a growing audience of nurses. "Floppy's heart would be broken if he weren't Toto."

"And I," he flourished dramatically, "would be the Cowardly Lion."

"No, the Wizard. Definitely the Wizard."

He boomed out, "I am Oz!" His eyes crinkled with pleasure. "Hmmm, the role grows on me. Maybe I will be." He handed her the small computer. "I've put all my notes in here. You're welcome to read them. It's amazing how much information and data I remembered when I put my poor fried brain to it."

"Your brain is not fried."

"Maybe not with the pain killers down to a minimum. How about flabby from lack of use?"

"Better."

"Take the computer home with you and keep it for me." He stretched.

"Excited?"

"Of course not. I'm an adult. I'm just getting out of the hospital tomorrow." He grinned sheepishly. "I feel like a kid waiting for Christmas and summer vacation rolled into one big holiday. I'd do a happy dance if I could."

"I'll do your happy dance for you." She placed the computer on the bed stand.

"You don't look very happy. What's wrong?" He squeezed her hand.

Her fingers twined with his, and she blinked tears. "I'm having difficulties with the authorities."

He paled. "You mean I can't come to your house."

"Yes, of course, you can come. I want you to come so much. It's the stupid rules." She shook her head. "There are restrictions."

"That sounds ominous."

"The plague laws. I must keep you inside my home, and you won't be able to leave except under government control. They've set up an area for you, and you can't leave it. It will have special sensors to pick up your physical condition, and if you leave the area, you'll be taken back here and never be allowed to come back to my home."

His voice faltered. "That sounds like prison."

She shrugged helplessly.

"Is this isolation to protect me from the plague?"

"Partially since you may not have natural immunity. My home has a sterile field generator to kill viruses like the hospital does."

His fingers tightened around hers, but he spoke evenly. "Exactly how bad is the plague?"

"It is almost non-existent among native adults. A small percent of babies without natural immunity die within hours of being born. I have been told that others, like yourself, who were stranded here because of faulty spaceships have a high death rate." She added hastily, "Because you have survived even though critically ill gives the doctors a strong belief you already have natural immunity."

"Or damn good standard immunity shots. When they wear out..." He shook his head. "I won't worry about that."

Her heart twisted with terror. "How long do your shots last?"

"Five years."

"Then before that time is up, I will ship more medicine in from Earth with Ilka's help." She smiled cheerfully.

"And I'll live a long and happy life imprisoned in your home."

She winced at his bitterness. "I am fighting. I know you would prefer freedom to safety from the plague."

"You know me pretty well, don't you, pixie?" He lifted her hand and kissed her knuckles.

Her insides fluttered. "A good scientist never prefers safety over freedom and exploration, and you are a great scientist."

"And so are you, as well as being a great lady. As prisons go, I guess I've lucked out with yours, and I shouldn't complain."

She smiled shyly. "Not prison, home. My home and now yours."

"HEY, bull, I brought you some beer for lunch." Hallie sauntered into the harem room and sat down their lunch tray on the table by the door. Wearing his green robe, Kellen curled in a tight ball on the bed.

She snickered. Sitting down on the edge of the bed, she nudged his shoulder. "Did I tire you out so, bull? Wake up and have lunch with me, then you can sleep."

He moaned her name, his body shivering under her fingers.

Her hackles rose, and she murmured a quick prayer. His forehead burned her fingers, his hair dripped wet with sweat. He stank of fever and illness. "Sweet Goddess, not the plague."

Bolting out of the room, she called the medics then forced herself back into the harem room. She fluffed and tucked fresh sheets over him then stroked his head. "Medical help's coming, Kellen. I'll be right here."

Lost in her own misery, she sat down at the table, flipped open a beer, and sipped. She'd become fond of the bull in their two nights together. If he'd been a woman, she would call him a friend.

The medic, fear in her expression, arrived quickly. The plague wasn't something most of them had ever seen. She forced him onto his back and began to poke and prod, taking a blood sample. Half in concern, half in determination the other woman wouldn't take liberties with him, Hallie stood over her and watched.

Finally, the medic straightened. "Stupid fool, this isn't the plague. He's an adult. He isn't even sick."

Sighing with relief, Hallie forced her fist open. "It took you long enough to determine that, and it's your profession. He's an offworlder. What should I have thought? Well, what is it?"

"Lotus withdrawal. Vomiting, chills, fever, violent seizures, intense muscle pains. Give him another eight hours of that hell, and he'll come out of it." The medic began to pack up her supplies.

"Can't you give him something to ease it?"

"He's just a man. Let him suffer. You act like you care."

Hallie fought another battle with her temper. "He's worth a fortune, and he belongs to Cadaran. You want to explain your actions to her if he's injured?"

The medic shivered. "No thank you." She filled the medical sprayer and injected it into his shoulder. "Vitamins and a relaxant. It won't help much, but nothing will with lotus."

Hallie escorted the medic out then signaled a cleaner robot. Returning to the harem room with it following behind her, she swathed Kellen in the fresh sheets, then picked him up, cradling him against her shoulder. She ordered the robot, "Clean the bed and replace the linens," then carried Kellen into the bathroom.

She slipped protective goggles over his eyes, closed her own, and stepped into the shower without bothering to undress either of them. The slight cold sting of the sound waves pounded her body, wiggling off the dirt and sweat.

After several minutes, she nudged the shower off, removed his goggles, then carried him back into the bedroom and settled him in the clean bed. Tossing away the sheets she'd wrapped him in, she eased the robe off his body.

For a long moment, she stared in rapt appreciation of his male beauty—the long legs, muscular thighs, chest, and arms, and the extremely talented staff which had pleasured her so much. Her fingers began to slid over him, examining as her eyes examined, but she could find no injuries or bruises. She rolled him onto his stomach, then stroked down his back, buttocks, and legs. No injuries. Despite two intense nights of pleasuring, she'd never even bruised his fragile Earther body.

How did Cadaran who was smaller and more graceful injure him when she did not? She shrugged and concentrated on his comfort. She dressed him in a bed tunic and pants then covered him with the bed linens.

The medication seemed to be taking effect; the tense jerk of his muscles was now a quiet shiver. She cursed the lotus. She'd been told it was a harmless will tranquilizer and mild aphrodisiac, not sadistic filth.

His eyes fluttered open, bloodshot green eyes staring at her through some hellish inner agony.

Forcing a smile to hide her pity, she stroked his black curls. She wanted to tell him the pleasuring he'd given her wasn't worth the price he now paid, but she feared he'd think she placed little value on that pleasuring, and that was far from true. "Can I get you anything?"

"Go away. Please."

Her mouth opened with shock.

"Don't see me like this. It gets much uglier. Let me keep my pride with you."

As a warrior, she understood although she didn't expect such pride from a man. She nodded and left him.

MARA'S nightmare swirled with jumbled images. A tornado carrying off a farm house. Dorothy. Oz. The Wizard, and the Wicked Witch. She was Dorothy, and Tristan the Wizard, then Tristan was Dorothy, and she the Wizard. Dorian Dalia's intense words of feeling from Tristan's obituary whirled through like tornado winds. Mara knew Dorian was the Wicked Witch, but Dorian was also Dorothy, and Mara was the Wicked Witch who kept Dorothy imprisoned. The Wicked Witch whose heart, not body, was melting.

Through all the images, underscoring them like music, was the sound of a woman crying. It was Aunt Em, it was Tristan's grieving mother, it was Dorian.

"No..." Mara tossed in her bed. "No..."

Mara was the Wicked Witch who made her cry, who held Tristan prisoner in Oz so he couldn't return home.

"No!" She jolted up in bed and stared into the darkness. Swiping away the sweat and tears on her face, she leaned back against the headboard and sorted out her dream and the message it gave her.

Even with government censors to pass through, she now knew how to tell Tristan's family he was alive on Arden. All the message would probably cost her was her scientific reputation and her career. All she had to do was break the great law her mother had instilled in her from the moment she'd first started her scientific studies.

And if she did send that message to his family... to Dorian, Dorian would come. Tristan wanted Dorian as his lifetime breeding partner, his wife.

Jealousy and desire scorched through Mara. Tristan wanted only kinning with Mara, and she felt kinning for him, but she burned, too. She wanted to breed with him, her legs around his waist, her arms around his shoulders, wanted his blue eyes to blaze with hunger as their bodies joined.

Heat flushed her cheeks, her nipples rising. She hugged her pillow to her aching breasts and belly. She wanted him to kiss her and fill her womb with his seed. She wanted his baby to grow within her and wanted to raise that baby. She wanted more babies. She wanted him to hold her in bed as he had once before, her head on his shoulder, his fingers in her hair, his scent and heat filling her. She wanted him forever.

Dorian would come, and Tristan would give all that to her, and Dorian would cure the plague and take Tristan away forever.

Dorian would cure the plague. Dorian would save Tristan from the harem and Mara's shameful desires. Dorian would tell his mother he lived.

Mara sighed. Would such good come of this message, or would Dorian blindly destroy Mara's career?

Thinking of what she'd have to do, Mara cringed. It was something totally alien to everything she believed in. As a scientist, she respected scientific truth above all things in her work, and if she betrayed that truth by stealing another's research, she'd never have another chance to redeem herself. In law, a woman could make restitution for a crime, pay a fine or go to jail, and return and start life afresh, but in science one deliberate lie destroyed a career forever.

Was telling Tristan's family of his survival worth that price?

Mara slid out of bed and fumbled her way into her study. She cut on her computer. She would write the message then decide if she should send it.

She typed the heading of a scientific paper, "The Oz Tunnel—From Black Hole To Quasar? by Mara d'Jorel."

Chapter 9

"Kneel and acknowledge me your better." Cadaran lolled back in her throne chair as Kellen crawled upright on the floor, his naked body still damp and quivering from the lotus she'd just forced into his system.

Standing, he rubbed his bruised jaw. "I acknowledge your right hook, you stinking bitch."

She beamed. "Why, how sweet a compliment, Green Eyes. My heart's all aflutter."

His eyes glowing with his hatred, he smiled back.

Her loins surged with damp anticipation. She pointed downward. "Kneel."

He visibly fought the command, but his body knelt before her.

"Bow your head." She giggled when he obeyed her. "I missed you. Did you miss me?"

"My joy would have filled the ocean."

"It's so nice to be appreciated." She patted his head. "My lieutenant tells me she thought you quite pleasant in bed. Pleasant, Green Eyes? I'm disappointed."

"Disappointed I didn't mangle her as you intended?"

"Mangle is too harsh a word."

"Brutalize? Rape? Injure?"

"Demonstrate how physical a male pleasurer can get. I thought you'd be perfect for the task. I'm disappointed."

"I won't do your dirty work, Cadaran. What the hell did she do to deserve the filthy trick you tried to play on her?"

Hiding her smile, Cadaran smoothed her black silk robe. "I was merely trying to give one of my officers a wider range of experience. Can you imagine she'd never been with a man before?"

"And would never want one again after I'd finished with her. You'd have made yourself another perverted manhater. Is that what happened to you? Did some big bad man mangle you?"

"I'm the only mangler in my relationships. No man's ever gotten the best of me."

"Lt. Hallie didn't deserve what you intended. She's absolutely loyal to you. Her naive hero worship of you is sickening."

"Coming to her defense? Don't tell me that plain, clumsy farm bumpkin's got to you?"

"A fellow human being was a nice change from what I normally bed."

Cadaran refused to let him see he'd drawn blood with that remark. "You are becoming quite tedious, Green Eyes. Fortunately, your talent in pleasuring hasn't ebbed yet." She pulled his head between her legs. "Pleasure me, slave. Pleasure me."

She arched into his face as his lips and tongue began to probe, his hands cupping her buttocks painfully.

Closing her eyes, she concentrated on the sensations he created. She stroked her breasts with one hand, the other twined in his hair, her nails scratching and digging into his neck.

As she drifted back down from the third intense journey into dark pleasure, she decided that very soon she'd ease off the throne and impale herself on his staff. Then she'd really show him why no man had ever bested her in bed or otherwise.

TRISTAN STIRRED uncomfortably in his wheelchair as he stared out of the ambulance flitter's window. The city of Galina with its new towers and pre-plague buildings had given way to suburbs. He could just glimpse among the trees prefabricated block houses, the morning sun sparkling brightly on their tiny round windows. Flowers, pink shrubs, and green and pink trees in the full brilliance of early summer surrounded the structures.

Beside him, Mara squeezed his hand. "Are you in pain? We can speed up and get you home quickly."

His legs and back throbbed in response, but he smiled. "Only mild irritation in comparison to what I've felt before. I'm enjoying the scenic route, especially since I may never see your world like this again. You have a beautiful world, Mara." He smiled to include his doctor and the driver in black. "And Ilka and....I'm afraid I don't know your name, driver."

The young woman with the big-boned, stolid features turned to him. "Lt. Hallie d'Leda."

He grinned. "Tristan Mallory. You have a lovely world, Lt. Hallie. A lieutenant in what?"

"Internal Security."

"Is that police or military?"

"Both. We keep internal order and maintain the quarantine."

"So no one can get off the planet."

"Yes..." Hallie again bit back the obvious "sir" that almost slipped out. She stared at his face with fascination then flushed when she realized the other women had noticed.

Ilka chuckled and patted Tristan's arm. "Blond hair and blue eyes are extremely rare on Arden. I doubt if most of us have ever seen both in one person."

"I see." Wonderful, he was a physical freak as well as a cripple. Maybe Mara could sell tickets to view him. He forced his attention away from the depression threatening to overwhelm him and concentrated on the world he might never be free to look at again.

The flitter lifted to avoid a forest, and they were away from the suburbs and into the open countryside. Meadows with an occasional small forest spread toward the horizon. Far beyond to the west were rugged young mountains. The flitter turned left, and they were sailing back over trees toward the suburbs.

After several minutes, Mara pointed toward a huge rectangular home with a large fenced area behind it. From its classical style and individuality, it obviously hadn't been prefabricated. "That's my home."

As the flitter circled, he could see light twinkling on water in the enclosure. "A small pond?"

"A swimming pool."

For a moment, he grinned exuberantly then remembered he wouldn't be allowed outside to swim in it. "My parents' home has a lake behind it. I used to swim and boat in it. I've always loved water."

"I do, too." Her forehead wrinkled with worry, Mara studied him as if sensing his mood.

He examined the front facade as the flitter settled to the ground. "You have a lovely home."

"*We* have a lovely home. It must not be grand in comparison to Earth, but I like it."

Hallie got out and opened the back entrance to the ambulance flitter, then propelled his wheelchair down the ramp.

He sniffed the clean unfiltered air with its aroma of plants and damp soil then closed his eyes, the sun bright on his face. "I've missed the sun."

Too quickly, he was being wheeled through the front door into the living room. Charming and homey, the room abounded in wooden furniture with brightly colored upholstery in earth tones, cheerful landscape paintings, and dozens of pink and green potted plants. Several tiny round windows near the ceiling lighted the room.

"The grand tour." Mara commandeered the wheelchair from Hallie and began to wheel him around the room telling and showing him family and personal history in the generations of bric-a-brac collected.

She pushed him through the dining room into the kitchen. The room was immaculate, the antiquated coolers and cooking units in perfect order. A bowl of kista, still glistening with moisture from washing, sat on the kitchen counter. He sniffed their fruity essence and smiled hopefully up at Mara. He'd been too excited to eat much breakfast.

She chuckled then held the bowl out to him. He forced himself to take only two. Mara turned to offer fruit to the others, but no one had followed them into the kitchen. Cupping his hand under his chin, he tried to eat neatly so he wouldn't spoil his brand new blue robe and pajamas. The kista's strawberry sweetness melted past his taste buds.

An older woman's voice, as tart as the kista was sweet, barked, "Those were for supper."

Mara answered with a commanding sharpness he'd never heard her use, "We only had two."

Tristan closed his hand guiltily on the leftover stems and smiled at the short grandmotherly woman who glowered above him.

"Novia, this is Tristan. Tristan, this is Novia."

"I'm pleased to finally meet you." He smiled with even greater warmth. "Mara talks about you with deep affection."

Novia didn't even try to disguise the cold hatred in her eyes although she nodded with surly politeness.

Mara's face tightened with pain. Tristan bit his tongue. An angry protest at Novia for hurting Mara would only make matters worse.

Squeezing the counter's edge with meaty hands as if warming up for his neck, Novia said to Mara, "That nurse is here. She's set up residence in *your* study."

"Thank you." Mara pushed his wheelchair into the hallway which bisected most of the house beginning at the front door. She motioned to a closed door on the left. "That's Novia's bedroom." She pushed open the second door. "This is my bedroom."

A large bed was shoved in the right corner, stacks of clothes piled haphazardly on top of it. Most of the other floor space was taken up by a huge desk with a computer and printer on it. The desk chair could barely be moved back because of the bed, and books and journals were piled under and around everything. Several very nice landscape paintings covered the wall. One high-set tiny window lit the room, and a small bathroom was to the left.

He'd never thought Mara such a messy person with her logical mind and neat appearance. "Why are all Arden windows so high and tiny. With your people's obvious love of nature, I thought you'd prefer huge picture windows."

"Tyrlins, a dangerous predator like an Earth tiger, can break through glass and most plastics."

"Even the luxel derivatives?"

"No one could afford luxel when most of our building was done. Most still can't. It has to be imported from Earth. Tyrlins roamed the streets at night during our early days. Later, we thinned them around the cities, but I've heard plague tales about tyrlins attacking the cities after Internal Security had been decimated by the plague. The big cats carried off the dead and dying, and the unprotected children."

Tristan shuddered.

"Well, this is my bedroom. I slept here when I was a little girl." She backed his wheelchair out of the room.

An image of the adult Mara sleeping, sprawled naked in this bed, struck him so vividly his loins ached. Perhaps it was just as well he was to be locked away in his own little room. Living and sleeping under the same roof with innocent, sexy Mara might otherwise lead him to actions he'd regret.

She wheeled him through the door at the end of the hall. The bedroom was huge and airy, glass French doors opening out on the fenced enclosure he'd seen from the air. Sunlight splashed across the white carpet toward the bed which faced the outer doors. A spacious bathroom was to the right, another closed door to the left.

"This is your bedroom."

All his images of a tiny, airless room vanished. "Oh, Mara. It's beautiful."

Her pleasure at his joy filled her voice. "We can have French doors to the outside in this room because of the garden enclosure—solid stone over twelve feet high." She motioned to the closed door to the left. "That will be converted back into your study when your live-in nurse leaves."

He shook his head at his own foolishness for thinking Mara messy. "This is your room, isn't it?"

"It's your room now."

"Thank you, Mara. Your generosity moves me so deeply...I don't know what to say."

Her hand settled on his shoulder. "Thank you was adequate. I pray you enjoy many happy years here, and everywhere else your heart wishes you to be."

He squeezed her hand. "I'd like to show you my home on Earth."

"The Goddess willing, you shall. I'll do everything in my power to see that you get home." She cleared her throat as if to fight tears. "Let me show you our garden. You'll enjoy it."

His heart jerked painfully with hope. "Will I be able to go out into the garden?"

"Of course. Anytime you wish."

His lifetime prison sentence suddenly seemed much easier to bear. "I'll be in that pool before you know it."

"Let me show you the garden." She wheeled him through the French doors.

Near the house, Lt. Hallie squatted, watching a white wood gazebo in the far left corner of the huge enclosure. Frowning, she stood when they approached. "You have a rab-cat. It's against the law to keep a rab-cat as a pet. They're a protected species."

"I know. He's a cherished member of my family. I have official approval to keep him." She called out, "Floppy, come meet these people."

His rabbit-sized ears flopping, a huge black house cat jumped off the gazebo and galloped toward them. He skidded to a stop six feet away from them and eyed them warily, his ears upright and quivering.

Mara said, "This is Tristan, Floppy, and this is Lt. Hallie."

Floppy examined Tristan with bright Kellen green eyes. A tremor of grief shook Tristan as he saw Kellen's intelligence and mischief in the cat's eyes, then he only saw a cat studying him with disinterest. Apparently, Novia wasn't the only member of Mara's family who didn't want him here.

Tristan opened his mouth to say hello, but the cat turned toward Hallie who lifted her hands to her head like rabbit ears and wiggled her fingers in several quick pulses.

Floppy plopped down on his haunches as if shocked then hastily returned the ear wiggle. He glanced toward Mara then began to wiggle his ears at Hallie in what seemed some complex semaphore.

Hallie turned apologetically to Mara. "I don't understand him. I only know the greeting."

Floppy's ears stilled, and he sat down completely, his ears laid against the base of his skull as if he'd understood her.

Mara asked Hallie, "How did you learn that?"

"Rab-cats live near my mother's farm. They'd always wiggle their ears like that when I'd see them." Hallie studied Mara as if noticing her for the first time. "You're the one who says rab-cats are human intelligent."

"Yes."

"K...A friend who's very interested in rab-cats would love to meet you. How did you get him?"

"I was out on Bryant meadow. Suddenly I felt this mental call for help. More of a terrified shriek. I just knew a child was in terrible danger. I began to run. I found a tyrlin over two rab-cats. I killed it with my laser. The mother rab-cat, I'm positive she called me, was dead, but her kitten was still alive, barely. I brought him home to my vet. Floppy has lived with me ever since. I've told him I'll take him back to his people when he's ready, but he wants to stay."

Tristan eyed the rab-cat. "Are you in psychic communications with him?"

"Not really. No more than I am with any human I feel kinning for. I think what I felt was more from the intensity of the situation than genuine communication. The rab-cats may talk like that to each other at distances, but I'm not certain. They have limited vocal cords. They don't even make normal cat noises, but they have an ear language. I don't know it, but Floppy and I communicate in our own fashion after several years together. Don't we?"

Floppy wiggled his ears in obvious agreement.

"Floppy, let's show Tristan and Hallie the pool."

His attention more on Hallie than Tristan, the rab-cat trotted beside Tristan's wheelchair toward the pool.

"We have a household garden near the gazebo," Mara said. "The other side of the enclosure has the pool and the flowers."

Tristan only had eyes for the long oval stone pool, easily Olympic in length. "I'm ready to go swimming now."

Mara chuckled. "Not today."

"Soon. Very, very soon. Swimming's good physical therapy for spinal injuries."

"You're absolutely right." Walking from the house, Ilka joined them. "I'm certain your physical therapist will agree. But right now you must rest from your trip."

He was exhausted and in pain from the simple journey, but he refused to admit it. "Can't I stay outside a little longer?"

Ilka chuckled at his little boy pleading. "Later. Now I want to check you over so Lt. Hallie and I can leave."

"Spoilsport." He grinned.

Mara wheeled him toward the bedroom doors.

Hallie asked Mara, "May I come again to see Floppy?"

"Floppy would like that very much."

Tristan's private nurse Benita was waiting by the bed.

When Mara pulled the wheelchair by the bed, Tristan readjusted the wheelchair into a reclining position and tiredly didn't complain that he could move himself when Hallie and Benita scooped him into the bed. He sat up and took off his robe with Benita's help.

Hallie picked up a white ceramic bracelet from the nightstand. "I'm sorry, but I have to put this on you."

"My bracelet jailer. Well, it beats the hospital." He gazed at the open bedroom door to the rest of the house he'd not go through again then held out his left hand and didn't flinch when the bracelet snapped closed with a vicious click.

Crying silently, Mara blinked hard and scrubbed at her cheeks.

Hallie nodded to him and left.

HALLIE stood at parade rest in front of Cadaran's desk at headquarters.

Cadaran flipped through her report on the vid screen then gazed up at Hallie with her huge sad eyes. "I see my hunch was right. Sending you to ferry the Earther to his new quarters paid off."

"Yes, sir. I think so." Hallie shifted nervously on her feet.

"I didn't think he was worth my interest when the doctors declared him terminal then a paraplegic, but he's stirring up a lot of trouble and support in the scientific community. What is your opinion of him?"

"He reminds me of Kellen."

Cadaran lifted her gaze from the report to Hallie. "Kellen is it?"

"That is his name. When I processed his file for you, it said 'Kellen Votrain.'"

"Yes, of course. How does he remind you of Green Eyes?"

"As you know, sir, before I became a lieutenant, I did a great many ferries between the harem and lottery winners and also between the different commons around the planet."

"You were well-regarded because you never fingered or damaged the merchandise, never had a successful escape, and you were always courteous to the lottery winners."

"Yes, sir. Well, I saw enough men to type them. There are the puppies, desperately eager to please and be liked. Then there are the lap cats, disgustingly pleased with themselves but willing to accept an owner's touch. The stupid placid ones are like cows who take anything as long as they're cared for. And then there are the rogues of each group who have gone bad for some reason."

Cadaran chuckled. "An adequate division system for the harem. What does this have to do with our two Earthers?"

"Everything, sir. Kellen and Tristan don't fit any of these categories. They're like us. They're like women in their sense of self and in their emotional strength. Kellen would make a fine trooper with his courage and fire. Tristan has..." Hallie paused, considering her impressions. "I was ferrying him to a harem location, and he acted as if I were taking him to preside over the Council. He handles himself with inner strength, dignity, and wisdom. He has incredible presence."

Cadaran's elegant black brows rose into her hair. "A man?"

"A man acts like that. Earth must be very different from Arden to make men act like women."

"That's why Earthers are such barbarians, Lieutenant. That's why they turned their back on us during the plague. Because of the men thinking they were equal to women."

Hallie nodded. "Yes, sir."

"What does he look like?"

"He's been brutally ill and still looks it—skin and bones. But he's fleshing out again and has good color. Very limited movement of his legs, but he's determined to regain use. He burns with determination."

Cadaran chuckled. "You still have no sense of men. Is he pretty?"

"With his blond and blue coloring and bone structure, I imagine he'd be beautiful in full health."

"As drop dead beautiful as Green Eyes if his Earther i.d. card is any indication." Cadaran smiled like a cat and brushed her lips. "He sounds like one of those who'd need my personal training before he's put into the harem."

Hallie thought of Kellen, the broken bones, and lotus. "I don't think so, sir. He lacks Kellen's spirit. All that dignity makes him rather boring."

Cadaran chuckled. "I'll be the judge of that. What of his patron Mara d'Jorel? What kind of relationship do they have?"

"She adopts stray kittens. She fusses over him like he's one of those injured kittens. All soft heart. She acts as if he's her intellectual equal. I overheard them talking in the hospital about quasars...?"

"An unusual stellar object which emits radio waves. And?"

"They were speaking rab-cat to me, but if she's as brilliant as her mother..."

"He isn't stupid. Are they breeding?"

"His nurse told me he can't. There's nothing in their behavior that suggests that Mara has any interest in him in that sense. None of the stroking, eye contact, or physical awareness I've always seen between lottery winners and their pleasurers."

Cadaran stifled an amused smile. "And I thought you were rather naive about men because you didn't frequent the Common."

"You don't have to be a cow to understand a bull, sir."

Throwing back her head, Cadaran laughed. "I guess not. So her main interest is his intellectual accomplishments as she claims."

"It would seem so."

"She's trying to gain permanent ownership. Thea d'Louisa is championing Mara's cause from her sickbed with a host of other major scientists. I've learned even Ilka d'Vida is trying to find converts in the Council. I'll have to keep watch on her. I don't like my officers plotting behind my back."

"Why all this fuss over a man? A crippled one at that."

"He has something rarer than blond hair and blue eyes, a fine brain. And an education of considerable merit. They seem to think he's on the verge of a discovery of greater financial value than Jorel's."

"A man can do that!"

"They seem to think this male freak can under Mara's protection."

Hallie shrugged. "He's worth nothing in the harem with no legs or staff. On the farm we say even castrated bulls have value—as meat. His best cut seems to be the brain. Let them have him and let Arden reap the profit."

Cadaran thumped her fingers on her desk and frowned. "A farm and Internal Security have different priorities. I don't trust them, and I don't want any man free from harem laws and protection."

"We can keep watch on them. Mara's housekeeper Novia doesn't trust him. She's a violent manhater and opposes his presence in the house. She told me she's only staying to protect Mara from his vile influence."

"A spy. A good thought. I'll contact her."

"I have permission to visit again, as a guest. I'll keep an eye on them. Did you know she has a rab-cat?"

"I have the report."

"Then it is legal? I was going to check that."

"You make a good cop, Lieutenant."

"Thank you, sir."

"Visit and see what else you can find out."

"Yes, sir." Hallie paused then asked, "Do you know what 'parents' are? Tristan used the term, and the vocabulary banks don't have the word."

"No, I don't."

"May I ask Kellen?" Hallie strove to keep her expression bland.

"Visiting his bed was a one-shot event, Lieutenant." Cadaran's face twisted with anger.

"I wasn't seeking that, sir. I assure you." Hallie couldn't explain she was far more eager to discuss Floppy with him over shared beers, but she didn't think Cadaran would understand such an interest in a man anymore than she'd understand the kinning, friendship, and respect between Mara and Tristan.

"I'll consider your request, Lieutenant. That will be all for now. I need to contact Novia and begin surveillance of that household. I've got a strong feeling about Mara d'Jorel. She wants to defy the harem system and destroy it as her mother tried to. I can sense it." Cadaran's eyes burned with zeal as she clinched her fist. "And I'll allow no one to do that. No one."

Chapter 10

Cadaran sprawled back in the desk chair of her formal office and watched Novia take in the elegant, intimidating surroundings which exemplified Cadaran's power as head of Internal Security. The old woman's eyes were huge as she settled timidly into the chair facing Cadaran.

"So kind of you to come, Novia." Cadaran smiled with studied warmth.

Novia nodded and twisted the hem of her tunic in her hand.

"I've always been a great admirer of Jorel d'Nissa. What a brilliant woman! Her early death was a planetary tragedy."

Certain of herself on this topic, Novia smiled with worshipful adoration. "The greatest scientific mind this planet has ever seen. One of the greatest human minds of all time."

"Absolutely. I watched her career with great interest, and I've watched her daughter's career, too. She seems to have a fine mind."

"Oh, yes! Perhaps not her mother's brilliance, but she will do great things for Arden. I sense it."

"A pity she couldn't have settled on a more sensible field than astrophysics for Arden's sake."

"Mara isn't very practical, but that's part of what being a genius is. You must follow your own dreams. Jorel's fellow scientists thought she was a fool in her research for the energy light converter and see how wrong she proved them."

"I fear in one genuine foolishness Mara might be following her mother too closely."

Novia studied her blankly.

"I've read Jorel's records about the time before Mara was born."

Color drained out of Novia's face. "I see."

"Yes. Even the greatest minds can have certain weaknesses. Even the great Jorel."

Her eyes downcast, Novia nodded.

"I don't want Jorel's daughter to make the same mistake."

"Neither do I."

"A soft heart is a dangerous weakness even with a great mind."

"Yes."

"This man she's tending..."

"Tristan. She says he's a great scientist." Novia sniffed with disbelief. "He's only a man."

"Men are dangerous. I'm afraid he'll take advantage of that soft heart and harm her."

Her eyes blazing with zeal, the old woman said, "I watch him. I watch him all the time to see he doesn't harm her."

"Thank the Goddess for that. I don't want him to hurt her, but I don't have the power to take him away from her. I worry about her."

"I watch him."

"Would you...Would you keep me informed about him? Let me know how their relationship is progressing. If I'm informed, I may be able to take him away before he harms her." Cadaran beamed with motherly concern and dignity.

Novia took the bait like a particularly stupid fish. "Oh, yes. I'll tell you all about them."

HIS eyelids drooping as he slowly chewed a bite of sandwich, Tristan leaned back in his wheelchair at the table in his bedroom. Afternoon sunlight from the French windows splashed across his strong features and his honey blond curls.

With a harsh mental admonition, Mara shook herself out of her besotted admiration of his beauty. Fortunately, he was too sleepy to notice her lapse. She wiped her lips with her napkin and put it in her empty plate. "If you get any more relaxed, you'll fall asleep in your lunch."

He chuckled and forced his eyes open. "Sorry."

"You exhausted yourself in physical therapy this morning. Do you always throw yourself so intensely in what you do?"

"Most things have come so easily I haven't had to work up a sweat over them. I'm paying for it now. I have to sweat blood over every centimeter of progress."

"Progress the doctors didn't think you could make. I have such admiration for your courage and strength."

"I have admiration for you, Mara."

"Me! I've done nothing of note. Except maybe the quasar paper."

He shook his head. "Your unselfconsciousness is incredible. Or should I say disregard of your own value. You are a warm and loving person who's sacrificed so much for me. I recognize that sacrifice if you don't."

"I..." She lowered her gaze to her empty plate as if fascinated by it.

"I'm not blind. Your little family doesn't want me here, and you're taking the brunt of their anger instead of me."

"Has Novia...?"

"No, she hasn't straggled me physically or verbally as she'd dearly love to. Her eyes and body language told me. And Floppy might not speak, but you'd hardly call him subtle in expressing his opinions."

Mara laughed. "No, not Floppy."

"Floppy's emotions I can understand. He's got a bad case of new baby syndrome. I remember that well from when Elaine was born."

"New baby?"

"I guess you wouldn't know about that being an only child. My two brothers are a bit older than I am so I was the spoiled baby in the family until Elaine was born, and suddenly she was the spoiled baby. Boy, was I jealous of her. She really got a double dose of the attention since she was the only girl. Girls are rare among the Mallorys."

Mara smiled, thinking of Tristan as a blond, curly-haired baby. "You mean Floppy is jealous?"

"Yes."

"I was afraid he would be. I told him your presence didn't mean I cared less for him, but..."

"Rab-cats must have as much of a problem controlling irrational emotions as humans."

"Novia's also got him convinced you will harm me." Mara bit her tongue in dismay.

"I'll what!"

"Novia doesn't like or trust men. She's totally irrational on the subject. I don't know why."

"I guess I'd better start plying my charms on her. Prove I won't murder or seduce you."

"Seduce me to do what?"

His blue eyes flickered with uncertainty. "Convince you to make love with me when it's against your best interests."

"What is 'to make love?'"

"Sexual intercourse."

"Oh, breeding." She wondered why breeding with him was against her best interests.

His expression thoughtful, he picked up his sandwich and ate. "At our evening meals when everyone's together, I'll try to earn their trust. Let them get to know me."

"You are very special. They will have great kinning soon. I know it."

He chuckled.

"Tell them about your family. Growing up. Tell them about Elaine and your mother."

His eyes twinkled as he gazed at her. "If I have women in my life, I can't be a total monster."

"Exactly. How did you get over jealousy of Elaine?"

"My parents paid special attention to me, and they let me share in watching over Elaine. I realized I wasn't the baby anymore, but I was a big brother. That made me almost a grownup. Later, Elaine and I became playmates and shared adventures. That finished the bonding process."

"I don't know how that can apply to Floppy."

"If he's as sensible as you think he is, he'll come around fast enough."

Mara nodded.

Tristan returned his full concentration on eating his sandwich. Very soon, his lids were drooping again. His last few bites of sandwich were in slow motion.

Her heart surged with kinning and tenderness as she stood. "Let me ring for Benita so you can have your afternoon nap."

He waved away the suggestion. "Let her have her lunch in peace. I'll put myself in. Not totally helpless."

"I'll help."

Flicking the chair out of manual operation, he motored over to the bed then lowered the wheelchair into a reclining position. He grabbed the bar above his bed and lifted to pull himself into bed.

Mara cupped his thighs as she'd seen Benita do and helped him ease into bed.

She didn't know what they'd done wrong, but suddenly they were both sliding downward. She had just enough sense to hold him and cushion his fall with her body. They hit the floor, Tristan draped on her.

The air knocked out, she blinked and stared up at his face, her arms around his shoulders.

Both asked, "Are you all right?"

Seeing the answer in each other's face, both laughed.

He smiled into her eyes and caressed her cheek.

Suddenly their shared humor at their foolish error became something else for Mara. She was conscious of his body weight, his chest rubbing her breasts, his thighs between hers, his musky male scent, the heat.

A terrible ache spreading from her breasts into her belly, she sighed. Only her terror of seeing his disgust kept her from lifting her thighs around his hips to assuage the throbbing dampness.

His eyes darkened with emotion, his face nearing hers. He was going to kiss her. She quivered, her arms tightening around his shoulders.

He cradled her head under his arm, his fingers lost in her hair, his face against hers, his lashes against her skin...His whole body stiffened, and he jerked his face away from her.

His fur upright, his ears back, Floppy crouched near them and snarled.

Tristan swore softly. "He's going to attack."

Fear surged through Mara. "Floppy, no! No! He wasn't hurting me."

Floppy's haunches quivered as he prepared to pounce, his green eyes glowing red with Tristan's death.

"No! He wasn't hurting me. I was trying to help him get into bed, and we fell. It was a silly accident."

The rab-cat's fur flattened, his ears coming up, but he didn't come out of his attack crouch.

She cleared her throat. "Would you please get Benita for me. I'm afraid to move until I'm certain Tristan hasn't hurt himself."

The rab-cat straightened, eyed Tristan as if warning him to behave, then trotted toward the bedroom door.

Sighing, she closed her eyes in relief.

"Mara?"

"Floppy was going to kill you."

"That little cat?" Tristan chuckled.

"You'd have been dead in seconds from mind touch. A rab-cat can kill a tyrlin."

"My God!" His arms tightened around her.

She returned the hug, barely conscious of their breeding closeness.

Benita walked in then. With her blustering, motherly humor, she quickly had them to rights. She tucked Tristan into bed and guffawed through an exhibition of how Mara should have turned her hip and balanced her weight.

Mara squeezed Tristan's hand and left him to his nap.

The terror still plaguing her, she wandered into her bedroom and plopped down at her computer. She stared at the article she'd finished the night before—Tristan's ideas with her name on them. These simple plagiarized words could be so costly. Loss of career. Loss of Tristan to Dorian and Earth. Loss of her heart if he left her. Loss of her life if the authorities discovered this act of treason.

She'd promised Tristan his freedom and Earth. She'd promised him happiness, and happiness was unlikely with her. If she were true to her promise and her kinning for him, she had no choice, whatever the cost to her.

Blinking tears, she cleared the screen and began the letter which would be sent with the article in the next mail.

TRISTAN picked up his computer keyboard from his nightstand and flicked it on then unfolded the big vid screen from the ceiling. He accessed the house monitor program and began his nightly bedtime check of the house, the closest he could come to wandering through the house as he would have in his own home. He switched to infrared scan for the dark living room. No one was in there, only furniture and plants. The kitchen showed a blank screen. Novia had cut off the kitchen camera monitor to keep him out even in spirit. In the dining room Sheba the cat was curled asleep on one of the chairs. Coalie the collie usually slept in Novia's room.

He didn't bother to check Novia's room or the nurse's. He flipped to what he really wanted to see. Her chestnut hair splayed across the pillow, Mara sprawled asleep on her bed, her sheet kicked away. Her thin white gown had crawled up to her thighs revealing long exquisite legs and dainty feet. Her guard cat Floppy was a black fur ball in his bed on top of her desk.

Unable to resist, Tristan focused the screen in close-up on Mara's feet then panned his way up her body. His loins ached as he remembered that body beneath him on the floor. He could just see through her gown her nipples and the dark triangle between her legs. He flushed with shame at what he was doing and focused the screen on her lovely face, even more innocent in sleep than awake. Her lips were slightly parted, her eyelashes flickering with dreams.

"Enjoying your mental porn? Or should I say voyeurism?" Kellen leaned back in the chair by his bed and rested his head on his arms.

Tristan jumped. "I wasn't imagining you."

"Well, I'm here." Kellen's eyes twinkled with mischief. "I must be your conscience. Isn't that a change of roles for me?"

"You have greater fondness for leading me into rather than out of temptation."

Kellen laughed. "What are you up to? Or should I just say 'up'?"

Tristan blushed like a schoolboy and tried a few pure thoughts to get himself out of his obvious predicament. Mara's body took far more than a few pure thoughts. "She put monitors in the rooms I couldn't visit so I could be part of the household."

"So you immediately took advantage by ogling her in her virginal bower."

"Only when she's dressed or asleep. I haven't sunk that low into depravity."

"Give yourself some more time with her just out of reach, and you'll see how depraved you get from frustration. You might even seduce her on your bedroom floor. If a chastity belt with rabbit ears doesn't kill you first." His friend chuckled wickedly. "Ought to be pretty easy with a woman who doesn't know what seduce means."

"My former conscience was more polite."

"You were better behaved back then."

"I wasn't going to seduce her. Only kiss her."

"And worry about her emotional reaction later. Remember what happened the last time you really kissed her?"

"I can't stop thinking about it. I can't sleep thinking about it."

"Nothing's changed. Or has it?"

Tristan sighed.

"You've finally stopped believing in fairy tales about true love, medical miracles, and rescue."

"It's been almost four months, and Dorian hasn't come. Maybe she doesn't love me enough to risk her life. I'm going to be stuck on this damn planet, in this room, for the rest of my life."

"There are uglier fates. Mara wants you. She's as hot and frustrated as you are. If ever a woman was ripe for taking, she is. You felt the way her body reacted—her nipples, the melting, the hunger in her eyes, the—"

"Enough. Don't talk about her like that."

"You wanted a woman who cared for the true Tristan, not the golden boy with the looks, money, and important family. Mara's seen you as ungolden as any woman ever has, and she hasn't run shrieking."

Tristan grinned. "No, she hasn't. She likes and respects the real me. Our friendship grows stronger the more we learn of each other."

"You respect her, like her, want her body. If she doesn't love you, she could. All she needs is a little encouragement and a proper introduction to lovemaking. Marry her and raise baby astrophysicists."

"I don't..."

"Love her?"

"I don't know how I feel." Tristan mangled his hair with his fingers. "She's so special, but my legs, and Dorian, and..."

"Dorian isn't here, she'll never be here for you, and Mara is. Your legs are getting better, and your most important working part is obviously in shape." Kellen beamed, wicked mischief dancing in his green eyes. "And consider the future. Mara is focusing all her attention on you instead of finding a husband. She's probably blowing her chances of marriage with anyone else. Hell, if this place is as sexually strict as you think, she's destroyed her reputation and any chance of a decent man wanting her. It's your duty to marry her and save her from such a loveless fate. Do you want her to be forced to conceive a baby from a test tube like her mother did? Or if she did marry, what would happen to you? Do you think some other man would want her to keep you here? And if he did, would you want to be locked in this room while she was giving that gorgeous, sexy body to another man?"

"You're still a pain in the butt sometimes, Kell."

Kellen grinned. "That's what friends are for, even dead ones. What are you going to do?"

Tristan shrugged.

"Well, you aren't going to be an invalid forever with a nurse fussing over you. It's time you started figuring that out. Mara and your will to survive have given you a future. Don't throw it away."

KELLEN pressed his ear to his bedroom door and listened. Finally, he heard the unmistakable rustle and thump he'd learned to associate with Cadaran entering her bedroom. He glanced at the clock by his bed. She would undress and be in here in ten to fifteen minutes.

He grimaced. She'd be in a particularly sadistic, horny mood tonight since she'd been out of town several days. Well, tonight would be his night for victory. Tonight he'd either escape or die trying.

Walking into his bathroom, he opened the linen closet and dug behind the clean towels the housekeeper and Cadaran never touched to find his supplies. He pulled out the bottle of ballard and kissed its rounded side. "Bless you, Hallie." He opened it and began to drink.

The alcohol burned its way down his throat and through his veins.

Putting the bottle down, he carried his other supplies into his bedroom and stashed them in appropriate spots then returned to the ballard and drank. After a quarter of a bottle, he rehid the bottle. He didn't want to pass the thin line between stopping the lotus' mind control and his ability to function soberly.

Sloshing liquid tooth cleaner around his mouth to mask the ballard on his breath, he prepared himself mentally. He'd waited weeks for this attempt so every item would be thought out, and so Cadaran wouldn't be able to blame Hallie whom he hadn't seen since he'd slept with her. Protecting Hallie was the least he could do since she was the closest thing to a human being he'd met on this filthy planet. He'd almost felt ashamed for using her so blatantly.

Although never religious, he closed his eyes and prayed fervently for freedom from this living hell, be that freedom escape or death.

He stretched to loosen his muscles before battle and sauntered into the bedroom. Tossing off his robe, he curled on his side, his back to the door, and pretended to be sleep.

Cadaran walked into the room with all her usual swaggering noise. She whispered, "Green Eyes, are you asleep?"

He didn't answer.

She giggled and sneaked toward him.

His bare buttock burned with lotus fire as she injected the poison into him. He groaned and rolled onto his stomach, burying his face into the bed sheets. Even the ballard didn't stop the fiery agony racing through his veins and nerves.

His fist tightened on the sheets, his fingers clutching, and his body convulsed with inner earthquake, then stilled. Blinking away tears, he wished her and the creator of lotus in hell.

Her mind trigger necklace scratching him, Cadaran rubbed her bare breasts into his back and purred in his ear, "Miss me, Green Eyes?"

"I'll never be that lonely."

"You'd better be nicer to me. I've already picked out your replacement. He's beautiful. Blond hair, blue eyes, great body."

"Give the poor bastard my sympathy."

"You'd better give yourself sympathy. The woman who wants you makes me look like a rab-cat with her kitten."

He shuddered.

"A real charmer is Lani. The richest woman on Arden. She buys men, and when she's finished with them, they usually aren't worth returning to the lottery. If there's any sexual life left in them, she either sells them, or gives them to the Common."

"What's that?"

"I believe you call them brothels on Earth." She giggled when he flinched. "Men like you are especially popular with my troopers." Her hand slid under him and stroked. He grew to agonizing hardness. "Remember Garnet?"

He'd never forgotten the soldier he'd killed when she'd tried to rape him. Her face and hands haunted many of his lotus withdrawal hallucinations.

Cadaran combed her other fingers through his shoulder length curls. "You're so beautiful and spirited. I hate to waste you on that stupid cow Lani."

"Then don't. Give me to some kind woman who'll treat me decently."

"But Lani's so rich. I'll make more on your one sale to her than I would your normal three or four year-long rentals to other women before the lotus burns you out."

"You personally?"

"I receive a large percentage bonus on all off-planet men in the harem."

"There can't be that many of us."

"You'd be surprised. With the asteroid belt, we get quite a few injured ships here. Not many men as pretty as you, though." She nuzzled his nape. "Let's pleasure. Sit up."

He sat up and shook his hair out of his face. He brushed it back. "I wish you'd have this damn hair cut."

"Men look so pretty with long hair. So soft and male."

A chuckle escaped. "We say the same thing about women's hair on Earth. Do all women have short hair, or only the military?"

"Civilians have hair any length they want."

"I'm a civilian. I want my hair cut."

"You're a man. You have no choice about anything." She wriggled her nose. "Pleasure me the way *I* like it, slave."

Clutching her buttocks, he pulled her into his lap and bent, taking a full purple nipple between his teeth. He tugged and nipped.

Moaning with pleasure-pain, she thrust herself into his face.

He attacked the other breast like a playful terrier, his fingers sliding between her legs and probing. She was already wet and open.

Very soon, she was rocking to meet his finger thrusts.

Using all he'd learned of her body, he worked her until she was mindless and limp. Easing her out of his lap, he put her on her hands and knees, her face away from the headboard mirror, then slammed full length into her from behind.

She cried out at the painful intrusion but gyrated back to meet his next violent thrust. He cupped her tiny breasts, squeezing, then one hand slid between her legs to their joining, caressing and pinching.

Bleating with orgasm, she jolted almost upright, knocking him backwards.

He shoved her back down and sent her over the edge again. Gritting his teeth against the agony of his arousal, he caressed her breasts then her shoulders and neck as he prolonged her orgasm, her body quivering and bucking into him.

Straightening slightly, he smashed his hand into the base of her skull. She slumped, taking them both down.

Laughing, he disengaged himself. He'd done it. He'd actually attacked her while under the influence of lotus.

Frightened for a moment he'd killed her, he checked her pulse, but it beat slowly against his fingers. He examined the necklace which controlled the pain stimulator in his prison bracelet, but he could find no opening. It must be electronically key-controlled, and she wouldn't have the key on her.

Well, later. Until then, he'd have to make certain she didn't zap him into submission.

His eyes never leaving Cadaran, he slid off the bed, and picked up her robe. He found the lotus injector and a small canister of the drug. He fitted them together, shoved the injector against Cadaran's bare butt, and injected the poison into her system.

A pity she couldn't be conscious to enjoy the lotus' fire. The first time was the most painful.

He wiped himself off with a towel, paying special attention to remove her vile essence, then began to dress. As he pulled his tunic over his head, his left hand flamed. He clutched his arm to his chest and shouted, "Stop that."

The pain stimulator cut off.

She sat on the bed with a stunned look on her face.

He chuckled and brushed back his curls. "Welcome to the joy of lotus, Cadaran. Welcome to hell."

"I'll kill you for this." She rubbed the back of her neck.

"No, you won't."

"No, I won't."

"Get dressed." He tossed the robe to her.

She pulled on the robe with jerky robot actions and tied it. "What do you want?"

"My freedom."

"There's no freedom on Arden for a man."

"If I can't find it, I'll be killed when they try to take me back."

"And me?"

"And you..." His face twisted. "I'm not a monster, yet. If you help me, I'll kill you cleanly with the dignity befitting a soldier. If you fight me, I'll return the favor for all the kindness you've shown me."

"How charming." Cadaran smirked.

"Better than you deserve, you bitch. Get up."

She came to her feet.

"Go to the computer, tie in to the central computer, and cut off my bracelet."

"I..."

"You must have the power and the codes to do it. Do you?"

She nodded.

"Then do it. No tricks."

Sitting down at the computer terminal where he could only get a few vid stations and the library, she tapped into Arden's central computer. He watched her face as much as the computer as she accessed the program she wanted. Her disgust at her inability to disobey the lotus was a minor yet sweet revenge for the sadistic sexual humiliation he'd lived through.

She typed in his real name then the requested code— "Green eyes."

He groaned. "I should have known. Are you finished? Can I leave the room?"

"Yes." She gazed up at him with her huge brown Madonna eyes. "What do we do next?"

"We raid your kitchen for supplies, take your flitter, and head for the mountains."

"May I change into my uniform? It seems more suitable to die in than this." She ruffled her robe.

"Nothing is suitable to die in, but you may. I want others to think you helped me escape. That should leave them wondering for a while and screw your reputation to hell for Arden eternity."

"As subtle a conniving sadist as I am, Green Eyes. You know right where to gouge."

"Let's get out of here. I'm damn sick of this room."

She motioned toward the door. "After you."

"After you." He grabbed her arm and forced her forward.

As they stepped through the door, agonizing pain smashed through him, and he was blasted back into his prison.

On his back on the floor, he shook his head to stay conscious.

Standing over him, Cadaran chuckled. "Nice try, Green Eyes."

"The lotus, you couldn't refuse me."

"I'm immune. Totally immune. Most women are with the local version of lotus."

"But you obeyed."

"I pretended to obey. I was curious about your plans. I wondered exactly how much you knew about our security. I found out. Hallie has been talking."

He shook his head. "Not her. The library. Suggest you look at the public files. The encyclopedia entry on the detention bracelet told enough for me to figure out the rest. It's used on other planets, too. I remembered some."

"Coming to the farm bumpkin's defense again?"

"Not a monster yet. She doesn't deserve blame for what she didn't do."

"I'll look into it. I am fair with my own troops, Green Eyes. That's one reason I am where I am."

He closed his eyes, relieved he wouldn't take Hallie down with him. There was enough information in the library to camouflage the information she'd given him. "What about me?"

Cadaran rubbed the back of her neck. "Since I'm not allowed to kill you, I'll send you to Lani sooner than I expected to. That's the same punishment but a lot slower, and a lot more profitable for me."

Chapter 11

Floppy lolled on the top of a nearby armchair like a tiger waiting for lunch, and Tristan was that lunch. The depressingly truthful image of Floppy killing him and Novia filleting him and frying him for the rab-cat's meal refusing to go away, Tristan glanced nervously at the staring rab-cat. He shuddered then turned back to the vid screen hanging in front of him in bed. He stifled a yawn and watched the capering animal puppets on the screen, who were singing about springtime and growing up.

He really should be working on his black hole equations, but he was limp from his morning torture session with the physical therapist, and he hated to admit it, but he'd become addicted to *Animal Crackers* in the hospital.

Thinking of his sophisticated colleagues' or even Mara's response to Dr. Tristan Mallory watching a children's show without a chaperoning child in sight, he winced. He'd become fast with the off button in the hospital, and if he was discovered with it on, he always pretended he'd been watching something else and had fallen asleep.

But, damn it, the show was wonderful. By Earth comparison, the graphics and effects were archaic, but the show was clever and funny with charming animal characters, and he'd learned more about Arden's plants and wildlife than he'd been able to from other sources. Two-year-old Peter would love it. He could almost feel his nephew snuggled on his lap, watching the show with him as they'd done on Earth with other shows.

Three-year-old Peter. His nephew had celebrated a birthday since he'd left Earth. Desolation and homesickness hit him hard. He forced himself to pay attention to the program.

Real wild rab-cats bounced across rocks in a mountain scene. He cleared his tight throat. "Floppy, rab-cats are on the vid."

Floppy's ears went up, and he hopped onto the bed with alarming quickness, but he studied the screen instead of murdering Tristan. His ears quivered and unconsciously mimed the other rab-cats'. When the sequence ended, his ears flattened on his head, and he sat down completely, his head slumped on his front paws.

Tristan rested a tentative hand on the cat's shoulders. "I know the feeling. I'm so homesick for my family I ache. But we have Mara as new family to love us. That helps."

Floppy studied him with Kellen green eyes as if reading his expression then turned his attention back to the vid screen.

Surprised he hadn't been rebuffed, Tristan eased his hand off the rab-cat.

When a sequence began about the letter 'A' and the sounds it had in reading, Floppy's ears went upright with interest, and he watched the capering letter as if it were prey.

Later, when the letter 'R' began, the ears went up again. Floppy sat beside Tristan through the whole program, and when it was over, he even wiggled his ears in farewell before he hopped off the bed and trotted into the garden where he usually sunned himself on the gazebo.

Tristan whistled to himself. Maybe his days as a probable lunch were over.

APPREHENSIVELY, Hallie entered Kellen's room.

Dressed in a simple white harem tunic and pants, Kellen lay on his side in bed, his hands manacled together behind his back. His chest rose and fell erratically as if he'd been exercising strenuously.

Her hands on her hips, Cadaran stood by him, her own face flushed with exertion, and smiled with a feral pleasure Hallie had learned to identify with personal victory.

Hallie came to a stop at the foot of the bed. "Sir?"

"Your prisoner is ready to travel, Lieutenant." Cadaran dusted her hands off. "All trussed up with enough sedatives to calm a tyrlin. He should give you no trouble."

"Men never do, sir." Hallie impersonally helped Kellen off the bed and to his feet. He wobbled slightly and studied her with bloodshot eyes as if he didn't recognize her.

Her heart twinged with pity.

Cadaran patted his butt and laughed, a cold hard sound that made Hallie's hackles rise. "Goodbye, Green Eyes. It's been a pleasure."

Kellen stared at Cadaran as if seeing an insect. "Go to hell, you stinking bitch." He spat on her.

Hallie jerked him backwards and toward the door before Cadaran could hit him. He stumbled, and she wrapped her arm around his waist and all but carried him out of the house. She cradled him gently into the passenger seat of her flitter and buckled him in.

She wasted no time before she was in her seat and powering the flitter up. Zooming upward, she headed toward her destination at top speed.

"Can't you let me see some of the countryside? A condemned prisoner's last request, and all that."

"You aren't condemned."

"Men don't walk away from my new owner. They're carted out."

Hallie said nothing. She'd heard of Lani's reputation among those who did the harem ferries.

"I thought you were my friend."

"As much of a friend as I'll ever be with a bull." She turned to look at Kellen, but he was examining the sky and the trees and meadow below like they were incredible attractions. She sighed.

When the flitter settled down at their destination, he gaped about at the farmland, meadow, and the nearby mountainous area. "Where's my new prison?"

"We only have an hour before we have to leave. Let's make the best of it."

His eyes were infinitely sad as he studied her. "I'm not on lotus. You'll have to rape me without it. Garnet didn't think she needed it."

Hallie swore violently. "I'm not..." She shook her head and slid out of the flitter, pulling a basket out of the back. "Lunch. I brought some beer." When he examined her blankly, she added, "Don't you have picnics on Earth?"

Not waiting for an answer, she spread out the blanket under a nearby lufta tree then opened his door and helped him out. He came to his feet with only a slight wobble from the drugs and sniffed the air like a hunting dog then stamped a foot, testing the grass and soil for their reality. He closed his eyes and turned his face to the bright sun. She said nothing when he began to walk around the meadow they were in.

She put out the food and arranged plates then began to eat her own meal.

Finally, he wandered back to her and held out his manacled hands.

She put down her fried chicken. "I can't take them off."

He sank down to his knees beside her on the blanket. "Please let me escape. Come with me. We can live in the wild. I'll even breed with you without the lotus if you want to."

Her throat tightened. "I can't."

"Please...I'll beg you, grovel anyway you want me to. I never groveled for Cadaran. Please. I can't bear this life anymore. It's killing me."

She shook her head.

"Don't you know what I live through? The lotus. It burns through you like acid and takes away your dignity, your humanity. The hell of withdrawal, again, and again, and again. The rape and humiliation, night after night. The beatings. Your wonderful commander gets her sexual jollies hurting and humiliating me."

"I've figured that out. She's still my commander, and I respect her professional abilities."

"Hallie, please." He shook back his black curls, his rab-cat eyes pleading. "My new owner is much worse. God knows what I'll have to suffer. Please free me."

She sighed and took a sip of beer. "The keys to your manacles are at your new owner's. It would take a power saw you can only find at a few places on Arden to cut them off. We might cut them apart, but the only way we could take them off is by cutting off your hands. The manacles have homing signals in them. Internal Affairs can find you anywhere on this world while you wear them."

"Then cut my hands off. It's worth it."

Realizing he was serious, she shuddered. "I don't have it in me to hurt you like that. Have some food. I'll feed you."

"I'd like some beer. I'm not hungry." He sipped when she held up the can and swirled it around his mouth. "I've missed that."

She let him empty the can then opened another.

He gazed up at the mountain with faraway eyes. "I tried to commit suicide after my second escape attempt failed. I realized death was my only chance for freedom."

"I saw the medical report." She finished the last bite of her fried chicken and forced herself not to look at the wrists he'd slashed. "My mother's farmhouse is just over that hill."

His gaze followed her finger. "Lovely country."

"Please enjoy what I can give you today. A family of my farm's rab-cats are here."

Recognizing her, the six rab-cats trotted trustingly into the open. She wiggled her hands in rab-cat ear greeting. Opening the basket, she took out fresh fruit from the cat plant then put it down on the ground nearby as a friendly offering.

The large male tabby sniffed at the egg-like white fruit then began to eat. The black female ate more daintily. Their kittens were more interested in Kellen than the fruit.

The oldest black male advanced sniffing as if sensing Kellen was different from the humans on the farm.

"He's a male like you," Hallie offered although she didn't think they understood Basic as Floppy did. "I'm female like your mother."

The kitten's ears quivered with excitement, and he walked up to them.

"Is this normal?" Kellen whispered.

"No. They've never come this close before."

The kitten stretched up on its back legs until it was almost face to face with Kellen, who leaned forward. The kitten batted at a black curl then gently touched Kellen's lids with the tips of its ears.

"It's your green eyes. They've never seen a human with eyes like theirs."

Kellen grinned. "They aren't color-blind. Hello, young man. I wish I had my hands free so I could return your greeting."

The young male danced away and began to excitedly wave its ears at the others who all trotted to Kellen and admired his eyes. Kellen admired back, his troubles forgotten. The rab-cats began to play around them.

Hallie let him watch the rab-cats and the summer afternoon until the very last moment then packed up the food and put it into the flitter. Kellen sat down in his seat without protest, his eyes never leaving the rab-cats, who'd scurried out of the way of the flitter.

After they were in the air again, he sighed. "When you worked on the farm, did you ever have a cow who was ill and in pain, but the vet couldn't help it?"

"Yes."

"What did you do to it?"

"We put it out of its misery."

"I'm in pain, and I'm being sent to be tortured to death slowly by a vicious, wealthy tyrlin in woman's clothing. Put me out of my misery. Certainly a member of your own species deserves the same kindness as a cow."

She shook her head. "I can't."

"I'll pretend to escape. All I ask is to die cleanly."

"I won't kill you. I can't. It's not in me to kill you in cold blood. I'll stop you some other way." She blinked tears. "I'm sorry I can't be a hero for you like you deserve. I'm too stupid and cowardly to do anything but my duty. I don't have the guts to throw everything away or even to give you the soldier's death you deserve."

He sagged, burying his face on his knees. "God help me. You were my last hope."

A BRISK tap of paw on his arm woke Tristan up. He blinked awake.

Floppy plopped down beside him on the bed and cut on the vid monitor. Tristan's black hole equations appeared on the screen.

The rab-cat hissed with displeasure.

Tristan chuckled and switched to the vid programs. *Animal Crackers'* opening music had just started.

Floppy's ears wiggled happily, and he sat down on his haunches to watch.

Tristan stroked the rab-cat's back. Floppy had become as addicted to the program as he was and would even cut it on if Tristan was in the garden or with his therapist.

The dancing animal puppets began to sing about helping mother around the house.

Tristan had assumed Floppy was waiting for more real rab-cats, the puppet version didn't interest him that much, but over the weeks they'd watched it together, no more rab-cats had appeared, and Floppy was still fascinated with the program. Tristan was just happy to have a common interest with Mara's beloved Floppy whose hostility had lessened even if he still watched Tristan around Mara like the chastity belt with rabbit ears he was.

Barely awake through most of the program, Tristan woke completely, sensing Floppy's excitement, when the animated letters "D," "O," and "G" chased each other across the screen to the carefully pronounced word "dog." The rab-cat quivered, his ears wiggling in complicated semaphore.

Floppy's reaction to all the cartoon letters wasn't because of their prey-like behavior! "Floppy?"

The rab-cat turned away from the screen.

"Do you understand those letters mean 'dog'?"

Floppy nodded.

"Does your race have written language like that?" He motioned toward the screen.

The rab-cat shook his head.

"This show made you understand the idea of written language?" When Floppy nodded yes, Tristan let out the breath he'd been holding. "Would you like me to teach you how to read and write human Basic?"

The rab-cat's whole body exploded into a "yes."

TRISTAN'S body slid against Mara's as he lowered himself into the pool beside her. His bare chest brushed her face then her breasts, the thin fabric of her bathing suit little barrier to his muscle and heat.

Trembling despite the warm water surrounding her, she wrapped her arms around his broad chest under his armpits as the therapist did.

His arms circling her neck, he floated beside her. "Are you certain you can handle me without the therapist?"

"We both have lifesaver rings if we get in trouble. They'll yank us out of the water and call for medical help if we need it."

His legs fluttered against hers. "Let me go."

She freed him reluctantly, her brain concerned about his safety, her body regretting the hugging closeness of their bodies. He began to swim, his muscular arms propelling him more than the weak kick of his legs.

Impressed by the improved movement of his legs which became better every day, she swam beside him. As happy as a dorph-fish frolicking in the ocean, he swam back and forth across the pool, then practiced weightless walking in the pool's shallow end by holding onto Mara's shoulders and pretending to walk.

Finally, he swam to the steps and settled down on a step low enough so he was in the water up to his chest. He laughed, his joy as sparkling as the sunlight on the water. "True freedom, no wheelchair. This is the life!"

Smiling, she joined him on the steps, her body a careful few feet away from his.

Breathing heavily, he leaned forward and massaged his thigh. "The skinny tree limbs are finally growing into trunks. Puny trunks, but trunks."

"Your legs are beautiful." Mindful of how that had sounded, she added mischievously, "But I still think your toes are prettier."

He lifted his right leg up as if it weren't a major accomplishment and wiggled his elegant toes. "My heart has always belonged to my toes, too."

She giggled.

Raising his arms, now tanned a deep honey gold after a month in the sun, the blond hairs glowing with sunlight, he stretched. "It's so beautiful today it reminds me of home when I was a kid. During summer vacation, we'd always spend the day on the lake. Swimming, canoes, sailboats, and skiing. Dorian had never enjoyed water before, her world's lakes were infested with a fish version of a tyrlin, so I taught her how to swim and everything else. Pretty soon she was dunking me."

His voice didn't catch or his face twist with unhappiness when he said Dorian's name as it normally did, but Mara wasn't certain if that was good or bad. "It would be wonderful to have brothers and sisters when growing up."

"It is. Why didn't your mother have more children? With a plague population to rebuild, big families must be popular."

Mara shrugged. "She never said. I guess she was so busy with her work she didn't want to bother. Maybe she thought one inferior daughter was enough."

"Mara!" He examined her worriedly.

She shrugged again. "It doesn't matter. I've accepted I can never live up to her expectations. She even fought my decision to concentrate in astronomy as well as physics. She thought I was making a terrible mistake since I could never leave Arden."

"You must follow your natural inclinations in science as well as in love."

She stared up into the sky, seeing night stars in the day sky. "The stars have always called me strongly."

"Me too. In earlier days, I guess we'd have been the ones to invent the telescopes or the rockets to follow that pull. Or written science fiction stories about them."

When she nodded, he took her hand and squeezed. "I've learned that you shouldn't let people's high expectations influence your self-worth. You do the best you can, and if that's not good enough for others, that's their emotional weakness, not yours. They're trying to validate their own self-worth through you." He smiled at her with such tenderness, her heart gave an erratic lurch. She returned the smile shyly.

Drawn by internal gravity, they leaned toward each other, Tristan's hand on her cheek, her own on the hollow of his shoulder.

As his chest rubbed against her nipples, she quivered, knowing he was going to kiss her lips. Burning bare flesh, his other hand stroked her back. She sighed and closed the gap between their lips.

Something slammed into the ground near them.

They both jumped at the loud noise and pulled away.

Novia, her face twisted with such hatred and malice Mara barely recognized her, glared at them from the French doors, a lawn chair crumpled beyond her feet.

WIND blowing off the Atlantic Ocean ruffled her long brown hair as Dorian slid out of her flitter. Her mind on the coming confrontation, she automatically noted the ocean rolling in at high tide just below the dunes the beach house was perched on and the raucous calls of the gulls wheeling above.

She stepped up on the porch and knocked on the door.

Elaine opened the door and greeted her with an undignified whoop of joy and a big hug.

Dorian returned the fierce hug, then they pulled away and examined each other. Elaine was brown and blooming, her tan making her long blonde hair shades lighter and her pure blue eyes shades darker. Dorian nodded with approval. "You look good. Beach air and research agree with you."

Ever the blunt member of the Mallory family, Elaine wriggled her nose. "You're too thin and pale. You aren't eating or sleeping properly." She tilted Dorian's chin. "And worry wrinkles are positively running around your eyes."

Covering the offending spots with her hands, Dorian asked, "Really?"

"Well, maybe not that bad, yet. You'd better clean up your act, or they will be."

"Yes, ma'am," Dorian answered meekly.

Elaine hugged her again then ushered her into the living room. "Come on in before I sound even more like Mom."

Settling down in a white wicker chair, Dorian placed her briefcase on a nearby glass table. Through the glass door facing the beach, the ocean seemed even closer than it had outside.

Smoothing her beach wrap over her legs, Tristan's sister sat down in the chair facing he and motioned toward the briefcase. "You look like you're ready to give a business presentation."

"I am. After a fashion." She wasn't ready to start. "How are you doing?"

"Well. This literary estate work suits me. I like keeping busy. Getting away from home is just what I needed. Here I don't keep expecting to see Tris walk through a familiar door and feel the gouge of pain when I realize he never will again."

Dorian nodded. "It's hard to believe he's been gone five months."

"It seems like yesterday, and forever. Why don't you spend some time with me? Getting away would be great for you, and I'd enjoy the company, especially yours. This place gets lonely."

"I can't now. I appreciate the invitation."

"You're still ripping yourself apart about Tris and David. That's not healthy, Dory. Why don't you come, and we can talk out some of the pain."

"The grief is always there, but that isn't what's bothering me." Dorian picked up the briefcase. "I might as well get this over with. I received this in the mail." She opened the briefcase and pulled out the letter and article. "Look at them carefully."

Elaine read the letter. "This seems straightforward enough. This scientist wants your specialized input on a project. Dad receives this kind of letter all the time."

"I've looked her up. Mara d'Jorel is an up and coming scientist in Tris' field. She's written a seminal paper on the evolution of the quasar. She's from Arden."

"The plague planet. I can see why she'd contact you like this."

"Look at the article."

Elaine read a few pages, her forehead wrinkled with concentration, before she gave up. "I'm a humanities major. Give me a break. I'll explain the literary significance of Oz, but you should talk to Dad about what she's positing."

"Before Tristan left, he was working on the same material. He used the Oz metaphor."

"Coincidence. The resemblance of a black hole sucking up debris to a tornado has been used before. I can quote at least six poetry sources without trying hard. The Oz metaphor is an easy jump."

"I took the article and deleted d'Jorel's name, then I showed it to your father. I told him I'd found it among my stuff and wondered if it was Tristan's. Justin read it and said it was. All the ideas were Tristan's, even many of the phrases, but someone else had cobbled it together."

Elaine leaned forward. "Plagiarism."

"Yes. But only Tristan, his father, and I had ever seen the material. He was still working on it when *The Helen* exploded."

"Well, let's fry this d'Jorel for stealing his material. She has no right to plagiarize."

"That was my initial emotional reaction, but..." Dorian pulled the flat holo base out of her briefcase and cut it on. A hologram map sprang into existence above the cube. She pointed. "This is Trigellan, Arden's sun. And this is where the debris from *The Helen* was found."

"They're close. So?"

Dorian leaned back in her chair and folded her hands in her lap. She struggled to keep her voice calm. "I've never said this, but I've never felt Tristan was dead. When David was killed, even before I was told, I felt his loss. It was like having a chunk of my soul ripped out. And before you say anything, you know I'm no fluff-brained romantic. I didn't make that up after he died. I felt it."

Elaine raised her hand in placation. "David I can understand. He was your husband, but Tristan wasn't...Were you sleeping together?"

Dorian colored. "No. But I would have known if he'd died. I know I would, and I didn't."

"Wishful thinking because we didn't have his body to bury."

"That's what I kept telling myself, but I began to do research. Did you know that over fifty ships have disappeared in that same quadrant of space in the last five years? Fifty ships, mainly small private yachts. That's ten times the normal average for any other human quadrant even putting the asteroid belt near Arden into the equation."

"A Bermuda triangle. Isn't that what these spots are called?"

"I've been in contact with some of Kellen and Tristan's spacer friends."

Elaine's golden eyebrows rose. "I hope you brought a laser pistol with you. Tris wouldn't allow most of those wild characters around me."

"I was safe enough. I had a good guide and protector—Captain Tor Orion. He's a smuggler and adventurer. Tristan respects and trusts him. Anyway, according to most spacers, that area has a reputation for being cruised by slavers."

"Slavers! Come on. This isn't the Spanish Main."

"Earthers like you don't know anything about the rest of the galaxy. Even on a dinky little farming planet like Gaynor, I heard stories that would curl your hair."

"Okay, so I'm sheltered, but slavers?"

"I researched Arden. Ever since the plague quarantine, all personal communication has been cut off. You can't send personal messages in, or out. Only scientific and business messages are allowed through."

Elaine lifted the letter from Mara d'Jorel. "This is rather cut and dried."

"According to the historical and medical documents on the Arden plague, over seventy-five percent of the population died. Of those, almost seventy-five percent were men. At the present time, the two biggest imports to Arden are computers and human semen."

"Which means male sterility or men are in short supply because of continued plague."

"Which means the planet is also in need of men."

"But new colonization isn't allowed on a plague planet."

"Exactly." Dorian beamed.

Elaine shook her head. "I see an outline of a horrifying theory in all this information. Do you want to give me your version?"

"Tristan and Kellen's ship was attacked by slavers, who blew it up after taking them off. They've been sold to Arden who needs men. Somehow, Tristan has gotten his colleague Mara d'Jorel to send this article to me since he can't communicate any other way. He probably tricked her into it. He's letting us know he's alive."

"All this from one article and letter?"

"Why send it to me? I've published work on the effects of space on the human body, but there are others with far more expertise. But I was helping Tristan with the very same thing she's asked me to do."

Elaine bit her finger in thought. "What does Dad think about this?"

"I haven't told him. You're the only member of the family I've told."

"Lucky me. Why?"

"I thought you could handle the news more rationally, and I wanted your input. Also, the Mallory men might stop me from what I intend to do. You know what a bunch of overprotective idiots they are."

"Uh oh! What are you going to do?"

"I'm going to Arden to find Tristan, or at least find out how this d'Jorel got his Oz project notes when they should have been blown up with him."

"But Arden is quarantined. If you land, you can't get off."

Dorian shrugged. "So what? David's dead. I have nothing holding me here anymore. I'm one hell of an immunologist, and Arden has one hell of an uncured plague. We're made for each other. Like Tristan and I are made for each other. If anyone owns Tristan, it's going to be me."

"You're going to buy him!"

"If necessary. Actually, I intend to steal him and whisk him off that filthy slaver planet."

"Plague, remember. Certainly you wouldn't risk bringing the plague back to Earth."

"Of course not." Dorian patted her briefcase. "According to my research, the plague virus has a year life span in its dormant stage. I've already picked out a suitable uninhabited planet for us. We'll Adam and Eve it for a year until we're certain we aren't carrying the plague, then we'll come home."

Elaine slumped back in her chair as if the enormity of what they were discussing had hit her. After several long minutes, she shook her head. "Tristan alive! That's such a seductive idea. I want to believe it."

"I do. I've even got Tor convinced, and he's one of the world's great pragmatists."

"You haven't mentioned Kellen."

"If I can get him out, I will. Tristan's my main concern."

"Tris won't leave without him."

Dorian's lips tightened as she recalled all the nightmare implications of Tristan's sexual slavery which had haunted her for the last weeks. "He'll come with me if I have to drug him and drag him aboard."

Elaine smiled dreamily. "Kellen was my first big crush. I would have died for him. Those black curls, eyes as pure a green as emeralds, and body that..." She shivered dramatically. "What a major hunk. He treated me like a sister. A major teenage ego smasher."

"Would you like to come with me? A year on a primitive planet with a major hunk? You aren't a naive teenager anymore."

"Kellen isn't really right for me, or me for him. Now, I do think of him as a brother." Elaine asked seriously, "Do you want me to come?"

"Would you?"

"If you need me, and it will help Tris and Kellen, you're damn right I will."

Dorian's heart surged with gratitude. "Your offer is tempting, but there's no need to risk you, too. Besides, I need a co-conspirator on Earth."

"What do you want me to do?"

"After I get Tristan off the planet, I'll send you a message through the ICC net so you can tell the family about what I'm up to, then I want you to take my information about Arden and the slavers and give it to Geoffrey. With his great contacts in the Earth Colony Congress...I want him to blow those bastards on Arden out of the water."

"A major political stink. You've got it with great pleasure."

"And if I don't contact you within six months, you can consider me trapped on Arden, and I want you to do the very same thing."

"Why don't we just throw all this information at the authorities to get Tris back?"

"If Arden is low enough to buy human slaves, do you think they'd worry about killing Tristan and Kellen to hide their tracks?"

"Oh." Elaine hugged herself. "I guess I am a sheltered Earther."

"Now for the messy part of this discussion. Finances. I've liquidated everything I own except David's farm. I still need over a hundred thousand credits. I want you to loan it to me with the farm as collateral. It's worth far more than that, but if something should happen to me or the ship I buy, and I can't pay you back, I want the family to have David's farm."

"I inherited that much from Tris in securities. We haven't had the heart to sell Tris' home yet. Sure, you've got the money. It will be well spent if we get him home, or even find out the truth about what happened to him."

"Good. The ship's going to cost a fortune, not even counting outfitting it with the medical equipment I'll need for studying the plague. Everything will be state of the art."

"It all sounds so easy, but won't you be captured immediately with all their protective sensors and things?"

"I don't think so." Dorian beamed. "The ship I want is a smuggler's craft, and I've been taking lessons in smuggling and piracy."

Elaine hooted laughter. "God help Arden, here you come."

Chapter 12

Thunder rumbled hard overhead. Mara jerked her head up, her attention diverted from the equation on the computer screen. A summer shower with all its unpredictability was ready to strike. She smiled, her mind already working on the equation even before her eyes found the screen again. She glanced at the computer clock.

Tristan! He would be up from his nap and in the garden, and his nurse had left over a month ago.

Mara bolted out of her room toward Tristan's suite. His bed, the room, and his study were empty as she'd expected.

Rain was sprinkling as she reached the garden. She glanced around then headed for the only real shelter against the sun and rain.

As the deluge began, she bounded up the wheelchair ramp into the large white wood gazebo. In the very center away from the blowing rain, Tristan sat in the lawn recliner and watched the downpour. The rain must have masked the sound of her approach because he jumped when she touched his shoulder.

"Afternoon, pixie." He smiled up at her.

Her heart gave a peculiar but pleasant half-turn as it always did when he smiled with such warmth. "I came to rescue you."

"I fear we both need rescuing now. I guess we'd better sit this storm out."

She nodded and picked up his metal crutches, placing them in the far corner. "Just in case of lightning."

Lightning struck nearby. She jumped.

"Afraid of storms?"

"Only lightning."

"Sensible lady. Thunder isn't dangerous." He eased over on the lounge. "Come here away from the draft. It's safer, drier, and the lounge is all plastic."

The cushion gave under her weight as she slid in beside him. He turned slightly on his side to give her more room and opened his arms. "Here."

Turning on her side, she rested her head on his shoulder as his arms settled around her waist. Her heart twisted again with a different kind of pleasure as her cheek rested on the silken fabric of his white tunic shirt. He smelled like Tristan and rain shower.

His hand rubbed against the sleeve of her robe. "Just get out of the shower?"

She blushed remembering what she had on, and didn't have on. "No, after our swim, I was showering and got an inspiration. When I finished, I slipped this on, sat down at the computer, and..."

"The afternoon and hours passed before the thunderstorm broke your concentration."

"Yes. I'm sorry I wasn't around when you got up from your nap."

"Don't apologize, pixie. I understand, and I don't need to be entertained every minute. I could have called you if I wished. Besides, I expected you'd have your nose in a computer screen. Those shiny golden eyes of yours had that peculiar twinkle of an idea waiting to be born."

"No one else understands that. I've lost friends because of my absorption."

"It takes one to know one. You've seen my peculiar twinkles before." His hand absently caressed her hair. "Our garden is beautiful in the rain. The lufta's leaves glow when wet, and the garden is redolent with its cinnamon scent."

"You've never said 'our' before. It's always been 'your garden,' 'your house.'"

"I guess I did. I'm ready to start my future, not bemoan the past that's gone forever."

"I'm pleased." She smiled into his shoulder.

He kissed her forehead. "I am, too."

The kiss fluttered through her like raindrops on bare flesh. She lifted her head. His eyes shimmered as they met hers, and she felt the attraction again between them. They were like binary stars circling each other, attraction pulling them together and apart at the same time.

Sensing she'd rip apart if these two stars never joined, she closed her eyes and nudged his lips with her own.

He moaned, "Oh, Mara," and his lips nudged back.

His lips caressed hers for an exquisite eternity, then his tongue tip flicked across the bow of her lips.

Her lips parted instinctively, and he entered with a gentle caress. Her body hot and cold in the same instant, she shuddered. His hand stroked her cheek in silent reassurance, his arm holding her against him.

Trusting that assurance as she'd always trusted him, she relaxed against him. Slowly exploring, he kissed inside her mouth with his tongue.

Groaning, her breasts aching, she melted deeper into the folds of his body. After another eternity of pleasure, she decided that perhaps she should be kissing back to return this wonder.

Her fingers wound in his hair as her tongue mimicked his.

A tremor shook them, their bodies so close Mara wasn't certain whose reaction she'd felt, then his lips left hers, trailing down her throat.

Her pulse throbbed erratically at his touch.

He moaned her name again and pushed away the fabric of her robe. His lips scalded her shoulder.

Trying to ease their ache with his heat, she thrust her bare breasts into him. His lips and tongue salved the top of her breast, but the pleasure/pain intensified.

She ground against him, her pelvis rubbing his. Through his clothing, his growing staff rubbed back.

Surprised, her insatiable scientist's curiosity present even in this wonder, she blurted, "Are you preparing to breed with me?"

He inhaled sharply then roared with laughter.

Seeing nothing funny about the question, she blushed.

As the laughter ended, the wondrous magic between them disappeared, and they were again two friends sharing a lounge in a thunderstorm. She bit her tongue and cursed her question.

Easing away from her, he closed her robe with two discreet fingers. "Oh, Mara, how I adore your unworldliness."

"According to my research, when a man's staff...changes, he's preparing to breed."

"Animals breed, pixie; people have sex or make love."

"What's the difference?"

"Breeding is cold propagation. Having sex involves physical pleasure and sating lust—sexual hunger. Making love involves tenderness, deep feelings like love, and physical and emotional pleasure. Conceiving a baby while making love is just a wonderful occasional side effect."

"Oh." Mara considered his definitions. "What were you doing?"

"Getting carried away with the situation. A man can't control that reaction sometimes. I only meant to kiss you."

Disappointed, she frowned. "You don't want to do any of those three things with me?"

"I didn't say that. I said I wasn't intending to do anything just now. Would you like me to?"

Her whole body flooded with embarrassed heat.

"That's not a question a gentleman should ask. I'm sorry."

"Have you ever...?"

"I've never bred or had sex. Many men do where I come from, but it's not my nature to divorce my feelings from sex. I've been deeply involved in every sense with several women."

Her stomach tightened into a painful knot. "Why haven't you married?"

"Something wasn't quite right with each relationship, and we parted."

She whispered, "Dorian?"

"We didn't have time to explore our relationship enough to know." He shrugged. "I think we would have. We've been great friends for years, and often that's the start of a loving and happy marriage."

"You mean you can feel kinning when you breed, I mean make love?"

"Of course."

"But kinning's family feeling. That seems wrong."

"Maybe I've misunderstood the idea of kinning. I thought it could mean deep personal friendship, not just direct blood relationship with the other person."

"It can, but..."

He smiled down at her. "You aren't a sister to me, Mara. I don't feel the same way I feel about Elaine, but my feelings for you are deep and strong. I would very much like to make love with you."

"You would!" She colored at the excited squeak in her voice. "You aren't a brother to me, but my feelings are deep and strong, so very strong. And I would..."

"Yes?" he prompted gently.

Burying her face in his chest, she whispered, "I would very much like to make love to you. Very, very much."

He chuckled and hugged her.

Lifting her face, she nudged her lips against his. When his lips nudged back, she asked for entry, her arms around his neck, her fingers in his curls.

He groaned this time, his tongue meeting hers, then groaned again when she rocked her body against his.

Their bodies met, as much a part of each other as rain binding with dry soil.

Despising the barrier, she tugged at her open robe to bring her body against his.

He quivered, tearing his lips from hers, and pushed away.

"Make love to me now, Tristan." She nuzzled his throat. "I want to be part of you with the rain falling around us in our garden."

"You know how to torture a man." He kissed her forehead. "Now isn't the time. I want our first time to be perfect, and these legs aren't ready for perfect. And I want it to be proper by the customs of your people."

Mara hadn't known breeding was only allowed in bed and wondered how Tristan knew this when she didn't. "Everything about you is perfect, but I will wait if you wish it."

TAKING each step with the help of his crutches, Tristan walked into his bedroom from his study. Novia stood in the middle of the room, directing the actions of the cleaning robots. She gave him a viperous glare for daring to come out of his study when she was cleaning his room. He asked politely, "May I speak with you a moment?"

"Mara wants me to communicate with you." Novia shrugged and plopped down on the edge of the bed.

Tristan settled into Sheba's favorite armchair. "If I had anyone else to ask this, I would. Even your library is no use to me. I want to know about your marriage customs."

"What's marriage?"

"The life contract between a man and woman. It involves deep shared feelings, a promise to be faithful and complete partners in all things, and a commitment to have and raise children in a loving environment."

"And you want this marriage with Mara?"

"Yes, I do. Very much."

The old woman cackled like a witch. "There's nothing like marriage on Arden. If a woman wants a baby, she gets it out of a test tube or buys herself a man. Mara's already bought you. Beggared herself doing it. Not that you're worth the money."

Tristan slumped back in the chair. "What!"

"And Mara swears you're intelligent." Novia shook her head. "Let me explain this simply. Men are property of the state in Arden. You are a man. Mara bought you for breeding purposes. These are your harem rooms. You are her bed slave. Is that simple enough, or shall I explain some more."

"I don't believe you. Mara wouldn't...She loves me. She must."

"She's too kind to hurt anyone, even a slave like you. She's developed a fondness for you, but that's Mara for you. Even fusses over her bed slave like she does her other pets." Novia beamed with malicious glee. "Excuse me. I must finish the living room." She ordered the robots out and followed them.

Novia's lies had been so outrageous they seemed believable. Tristan shook himself out of confusion, lifted himself to his feet with his crutches, and hobbled in search of Mara.

In his agitation, he didn't realize he was going through his taboo bedroom door until he'd already stuck one foot through. Electricity shot through him, and he was blasted backwards.

He screamed as he smashed into the floor. He must have blacked out because when he opened his eyes Mara was kneeling beside him on the floor, her face dead white. She caressed his head. "What happened? Should I call Dr. Ilka?"

"That door has an electrified forcefield on it."

"I know. Your bracelet monitor activates it."

"I thought I was under house arrest, the honor policy, and I've been in jail instead. I've been in jail in this house for three months, and I didn't know it." His laugh cracked.

"This isn't a jail. You've done nothing wrong."

He sat up. "No, it's a harem room. That's what Novia called it, a harem room."

Her face turned even whiter. "Yes, it's called that."

"My God, you did buy me! I'm nothing but a bed slave you've been jollying along until breeding time."

"No!"

"You didn't buy me?"

"Yes, but..."

Black despair and anger engulfed him, and he saw the sham of the past months and the woman he'd wanted to marry. "Get away from me. Get away. I never want to see you again."

MARA crept into Tristan's bedroom like a thief. Moonlight spilled through the French doors, coloring the room with silver and lighting her steps to Tristan.

He curled on his side in bed, a sheet draped haphazardly across his loins and legs. Moonlight burnished his curls, lashes, and beautiful features and lovingly traced his muscular chest and arms with quicksilver.

Her heart twisted with tenderness and loss, the emotions threatening to shatter it into pieces. She blinked tears. For the last two weeks, these midnight visits were the only opportunity she had to see him. If she tried to speak with him, he'd turn his back on her and ignore her, his icy hatred an unbreakable barrier between them. He wouldn't listen to her explanation of why she'd bought him, and he refused to eat in her presence, although from his thinness he didn't appear to be eating much alone either.

He even refused to work with his physical therapist, but Floppy had told her he was still swimming. Floppy was the only member of the family Tristan communicated with, their lessons continuing unabated.

Tristan had redefined her life, her very identity, over the last six months, and without him, she was adrift without purpose, even her research meaningless.

He slept so peacefully she leaned toward him, careful not to wake him, and brushed a kiss on his forehead. As she straightened, his arm clutched her waist and dragged her into his bed. She squeaked with surprise.

Hovering above her, he pinned her arms over her head. "Aren't slaves allowed to sleep unmolested around here?"

"I was checking on you and just..." She lifted and kissed his forehead. "Nothing more."

"Too damn much." He stared down at her body.

She lifted slightly but couldn't see what interested him, only her nightgown plastered against her body.

His eyes glowed with a cold hunger she'd never seen before, and her nipples tightened and rose under his scrutiny. His staff stirred against her thigh.

His breeding feelings seemed very different from their other times together. Hunger and anger twisted together. "Tristan?"

Her voice broke his trance-like fascination with her breasts. He freed her left hand and cupped a breast. Her heart pounded against his fingers. His voice was a harsh rasp, "You bought me for straight animal breeding. I guess I'd better start earning my keep. Breeding it is."

"But you said only animals breed."

"Only an animal would keep slaves." He jerked her gown upward to her waist and slid between her legs as he opened his pajama bottoms. His staff stirred against her. Ripping open the fastening of her gown, he cupped her breasts with hot hands, his face descending toward them.

Sighing, she wished this mating could be as it would have been in the gazebo. His hurt filled her. Both arms free, she wrapped them around his neck and kissed the top of his head.

He buried his face between her bare breasts. "Damn it. You aren't afraid."

"Why should I be afraid? You won't hurt me."

"Don't you know what rape is?"

"Forced breeding?"

"Yes, and this is it. You're supposed to be afraid."

"It's against your nature to hurt me. You're gentle and kind."

He groaned and rolled off her, burying his face in the mattress. His chest heaved with the bottled emotions of the last two weeks.

She rested her cheek against his shoulder blade and held him, tears streaming down her face, as she shared his pain.

"Damn you, you're right. I can't hurt you. I could never hurt you. Even if you deserve it."

"I have such kinning for you, Tristan."

"Then free me."

Sniffing, she scrubbed at her cheeks. "I wish I could. I do own you, but it's to keep some other woman from owning you. That is the only kind of freedom I can give you on Arden." She sat up so he wouldn't think she was seeking breeding. "You don't have to breed with me, or have sex, or make love. Never. I only sought it when you said you wanted it too."

Closing his pajama bottoms, he flopped over, sat up, and leaned against the headboard. He studied her open gown a moment then fastened it with shaking fingers. "Okay, I'm ready for the official explanation. Tell me what kind of hell planet I'm stuck on, and what my options are."

She explained about the plague, the development of the harem, and about the present version.

Tristan shook his head. "And no one tries to change this archaic system? Certainly the emergency is over."

"We have a problem bringing our percentage of men to equal levels. They're more susceptible to plague. Plus, our system is so structured now the bureaucrats don't want to change it and risk losing power. We have enormous graft and incompetence. And if you speak against the harem or the system, you're branded a traitor and thrown into prison. Some have been executed. Only my mother's fame and the planetwide respect for her brilliance kept her from being imprisoned when she fought against the harem system."

"What a charming world."

Mara nodded. "But there are ways to use the system to our advantage." She told him about her six months of effort to free him from the harem—Thea d'Louisa and the other major scientists who sided with them and who had kept him under her protection, and about Dr. Ilka and the black hole equations. Not wanting to offer him false hopes, she didn't tell him about the plagiarized article she'd sent to Dorian. It had been two months with no response. Dorian had probably tossed it in the recycler without reading it.

"So our major opponent is this Cadaran, head of Internal Security?"

"Yes."

"I'll have to think about this. I have some experience in bureaucracy and politics. We have to make my freedom more profitable to her and the state than tossing me back into the harem in a year."

"Ten months, twenty-two days."

"My how time flies when you're a sex slave." His expression closed for a moment. "If going through channels doesn't work, would you help me escape?"

"You can't flee off-planet."

"I accept that. I won't carry the plague home. Aren't there places on this planet I can hide?"

"The mountains. But the tyrlins live there."

"A tyrlin is preferable to being tossed into the lottery again. Will you help me?"

"On the day I met you, I swore I'd free you if I had to tear the government apart. That promise was for a colleague named Dr. Mallory who had a brilliant way with black holes. For Tristan, prison breaks, tyrlins, or anything else."

He kissed her palm. "Thank you, pixie. I'm sorry I refused to listen to your explanation about the harem. You're as much a prisoner in this situation as I am, and you've taken terrible risks. Thank you."

"You're welcome. I'm sorry I didn't tell you the truth, but I knew the truth could only hurt you."

"I wouldn't have fought to stay alive to be a slave. Perhaps you should have told me."

"You aren't going to be a slave."

He squeezed her hand. "I've been a roaring fool. You shame me with your trust. I should have trusted in your goodness when Novia told me the truth. You aren't exactly Simon Legree."

"Who?"

"I'll explain some other time." He studied the moonbeam pattern on the ceiling. "The worse hurt was...I didn't think you cared for me. The real me. I thought I was even less than a golden boy to you. A sex slave." He shuddered. "A new low even for me."

She had a vague sense of what he was talking about. "Other women cared only for your beauty? What fools. Your brains are much more attractive, and your heart is even more beautiful." She smiled coyly. "But your most attractive feature are your toes."

He chuckled and opened his arms. "I've missed you so much. These last two weeks have been empty without you."

Settling into his embrace, she rubbed her cheek against the hollow of his shoulder. "I have no life without you, Tristan. Even the stars don't twinkle without you."

Curled against each other in contented companionship, they remained silent for a long time. Finally, he brushed a kiss on the top of her head. "What do you want, pixie? I mean between us?"

"I cherish every day I spend with you and our little family. I'll cherish whatever comes."

"You certainly don't pressure a man into making declarations. Can I make perfect love to you tonight?"

She nodded into his chest. "I would very much like to make perfect love with you. Very, very much."

Chapter 13

Stars covered the sky like frost on black velvet, their twinkle dimmed only by the full moon's light. The scent of cinnamon lufta and sweet meadow grass drifted past, making the swimming pool's surface tremble as Mara trembled. She shifted nervously on the raft she and Tristan knelt on.

Loosening the raft, Tristan pushed it away from the side of the pool. It drifted. He slipped off his pajama bottoms, balled them, and tossed them overhand with unexpected skill onto his crutches on dry land.

He joined her and wrapped his arm around her waist. "Don't be concerned. This raft could take three kids jumping up and down on it and wouldn't tilt or roll, and it's even bigger than my bed."

"We would only get wet," she answered matter-of-factly and stared at the moonlight dancing like ghostly maiden's hands across his hair, magnificent body, and staff. She flushed, her insides fluttering with excitement.

"Oh, nerves. Well, I have them too, pixie."

"You do?"

Nodding, he squeezed her waist. "Let me show you why I wanted to come out here." He stretched out on his back and opened his arms. She nestled against him, her head on his shoulder, his arms around her. The raft's fabric was warm and soft against her bare arms and legs as it molded itself to her. The water rocked them. "Look around."

Moonlight and stars reflected off the pool's surface and through the clear fabric of the raft.

She gasped. "We're floating in the night sky."

"Two lovers on a magic carpet. Romantic astronomers on a trip to the moon."

"This is wonderful!"

"I was out here one night like this, and thought of you, like this. I didn't sleep much that night aching for you."

"Men ache too?"

"Yes." He moaned into her hair, "Oh, yes."

Unfastening her gown, she sat up and pulled it over her head. She shook back the hair cascading around her shoulders and tossed the gown away. She smiled shyly and opened her arms. “I can’t bear to see you in pain.”

His eyes twinkled like the stars as he studied her, his gaze traveling from her full breasts to her waist to the legs tucked under her. “You’re so lovely.”

“I am?”

“You are. Beautiful and brilliant and wonderful.”

She blushed but held out a foot and wiggled her toes. “And my?”

“Not as pretty as mine, but you can’t have everything.”

Giggling, she swatted his arm.

He pulled her gently down beside him and leaned over her. Wrapping her arms around his neck, she nuzzled his face. “Tristan, I...”

He nuzzled back to prompt her.

“I don’t have the words to tell you what I feel for you. I don’t think they exist on this world, but I...”

“Show me, pixie. Show me.” He settled against her, his chest rubbing her breasts.

Sighing, her nipples hard and aching, she kissed him.

He touched her as his lips and tongue touched her. One hand swirled against her breast; the other wandered up and down her hip and thigh. The tickling warmth ignited small flames which whirled downward to her core.

Shivering, she twined fingers in the curls at his nape, her other hand tracing the line of his jaw to his neck. A memory of touching him like that for the first time in the hospital appeared then vanished like stars on the water.

His chest against hers, he rocked, and she jolted, fire shooting inward from her breasts. “Oh, Mara. Beautiful, sexy Mara.”

Her heart slammed into her ribs as he slid down her, his lips and tongue lathing wet kisses down the straining cord of her neck to her shoulder.

His lips found her nipple. “Tristan!”

Chuckling, he suckled harder, a hand kneading her other breast.

She hugged his head to her, the stars above swirling dizzily, as he made slow and lavish love to each breast.

Her knee came up without her volition, and she stroked his leg with her own, her pelvis swaying against his outer hip.

Moaning, he slid downward again. His nose found her navel and twisted. She giggled then gasped when he kissed her belly. His fingers circled up her inner thigh. She parted her legs at their tickling insistence. One finger found her center of pleasure and traced it. She stiffened.

Tristan moaned her name, resting his head on her belly, and traced upward again. Goose bumps exploded over her body, and her pelvis ticked against his hand. His thumb rotated gently, his hand holding her.

Flame swept across her, yet she was liquid and limp.

He kissed where his thumb had touched.

Crying out, she thrust upward.

Caressing her hips in reassurance, he kissed her with his lips and tongue.

Whimpering and clutching his head, she sagged back. He taught her delight until she writhed against him, unable to bear the sweet torment, then he taught her a greater pleasure still, the torment even greater. When she could bear no more, she tensed then arced upward. The stars overhead exploded and burned through her.

Her rasping breath brought her back to earth.

Tristan slid up beside her and cuddled her. Shivering, she circled his neck with her arms and buried her face into his shoulder. His unique scent enveloped her like his arms. "Oh, Tristan!"

He kissed her head. She nestled against him, sharing their wondrous emotional closeness and the magic he'd given her, but very soon, she was conscious of his staff against her thigh, its heat prodding her. She sighed, pleased the sweet torment had returned, and wrapped her upper leg over his. She kissed his nipple as he'd kissed hers.

His body twitched, his heart smashing erratically against her lips.

"Does this please you?"

"Oh, yes."

"May I?" Her hand slid down his belly.

His voice was a breathy sigh. "Please."

Desire to pleasure him and curiosity moved her fingers downward. She explored with tender fingers, discovering texture, shape, heat, and strength. His hand covered hers and taught her movement.

She smiled as he quivered to her continued caress. His body crackled with breeding tension as hers must have when he'd pleasured her. If she could return to him what he'd given her, she asked nothing else. She nibbled kisses across his chest.

"No more. No more." He eased her hand away from him and rolled them until he was on her. His weight intensified the painful yearning in her belly.

Smiling up into his eyes, their blue so bright with tenderness and desire she could see it in the moonlight, she lifted her knees around his hips. "Make love to me, Tristan."

He gazed at her as he had in her dream of breeding and kissed her.

Her tongue meeting his in a slow dance, she relaxed under him. His hand slid between them and caressed her.

The ache grew until she thrust her hips in that sweet torture, then his staff caressed her too. The torment grew.

She moaned his name, then his staff gently entered her.

"Oh, Mara. My beautiful, darling Mara."

Stilling, her arms tightening around his shoulders, she savored the sensations. A moment of pain, then fullness and throbbing heat.

His arm cradled her head, and he kissed her temple. "Mara?"

"Breeding with you is beautiful, Tristan."

Chuckling, he nuzzled away her happy tears. "This is making love, pixie, and I haven't even started yet."

She opened her mouth to ask what he meant, but his staff nudged forward. She blinked as it nudged again, then again, filling her more completely. Slight pain followed each movement, but the pleasure was more intense. Her arms tight around his shoulders, she relaxed beneath him.

His staff nudged again as he groaned, "Perfect," then began to leave her.

Something seemed missing from this mating, and she almost protested, but his staff eased forward again, sensations surging through her. "Oh!" Her eyes opened wide with understanding and excitement.

Throwing back his head, he laughed. "Yes, oh, my unworldly pixie. *My* pixie."

"Oh, yes." She lifted and nibbled kisses across his sweaty face. She wanted to say he belonged to her now, too, but she feared he'd think she meant the harem.

He thrust forward with controlled power.

Her instinctive woman's body knew more than all her scientist's research. Her hips began to meet his. They ground together in a lingering dance of tender pleasure, the raft rolling beneath them.

His hands leisurely stroked her breasts, hips, and face as his lips trailed over her face, neck, and even made a teasing goose bump visit to her ear.

She giggled, and her hands joined the exploration, discovering him as he learned her. His skin changed texture from his coarse browned back to his baby smooth buttocks which tensed and quivered with each thrust within her. When her finger tips traced the small of his back, he groaned, but it was an excited groan. She did it again.

"Teasing, sexy little pixie." He retaliated by licking her breast then suckling.

Trying to force her whole body harder against his, she whimpered. Her legs wrapped around his hips, and she oscillated against him.

The power he'd controlled for so long broke free, and he plunged into her, again and again, with breathtaking intensity.

Her body bucked against him as all the sensations within began to nova.

The raft seemed to be spinning upward, night sky and stars a blur. The moon careened past them, and they were floating in space.

Star flame melted them into one whole being, then there was nothingness.

"Tristan!"

He held her through the flame and beyond, his seed filling her womb.

Mara rediscovered herself. Tristan sagged against her, their bodies still linked and quivering from the intensity of what they'd just shared.

Caressing his hair, she nuzzled his cheek.

He finally nuzzled back. "Mara?"

"That is an interesting way to sail up to Oz. Black holes and quasars will never top it as a transportation method."

Chuckling happily, he rolled sideways, taking her with him. "Oh my sweet, funny pixie."

She nestled into his chest and shivered as the night wind whispered across her wet skin. She was his, and he was hers, and no one—not Cadaran, Dorian, or the entire Arden Council—would take him away from her. No matter what she had to do to keep him.

TRISTAN composed his face as he heard the approach of his enemy. Holding onto the arms of the chair, he came to his feet, wobbled a moment before his legs held, then tugged his best pants and shirt, cut in his favorite Earth style, into place.

Mara walked into the bedroom with the elegance and serene power of a queen. His heart surged with admiration. No one could guess, least of all their enemy, that Mara had thrown up her lunch from tension about this meeting.

Cadaran strolled in with the certainty of a hunter in her own territory. She stopped just inside the door and stared at Tristan. Tall and slender with a boy's figure in an impressive black with gold braid uniform, she had huge, sad brown eyes framed by military-short black hair. She smiled like an urbane panther, her eyes crinkling with amusement.

He nodded with equal urbanity. "Thank you for coming to see me. I would have come to see you, but..." He grinned and held up the wrist with his detention bracelet.

"Quite all right. I've been curious to meet you." She stripped him with a lingering look. "Your Earther i.d. didn't do you justice."

"Official i.d.'s rarely do anyone justice. Please have a seat." He waved at the chair in front of him.

She smirked politely and settled into the chair. Mara sat down unobtrusively in a chair facing them both. Only when they'd both taken seats, did he allow himself into his own chair. Holding onto its arms, he eased down, using every bit of strength and control he'd gained through months of therapy.

Cadaran's eyes flickered around the room and stopped on the bed then out to the garden. "Nice little harem suite you're sharing. Largest, most open one I've ever seen. It must have cost a fortune to put the forcefield generators up."

"Two fortunes," Mara replied dryly.

"Indeed."

Tristan leaned back in his chair and crossed his legs. "Fortunes are one matter I wish to discuss with you."

The urbane panther in her lips and devil cold in her eyes, Cadaran smiled. "We've earned a pretty credit on your first sale, and I look forward to many more sales in the future."

He chuckled. "You haven't gotten where you are by limited thinking. You know I have far more value otherwise. I'm certain with your extensive information network you already know what I can offer Arden."

Cadaran held out a hand and admired her nails. "I have heard rumors."

"Jorel's energy converter, which provides Arden with sixty-five percent of its off-world credit income, is nothing in comparison to what my black hole equations can bring."

"My experts tell me they're many years from possibility."

"Have they seen my notes?"

"No."

"Then they don't know. Before *The Helen* was destroyed, I would have said ten years, but Mara and I have discovered our work on black holes and quasars blend together perfectly." He latticed the fingers of both hands to demonstrate. "Together, they form a more complete answer. We should have our answer in a few years."

"And after that?"

"The possibilities are endless about how we can manipulate them for different practical applications. We can spend the rest of our lives creating new sources of income for Arden."

Cadaran shook her head. "And what do you expect to get out of this?"

"Freedom from the harem. I'll stay here willingly with Mara to work together."

"And breed together."

"Yes, and we'll give Arden something of even greater value than the equations. Children born of such bright parents and raised in a loving, intellectually stimulating environment will surpass us both. Does three or four Einsteins interest you?"

Blushing, Mara added, "He was the greatest scientific mind the human race has ever seen."

Cadaran waved away Mara's comment. "I know who he was."

"My family on Earth is very important. If you'll let me get in touch with them, I can offer Arden other things of value. My oldest brother designs the finest computers in the galaxy. Most of them haven't been allowed off Earth, until now. My other brother has a top job in the Earth Colony Congress and all the power that implies. My father is head of the Science Foundation which is a galactic version of your Jorel Foundation. He could tout your scientists."

"You're—"

"Dead. I know. I read my obituary in a scientific journal." Tristan staunched the pain he felt for his family's grief before it reached his face. "Arden can announce you just found me living in the mountains. I jettisoned out of the ship in the escape pod before it blew up."

Cadaran chuckled. "You are very good. Are you certain you're a scientist?"

"Where I come from, a scientist must be a politician. And I learned the rules of power watching my father."

"And if we won't allow this miraculous return to life?"

"You'll lose my family's influence as well as their help in utilizing the equations to their maximum financial benefit. But, if necessary, I'm willing to allow Mara total credit for the research."

"Very generous. If that's all, I must be going." Cadaran stood.

Tristan levered himself up to his feet.

She gave another panther smirk. "You have fire and beauty. I'll enjoy bedding you myself when this sweet little baby scientist finishes with you in ten months."

A chill shot down his spine. "I've just offered Arden unlimited wealth and galactic power, and you toss it away."

"A man is only a man on Arden. Especially men like you. You can offer us nothing." The cold in her eyes flickered a moment, and he saw her soul before she turned and walked out of the room.

He shivered. He'd expected pragmatic greed, but he'd found a hatred for men so insane nothing could sway it.

ON GUARD duty, Floppy sat on the railing of the gazebo and watched the sun-drenched garden.

Mara moved Tristan's crutches and slid into the lounge beside him. He wrapped his arms around her and kissed her. She sighed, nestling into his body, and returned the kiss but forced herself to pull away when his lips left hers. They hadn't come out here to make love.

His ears quivering, Floppy studied them now. After a man to man talk with Tristan, the rab-cat had accepted the humans as life mates and trusted Tristan with her, he even accepted that Tristan, not he, would share the same bedroom every night with Mara, but he was fascinated by their kissing.

Mara sighed again. A pity Novia hadn't taken their relationship as easily as the rab-cat.

Tristan asked, "Well?"

"I can find no monitoring devices, and Mother's anti-bugging devices haven't been touched. Cadaran hasn't been watching us."

"How could she know we're sleeping together? Are you certain you've told no one?"

"No one."

"Patta?"

"She would insist on every detail. I thought it wiser to say nothing."

"Charming."

"She doesn't understand. She's had no chance to learn the difference between breeding and making love. About what a man and woman can feel for each other."

"Ilka? A physical?"

Mara wondered if he knew about the bimonthly pregnancy test she was required to take. "No, not yet."

"That leaves Floppy and Novia who could tell. Floppy?"

The rab-cat shook his head vigorously and hissed with disgust.

"He was only teasing, Floppy. He knows you and Novia wouldn't betray me."

"But Novia would betray me. She hates me."

"But I would be harmed."

"Can she see that behind all that hate?"

"I don't know."

"We can't trust her anymore. If she finds out about our escape plans..."

The last of Mara's childhood ripped away, and she blinked tears of loss. "We won't trust Novia anymore."

"I'm sorry, pixie." He kissed her head.

"Escape is our only option?"

"Unless we can get someone of greater power than Cadaran to back us, yes. Ilka hasn't had any luck in that direction. The whole Council is under Cadaran's thumb."

"She reminds me of a tyrlin. Crazy mean."

"Did you really kill one of those giant cats?"

"Yes. I drew it away from Floppy and blasted it when it pounced at me."

Tristan shivered.

"I won't blast you, even if you pounce on me." She caressed his hand tucked against her tummy.

He chuckled. "I already have, and you yawned with terror at my viciousness."

She giggled then became serious. "Floppy's people will take us in and hide us in the caves in the mountains. Won't they?"

The rab-cat nodded.

Tristan groaned. "All we have to do is disconnect this damn prison bracelet, get supplies, and leave."

"We're making progress with the bracelet."

"Yes, my naughty little hacker. We are."

Even though he was teasing her, she defended actions she was still uncomfortable with. "I was curious if my new computers were powerful enough to gain access into the antique government computers, and one thing led to another. I didn't intend to do anything illegal when I broke into them."

"Until you met me, and I led you into a life of civil disobedience."

"I don't regret a moment of it. I love my world, but the harem is wrong, and putting you in it is evil."

She felt his inner quietness and determination even before he spoke. "If I can't escape before Cadaran comes to take me.... I'd rather be dead than accept that life."

"I know."

"Then you'd help me?"

"Yes, but it won't happen. I'll feed her and the Council to a tyrlin first."

He laughed. "And you would."

"Damn right I would."

"You'd make a fine little rab-cat, all soft and purry, until someone's in danger then pounce, no more tyrlin. Wouldn't she, Floppy?"

The rab-cat nodded, his green eyes gleaming with mischief.

Tristan blinked tears. "Oh, Kellen. How I need you right now."

"Tristan?" Mara sat up and swiped away his tears.

"Don't mind me. I'm not going crazy. Kellen had the biggest, greenest rab-cat eyes you've ever seen, and they glowed with as much of the rogue as Floppy's."

"Oh. I didn't know a human could have green eyes." She settled back against Tristan's shoulder, but her mind refused to return to the problem of his detention bracelet. Some piece of information was trying to rise to the surface of her mind but couldn't quite make it.

Tristan stroked her hair, his own thoughts far away.

"Oh!" She slid out of his embrace. "I'll be back." She bolted off the gazebo and flew into the study. Even before she sat down at the computer, she began to type access codes.

After accessing the harem file, she entered the search function and typed in the information she wanted, but "Unable to locate file" appeared on the screen. A number of variations on names brought no success. She bit her finger. Patta had mentioned green eyes, and his name had been in Earth form. Mara had intended to check the file later, but Tristan's picture had appeared, and over six months later, she still wasn't back in her right senses.

She'd get into the other files sideways, the same way she'd found Tristan, who hadn't been in the regular catalog. She asked for a search on a genetic pattern with green eyes and high intelligence quotient.

Biting her finger, she waited.

Tristan hobbled into the study on his crutches. "What's wrong? I thought you were ill."

She darkened the screen before he saw it, got out of the chair, and helped him into it. "You'd better sit down. I've found Kellen. He's on Arden, and he isn't dead."

Chapter 14

Mara's hackles rose in instinctive revulsion when Lani opened her front door. Lani's highly decorated face had a peculiar bloated look to it, the skin waxy, like some pond amphibian, and her unfocused brown eyes held a dangerous animal intelligence. Her hair swept upward in a complex style, and her clothes were the latest fad, yet she stank of body odor.

Mara forced herself to walk into Lani's overstuffed living room,which was as expensively decorated and ugly as its owner. Many of the peculiar furnishings must have been imported from off-planet.

"Do have a seat." Lani snickered as if she'd said something witty.

"Thank you." Mara perched on the edge of a luxel chair.

"To what do I owe the honor of a visit from Mara d'Jorel. The great Jorel." Lani's voice caressed her mother's name like a new possession.

"I—"

"I invited your mother to my parties. But the great Jorel never came. Never."

Mara smiled politely. "Mother didn't go to parties. It was one of her little eccentricities. We scientists are known for them."

"She could have come to *my* parties. Will you come to my parties?"

Patta's gossip about the wealthy, idle crowd with their fondness for drugs, alcohol, and each other surfaced in Mara's memory. She blushed. "I never go to parties myself. But I might make an exception when my contract on my pleasurer is over." She waved her hand with sophisticated amusement. "You know how it is. Most of my time is spent at home now."

Lani guffawed and winked. "Know what you mean exactly." She glanced over at a clock. "Got an appointment. Looking at the new consignment of men."

Mara bit her tongue to slow her comment. "I thought you already had a pleasurer."

"I do, but..." Lani yawned. "You know how it is."

"One man does get boring, but mine is rather sweet in his own stupid fashion. It takes so little to please him. He's like a child." Mara fought her inclination to grimace at her lies. "Speaking of whom, that's why I came to see you. My pleasurer is a great friend of yours, and he begged me to bring him a message. May I see him for a few minutes?"

"See Greenie all you want..." Lani snickered. "If you know what I mean. I've got to be going. Got to convince them to let me have another even if's not time yet. You will come to one of my parties?"

"As soon as I return my pleasurer. Unless of course there's a baby on the way. Then I must curtail parties."

"Can't have a kid. Never could." Lani shrugged and blinked drunkenly as if the drug in her system was becoming stronger. "Let yourself out. All servants off today. Bye."

"Goodbye. Thank you. Trissie will be so pleased." Mara stood.

Lani pointed toward the left then staggered out of the room.

Mara allowed herself a shiver of revulsion then went into the hall to the left. She opened half a dozen doors before she found the harem room, the smallest, most claustrophobic bedroom she'd seen. It even lacked a window. An enormous bed dwarfed the room, the bed dwarfed by a lacy red canopy. The room itself was a nauseating pink with gold highlights.

On the bed, black curls cascading down his muscular shoulders, a naked man sprawled on his stomach as if asleep.

Her breath caught at his beauty. She cleared her throat, but he didn't move. Sitting down on the edge of the bed, she leaned forward and nudged his shoulder. He was as tall but more slender-boned than Tristan. "Kellen?"

Flopping over, he opened his eyes.

For a moment, she stared at his magnificent nakedness then forced her eyes up to his face. After she saw his strong, perfect features and rab-cat eyes, she had no desire to look elsewhere. "Kellen?"

His eyes dim, he studied her blankly. He was pale, his features too sharp from lost weight, and a fine sheen of sweat covered his face.

Her heart twisted with distress, and she caressed his forehead. "You've been ill."

"Guess you could call it that."

"Here. You shouldn't get chilled." She picked up a gauzy green robe from the foot of the bed and tucked it around him.

"Didn't think I'd be put up on the auction block so soon."

"Would you like something to eat or drink? I can find you

something."

"How did an angel like you end up in this hell?"

His forehead didn't seem hot under her hand, but he was babbling like a fever. Her eyes narrowed. "Has that human filth been pouring drugs in you?"

He laughed with genuine amusement, the sparkle of humor and intelligence Tristan had spoken of glittering in his eyes. "Yes, that human filth has. Among other atrocities."

Anger flushed her face, but she could think of no curse vile enough to express her fury.

His eyes were so intense they made her feel peculiar inside. "You're as beautiful as a Tenly sunset."

"Tenly is the fourth planet of the star Tarny, but I didn't know it had pretty sunsets."

"As pretty as any I've ever seen. All purple, red, and green with streaks of silver."

"I would like to see that."

"So would I." He sighed, then his expression closed. "As owners go, you'd be a definite trade-up." His eyes liquid and beckoning, he smiled. "Come here, and I'll give you a free sample to encourage the sale."

He pulled her onto him, molding her body to his, and plundered her mouth with his tongue.

Her scientific curiosity stifled her instinct to pull out of his arms, and she relaxed and let him kiss her. His hand caressed her back and tugged at her tunic top. She compared his kissing technique favorably to Tristan's, but it lacked some vital ingredient she couldn't define.

His hand found the bare skin of her back and slid into her pants, cupping a buttock. Her eyes jerked open. He was preparing to breed with her.

Suddenly her heart told her what her curiosity and the kiss lab test hadn't. She pushed at his shoulders to lift herself and yanked her lips from his. "No!"

"Please. I'll make you so happy," he pleaded. "You won't even have to drug me to make me perform. I'll do anything you say. Just get me away from this hell."

She blinked tears at his pain.

"Let me kiss you again. I'll make it better this time."

"There's nothing wrong with you or your kisses. The only man I ever want like that is Tristan."

His mouth opened as if to beg again then snapped shut.

Freeing herself from his arms, she sat up with her legs tucked under her. "Hello, Kellen Votrain. I'm Mara d'Jorel, Tristan's...friend."

He shook his head slightly as if testing his consciousness. "Tristan is dead. He died almost seven months ago."

"When *The Helen of Troy* was attacked by space pirates. He told me to give you this message to prove myself— 'I'm still a damn fool, and you're still the only brother my parents didn't have.'"

Kellen's face blanched. "You have seen him. I thought the last withdrawal was worse than usual. I'm dead, and you're an angel. You're better than I deserve, but take me."

She took his hand in hers. "Tristan isn't dead. They lied to you, and they lied to him about you. We thought you were dead until a few days ago."

"He isn't..."

"No, he isn't. He's been on Arden the whole time." She squeezed Kellen's hand.

"Well, God help him. I thought he was better dead than on this hellhole of a planet."

She pulled out the computer data cube from her pocket and handed it him. "A vid message to you."

Kellen grabbed it and scooted past her toward the computer terminal. Mara draped the robe over Kellen's bare shoulders to keep off the chill while he sat at the computer then unhooked the electronic finder on her belt and began to scan the room for bugs and monitors as Kellen watched the message from Tristan.

Tristan's voice followed her around the room as he greeted Kellen and told him of the seven months since they'd parted. The words, especially about the last months, had been carefully chosen in case Lani or Cadaran was to see the tape, but Tristan's kinning for Kellen and his humor filled his voice and his image on the screen.

Kellen finished the thirty minute message then started it again as if he couldn't quite believe what he'd seen. Mara checked the house for others then returned to the harem room and sat on the edge of the bed to wait.

As the message finished a second time, Kellen stood and blindly slipped into the robe, tying it closed, then stumbled over to the bed and sat down beside her. "He really is alive. You saved his life then bought him."

"I did buy him, but...It's not that way between us. It's..." She gazed into Kellen's eyes, hoping he'd understand the feelings she didn't have words for.

"It's like that, is it?"

Blushing, she nodded.

"He always was a lucky bastard. Well, thank you for Tris' life and the happiness and health I see in him. A pity you can't buy me too."

"I would if I could." She flipped on the electronic finder, but the sensor remained negative. "We're not being bugged. There are things Tristan couldn't say in the message in case someone else saw it. We intend to escape into the mountains, and when we do, we'll come for you."

"But the..." Kellen held up the wrist with his detention bracelet.

"I have the finest computers on Arden, and we have two of the finest minds. We'll open them."

"Hal...I learned that they're controlled by a central computer. Each bracelet has a code word to control it. Only Cadaran has the master list of codes. The forcefield itself can't be shut down."

"Thank you. That will help us a great deal."

"Don't take forever. I won't survive much longer. I've lasted longer than most. Either Lani will deliberately kill me through her inevitable rich-bitch boredom so she can buy a new man, or she'll burn my brain or body out with the drugs and the..." Kellen gazed into Mara's eyes. "Don't ask me what she's done to me. You have the innocence of an angel, and I won't soil it with her filth."

"Keep fighting. We won't fail you, or ourselves."

Kellen nodded, then turned his head, his curls obscuring his face. "Please don't tell him the truth about me. The drugs and the abuse. Or that I'm falling apart. Tell him I'm still spitting in their eyes and whistling. Knowing the truth would eat him with worry."

"I know. I won't if you wish it."

"Very much."

"He also asked me to give you this." She wrapped her arms around Kellen and hugged him. He jerked and almost fought her embrace then buried his face in her shoulder and hugged her back. His inner pain a knife through her heart, she blinked tears and brushed a kiss on his head. She whispered a prayer to the Goddess for his safety and rescue then released him. She swiped at tears and beamed at him.

Kellen's face had closed again as if he'd tightened control on his emotions before he fell apart.

She considered everything Tristan had told her to say, but she couldn't think of anything she'd left out but her own very important question. "Arden doesn't use the same form of Basic as Earth, and there are Earth words I need. How do I tell a man that I want to make love with only him for the rest of my life, have children with him, laugh with him, and cry? How do I say I'll live with him through anything or die with him just so we can be together?"

"Leave it to Tristan to find you in this hellhole." Kellen brushed back his black curls, his rab-cat eyes glistening. "The words are simple. All you say is 'I love you.'"

STANDING behind Tristan who sat at the computer in their study, Mara held him in a loose hug while she watched him activate the program he'd spent days writing into the computer. His body tense against hers, he paused and swiped at his sweating forehead.

She brushed a kiss on his head. "That had the final Trojan horse?"

"Yes. We'll reroute through so many other computer systems that, even if Cadaran does discover we're breaking into her personal computer, she'll never be able to trace it to us."

"I certainly hope not."

He chuckled. "Trust me, or better yet, trust my brother Geoffrey. He got his start in computers by breaking into them."

"What!"

"For his first job, he tested other computer experts' security programs to see if they could be cracked. Most of them could, and he'd redesign them. Some of his security programs are fifteen years old, and no one's broken into them. That's a major record." Tristan's laugh rumbled through her like a caress. "He taught me everything he knew, and I helped him. Even an expert can't quite achieve what a devious teenager can."

"You were a devious teenager?"

"Very. He rerouted my deviousness into helping him."

"Another Trojan horse?"

"Exactly. Well, here goes nothing." Tristan engaged the program.

Mara closed her eyes, half expecting sirens to go off and Internal Security personnel to pour into the room. The computer only purred away like a contented Floppy.

Tristan squeezed her hands at his heart. "Don't you trust me, pixie?"

"This is not a teenage game. They could take you away from me for this."

"Among other things like being shot for treason."

"That would be an act of kindness if I lost you."

Information began to pour across the screen as their computer stored it, then "task finished" appeared on the screen. He broke their connection to the other Arden computers. "To cut down the risk and the amount of time we were connected, I asked for the information files she'd stored in her computer in the last two months. I figured with such an active lottery system, she'd have to access and change the bracelet code fairly often."

He requested the list of the files they'd stolen.

It took them over two hours of deciphering file names and glancing through files before they found what they wanted.

Mara stirred restlessly in the chair beside his as he found his own file and password.

Tristan swore. "'Blue boy.' What an original thought." He inserted his code word into another program he'd stolen and engaged it. "Here goes." He held out his hand to her.

She clutched it and prayed for success.

The computer beeped and printed, "Task completed."

She let her breath out.

"Well, I guess I should test it." Getting up, he hobbled into the bedroom.

Acting as a sentry against Novia's prying, Floppy sat at the bedroom door. He wiggled his ears in greeting.

Tristan asked, "Novia still gone?"

Floppy nodded.

"Well, here goes. Don't let me fall on you."

Her heart slamming against her ribs, Mara prayed.

Flinching against the expected pain of the electrified forcefield, Tristan stuck his detention bracelet into the open door. Nothing happened. He hooted with joy, then stepped through the door into the hall for the first time.

The floor swayed dizzily, and for a moment, Mara thought she'd faint, then she was through the door and in Tristan's arms.

He kissed her.

The universe twirled as her body melted against his, then his lips left hers, and he gazed toward the front door. He whispered, "Novia."

Nodding understanding, she ran toward the kitchen to delay her housekeeper until Tristan could return to the bedroom.

All bluster and fuss, Novia was unloading fresh produce from the flitter. Mara helped her unload the storage bins and carry them in. She asked about Novia's shopping success at a local farm. When Novia began her standard diatribe against Tristan, Mara merely nodded although she didn't really listen until Novia sighed and shook her head.

"You're a fool, little one. A fool. He'll leave you, and where will you be then?"

"I won't let them take him. Never."

Novia snorted and shook her gray head. "They always do. They always do. What makes you think they'll change two hundred years of rules for you?"

"Then I'll change the rules." Mara bit her tongue.

"No one changes the rules, not even the great Jorel. And she tried over twenty-two years. They defeated her too."

Mara stowed away the last of the vegetable bins in the cooler. "I must go back to Tristan. We're working on our quasar project."

When she reached the bedroom, Tristan was stretched out in bed with Floppy sitting beside him. Tristan smiled and opened his arms.

"Did you?" She glanced toward the study.

"After only a minute of freedom, I'm an official prisoner again so they won't suspect anything. Come here, we have some celebrating to finish."

"It's time for your afternoon nap. I should leave." She smiled coyly.

"Nap like hell." He ordered, "Come here, pixie."

"If you insist."

"Definitely."

She eased up on the bed and rested her head on his shoulder.

His arms circled her as he kissed her head. "In just a few days, you, Floppy, Kellen, and I will leave here."

Her heart ached at leaving her home and Novia, and she almost asked him to delay since they still had months left on their contract, then she thought of Kellen. "A few days to finish getting our supplies together." She wanted to add the words Kellen had taught her, but they caught shyly on her tongue as they always did when she wanted to say them.

"Our freedom may be short, but I promise you it will be sweet."

He kissed her. She blended against him, her hands caressing his ribs and twining in his blond hair. That sweetness blossomed between them, as beautiful as the first time yet subtle with many nights of pleasure. She wrapped her upper leg around his hip and fiddled with the fastening of his shirt.

His lips left her, and she became aware of curious eyes on her back. She blushed and shook the hair out of her face.

Tristan chuckled huskily. "Floppy, please close the door on your way out."

His curiosity about human breeding still unappeased, the rab-cat sneezed with disgust and hopped off the bed. The bedroom door slammed closed.

"I never thought I'd look forward to that door closing me in," Tristan said.

"Only with you. Only with you."

"Oh yes, pixie. Only with you."

TRISTAN blinked awake. He sat up in bed and studied his bedroom. The afternoon sun and shadows were several hours later than when he'd fallen asleep. A voice deep within said something was very wrong, but he couldn't see anything out of the ordinary.

He'd been helping Floppy with the child's reading lessons they'd borrowed from Arden's computer library. Despite the loud beeps and whistles of the computer lesson, his eyes had begun to droop and....

He grimaced. It didn't look like he'd ever get over his need for naps. His health was almost perfect now, and he didn't have to murder himself in therapy, but the heavier gravity stressed his Earth body and heart so much he was exhausted by the middle of the day. Naps seemed a permanent addition to his day.

Floppy and his computer were gone. Mara must have removed the computer since Floppy couldn't, and a sheet was draped over him. Everything was as usual after dozens of naps, but anxiety prickled.

"Mara! Mara!" He slid out of bed and walked into the study. Empty. So was the bathroom.

Opening the French doors, he called her name again then Floppy's since the rab-cat often sunned himself at this time of day.

When no one came, he stalked toward the open bedroom door and almost walked into the electrified forcefield. He jerked to a stop and shouted their names.

Panic, even more intense because he couldn't logically give its cause, surged through him. He shouted for Novia. His voice echoed through the house.

"Damn!" Recalling the house monitors he hadn't needed since Mara had moved into his suite, he punched up the monitors on his bed computer. The living room. The dining room. The kitchen. Novia still had the monitor cut off in there. Everyone could have been murdered in there, and he'd never know. Mara's old bedroom. Perfect. She often worked in there while he napped so she wouldn't bother him.

The room was empty. She wasn't at her computer or on the bed. The bathroom door was open, and he couldn't see....

A human hand, palm up, lay on the carpet at the corner of the screen.

"Oh, God!" He redirected the monitor.

Mara sprawled on the floor by the bed.

He focused on her face. She seemed to be breathing, but her skin was as white as the carpet except for a telltale rash from her jaw line down her throat into her tunic top. The rash would extend to her breasts.

"No, they couldn't have been that inept. Certainly my records..." Tristan swore and punched up the intercom to the kitchen. "Novia!"

The link snapped like someone had shoved their fist through the kitchen intercom control.

He hit the master switch. "Floppy, come quickly. Mara needs you."

If Floppy was with Novia, he wouldn't be able to hear that. Mara had only one chance at life. But Novia was in the house and would tell Cadaran.

"Cadaran and Novia be damned. And me too." He cut off his bracelet at the government central computer and walked as fast as his legs would allow him to the kitchen. He shoved open the door.

Novia was processing tomatoes at the worktable. Shocked, she squeezed a tomato into mush in her hand and gaped at him. Her cheeks reddened with emotion. "You!"

"Get Mara's doctor here. Now. She's dying." He spun and walked to Mara's bedroom. Floppy charged past him into her bedroom. She hadn't moved. He fell to his knees beside her and rested his palm on her forehead. She burned with fever. "Mara?"

Floppy sniffed her and brushed her cheek with his ear. His keening moan filled Tristan's mind.

Lifting her by the shoulders, he hugged her against his chest. Her face scorched through his shirt. "Oh, pixie."

"What have you done to her?" Novia towered over him, a kitchen knife in her hand. "Get away from her, or I'll kill you."

"Could I do this?" He eased Mara into his lap and unfastened her tunic. The rash was brighter against the ivory of her shoulders and full breasts.

Novia recoiled in horror. "By the Goddess, what is that?"

"Starsus plague. Have you called the doctor?"

"No, I..."

"Tell them what it is. Dr. Ilka is your best bet. She'll believe me. Hurry. Mara doesn't have much more time."

Novia's face twisted with distrust, uncertainty, and shock.

Floppy bit her ankle.

She jerked and bolted out of the room.

Tristan laughed wearily, thinking how much Mara would have appreciated Floppy's gesture, and brought her back into his embrace.

Floppy hissed unhappily and rested his head on her stomach.

Novia finally came back. She dropped to her knees beside them and took Mara's hand in hers. Age and grief etched her face as she met his eyes. "I called Dr. Ilka and told her what you said. She said she understood. She's coming."

He closed his eyes with relief. Any other doctor on Arden would have treated him as a stupid male and ignored the information until it was too late. "Good."

"What's this starsus plague? I've never heard of it."

"Kellen and I probably brought it to Arden. We've both had it. We must have yearly shots of a form of adrenalin, or we become active carriers again. It was on our permanent medical records." He touched the info chip implanted at the base of his skull. "I guess your medical people didn't understand."

"Then you gave it to her?"

"Yes, or..." He bit back Kellen's name.

"You survived."

"If treatment is soon enough. Otherwise, it's fatal. Starsus did to Vega Two what your plague did to Arden. They found a cure for it."

Mara stirred and opened her eyes, looking up at him as if from deep within a hazel pool. She dampened her lips with her tongue.

Blinking tears, he smiled at her. "We're all here, and Dr. Ilka is coming. Just rest, and you'll be better soon."

Her lips twitched as they always did when she knew he was lying. "Wanted to say..." She took a deep breath as if focusing dwindling energy. "I love you, Tristan."

His heart twisted. "Oh, pixie. Where did you learn that?"

She mouthed Kellen's name. "I do."

"I knew, pixie. Even when you didn't have the words for it."

"Leave now. Before I die. They'll take you away then. Safety. The mountains with Floppy. Safety for you and Kellen."

He shook his head.

"Please. Now. For Kellen."

"You aren't going to die."

"Novia?"

"Here, little one." Novia sniffed and squeezed Mara's hand.

"Last wish. Help him. Don't let them take him. It will kill him. Please."

"Save your energy, child."

"Please."

"I'll help the devil himself to make you happy, Mara. Even this devil."

Mara smiled, and her free hand rested on Floppy's shoulder. She sighed, closing her eyes, and her limp hand slid off the rab-cat.

Tristan cleared his tight throat. "She's unconscious."

"Get out of here."

"I'm not leaving her."

"Do you want them to know you can get out of that room?"

He blinked with surprise.

"A promise is a promise."

Tristan hugged Mara more tightly, torn between safety and need. If she were to die without him....

Novia growled like an ill-tempered cat. "Take her with you then if she can be moved."

"She can." He cradled Mara and with more concentration and courage than he'd shown in therapy, he stood up and carried her into their bedroom.

Chapter 15

Tristan raised Mara's shoulders up and slid behind her in bed until she was propped up by his body, then he smoothed her nightgown back into place. Her essence filled his nostrils as he buried his face in her tousled hair.

After a token wiggle of resistance, she sagged weakly against him. "You don't have to do this."

"Hush, pixie. We want to do this. Don't we, Flop?"

The rab-cat nodded, opened his mouth, and dropped the comb into Tristan's waiting hand. Tristan began to comb the tangles from her hair.

She blushed, her flawless complexion no longer marred by the red rash.

He chuckled. "You beat everything. You spend your life fussing over us. Long months tending me when I was as helpless as a baby, then can't understand when we spend a few days fussing over you."

"It's not the same thing."

"Of course it is." Finished with her hair, he returned the comb to Floppy and started to slide out from behind her so she could lie back down.

"Don't. Hold me."

"Anything for the most beautiful sick lady on Arden." He let her nestle against his chest then wrapped his arms around her waist.

When he kissed the top of her head, she sighed happily. "I've missed this."

"So have I, as well as something I can't mention with the child present."

Mara giggled. Floppy sneezed with displeasure and curled up against her, his chin resting on her leg.

Her body relaxed, and very soon, her breathing had slowed.

Tristan stretched back into a comfortable position and fought his own inclination to follow her into sleep. He still felt the exhaustion of the days they'd spent watching over her during her illness' crisis.

Novia walked in, then stopped and started to back out.

He whispered, "Come in and join a family cuddle."

Novia studied them uncertainly then, seeing Floppy, came forward. "I think I will." She sat down in the chair by the bed and placed on her lap the small box she'd been carrying.

Mara woke as easily as she'd drifted into sleep. Smiling, she held out her hand to Novia, who kissed her palm. "Little one, I was so afraid."

"I'm better now."

Novia released Mara's hand then clinched the box on her lap, her fingers working convulsively. "Do you feel like listening?"

Mara nodded.

Sensing intimate matters, Tristan asked, "Would you like us to leave?"

"No. You have the right to hear this." Novia turned to Mara. "I've been thinking these last days while we watched over you. He's been half crazy with worry over you. Took more than his turns sitting by you in case you went into seizures. He wouldn't leave you after we found you even if they found out he'd escaped. I had to order him in here with you."

"We share great kinning."

"I didn't think a man could have those feelings." Novia corrected herself, "I didn't think another man could have those feelings. I prayed it wouldn't happen again. That the same tragedy wouldn't destroy your life, too."

"Another man?" Mara reached for the hand Tristan had tucked against her tummy. He squeezed her hand in his.

"Your mother never told you the truth. At first it was because she couldn't bear to speak of it, then she decided it was for the best. She let you make the wrong assumptions about your origins."

Mara stiffened against him. "What are you saying?"

"Jorel won the right to a man in the lottery. She was just like all the other women on Arden. She believed in the harem way of life. She had a chance to meet her choices, the lottery wasn't so big then, and she met Adam Mark Randell."

Mara gasped. "That's an Earther name."

"He was. His ship was hit by an asteroid in the belt, and he crashed here."

Tristan's memory nudged. "I've heard of him. He was a respected explorer and astronomer. He disappeared over twenty-five years ago."

Novia nodded. "He was new to Arden when she met him. He'd just learned a man's role on Arden, and he'd accepted it. He didn't like it, but he accepted it. Then he met your mother, and she met him, and nothing was ever the same."

"They loved each other?" Mara whispered.

"That's what they called it. I called it madness and hunger. But Adam was a winning man—all smiles, charm, and excitement. And he was brilliant and sophisticated in a way no one on Arden could ever be. Jorel lost herself in him. He even charmed me." Novia's smile softened her face. "What a wonderful, spirited creature he was with his great kinning heart and laughter.

"Jorel couldn't accept that they'd take him away from her. She fought to hold onto him, but no one ever wins that fight. They had no chance to win that fight, and they knew it. On her next government pregnancy test, she tested positively for you. The next day, they were going to take him back to the lottery." Novia blinked tears. "He killed himself before they could."

Mara whimpered with pain and sagged against Tristan, who held her tightly.

Novia opened the box. "Your mother wanted to die too, but she held you inside her, and you were part of Adam. We secretly named you after your father."

"Adam Mark Randell. Mark Randell. Ma-ra." Mara blinked tears.

"Jorel swore then that she'd destroy the harem so no one else would suffer what she'd suffered. She believed the harem was a mockery of the truth of a man and woman's relationship. She began to dig for information through stealth and bribery, and she threw herself into her work.

"Gradually, she found the ammunition she needed, and she gained fame and wealth with her converter, but there was you again. If she used that ammunition, you would be destroyed. She didn't care about herself, she was totally embittered with life after losing Adam, but she couldn't risk you. When she knew she was dying, she gave me all the information she'd collected, she collected it until the day she died, and told me to give it to you if you ever became pregnant or found your Adam, and they were going to take him away. She wanted you to have the ammunition she didn't have."

Mara shook her head. "Why haven't you given me this?"

"I kept praying it wasn't the same. I knew you would destroy yourself fighting the harem. I thought you'd learn to hate him, as I've hated him, for the destroyer he is, and you'd stay safe." Novia's shoulders sagged. "But he's not a destroyer, and when you wished his freedom with your dying breath, I knew Jorel would want you to have this. You have the right to fight for him even if it means your death." The old woman rustled around in the box and pulled out a holograph. "This is Adam."

Mara's hands trembled as she took the picture. She stared at it. "He has beautiful blue eyes like Tristan's."

Tristan shivered, seeing Mara's face and pixie smile of mischief in the other man as well as her chestnut hair.

Mara whispered, "He's my father. This was my father," cradled the picture against her chest, and began to sob from loss.

TRISTAN knelt by Mara's armchair and tucked the blanket draped over her lap around her bare toes. "Are you certain you're ready for this?"

Mara sighed, tears threatening to erupt again, and rested her head on the back of the chair. She forced herself into calmness. "Yes, I must. I won't let them take you away from me the way they took my father. This is my ammunition to keep that from happening."

He settled in the chair beside her. "While you were sleeping, I found this in the box." He placed a sealed envelope in her lap.

Her name was written on it in a bold hand. "Mother's handwriting." Her hands trembled as she opened it and pulled out the letter within, also handwritten. The letter blurred through her tears. She blinked hard and cleared her throat then began to read aloud to share its contents with Tristan. "My dearest Mara, Since you're reading this, you are experiencing one of the two great moments in a woman's life—giving your heart to a man, or awaiting your child. How I wish I could be there to share this happiness with you. For it is happiness, even the pain within both moments is happiness. Remember that when the pain seems too hard to bear.

"Novia will have told you about Adam. With the wisdom you've gained, I hope you can understand the inner demons and angels who drove us together and wouldn't allow us to part. Adam told me that his religion believes that a man and woman who love each other will be together in the afterlife as we believe mothers and daughters will be together. If this is so, I've finally found the peace and happiness with Adam I couldn't find on Arden."

Mara cleared her throat again.

Tristan rested his hand on her shoulder and smiled at her.

Her answering smile faltered a moment then held. She returned to the letter. "In my grief over Adam's death, I sought revenge against

Arden. My revenge is within this box, but I dared not use it for your sake. Use it well and wisely for your own safety and happiness.

"Briefly, here are my discoveries. Men within the harem are used as bribes to control government officials and wealthy, influential citizens. They are also part of the payment for those of wealth who control offplanet shipping and bring in luxury items and drugs. In the years since Cadaran has gained control of Internal Security, this practice has grown more widespread and sophisticated, and she's already gained staggering power. Beware of her for, by now, she must control much of the planetary government."

Tristan swore. "I can believe that."

Mara read aloud, "This widespread use of men has increased the need for 'prime pleasurers' of beauty or exotic attractions for the wealthy and powerful, and Cadaran has fed this need by running slaving operations which attack ships in the nearby shipping lanes."

"My God!"

As her thoughts followed his, Mara blanched. "Slavers attacked your ship! That would explain how you and Kellen ended up on Arden."

Scowling, Tristan stared blindly at his legs.

She rested her hand on his.

He blinked back into the present. "I'm fine. Please continue."

"Men are used and abused at an appalling rate, and Cadaran and others are willingly blind to those abuses and the frequent deaths of these men. Thank the Goddess that my Adam did not live to see such treatment.

"As shameful as this treatment is, it extends to far more than off-world slaves. Our own children are thrown into this filthy system. I have discovered that newborn boys don't die of the plague. They are stolen from their mothers at birth to feed the harem's insatiable appetite for men. Teenage boys don't volunteer for the harem as we have been told, but are trained from childhood to accept that life. The government knows that a woman would not willingly part with a child for the harem, and knowing a boy child and raising him, how could that woman accept the harem as his fate or accept the harem at all? If you hold my grandchild within you, please take care and don't allow them to snatch him from you."

Shivering, Mara clutched her belly. "That is the most evil thing I have ever heard. My neighbor Jane almost died grieving for her little boy, and...For them to take my baby..." Her face flamed with anger.

Mara literally shook herself and forced herself to pick up the letter again. "The most shameful secret of all is the last. None of this need ever have happened. Our babies have been torn from us, and our men have been wasted in an evil system merely for bureaucrats' greed and not for the sake of Arden. Mara, the plague doesn't exist. It hasn't existed for over a hundred and eighty years. Twenty years after the first outbreak, the plague virus mutated into a harmless form. The harem could have ended, and we could have regained the stars many generations ago.

"When the government found out about the virus, it knew that its control of the harem and the women of the planet through the harem would be over if the population and the galaxy knew so it stayed silent. Only a few key members of the Council and Internal Security know this truth, and they do not share it. May the Goddess refuse their eternal souls for this greatest of lies."

Mara's voice trailed into silence as she tried to grasp the enormity of what her mother had said. Her whole culture was based on a lie. She'd lost her father and his love through a lie, Tristan had nearly died from that lie, and her mother had lost her Tristan because of that lie.

An emotion alien to her nature boiled through Mara to her very soul, and her fist tightened. "I hate them. I hate them."

"We'll destroy them for this. I promise that."

She continued reading the last of the letter. "Don't let your anger and hate destroy you as it destroyed me. I never knew happiness except through you after Adam was gone, but I did know great happiness with you. Your father asked me to tell you that he loves you, and he's with you in spirit. He'd be so proud of you with your gift and passion for the stars, the same gift and passion he had. I'm so proud of you, too. What a splendid scientist and woman you are. Jorel."

Mara sagged. Love and hate, and grief and gain surged in such a confusing mixture she was exhausted. "Momma did love me, and she was proud of me. Her grief was for Adam, not my failure."

Lost in his own thoughts, Tristan ignored her as he'd never ignored her since they'd become mates.

She trembled with a foreboding of loss.

He jolted to his feet and stared out at the garden and the night sky. "I can go home! Nothing here holds me. I can go home."

MARA peeked out of the bathroom. Tristan lay in bed, his hands behind his head, and stared pensively up at the ceiling. His thoughts were far from Arden as they had been for the fifteen days since they'd read her mother's letter. He was thinking of Dorian.

Well, he was hers, not Dorian's or Arden's, and she would fight for him in all arenas, even bed. She straightened the filmy robe she'd copied from Kellen's with its erotic, tantalizing views of his bare body and fluffed her perfumed hair. She threw her shoulders back so her breasts thrust against the gauzy fabric and sashayed to the bed.

Her face flushed with anticipation, she smiled down at him. His bare chest was magnificent, muscles coiled under tanned honey skin. Remembering the feel of that chest rubbing against them in breeding, her nipples rose to hard, aching points.

Barely glancing toward her, he politely tossed open the covers.

Kneeling on the bed beside him, she pushed back the sheet, exposing his body. She sighed with appreciation and caressed his chest. "You are so beautiful, Tristan."

"How would you know? I'm the only man you've ever seen."

"I've seen pictures from the harem catalogs of naked men. Many men. And I have seen Kellen. He's beautiful, too."

She'd finally gotten Tristan's attention. He spun toward her. "You saw Kellen's body!"

Wondering why this information upset him, she replied, "He was naked and sleeping without covers."

Tristan's bright blue eyes shimmered with some deep emotion. "You think he's beautiful?"

"Yes. He has a splendid body and well-proportioned features. I especially like his eyes. They are so like Floppy's yet make me feel peculiar inside with their intensity." She cocked her head. "You should grow your hair long. It would be very becoming. Very sensual. It would frame your face and eyes. I can imagine the tickling, pleasing feel of it on my breasts and thighs when you make love to me." She ran her fingers through his short curls. "Kellen and I have been growing our hair for the same length of time, yet his black curls are longer than mine."

"What!"

"It is the fashion for men here."

"I won't be here long enough to grow my hair, thank you. Kellen and I are getting the hell off this planet as soon as I can steal a spaceship."

"*We* steal a spaceship," she corrected. "You and I. We will discover a way very soon."

Tristan sagged. "The damn bracelet was easier than the ship. Two weeks of research and reading Cadaran's personal files for information, and no luck."

"We will steal the ship. We won't be stopped now. I swore I'd get you home, and I will."

"You're very good to me, pixie. Thank you."

"I love you, Tristan." She almost blurted her secret, but some inner sense told her the time wasn't right. Smiling seductively, she untied her robe and pulled it away from her naked body. "And I want to make love to you very, very much." Leaning forward, she nibbled a kiss on his lips.

He nuzzled her and groaned happily. "You smell wonderful. What is that?"

Draping herself on him, she lathed wet kisses across his cheek. "Lufta flower and my personal pheromone." She bit her tongue to keep from giving scientific footnotes about her research into sexual scents.

His arms encircled her shoulders as his growing staff nudged her thigh. "You make me so hot, Mara."

Deciding he wasn't talking about the room temperature, she smiled and licked his ear. He started to roll over onto her, but she stilled him with a touch. "Tonight, I make love to you." She began to slither down his body with exquisite slowness, her lips and hands paying tribute to each beloved, beautiful inch she passed.

She lavished kisses and caresses on the sensitive spots she'd discovered in their lovemaking—the spot beneath his ear, the hollow below his armpit, his nipples, and naval. He jolted beneath her.

Her fingers found his staff and stroked as he'd taught her, then her lips began a careful exploration of his reactions.

"Mara!"

At his excited cry, triumph surged through her. Since the letter, he'd been as generous with tenderness and passion as he'd always been when they made love, but he'd held back some part of himself. Tonight, she would regain that emotional commitment.

Writhing, he tangled his fingers in her hair as she took him in her mouth. She pleasured him to the moment before he could bear no more then lavished kisses across his thighs and belly then pleasured him again to the point before release, pulled away, then pleasured him again.

He thrashed so violently he nearly knocked her away.

Sliding upward, she joined herself to him, his staff filling her to joyous completion. She held onto his shoulders to keep herself upright and began to undulate in a slow rhythmic pattern.

His eyes clinched against the pleasure, he tensed beneath her. The rasp of his breathing filled the room.

Leaning forward, she nuzzled kisses across his face. "You are so beautiful, Tristan. Your body makes mine ache with wanting. I love your staff within me. Can you feel how I throb around you? That is joy. I want to hold you within me like that and never let you go. I want your seed to fill me and blend with me. I want blue-eyed babies with curly hair..."

Her fingers slid down his chest and up again, and she tensed around him, her rhythm faster in response to his. When they could bear no more, she ground against him, holding him fully within her. She whispered, "I love you, Tristan," then they were both sailing upward.

Somewhere after eternity, he lifted slightly, pulling the sheet up over them both. She sighed happily and nestled against him.

"Oh, Mara, where did you learn to do that?"

"From you. I just did to you what you do to me."

"It worked." He chuckled lazily.

She smiled. She might not have regained his total commitment, but she'd certainly gotten his mind off Dorian. Now for the final surprise. "Tristan?"

"Mmmm hmmm."

"I have a wonderful gift for you."

His deep laugh rumbled through her. "You just gave me one."

"This is much better." She raised slightly to see his expression. "I'm pregnant."

Humor left his face to be replaced by blank dismay. He sat up so suddenly she slid to the mattress with a thump.

"Are you sure?"

Her heart quivered with trepidation at his unexpected response. "Yes. I have sensed the baby from the first, but I didn't want to tell you until I could be certain. I didn't want to disappoint you. I have passed the home pregnancy test twice."

"You haven't seen a doctor?" He scowled like a lawyer looking for a loophole.

"A doctor would report me to the government, and you'd be taken away within a day."

"How long have we got until the government finds out?"

"Six weeks until I'm tested again. Dr. Ilka tested me when I had starsus before she would treat me." Brushing back her hair, Mara sat up and met his eyes.

"When was the baby conceived?"

"While you were comforting me after I found out about my father. I'm glad it was then. I've never felt closer to you than those moments."

"Do you feel all right?"

She nodded. "I'm strong and healthy, and Mother and her mother had easy pregnancies. My doctor once said I should have the same."

"Thank God."

She'd expected shock and happiness, not dismay. Didn't men desire children as desperately as women did? "Don't you want a baby?"

"Of course I..." He mangled his curls with his fingers. "The timing's lousy, that's all. Trying to escape and..."

"Going home to Earth. The baby and I won't slow you. I promise." He was thinking of Dorian and the babies he wanted with her. A tear trickled down Mara's cheek. "I have to leave here. I won't let them steal our son for the harem."

"Of course not." Tristan pulled her into his arms and kissed the top of her head. "Oh Mara. My beautiful pixie. I won't let them take him. I'll take good care of you both."

Sniffing, she buried her face in his chest.

He lay back down, taking her with him, and pulled up the sheets around them. He nuzzled a kiss on her ear. "You sure know how to knock the breath out of a man with your little surprises." He said nothing else, and when she finally drifted into sleep, he was still awake, his uncertainty a barrier between them.

Chapter 16

Her heart hammering, Dorian studied the twelve-foot stone fence. Moonlight sparkled across its stones and laced a nearby ludicrous pink tree with silver. The wall was all that separated her from Mara d'Jorel and the answers she'd sought for months. Even if she had to resort to illegal truth drugs, Mara would tell her where Tristan was, and she was getting him off this slaver planet.

Her arrival on the planet had been anticlimactically easy after four months of worry and planning. With her ship's sophisticated anti-detection systems, she'd landed without the government noticing and found a public vid-phone near a small town. It had given her Mara's address and even printed a map to this house. Her ship was now several miles away by a grove of trees.

She resettled the body harness of the anti-gravity unit which had helped her make the walk from the woods. She'd trained for the higher gravity for months, but she still felt the strain on her heart and muscles. She turned up the unit's controls until she floated then began to climb the wall.

At the top, she paused, breathing heavily, a tiny part of her mind admiring the beautiful late summer garden and house below, then she unholstered her gun and jumped.

Landing gently on her feet on the ground, she readjusted the unit to its original setting and headed toward the house and the French doors she'd noticed from above.

Her hand on the door, she whispered a brief prayer for courage and good fortune then pushed. It opened easily. She was in a large bedroom. Pausing, she waited for her eyes to adjust to the greater darkness then crept toward the bed and its inhabitant.

Tristan! Stunned, she jolted to a halt.

He sprawled on his side in the bed, moonlight shimmering across his blond curls, well-remembered features, and down his muscular chest and arms.

Her heart twisted with all her years of love and with astonishment. Until this moment, a small part of her hadn't believed he was alive.

Her knees wobbled, but she forced herself into calmness and stared to convince herself she was seeing true.

She holstered her gun. Without having to drug his location out of Mara d'Jorel then finding him, she'd be able to get him off-planet before the sun came up. She strode forward.

He wasn't alone in bed. Half hidden by the sheet, a woman's arm possessively circled his waist. She curled naked against his back, her face almost buried in his curls.

Dorian stopped again in jealous amazement. She'd imagined Tristan's owner some wealthy dissipated monster, not a young beauty with a gentle, intelligent face.

Cold hatred replaced jealousy as Dorian remembered the harem and the drugs and brutality which had forced Tristan into this woman's bed. Dorian tapped his shoulder.

His eyes crawled open then widened.

She covered his mouth before he said her name, motioned him into silence, then pointed toward the garden.

He eased out of bed, slipped on a robe, and followed her into the garden without looking back at the owner he'd left sleeping.

Dorian moved far enough away from the house so they couldn't be heard then threw herself into his arms. He hugged her fiercely and buried his face in her hair.

"Oh, Dory! Dory."

Mumbling his name, she stroked his shoulder in comfort. "Everything's going to be all right now. Everything. I'm getting you away from this filthy world." She lifted her face for his kiss.

His eyes hazy with emotion and confusion, he cupped her cheeks as if uncertain of her reality.

"I'm really here." She brushed her lips against his.

He kissed her gently back.

Some instinct kept her from deepening the kiss. She brushed kisses across his face. "I've missed you so much, Tristan."

"Oh, Dory." His arms tightened around her.

"I'm taking you home. Forget all you've suffered here. You don't have to see that woman again. I'll drug her so she'll not wake too soon, and we can leave."

"You're too late."

At the other woman's voice, Dorian spun, drawing her laser gun, and fired at Tristan's owner.

"No!" Tristan grabbed Dorian's arm.

The other woman cried out as the laser bolt flashed over her head.

His hand still manacling Dorian's wrist above her head, Tristan gaped wildly at both women. His eyes shimmered in the moonlight as they met Dorian's. "You're real. I thought you were only a dream."

"I'm real."

"Are you crazy? Mara's our friend."

Dorian yanked her hand free, holstered the gun, then rubbed her sore wrist. "She's your owner. She paid for you, didn't she?" A painful doubt crossed Dorian's mind. "Or do you sleep with her willingly?"

Tristan flushed. "Yes, and yes."

"The Tristan I knew wouldn't sleep with a woman who bought him. Are they drugging you?" She peered at his pupils.

Mara laughed with amusement and joined them. Moonlight shone through her sheer robe, highlighting her disgustingly splendid figure. "Am I drugging you, Tristan?"

"No!" Tristan backed away from them both and rubbed his temples with his hands. "This certainly has been my night for surprises."

Mara nodded at Dorian. "I'm Mara d'Jorel. I see you got my message."

Dorian and Tristan both said, "Your message?"

His owner's smile twisted with mischief as she met his eyes. "I sent your Oz Tunnel paper to her with my name on it as if I were seeking technical consultation. If she were as intelligent as you believed, I knew she'd understand it was from you."

"I did, and here I am."

"I expected you much sooner. I'd given up on you." Before Dorian could defend herself for the three months she'd needed to get the ship and the month to fly here, Mara asked, "Are we to leave tonight?"

"Yes, before dawn. Wait a.... *We*?"

Tristan had finally come to grips with the last minutes' shocks. He asked briskly, "How many can the ship hold?"

Dorian did some fast calculating. "Six humans if we crowd in, but I only have food for a year for three."

"A year?"

"The Arden plague has a dormant life span of a year. I've picked out an uninhabited planet we can live on until it's safe to go home."

"No problem then."

Mara squeezed Tristan's hand. "I'll leave you two together. You have a lot of catching up to do. I'll go wake Floppy and Novia and finish our packing."

Dorian watched her return to the house. The other woman had the same jealous, worried expression she must have. "Tristan?"

He hugged her again. "It's so good to see you. Is everyone all right?"

She buried her face in his chest. His clean male aroma was marred by perfume and the other woman's sexual scent. "Your death was a terrible blow, especially to your mother, but that Mallory courage brought them all through."

"Thank God." He studied her with solemn blue eyes. "And you?"

"It would have killed me except I just knew you weren't dead even before I got that plagiarized paper. What's happened to you, Tris? Why are you so cozy with this slaver?"

"Mara isn't..." He took her hand and led her to some chairs by a huge swimming pool. He settled in a chair beside hers, held her hand in two of his, and began to talk.

Fighting her inclination to take him in her arms to ease the terrible pain he'd suffered, Dorian sat silently through his recital of his last eight months on Arden. Her hatred of Mara turned to grudging respect and fear for a rival she might not defeat. When he finally sputtered to a stop, she asked, "Why are you sleeping with her?"

"I care very deeply for her, I... desire her, and I'd given up hope of going home to you until a few weeks ago. By then we'd already..." He added bleakly, "She's pregnant."

"Wonderful." Dorian stared inward in thought. "So that's why you want to take her with us. To keep the child out of the harem if it's a boy."

"A Mallory child? You can bet it's a boy. That's part of it. Mara will be executed for treason for helping me if I leave her."

"Then she'll come."

"She, Floppy, and Kellen."

"Who's Floppy, that cat creature?"

"The local intelligent life form. Floppy, Mara, and I had a long talk about it, and Floppy has convinced us he should come. He wants to see Mara properly settled, even if he can't come back to Arden. Novia intends to stay here and take care of Mara's animals and house. She's in no danger from the government, and she insists she's too old to be chased over the galaxy."

Dorian rubbed her temples as Tristan had earlier. "All this makes my head spin. No plague, your injuries, your kind-hearted owner with her baby..."

Something black and small bounded out of the darkness from the house and jumped onto Tristan's lap.

Tristan rubbed the long-earred cat's head. "Dorian, this is Floppy. Flop, this is Dorian. We grew up together."

The cat wiggled its ears genially and studied her with intelligent green eyes.

"Hello, Floppy."

The cat tapped Tristan's bare arm for attention then stared toward the house.

"Mara wants to see me?"

The cat nodded then motioned toward Dorian with his paw.

"Both of us are wanted," Tristan decided and stood, putting the cat on the ground.

Dorian followed them back into the lighted bedroom. The room was charming and homey with its antique furnishings. Wringing her hands, a short elderly woman cried in a chair near the bed with a tabby cat and black collie curled for comfort at her feet as if they sensed the imminent cataclysm of their cozy world.

Dressed in an attractive yet practical pink tunic and pants, Mara settled data cubes beside a small computer in a briefcase on the bed. She smiled at Tristan, her face serene with decision despite tears streaming down her cheeks. "I've put out clothes for you in the bath. Decide if there's anything personal you wish me to pack. Your clothes and work are packed."

Tristan nodded. "You and Flop are the only things I want to take with me." He brushed a kiss on an old woman's head then went into the bathroom, closing the door behind him.

Dorian shifted awkwardly on her feet. "May I help?"

"No, thank you." Mara blinked tears, her voice husky. "Forgive my manners. Dorian, this is my housekeeper Novia. She helped raise me and is like my grandmother."

Novia glared at Dorian and blew her nose on a tissue with a fierce honk.

After half an hour, everyone was ready, the six travel bags and a large briefcase packed in Mara's flitter. More a follower than leader now, Dorian settled in the back seat as the others exchanged hugs and kisses and final words of farewell.

Her throat tightened in sympathy. Mara was leaving the only home and family she'd ever known for an uncertain future. Dorian remembered the same feeling when she'd left her home world as a young teen to go to Earth for her education.

Novia asked Mara, "When should I contact the authorities about you?"

"Wait a day as we discussed, but I don't think you'll have to. I've arranged for all hell to break loose on Arden tomorrow morning. The government won't have time to worry about me and one harem male."

The rab-cat hopped into the back seat beside Dorian and sat on his haunches, his ears erect and quivering with excitement, then Tristan joined them.

With one final wave and a lingering examination of her home and Novia, Mara slid into the driver's seat and powered up the antique flitter.

Tristan turned to Dorian as they lifted off. "We're getting Kellen then going to your ship." He leaned forward and patted Mara's shoulder in comfort. "They'll be all right, and when we get settled on Earth, we'll send for them to stay with you."

"I know." Mara brushed at her tears.

"What did you mean about hell breaking loose?"

"I am giving Mother her revenge and taking some of my own for my father, and for you. I wrote an open letter to the women...people of Arden, much like the letter Jorel wrote me, telling of the abuses of the harem and about the lies about the plague. It is the introduction to all the data of their corruption Mother found and we found in Cadaran's personal files. I put all of it on the computer lines. Everyone can see for themselves what their government has done to us."

"The government can delete that easily enough."

"No, they can't. It's in a computer virus program, three virus programs. It will spread to every computer on Arden and hide to spread again so they'll never completely delete it. Each time someone uses her computer, that letter will be the first thing she sees."

"That will cause government collapse?" Dorian asked. "I thought the women didn't care what happened to the men in the harem."

Mara's voice shook with repressed rage. "Many might look away from the abuses of the harem, or even being quarantined without cause, but they'll never forgive the stealing of our babies. Every woman who has lost a boy, or whose mother lost a boy won't rest until that child is back, and the harem destroyed. Over thirty percent of the adult female population has lost a child, even more have lost a brother."

Tristan chuckled dryly. "Novia won't have to worry about them bothering her about us. The government will be too busy trying to escape lynching."

Mara nodded. "I examined your program for releasing the detention bracelet and Cadaran's personal information on the system. I've destroyed the bracelet system. All men are free now from the bracelets. I included that information in my letter."

"Remind me to stay on your good side, pixie."

The flitter settled in a parking area by a huge sprawling house. Mara got out and rested a suitcase on a sling over her shoulder. "I have heard that Lani can't keep live-in servants because of her wild parties and the...things she does. The door should be unlocked so we won't have to ring."

"Another program?" Dorian asked, joining her, Floppy, and Tristan at the front door.

"No, more gossip." Mara opened the door. "I must thank Patta, if I ever see her again." She stepped into the darkened living room and called out, "Lani."

Flicking on the light, Dorian winced at the terrible tasteless clutter of Earth junk in the room.

"Lani." Mara headed through a door on the left.

The others hastened after her into the lighted hall.

Mara jolted to a stop. A naked woman stretched on her back on the hall floor, her head thrown back, snoring.

Kneeling by her, Dorian checked her pulse and peered in her dilated eyes. The woman's face was bloated and waxy from the terminal stage of pleasure drug addiction. Dorian shuddered with distaste. "Out cold."

"Lani has tried every pleasure drug in the galaxy." Mara stepped over the woman and walked toward an open bedroom door.

"Most drugs more than once," Dorian whispered under her breath and hurried after them.

Tristan swore violently as he turned into the bedroom. Dorian peered around him.

A naked man hung from his hands above the bed, his sagging head and body attached to a slender mechanized frame which controlled his body shape. The device was like something out a violent sexual deviant's wet dream.

Her stomach turned over.

"Kellen!" Tristan was on the bed, his gentle hands freeing the unconscious man. Kellen fell into Tristan's arms.

Mara touched Dorian's shoulder to get her attention then handed her a med-kit which looked old enough to belong in a medical museum. Dorian stared at it in disbelief.

"Dory!" Tristan eased his friend onto the bed.

Dorian brushed back long black curls from Kellen's face and began her examination. Bruises and burns ran across his chest and back as if he'd been beaten and tortured, and his eyes were dilated with drugs. She took a blood sample.

He jerked, his eyes flying open. They widened as if she were a monster, and he shrieked and backpedaled away from her.

Tristan touched his shoulder. "Kell?"

"Tris!" Kellen threw himself into his friend's arms. "I knew you'd come. Only thing that kept me alive."

Running her medical diagnostic scanner above Kellen's body, Dorian let them greet each other. She studied all the information the equipment gave her.

Meeting her eyes in question, Tristan stroked Kellen's head. Kellen still clung to him like a hurt, frightened child seeking refuge.

Dorian understood his question. "Mind control drugs. They enhance fear and pain. He's still under the influence. There's nothing physically wrong with him I can't fix on the ship." She didn't add the emotional damage from rape and abuse would be much harder to repair. "Let me cover the marks on his chest and back, and we can get him out of this filthy place."

Nodding, Tristan released the catch on the porcelain detention bracelet on Kellen's wrist, removed it, and smashed the bracelet into the wall.

Dorian spray bandaged Kellen's back.

Tristan eased Kellen onto the bed.

She leaned over him, but he scrambled backwards to the edge of the bed.

"This is Dorian." Tristan rested a gentle hand on Kellen's shoulder. "Remember her. I've talked about her so much. She's a doctor, and she's taking care of your injuries."

Smiling warmly, Dorian gazed into Kellen's bright green eyes. Her heart surged with tenderness, then she became enraptured by his eyes and his strong perfect features framed by black curls. God, he was handsome.

He must have sensed her intense sexual response because he scurried backwards against Tristan.

Dorian cursed herself. "Here." She handed the spray bandage applicator to Tristan, who applied it.

He looked around the bleak, ghastly pink bedroom. "We need some clothes."

Mara opened her suitcase and brought out clothes. "I had these made for him. In the same Earth style you prefer. He has enough clothes and supplies for the trip to Earth."

"That's my pixie." Tristan beamed at Mara and accepted the shirt, pants, underwear, and shoes.

Silently cursing the other woman's competence and her own incompetence, Dorian slid away from the men before she screwed up any more than she already had.

Fully dressed, Kellen came to his feet with Tristan's help then wobbled toward the door with blind determination. He flinched as if expecting pain as he crossed the threshold but didn't slow his pace until he reached his owner sprawled in the hall. He lifted his foot as if to kick her then put it back down. "With Cadaran, I had someone to fight against. She never broke me, but this one..." He shuddered. "There's nothing human inside her anymore. All humanity was burned out by the drugs and over-indulgence. How can you fight against a brutal slug-like thing? She won."

Tristan squeezed his shoulder. "You're still alive to escape. You won after all. Let's get the hell off this planet."

Kellen grinned. "Yeah."

To save Kellen from her female presence and point the way to her ship, Dorian sat in the front of the flitter with Mara. Kellen and Floppy spent the trip in mutual fascination with each other. Only the sight of her ship brought Kellen back to reality. He whistled. "What a beauty."

"She's a fast craft with all the smuggler amenities. I call her *The Trojan Horse* in honor of your *Helen of Troy*. And for obvious reasons."

Kellen chuckled at the classical joke. "Very apt."

They loaded the suitcases on the ship, sent Mara's flitter back home on automatic pilot, then boarded. Dorian strapped herself in the captain's chair in the control cabin then glanced back. Tristan had settled the others in flight chairs and was fastening his own belt.

Mara's eyes were huge with excitement and fear as she clutched the rab-cat in her arms to secure him against take-off. Kellen seemed to be fighting an inclination to pass out and a desire to take over the controls.

"Here goes." Dorian pushed the data cube for an illicit atmosphere departure into the navigation computer, flicked on the engines, then they were lifting gently toward the Arden night sky.

Mara gasped with wonder when they left Arden's atmosphere, and the stars jumped in brilliance like glass suddenly transformed into diamonds, then they were all silent as they waited for pursuit.

EVEN after hours in fast flight, no one seemed eager to leave the control cabin. Tristan and Mara got up to eat and relieve themselves but quickly returned. Kellen sprawled in drug-induced sleep in the chair he'd first taken, and Floppy explored the ship to his satisfaction then curled up in an empty flight chair by Kellen.

All of them knew that this ship was fast, but its engines couldn't maintain that speed for long periods. Arden's huge fighters didn't have as great a speed, but they could maintain their top speed almost indefinitely.

A tortoise would always catch up with a hare with its fast occasional bursts of speed even if the hare had a head start. And Arden's tortoise was heavily armed and had forcefield protection, and their ship didn't. They'd have no chance making it straight to Earth if pursuit came. They might not even reach the unlikely safety of the nearest military outpost.

Ten hours into the flight, the *Horse's* sensors at their furthest scanning point picked up an Arden fighter coming after them. They needed to find a place to hide before the other ship reached them, or they were dead.

Chapter 17

Sliding off the examination table in the ship's infirmary, Mara began to dress. "How is the baby?"

Hostility crackling around her, Dorian shifted uneasily on her feet and studied her instruments' readings.

Mara sighed. Dorian had as much right to dislike her as she did Dorian. But, somehow, she didn't hate the other woman. She was too numb with grief for all she'd given up and would lose when Tristan walked away from her. When Dorian said nothing, fear stabbed Mara. "The baby is healthy?"

"What?" Dorian blinked and dragged her attention back to Mara. "Yes."

Mara sagged with relief.

Someone knocked on the infirmary door. Dorian glanced at Mara, who was now fully dressed, then unlocked the door. It slid open.

Tristan stood hesitantly at the door and brushed back his hair as if nervous. "May I?"

Dorian motioned him in.

"I helped Kellen get cleaned up and put him to bed before he passed out again. Flop's watching him for me."

"If he's completely under, I'll tend his injuries and check him out. If you'll assist?"

"It would be best," Tristan agreed.

"The drugs he's on..." Dorian rested a hand on his shoulder. "Withdrawal's going to be ugly."

"God damn them for what they did to him."

Dorian glanced at Mara as if she held her personally responsible for Kellen, then her face softened again as she met Tristan's eyes with an intimacy which wounded Mara worse than the personal dislike. "And the withdrawal isn't the hard part. The emotional healing will be much more difficult. As difficult as your own recovery from the massive trauma of the ship attack."

"I'll be there for him. He won't face it alone." Tristan's gaze shifted to Mara a moment, then he studied a medical monitor on the wall. "I'll bunk with Kellen. He shouldn't be by himself."

Suddenly weak-kneed, Mara sagged against the examining table. She couldn't have borne being so close to Tristan and Dorian if they'd become lovers. Even the thought of it ripped at her heart and pride.

"About..." Tristan wet his lips. "Did Mara's examination?"

"She's pregnant all right." Dorian frowned.

Tristan scowled in return, then he glanced at Mara and his face became politely neutral as if he were aware of hurting her. "And their health?"

"Excellent."

Mara asked Dorian, "And this earth-normal gravity?"

"The ship's gravity shouldn't be a problem. If it were heavier than you're used to, it would be dangerous. You might experience dizziness and nausea at first or if you over-exert, but otherwise, you should be fine."

"We can raise it if..." Tristan said.

"No need." Mara smiled. "I know it must be more comfortable for everyone else."

"I feel positively normal for the first time since the accident," Tristan admitted. "Like heavy shackles have been taken off."

"They were." Dorian clinched her fists.

"In comparison to Kellen...My last eight months have been a vacation on a pleasure planet."

Anger surged through Mara. "Thank you for such a lovely compliment."

Tristan flushed. "I wasn't referring to...I meant the injuries, the government and the harem, being unable to contact my family, Kellen's death..." His gaze met her eyes for the first time since he entered the room. "You were the only bright spot, pixie."

Mara smiled shyly back.

"I'm sorry about...God, I never meant to hurt you like this." He turned and mumbled something about checking on Kellen then bolted out of the room.

Dorian picked up her med-kit. "I should go see to Kellen now."

Mara watched the other woman leave. For the first time in her life, she felt totally alone.

SPACE was nothingness with nowhere to hide.

Tristan sipped his beer and stared at the forward viewing screen he was seated in front of. Stars twinkled in the nothingness, their seeming closeness an illusion. Nowhere close to hide and their enemy narrowed the distance between them with each passing hour.

Something shuffled behind him. He turned his chair.

In his pajamas, Kellen staggered toward him. Tristan forced himself to remain in his seat to save Kellen's pride. "Dory brought our favorite brand of beer. Want one?"

His friend all but fell into the control chair beside him and gazed hungrily at the stars in front of them. His face was gray and sharp with suffering, and his black hair, now cropped short, dripped with sweat. "Yeah."

Tristan picked up the extra can on the floor and flipped it open. "The disposal unit's to your left if you need it."

Smiling grimly, Kellen took the beer. "Just might. Maybe beer'll stay down."

They drank in companionable silence for several minutes, their eyes on the stars, before Kellen spoke. "Hope I didn't keep you awake."

"No. I was edgy." Tristan didn't add, "I'm as horny as hell, and the bed was as empty as these stars without someone to cuddle with."

"Sorry you had to see me like this."

"Don't be a damn fool. Another beer?"

Kellen grinned. "Love you too, Tris. No thanks."

"Something to eat?"

"In a bit, Mom."

"If you want to talk?"

"Not now. I can't..." Kellen shuddered. "Not now."

"The offer stands."

"Soon," Kellen promised. "Same offer to you."

"I'm ashamed to complain."

Humor sparkled in Kellen's eyes a moment before fading behind the pain and weariness. "Minor bitching's all I can handle now."

"Mara's pregnant."

"And congratulations aren't in order?"

Tristan shook his head. "Maybe before I found out I wasn't trapped by the plague. And by then she was already..."

"Knocked up." Kellen shrugged. "See her settled on Earth then wave bye-bye. She's an adult. She'll survive."

"Yeah," Tristan agreed morosely.

"Still interested in Dorian?" Kellen flinched slightly as if the name were painful.

"Of course."

"An angel who fought a planet of devils for you, and a woman gutsy enough to sneak onto a plague planet to rescue you from slavery. A rough choice between two such extraordinary women."

"I've already made my choice. I made it before I left Earth."

"Did you?" Kellen didn't sound convinced.

"Yes." Tristan stirred uncomfortably. "We need to make plans." He pointed at the sensor screen. The blip that was the pursuit ship had gained slightly on them since they'd spotted it.

Kellen groaned. "If they catch us...They're not taking me alive."

"Me neither. I'd as soon not come to that point."

"I want them to pay. I want that whole damn planet to pay." Kellen slammed his fist against the screen.

"To do that we much keep out of their reach."

"We don't have the firepower to attack or even defend. We need to find heavy artillery—a military base or ship. Or a place to hide."

"The nearest base is on Sparta. By my calculations, they'll catch us before we reach it."

Growling unhappily, Kellen leaned back in his chair as if deep in thought. He sat up suddenly. "The ICC net."

Tristan nodded. "That's what I thought. We have Dory's credit card. The nearest ICC transmission station to Earth is on Scarpia, just over a week away."

"Can we make it?"

"Less than an hour to spare ahead of them."

"And how do we convince anyone to believe us in that time?"

"Dory told Elaine what she was up to. We contact Elaine, and she contacts Geoffrey, and from there..."

"The most important ears in the Congress. But that's long term help. It'll take forever for the military to get the commands, let alone reach us."

Tristan nodded. "Then we'll have to make time. We'll either hide on Scarpia among the colonists, or we make sure the Arden fighter doesn't leave Scarpia when we do."

HALLIE dragged her gaze from the vid screen of her private reader and the open letter she knew by heart and stared at the window of the control cabin of the fighter. Blind for the first time to the unique wonder of deep space, she sighed.

She didn't know what to do. This open letter to Arden from Mara d'Jorel had finished upsetting her view of life that Kellen had started.

She didn't want to believe the accusations in the letter, especially those about Cadaran, but she must. Too much of the evidence included with the letter meshed with her own experiences with Cadaran. She'd just been ignorant of what those experiences had meant.

Cadaran, the woman she'd respected above all others, the woman she'd secretly loved and desired for several years, was the most despicable of all villains who'd not only betrayed the moral codes of the Goddess, but also Arden's people.

Hallie bit her lips. What should she do about it? Her long standing sense of duty to her commanding officer warred with her moral obligations.

None of the other soldiers aboard the Arden fighter had seen this letter. She'd copied it off the headquarters' computer just before Cadaran had ordered her to organize the pursuit off-planet, but she'd shown it to no one, not even Cadaran. Especially not Cadaran. Should she show it to the troopers? She would be instigating mutiny if she did.

"Damn!" Cadaran's voice jolted her back to the present. She flipped away from the letter.

She turned. "Sir?"

Cadaran bent over the scanner screen. "They've changed course, and you've not compensated, Lieutenant. You've given them a greater lead."

"Sorry, sir." Hallie programmed in new coordinates.

"The most important capture of my career, and I'm stuck with a bunch of planetbound troopers. What I wouldn't give for one of my attack crews."

"Yes, sir. I'm sorry none were available in time."

"You seem less than enthusiastic." Cadaran raked her with her gaze.

"I don't mean to, sir. This week in space on double duty has been wearing. I'm tired."

Cadaran smashed her fist on the console. "But we're gaining on them, we're gaining. Another day, and we'll have them. Then I'll..." She smiled with feral pleasure. "I'll teach both those men and Mara d'Jorel a lesson they won't forget." Cadaran patted Hallie's shoulder. "We must get them before the other colonies learn they've escaped. The Colony Congress could take away our right to protect our own skies if we don't. They could even blow up Arden to make certain no one else can spread the plague."

"Yes, sir."

Staring at the scanner screen, Cadaran muttered, "We've almost got them. We've almost got them."

Hallie studied the blip too and thought, "Run, Kellen. Run fast so we won't catch you."

MARA sat back from the vid screen and stretched wearily. She yawned and gazed out of her tiny cubicle. Just beyond was the control room. If she turned the other way, she could see the passageway which bisected the ship.

She could watch everything going on in the public areas, but no one could see her. She sighed. That was an apt description of her life on this ship.

Kellen and Floppy were in the control room. Kellen leaned over Floppy and his tiny computer on the table and studied the screen where Floppy typed then looked up at the rab-cat. "And how do you say that?"

The rab-cat wiggled his ears in a complex pattern.

"Oh, I see." Kellen rested his hands on his head like rab-cat ears and clumsily repeated the pattern.

Floppy nodded and gazed in admiration at Kellen.

Mara turned away. Kellen had been a man possessed for the last week. He'd spent most of his waking hours with Floppy deciphering the rab-cat's language. He acted like a starved scholar offered a mental feast in his quiet moments, like a tortured man fighting horrible memories at his worst.

Floppy seemed as inexhaustible. His crude communications and silence with the humans had ended with Kellen. And with the communication came the slow pulling away from Mara. The kitten she'd rescued had finally matured, and his attention had shifted from mother to the outside world. The logical scientist in her was pleased that Floppy sought others, the mother within her grieved at the loss.

That loss among so many others.

Blinking tears, Mara forced her attention back to the vid screen and the Earth history she was reading. She'd spent the last week studying Earth's culture, literature, and history. She'd had nothing else to do. The others sought conversation with each other, catching up on lost time and old memories, and she could only listen to stories exchanged about people, places, and events she knew nothing about. Tristan had become a polite almost stranger with her, Dorian civil and disinterested. Oddly, it was Kellen who sought her out.

When she kept her physical distance and moved with the slow care she would have used with a half-wild animal, he relaxed enough to ask her about Floppy's past, and he would tell her stories of talking with Earth dolphins and other magical creatures.

He also gave her hope. He was the only one who believed that Tristan might seek her rather than Dorian as his wife. Kellen would not explain his reasons and would only smile mysteriously as if he knew something the others did not.

Mara clung to that hope with her whole heart although her scientist's brain chided her for a fool. She'd intended to fight for Tristan, but her readings of Earth literature and the form they called the romance told her how foolish this was. She'd thought she'd understood love and the relationship between men and women, but she'd discovered her error. She knew nothing and understood less. She had no chance to defeat Dorian with her lifetime of knowledge of the intricacies of male and female relationships.

Down the passageway, laughter drifted from the galley toward Mara—Tristan's soft, sexy chuckle followed by Dorian's amused laugh as they shared a private joke.

Mara buried her face in her hands and would have wished herself dead except for the child within her.

MARA stirred restlessly in her flight chair and held her breath as Kellen maneuvered their huge ship through the rugged canyon, the narrow canyon walls seeming inches away from the side of the ship. A slight miscalculation, and they would crash.

As if a tiny flitter landing on a paved parking spot, the ship slowed then settled beneath an overhang of rock and between several outcroppings of boulders.

Kellen powered down the ship and brushed his hands as he stood up. "They'll have the devil's own time finding us now."

"That was splendid." Mara applauded.

Laughing, Kellen bowed.

"Very good, Kell," Tristan acknowledged from the chair beside him.

"When you've got it, you've got it." Kellen bent and picked up Floppy from a flight seat. The rab-cat's ears and eyes were busy telling of his own admiration for Kellen's pilot virtuosity. Floppy purred and rubbed his cheek against Kellen's brown shirt.

Mara stifled a surge of jealousy at the natural ease between man and rab-cat.

Fastening a laser pistol belt around her waist, Dorian walked into the control cabin. She fastened the holster to her pants at her thigh. "I'm ready."

Kellen studied Dorian with a fascination mixed with pain.

Floppy met Mara's eyes then began to talk with his ears to Kellen.

"Not so fast." Kellen watched the rab-cat. "I don't..."

Mara didn't know the rab-cat language Kellen was learning so rapidly, but she did know Floppy. "He wants to come with us. Me particularly. He wants to protect me."

Floppy nodded emphatically.

Tristan patted Mara's shoulder for the rab-cat's benefit. "I'll watch over her for you. We can't risk anyone on the planet seeing you. If they realize we're from Arden, they'll shoot first, fearing the plague. You can't come from any place but Arden."

Floppy tucked his ears down.

"You'll never pass as an Earth cat, Flop. Even with an ear bob." Kellen put him on the floor. "We need you to guard the ship for us. You can let us know if they find the ship."

Hopping onto the captain's chair, Floppy pointed at the buzzer attached to the communications system. He nodded and began to watch the sensors and the outside view screens with a predator's patience.

Mara brushed a kiss on his head. "See you soon." She smiled warmly at Kellen and Dorian. "The Goddess watch over you." She followed Tristan, who opened the ship's outer door and helped her down. The air was sweetly alien with bizarre plant and soil scents, and she could just see some evergreen-like twisted trees. The sky was a peculiar yellowish shade of blue with dark clouds. She stamped, testing the ground, and grinned. "My first new planet—Scarpia."

Tristan laughed. "But not your last, pixie."

"I certainly hope not." She glanced back at the ship's opening. "Aren't they coming?"

"They'll wait until they see where our pursuer lands, then they'll head in that direction."

"To buy us time." Mara shivered.

"Let's not waste our hour head start. Let's do what we came here for." He gave her his hand, and they began to scramble down the slope to the canyon bed.

She concentrated on her footing and her balance. Her body had grown used to Earth standard gravity on *The Trojan Horse*, but her physical reactions were still clumsy, every action exaggerated, and fast movement made her sick on her stomach.

While her movements were hindered, Tristan walked with a natural ease he'd not had on Arden.

When they reached the bottom, he released her hand and began to stride forward along the rocky trail. Her hand curled regretfully at the lost contact, and she matched his step at his side.

Tristan said, "When we reach the town..."

"I have been studying Earth customs on the ship. And Earth history and literature. I won't make any mistakes."

He flashed wary blue eyes at her through his blond lashes. "I'm sorry I've spent so little time with you on board. You've had little to do but read for ten days."

"I understand. Kellen needs you." She bit her tongue to hold back the pathetic gratitude she felt that Tristan was sharing Kellen's cabin, not Dorian's. "Kellen is much better. He seems so much like the man I imagined from your stories."

"He's very strong, but I don't know if he'll ever be that man again. The brutality he..." Tristan grimaced. "I don't know if he'll ever be comfortable with a woman again."

"He needs to find a special woman who will reteach him the difference between having sex and making love."

"Are you volunteering?" Tristan's tone was sharp.

"I have great kinning for Kellen, not just because he's your closest friend, but also because of his warmth of spirit, courage, and his hurt. Still, I don't feel any breeding feelings toward him. None at all. I would be the wrong woman to help him."

"Well, you'll meet other men you'll have breeding feelings for. I'm not the only man in the galaxy. I'll give you that chance to find your man."

"You are the only man I want. Even if I meet hundreds more."

"How do you know?" He chuckled bitterly.

"How do you know which answer to a difficult theoretical equation is the right one? You just sense it. Intuition or instinct tells you."

He shook his head. "Well, I'll see you properly settled in a new home on Earth and help you with the baby."

"I have read a male child needs a father influence. Thank you." She stiffened her back with pride, her heart aching, and kept walking.

"Frontier planets like Scarpia aren't like Earth in customs. Far from it. I'm ashamed your first view of other human worlds is a violent place like this. The social structure is primitive with little power or protection for women. Just do what I tell you to do. Don't look directly into a man's face or speak to him unless I include you in the conversation. Act like you belong to me."

Her eyes widened. "Is this a slave planet, too?"

"No, but close. A woman is under a man's protection as his wife or daughter, or she's free for the taking. Either as a prostitute or for forced marriage."

Mara touched the laser pistol hidden under the hip folds of her tunic. "I do not wish that. If I must belong to anyone, I prefer you."

"It shouldn't come to fighting over you. The social customs are primitive by Earth standards, but most people on these planets follow them. Few men try for the protected women."

As they reached the end of the canyon, the land opened up into a huge rolling, grassy valley rimmed by great mountains. In the distance, she could see a town of one and two story buildings. After twenty minutes, they reached the edge of the small town. The buildings were shabby prefabs from off-world or huts built of native timber and clustered together on dirt streets. Dingy red dust floated and covered everything. The scene reminded Mara of a painting she'd seen about a period of Earth history called the Old West.

Tristan took her right hand in his left, freeing his right for the pistol conspicuously strapped on his hip, and began to walk down the street.

Mara kept her eyes down but saw everything through her lashes and sidelong glances. Men were everywhere! Standing on wooden walkways by public buildings, entering and leaving buildings, kicking the dust around her on the street. So many men in one place was frightening and exhilarating, and the air had a subtle, dangerous tension she'd never felt in her society except when the tyrlin were prowling.

From the walkway, a man whistled loudly. She glanced at him, he watched her with a peculiar unpleasant smile.

Tristan's hand tightened in hers. He said through clinched teeth, "That whistle was a compliment to your beauty."

They turned off their street onto a much narrower one with fewer men then turned into another street, narrower and dirtier still, with few public buildings.

Tensing, Tristan pulled her against the side of building and stepped in front of her. Three men faced him. All were big, their garments dirty by the standards of the other men she'd seen, their hairy cheeks long without a depilatory.

Tristan faced them, his male strength, courage, and self-assurance an almost visible barrier, and rested his hand on his laser pistol's butt. "She's my wife. Earth legal."

Two of the men shuffled uneasily on their feet and lowered their own eyes.

Mara recalled her readings on the male order of a pack of tyrlin and how one powerful male controlled the less powerful and had his pick of the females. Sudden insight into the human male personality struck her.

She smiled secretly as the men began to back away from Tristan. Her male was obviously superior to other males in their opinion as well as hers.

The third man held his ground and slurred, "Want her. Pay for her."

"Where I come from you don't sell your wife, or rent her."

"Want her." The man staggered forward.

Mara's hackles rose as she sensed he wasn't really drunk, but before she could shout a warning, the man charged toward them.

Tristan was waiting for him. He smashed his fist into the other man's stomach. The man bent double and gasped "ooof," then toppled to the ground.

The other men rushed toward Tristan.

Reminding herself she must follow the customs of this planet, Mara stifled her instinctive move to help Tristan. She backed against the wall, her hand on the butt of her hidden pistol, and kept watch for others. Tristan really didn't need help. He ducked, dodged blows, and smashed at the other men with his fists. Mara cocked her head in curiosity. He seemed to be having a wonderful time. Why would fighting someone be fun? Another curious animal aspect of the male personality perhaps.

The man on the ground stirred then crawled upright. His hand sought a weapon tucked in his belt as he eyed Tristan.

Mara glanced around for witnesses, grabbed the man's shirt and belt, and threw him. He slammed head first into the wall, slid down, then stayed down.

Deciding violence against someone who meant a loved one harm involved a certain satisfaction, she dusted off her hands then waited for Tristan to finish off the others.

The last man up swayed under Tristan's blow to the chin then fell on top of his friend.

Tristan glanced at the man she'd thrown then studied her as if guessing what she'd done. She smiled demurely, her lashes lowered.

"Come, pixie." He gave her his left hand. "That will teach them to stay away from women from heavy gravity planets."

"And their men."

After several streets as dirty and narrow as the others, Mara could see a huge communications tower and dish ahead of them. Tristan led her into the tiny attached prefab building with the Intragalactic Communications Company's logo on it. The communication computers purred and blinked in the corner of the room as messages were relayed from other planets' communications dishes to this one then sent on, but the dust and neglect in the tiny office showed few messages came in or out of this office or planet. An older man with grizzly gray hair sprawled asleep on a recliner chair in front of the equipment. He snorted awake at their entrance and sat up.

"Hello," Tristan said politely. "I'd like to send a message to Earth."

The man eyed them both. "You're new here."

"Tristan Mallory and my wife Mara. We just arrived." Tristan shook his hand.

The man ducked his head politely. "Mrs. Mallory."

Mara ducked back, hoping that was a suitable greeting.

"Why didn't you zip the message to me through your ship communications? I'd have boosted its strength and relayed it if you had the proper credit account."

Tristan held out Dorian's charge card. "I do, but we wanted to touch ground. We've been in space for some time." He didn't add that Cadaran could blast them out of the sky using that communication to pinpoint them.

The man chuckled. "Must have been up for a long time to want to come to a place like this."

Tristan handed him the data cube with their call for help to Elaine on it. "We're in a hurry."

"Seen about as much of this place as you wanted to, hmmm." The man chuckled again, took the data cube, and began to fiddle with his equipment.

Picking up a news story printout, Tristan scanned the headlines.

"Welcome to keep the paper, if you want. It's way out of date."

"So am I." Tristan shoved the paper into his pocket.

Mara wandered to the dust-encrusted window and peered out through the one tiny attempt at cleaning. As if fighting gravity that wasn't present, a figure in black loped away from the communications tower. "Cadaran!"

Explosive noise surrounded them as dust and tower blasted toward their building. Tristan grabbed Mara, pulling her to the floor. His body covered hers as the room began to collapse.

KELLEN leaned over the boulder he hid behind and peered through his stereoscope down into the tiny valley. The Arden fighter, every monstrous foot of it, sat in the flat field that had been some miner's garden. He could just see beyond the fighter a well-constructed hut of native timber.

One of Cadaran's blacksuited troopers leaned against the fighter's closed entrance as if basking in the warm afternoon sun rather than being on guard duty. No other troopers were in sight. With Cadaran in search of them or within the craft, he decided.

He handed the stereoscope to Dorian. She nodded thanks and studied the scene with the same careful professional attention. Sunlight sparkled through the long braid of brown hair down her back and accented the fine bones of her face. Her brown jumpsuit tightened against her breasts as she leaned forward.

His body awaiting the lotus pain his brain knew wasn't coming, he flinched as desire surged through him. She was so beautiful with the wild spirit of a fighter and the tenderness of a healer. He swiped away the sweat on his palms on his thighs. "Ready?"

"Yes."

"If they catch me before I plant this," he hefted the explosive pack, "and I'm near enough to damage the ship, I'd consider it a great personal favor if you'd ignite it with your laser pistol before they take it away from me."

Color disappeared in her cheeks. "But..."

"Don't let them take me back alive, Dory. It's a cleaner way to die than what I'd go back to, and it would give Tris a head start."

"I won't let them take you back."

Sensing he wasn't getting any other promise, he nodded. "Good enough. The Goddess watch over you, Dory."

Using boulders, scraggly twisted evergreens, and shadows as cover, he began to climb down the rugged trail toward the cabin. He concentrated on silence and stealth, not on the sick fear of returning to

Arden if caught.

As he reached the foot of the mountain , he ducked behind a small boulder. The guard hadn't wiggled. Her arms tucked under her breasts, she leaned back against the fighter's door. The fighter was wedged-shaped, two exhaust jets attached as cylinders along its sides. Laser turrets studded the top like metal warts.

The exhaust jets' tubes were his best bet to place the explosives, he decided. Repairs would take over a week before that ugly monster could become airborne again.

With infinite slowness and care, he began to drift from bush to boulder to shadow around the far side of the fighter away from the guard. He kept out of sight of the ship's ports. Most fighters had sensors for space but not for the ground, but the troopers within could see through the ports.

Sweat soaked his clothes as he neared the exhaust tubes. He ducked down, hunkering against the ship's back, and flipped on the detonator of the explosive pack. He slid it gently into the tube.

A woman shouted, "Halt."

Dropping the pack, he grabbed for his pistol as the woman lifted up out of a repair hatch above him. He had only time to realize her pistol was trained on him and to recognize her as Hallie before his own pistol was leveled at her.

In the instant of hesitation, something smashed his head from behind, and he fell.

A knee landed on the small of his back pinning him, and someone pried his gun out of his hand as he struggled. She ground his face into the dirt, then he was jerked upright, his right hand twisted behind his back, an arm around his throat. He shook his head to stop its ringing. The trooper behind him snickered. "Ain't he a pretty one."

Hallie shimmied down the side of the ship. "No touching, Ava. The last trooper who tried that he killed. Didn't you, bull?"

Kellen spat the dirt he'd eaten. "Yes. Hello, Lieutenant. Still licking that bitch Cadaran's feet, I see."

Hallie glanced at the trooper. "And still wagging my tail about it. Sorry to see you again."

"Feeling's mutual."

Hallie gingerly pulled the detonation device from the jet exhaust and disarmed it. With a deep sigh of relief, she put it on the ground. Pulling cuffs from her pocket, she walked over to him . He fought them as they pried his wrists together behind his back and manacled them.

"See if there's more fugitives." Hallie motioned toward the mountainside.

Her weapon drawn, the trooper began to search the area.

Hallie's hand settled in his and gave a gentle squeeze of reassurance. "I won't let her hurt you." She rested her hand on his back and began to nudge him toward the cabin.

"Better to die here than Arden."

"You aren't dying in either place, Kellen."

"Then let me go."

"I can't. As long as Cadaran is chasing after you and Tristan, she isn't at home stopping the rebellion she doesn't know about. Mara d'Jorel's letter must have ignited a revolution."

"So you've turned against her."

"Give a girl enough time and evidence, and, even if she's a stupid farm girl like me, she'll get the point. I'm sorry I have to keep you, but I have to keep her trust. I'll just do my duty and hold tight."

"Sometimes just doing nothing isn't enough. That's all you've done so far and little good you've done by it. Will you do nothing when Cadaran comes back and takes her frustrations out on me? You remember how gentle she was with me."

Hallie inhaled hard. "I can't release you."

"As friends go, you sure as hell aren't much, Hallie. I hope you have nightmares about me for the rest of your cowardly existence."

Her voice was dead quiet. "I already have."

A flash of brown out of the corner of his eye. He didn't look although he sensed Dorian running toward them to get a clear shot at Hallie.

He shrugged mentally and dropped to give her that shot.

Dorian slid to a halt and aimed at Hallie's middle. "Release him."

"He's all yours. My pleasure." Hallie sounded as if she meant it.

Careful to keep himself out of Dorian's line of fire, he came to his feet and held out his manacled hands to Hallie.

A flash of black beyond. He shouted, "Behind..."

Hallie shot Dorian as she spun.

His scream of negation ripped from his heart as she crumpled. Sobbing, he collapsed to his knees.

THE ROAR of the building's collapse finally stilled. Darkness and dust surrounded Tristan as he lay on the floor. His shoulders and back stung where debris had hit him, and his lungs ached from the dust.

He blinked dirt from his eyes and lifted slightly. The boards covering him wiggled. Mara stirred beneath him. "Pixie," he whispered hoarsely and levered himself off her with his arms.

Sneezing, she tried to crawl upright.

"Don't move."

She sank back down. "Are we trapped?"

"I don't know. You okay? I didn't hurt you?"

"The baby feels fine. I'm used to your weight."

He flushed, aware of her sweet little rump beneath him. He ordered his body to behave. "Not like this you aren't."

"No," she agreed sadly. "How do we get free?"

"Cautiously. Shield your head with your arms."

When she did as he told her, he wiggled forward and began to nudge and push at the boards around them. If memory served him, he was facing the wall where the door was.

The boards clattered and slid at his touch. One smashed toward his head. He knocked it away and burrowed forward like an earthworm traveling through twigs. A large chunk of wall stopped him. He explored it with his hands. Not much bigger than a yard square. Lifting himself, he traced its top edges in search of other debris. He could feel nothing above.

If he pushed it away, nothing should land on his head. He shoved. As it fell, sunlight blasted him.

Blinded, he blinked tears then stared blearily at the door. Its frame was bowed open from the building's collapse, and the door hung on one hinge. It was a sorry excuse for an opening, but it was an opening.

He grinned then crawled cautiously backwards through the tunnel he'd created in the debris until he reached Mara.

Her hand clutched his ankle. "Tristan?"

"Can you follow me?"

"Yes."

He eased back out, Mara behind him. She kept her hand on his ankle to guide her in the darkness. Tristan squinted as light hit him again, and he was through the door into the open. He stood stiffly then turned.

Mara crawled out of the hole. He reached down and lifted her to her feet. She wobbled slightly then buried her face into his shoulder.

For a moment he hugged her tightly then released her. She smiled at him. Red dust and white plaster covered her, but he could see no injuries. "You sure you're all right?"

"I'm fine. You?"

"Nothing worth mentioning."

She caressed his cheek. "You look like a sugar-powdered gingergirl cookie."

Her touch was fire and ice down his spine. "You too, pixie."

A group of locals charged down the street toward them. One shouted, "Where's Fred?"

Remembering the ICC operator, Tristan pointed to where the old man had been when the tower hit them.

The men began to rip at the structure. The twisted metal of the tower snaked through the broken boards where the man had stood.

"Stand back, pixie. Where it's safe. I'll help them."

She nodded. "Take care."

Tristan helped the men dig out the ICC operator. Miraculously, he was unhurt. His body had been shielded by the recliner he'd spent so many bored hours on.

Brushing off his hands, Tristan walked back to where he'd left Mara. He searched the small crowd of onlookers, but she wasn't among them.

His heart smashed into his ribs as he remembered the men who'd tried to steal her earlier. They must have her again, and they'd either gang rape her or sell her to a local brothel for....

Sick horror washed over Tristan at the possibilities.

A flash of black caught his eyes beyond the crowd. Cadaran stood in the shadow of a nearby building and smiled at him like a panther after a bloody kill.

HALLIE shoved Kellen into the darkened miner's cabin. He stumbled inside, too numb with horror to fight her. He sniffed back tears. "Damn you. Damn you. I begged you to kill me, and now you've killed her."

"She something to you?"

"Tristan's sister."

Ada came in behind them with Dorian slung over her shoulder like a dead animal.

Hallie said, "I used a muscle stunner, Kellen. She'll be fine." The trooper dumped Dorian's body off her shoulder onto the small bed in the corner.

"Down." Hallie pushed him to his knees at the foot of the bed. "Put your head between your legs and don't move, or I'll stun you too." She backed away from him.

His manacles released by remote control, but before he could come to his feet, the door slammed closed.

Stumbling upright, he rubbed his wrists then sat down on the edge of the bed. Dorian sprawled on the bed as if asleep after a night of passion. His nostrils flared as he touched her breast. Her heart beat sweetly against his fingers. He straightened her body and rested her head on a lump of pillow. His fingers trailed down her braid as he brushed a kiss on her forehead, then he started a careful examination of the room in search of weapons or escape. He didn't expect to find either, but it would keep his mind off the prison claustrophobia the small room gave him.

After many long minutes, a shaky voice asked, "Any luck?"

He glanced at Dorian, who watched him from the bed. "No."

"Sorry I blew it."

"I couldn't have done better. Only killing them would have been better." He concentrated on his search again. After several minutes he glanced toward Dorian.

In a tight shivering knot, she huddled on the bed as if freezing.

Striding to the bed, he rested his hand on her face. The skin was damp and cold. "Damn, you're in shock." He swore again. "That stunner must have been set too high. Why didn't you say something?"

She shrugged.

"Come here. I'll warm you." He sat down on the bed and opened his arms. He forced himself to relax when she settled against him, her own body stiff as if she feared upsetting him. He stroked her hair. "Relax. I know you won't molest me." His body quivered as she nestled into his chest. "At least my brain knows."

She burrowed her face into his shoulder. His fingers traced the nape of her neck. A shiver that wasn't shock went through her. An answering jolt of pain ripped through Kellen. He bit his lip and fought his instinct to flee her.

When he could control his voice, he said, "Sexual chemistry's hard to explain between a man and woman. It's there or it isn't."

He felt the heat of her blush through his shirt. She mumbled agreement.

"I never felt it on Arden. Not for that bitch Cadaran, or Hallie, or for Toadface and her sadistic friends."

"Friends?"

"Don't ask." He forced back nightmare memories. "The lotus on Arden doesn't just control sexual desire. It makes desire agony, the act itself torture."

Dorian glanced up at him with soft, sympathetic brown eyes.

"And Toadface gave me other drugs to enhance pain and fear. She couldn't feel anything anymore so she fed off my emotions."

"Sick."

"Yes, she was." He sighed. "And so you see, sexual desire means pain to me. I feel pain when I desire a woman."

"A trained behavioral response."

"Like a rat in a maze," Kellen agreed.

"With therapy you can relearn how to enjoy desire."

"Give the rat a cookie instead of a shock." He sighed again. "Perhaps. Or perhaps this rat's too messed up to ever save."

"You're worth a try. You're very brave. Why are you telling me this?"

"I didn't want you to die believing I thought you were.... I wanted you to know it wasn't your fault I back away. This biochemical attraction between us.... I can't control it, and you can't so I back away."

"I understand, Kellen. I'm sorry."

"I am, too, and I'm sorry I got you in this mess."

"Not your fault." She yawned.

"That's the shock wearing off. You're trembling less. Rest, and I'll make escape plans."

Her body relaxed completely against his, her arms circling his waist.

He managed to stifle his flinch before she felt it, but phantom lotus pain ripped through his loins. He counted to fifty and stared at the ceiling of the cabin. Gradually, the ceiling beam patterns began to make sense.

"Wake up, gorgeous." He nudged Dorian's shoulder. "I think I just discovered our way out of here."

Chapter 18

The Arden security officer gripped the chain between the manacles which pinned Mara's hands behind her back, and shoved Mara down the alleyway. She stumbled forward and shook her head in bewilderment.

One moment she'd been watching Tristan rescue the old man from the collapsed building, then she'd been grabbed from behind, cuffed, and forced away. She'd tried to scream for Tristan, but the woman's hand had muzzled her.

They'd been walking for ages through the streets. Mara wondered if they were lost. "Where are we going, officer?"

"Veta d'Vira. None of your damn business, traitor."

"Oh, we are lost then."

Veta grunted unhappily, and her hand clamped down on Mara's wrist.

Mara blinked tears of pain, but her mind cleared for the first time since the explosion. Tristan would find her, and if he didn't...Well, if he didn't, she'd do everything in her power to see that Cadaran couldn't pursue the others off this planet. Then she'd stay alive until Tristan brought back rescue from Earth for her and their baby. He wouldn't desert them.

Ahead, a door swung open into the alleyway, and a huge man in dirty miner's clothing stepped out. Mara plowed into him.

Backing up, the man uttered strange words she'd never heard before but which sounded like curses and glowered belligerently at them. "Women!" He studied Mara with a warm grin, then his gaze drifted up to the large soldier who held her prisoner.

His expression changed to stunned blankness as if he'd been hit on the head with a board. He had freckles, curly red hair, and a plain open face.

Mara glanced up at her guard to see what she thought of this strange man. Veta had the same expression of concussed wonder on her face, her jaw slack.

"Ain't you a big, pretty woman," the man finally said to Veta.

The security officer ran her eyes down the man's enormous frame. "Big and beautiful."

They exchanged a long, knowing look, then the man opened the door. "I live here."

Veta pushed Mara ahead of her, as if an afterthought, and they entered the building.

From the looks of the shabby hallway and the smells and sounds, this must be some kind of boarding house, Mara decided. The man ushered them up some rickety wooden steps to the second floor. He unlocked a door, and they stepped into a parlor. A broken couch which once had been floral sagged against the wall, and a chair and table perched near the window. The floor was wood with a dust-colored rug on it.

The man closed the door and locked it then shuffled nervously on his feet. He'd kept the same blank look. Mara finally recognized the expression and the emotion behind it. She must have had the same stunned wonder when she'd seen Tristan's picture, and her whole existence had been changed forever.

"Name's Owen."

"Veta."

"She want to join us?"

Mara blushed as she understood his meaning. "No, thank you. I have a husband."

"She's my prisoner." Veta lifted Mara's arms and showed him the manacles.

"Oh." Owen turned as if forgetting Mara entirely and began to pull his shirt over his head. He walked toward another room.

Veta glanced around, dragged Mara to the chair at the wall, uncuffed her right hand, and rehooked the manacle to a piece of pipe which extended from the wall.

The blankness replaced by eagerness, Veta strode toward the bedroom, shedding uniform as she went. The bedroom door closed behind her.

Mara yanked at the manacle, but the pipe wouldn't give. She glowered. Somehow or the other she was getting out of here.

HIS gun at ready, Tristan ducked into the shadows of a building and peered around its corner into the street. No one moved past the dilapidated shacks beyond. Only the ever present red dust blew gently by.

He leaned against the building, feeling the wood through his sweat-soaked shirt, and rubbed tiredly at his forehead. He'd been dodging Cadaran and her Arden goons and searching for Mara for twenty minutes with no luck. Cadaran always stayed just behind him. Could she be trailing him in hopes he'd lead her to Kellen and Dorian? It'd be a cold day in hell before he'd do that.

Another possibility struck him. Could Mara have run when she'd seen Cadaran, and Cadaran expected him to find Mara? Not likely. Mara would have shouted a warning. But if she couldn't give warning, she'd have drawn Cadaran away. Tristan grimaced. That was far more likely to be the case.

How could he find Mara in this maze of shacks and buildings? She could be anywhere. He tried to force his mind to work, but it remained stubbornly numb. What he needed was a homing device. A homing....

He inhaled hard. Floppy! Several days before he'd overheard...deliberately eavesdropped on Mara and Kellen in intimate conversation, more out of concern for Kellen than.... Tristan shook himself away from contemplating the surge of jealousy he'd felt and tried to remember the conversation.

Mara had been talking about Floppy. She'd said that rab-cat kittens and their mothers had a natural homing signal between them so they could find each other anywhere. Mara didn't have the ability, but Floppy could find her. She'd said something about playing hide and seek in a nearby meadow and....

Tristan bit back an exclamation of excitement. He'd make sure he'd lost Cadaran, then he'd go back to the ship and get Floppy. He eyed the street, but it remained as lifeless as before.

He raised his gun and darted across the street into the darkness of another building's shadow.

Cadaran waited there for him. Her gun drawn, she smiled and fired.

His gun flew out of his hand. He slid to a stop and flexed numbed fingers as he met Cadaran's eyes.

She beamed at him and holstered her pistol. "It's taken a while, but I've finally found you."

"Where's Mara?"

"In the brig of my ship by now." Cadaran pounded her fist into her other hand. "It's time you learned a lesson about the way a man should behave."

Tristan tensed and waited for her attack.

"Well, looky here. Ain't you a beauty." One of the men who had tried to steal Mara sauntered from an alleyway and leered with broken teeth at Cadaran. "Come here, boys. We got ourselves some fun."

Tristan backed into the shadows.

The other men limped out and circled Cadaran like wolves around a lamb. "Ain't she a nice'un," the smallest muttered.

Cadaran glowered at them as if they were a minor irritation. "Go away."

One chuckled nastily.

Tristan scooped up his gun and studied its indicators. It was dead.

The men moved toward Cadaran. Tristan considered going to the rescue, but he decided against it. These men deserved what Cadaran was going to do to them.

Turning, he began to run away. Behind him, he could hear Cadaran's cold laughter and the men's cries of pain.

He only stopped a few times to check for pursuit on the way to *The Trojan Horse*. Finally, he staggered up the canyon to the ship. The door opened, and Floppy studied him from the entry.

Dragging himself inside, he slid to the floor. The door closed behind him. The rab-cat's ears began to wiggle in question.

Tristan didn't have to know the ear language to know what Floppy wanted answered. "Cadaran captured her. I don't know where she is. Can you find her?"

The rab-cat nodded.

"Have you seen Kellen and Dorian?"

Floppy shook his head.

"Damn, I hope she hasn't gotten them, too. Give me a moment, and we'll go." He chugged down a quart of water and replaced his damaged weapon with another then returned to the control room.

The rab-cat waited at the door. He wore the collar with the remote control key to the door that Tristan had made for him. "Good. You might need it if something happens to me." Tristan took his own key. "Let's go find Mara. We'll get her back safe, whatever it takes."

Floppy nodded and followed him out of the ship.

KELLEN ran his hand down the side of the wood wall of the miner's cabin near the wood column. He grunted with satisfaction. "Found it."

Dorian shifted on the bed, her arms tucked under her breasts. "Are you sure?"

"Most miners have an escape passage. Or at least the smart ones do. Whatever world it is, whatever they're mining, there's always someone who'll try to take it away." He pulled the hidden switch downward.

Something rattled over his head. She stared upward in amazement as a trapdoor opened in the roof and a rope ladder fell down toward them.

"Nice!" Catching the rope, he tugged it. It was tied firmly to the roof. "Good engineering. Most just dig an escape tunnel." He bowed. "Ready to escape, my lady."

"Happily, milord." Smiling, she sashayed to the ladder and began to climb upward. He followed closely behind her. Reaching the roof, she crouched down. Below, the large guard called Ada leaned against the cabin door. The Arden fighter appeared deserted, no other guards in sight.

Kellen crawled to her and studied the ground. Sunlight flashed in his dazzling green eyes and across his classic features. He pointed behind them. Another ladder waited to be unfurled down the back of the cabin. He handed her a potato.

Lifting an eyebrow and wondering why he'd taken the poor miner's food, she examined it. He pantomimed throwing it past the guard then motioned to himself then to the ladder, then mimicked a karate chop.

She gave a thumbs up in agreement and for luck. Grinning, he pulled several more potatoes out of his pockets and placed them beside her then crawled to the ladder, hurled it over the side of the cabin, and began to climb downward.

Dorian listened to his almost silent descent. He might have emotional problems, but he was still damn good at what he did, as good as Tristan's stories about him.

Lifting a potato, she sighted a water bucket just beyond the far corner of the cabin and threw.

With a rattle, the bucket fell over. Ada jolted upright and stalked toward the noise with her weapon drawn.

Kellen crept up behind her and clipped her across the neck with his hand. She turned as if he'd barely tapped her and grabbed at him. He jumped back.

After shoving the potatoes in her pocket, Dorian shimmied down the ladder. When she reached the ground, she ran around the corner of the cabin. Kellen and Ada faced each other, circling like wary fighters. They struck at each other with fists and legs, but each dodged the worst blows.

Dorian glanced around wildly, looking for something to even the odds. Their weapons were piled near the door with her stereoscope binoculars.

With his foot, Kellen slashed into Ada's knee. Her legs buckled. As she hit the ground, he kicked at her face. Rolling, she scissored his legs with hers. He fell. They tumbled together, kicking and punching.

Closing her hand on her pistol, Dorian set it for heavy stun and aimed.

The fighters lumbered to their feet and began to smash at each other. Kellen seemed more intent on pummeling the woman than on escape. His hatred smoldered in his eyes and in the vicious movements of his body.

Dorian hefted another potato in her free hand and bounced it off Ada's back. The big woman backed away from Kellen and stared about like a big, dumb animal.

Before Kellen could close the gap between them, Dorian fired. Ada fell like a toppled tree.

He kicked at her but missed. "What the hell...I was winning."

"Let's get out of here before they come back."

"What?" Kellen gaped at her as if drunk on emotion.

She tossed him his gun and hung the stereoscope on her hip. "Let's go."

"Oh." Kellen gazed around them. "The explosives?"

"They're gone." Dorian tugged his sleeve. "Let's go!"

Anger flared in his eyes. "Don't touch me."

Dorian tossed her braid in disgust, turned, and began to run toward their ship. She didn't look back to see if he followed, but she could hear the sound of running feet behind her.

GIGGLES and deep male grunts reverberated from the bedroom into the parlor. Flushed with embarrassment and a strange edgy excitement, Mara examined the pipe her manacle was anchored to. The metal tubing extended from the wall to the ceiling, traveled vertically three feet, then curved back into the wall. It was of one piece and the metal seemed thick and in excellent shape. It must be some form of heating element.

Standing, she grabbed the pipe and yanked with all her strength. The pipe groaned, and the wall plaster crumbled against her assault, but the pipe wouldn't break free.

Perhaps she needed something to pry with. She glanced around.

The only things within reach were the chair and table. The table moved solidly to her touch. It wouldn't break apart easily, and the process would be so noisy that even the preoccupied couple in the next room could hear it.

The wooden chair, held together by glue and bolts, was a possibility. Grabbing two legs, she jerked outward as if she were pulling apart a wishbone.

Her arms and shoulders throbbed with the effort, but the chair remained maddeningly whole. Disgusted, she put the chair back.

She stared out the window at the alley below. Her gun drawn, Cadaran slunk down the alley as if in search of someone. Mara jerked away from the window and hid behind the drapes. Certainly Cadaran couldn't have trailed them here, could she? Mara shivered with superstitious dread. The woman was unnatural in her ability to hound them.

Mara's heart pounded for several minutes, then she relaxed slightly. Cadaran must have passed, or she'd be here by now. Mara glanced up at the dust red curtains and noticed the curtain rod—a slender metal pole.

Stepping up on the chair, she flipped open the curtain assembly and lifted the rod out. The curtain fell to the floor, and she held her treasure.

Hopping down, she inserted the bar under the pipe, and pried. Wall collapsed under the tip of the bar—she grunted with effort—and the wall fell in with a quiet puff of white plaster.

Gasping, she studied her work. The inner wall around the pipe had broken apart, revealing the wooden outer wall of the building, but the pipe wasn't even dented.

Tears of rage burned down her cheeks. Just within the wall, the pipe was joined to another by some kind of twisted ring of metal.

Mara explored the ring with her fingers. It gave slightly. She began to twist it open.

The heating must come from hot water forced through the pipes, she decided, her fingers pausing. She could be setting herself up for a nasty burn. But it appeared to be summer in this hemisphere of Scarpia, and the pipes were cold. It was an acceptable risk. She began to twist again. The ring was rusted, but it finally gave under her assault.

The ring slid downward, and the pipe came apart. Mara grinned and began to shove the manacle toward the opening she'd created. Finally, she was free.

What now? Clasping the dangling manacle in her hand, she glanced toward the bedroom door. Veta was moaning "oh," and "Owen" in a high pitched wheeze of pleasure, and the male grunts were louder and faster. She'd better get out of there before the inevitable conclusion was reached.

Veta's uniform was piled by the door. Mara bent and examined the pockets. She found the electronic key to the manacles and freed herself. On the bottom of the pile was her gun.

Lifting her eyes upward, she thanked the Goddess for this gift. Love at first sight and the Goddess had gotten her into this mess with Tristan, and Veta's love at first sight and the Goddess appeared to be rescuing her. She hoped Veta had sense enough to know what she'd found and not leave it to pursue Mara and return to joyless Arden.

Picking up the gun, Mara hastened to the parlor door. She unlocked it and peeked out into the hall. She didn't relish having to face any more amorous miners like those in the alley.

The hallway was empty so she slunk out and crept down the steps to the exit. Some man in a nearby room sang a slurred song which seemed to be about breeding with a four-breasted alien. Giggling with embarrassment, Mara opened the exit door a crack and peered out. The alley was empty, but Cadaran had been by minutes before.

Mara's palms sweated as she lifted her gun and stepped into the alleyway. If Tristan thought she'd been separated from him, he'd assume she'd head toward the ship so that's where she'd go. But in what direction was the ship? On Arden her sense of direction was perfect, but on this new planet she was as confused as Veta had been.

She glanced up at the afternoon sun, did a little calculation on movement and time passage, recalled its earlier location, and headed down the alley toward the ship.

At the entrance of the alley, she paused and studied the terrain beyond. The street was empty, heat beating down on floating dust, and an insect droned sleepily. Most of the colonists must be indoors during the hottest part of the day. Mara mentally chose her route to provide maximum cover and escape routes then began to dart from hidden point to hidden point until she reached another alleyway against Lolly's Bar— "We treat men extra good." She paused, breathing heavily, and glanced behind her. Cadaran trotted down the street toward her.

Mara whimpered with panic but forced herself to be calm. Just beyond was the side exit to Lolly's Bar. She tested the knob. The door opened. Slipping in, she closed and locked the door, then leaned against the wall, her heart threatening to slam itself out of her chest, and listened.

Cadaran's footsteps paused at the door, the knob twisted, the door shock, and the footsteps moved onward.

Sagging with relief, she examined the room she was in. Small tables, chairs upended on them, filled the big, empty room. A bar was in the far corner with liquor bottles and a big mirror behind it. In the other corner in the shadows, a woman sat at a table with a glass of amber liquid in front of her. She stood and stared at Mara. She had strange red coloring on her lips and cheeks, and her eyes and lashes were darkened. Her long, red glittering gown showed more of her breasts than it hid, and a slit ran up its side exposing most of her leg and thigh. Mara wished she could show Patta that dress.

The woman eyed Mara up and down in a rather intimate manner and sipped her drink. She spoke in a husky voice. "You've come to the right place, honey. You've got the look of a woman who can please a lot of men. Please them the way they want it."

Mara gulped nervously. Perhaps this was not the safest of sanctuaries after all.

TRISTAN ran down the canyon trail, his eyes half on the rocks beneath him, half on the blur of black fur who was Floppy. The rab-cat charged forward with the absolute certainty he could sense Mara ahead among all these rocks and the people below.

With no other hope of finding Mara, Tristan had to put his own faith in the rab-cat's ability. He kept moving from sheer force of will, his energy long exhausted. The possibility that Cadaran could be hurting her or some man could be raping her fueled the sick panic which wouldn't feel exhaustion.

The rab-cat slid to a stop, glanced back at Tristan, then darted up the almost sheer side of the mountain.

Stopping, Tristan fought for breath. "I can't follow you. It's too high."

Floppy didn't slow. He sprang from rock to boulder like a sure-footed ion-propelled mountain goat. Tristan shook his head in admiration. The rab-cat's natural speed and agility had increased remarkably on this world with its lighter gravity. Floppy reached the top of the mountain and stopped. He sat down, his long ears wiggling as if he were thinking aloud. He studied the terrain below in the direction of the town. Could Mara still be there instead of in Cadaran's ship among these canyons?

The rab-cat gazed down at him and motioned with his left paw toward the town. Tristan nodded and began to run in that direction with new speed.

After several minutes, Floppy passed him again and took the lead. They didn't lower their pace, reckless of the terrain and possible ambush, until they reached the edge of town.

Floppy slowed to the fast walk of a lion following certain prey. His gun in his hand, Tristan caught up with him and strode by his side.

The streets were still almost deserted, the heat pounding down on the dirt streets and buildings. The few people they passed ignored the rab-cat.

Tristan held his breath at each passing. If someone were to connect Floppy to Arden and the plague, they'd be killed by hysterical people without questions asked.

Floppy paused at the corner of a ramshackle hotel and an alleyway. His nose quivered as if he scented something.

"Mara? Is she inside?"

The rab-cat shook his head indecisively.

"She has been there? You smell her?"

Floppy nodded.

"She's not there now?"

The rab-cat nodded and pointed at the building with his paw.

"She's in that direction?" At Floppy's nod, Tristan smiled. "Let's go around the building." He tightened his grip on his laser pistol and walked into the alleyway. Above him through an open window, the squeak of bedsprings, the grunts of a man, and the happy squeals of a woman as she reached orgasm drifted downward.

Tristan's loins ached as he remembered Mara's breathy cries of "Tristan" as she tightened around him, her body tensing with release, and the shy "I love you" as she cradled him afterwards.

Biting his lips and forcing his attention back to the present, he stopped at the alley's exit and examined the street beyond. Floppy pointed at a building further down the street on the other side.

"She's in there?"

Floppy nodded decisively.

Tristan frowned. Lolly's Bar. And from the look of it, probably a brothel, too. Damn them. Damn them. He'd make any man who touched her pay with his life.

His ears going back, Floppy snarled as if sensing Tristan's

emotions.

Fighting his anger, he whispered, "That's a dangerous place for her. They'll hurt her. Let's get her out."

Picking out his route, he darted out of the alley toward the nearest patch of shadow. He paused, looking for enemies, then continued onward down the street, followed by a furry black shadow.

He decided against a frontal approach. Stopping at the alley door, he tried the knob. The door was locked. He held his breath, clutched the knob, and shoved with his shoulder and arm as Kellen had taught him. The wood frame shattered at the lock. The door swung open.

The rab-cat slipped in ahead of him. Tristan shifted his pistol and prepared to charge forward shooting. Floppy stuck his head out and motioned with his ears for Tristan to come in.

The barroom was empty. Tristan closed the door behind him and propped a chair against it in case Cadaran was behind him.

Floppy circled the room once then bounded up the steps in the far corner. Tristan cursed the rab-cat's rashness and charged up after him. At the top a hallway extended through the building with rooms on both sides.

The rab-cat trotted confidently to the last room on the left and impatiently ordered Tristan to open the door.

Tristan put his ear to the door but could hear nothing. With infinite slowness, he twisted the knob then pushed the door open.

His eyes blazing, Floppy exploded into the room with Tristan at his tail. Both stopped in confusion.

Mara sat in a rocking chair, a red-headed toddler asleep in her lap. She motioned them to silence and lifted the child. A woman in a sleazy red dress stepped out of the shadows near the bed and accepted the child with a warm smile. She eyed Tristan with lusty approval, winked at Mara, then exited the room.

"Pixie?" His voice was husky with weariness and surprise.

"Wasn't he beautiful? He's a little boy. I've never held a little boy before." She blinked tears and threw herself into Tristan's arms. "I'll not let them take our child. Never. Never. I'll fight..."

Tristan hugged her stiffly. "Nothing will happen to your child, Mara. We won't let it happen."

"They captured me, but I escaped. Lolly hid me."

Tristan chuckled. "Flop and I came to rescue you, ready to face tyrlins and Cadaran, and you didn't need it."

"The effort and the company are appreciated."

Now minus the baby, Lolly paused at the door and examined Floppy. "What the hell kind of cat is that?"

"The long-earred larot. A new breed from Earth," Tristan said, stepping away from Mara.

Floppy stared coldly at him but twined against Mara's ankles and purred loudly like a friendly tom.

"Ain't he a darling." Lolly bent over, giving a spectacular view of her breasts, and stroked Floppy's head. "Want to sell him?"

"My wife would rather sell me."

Mara choked back an hysterical laugh.

Lolly straightened and winked at Mara. "Want to get rid of either one, and I'm your first bidder."

"No thank you. Both are too precious to me." Mara rested her hand on the other woman's arm. "And thank you for your help."

"Any time, honey. We girls got to stick together in a place like this. Especially with the little'uns to think of."

"Thank you," Tristan said. "God bless you for hiding her." He led Mara out of the room and down the steps with Floppy at their heels. "What did you tell her?"

"Very little. For her own safety. I told her about those men. Her husband was out looking for you to bring you here."

"Good thinking, pixie. Did they hurt you?"

"No. I'm very tired."

"Me, too. Let's get you back to the ship, I'll find Kellen and Dory, and we'll get off this damn, dusty planet."

As they reached the barroom, Tristan remembered something he'd promised himself months before. "Do you dance?"

Stopping, she studied him as if wondering about his sanity. "I took ballet until I started college at sixteen."

"Waltz?"

"I have seen it done. It is very beautiful."

"Would you dance with me?" He bowed.

"Tristan?"

"Please, pixie?"

"Very well."

He gathered her in his arms. "It's like this." Humming his favorite Strauss waltz, he began to dance slowly.

After just a few stanzas, Mara followed his lead naturally, and they began to waltz across the barroom floor.

Her hazel eyes met his in question, and he smiled down into them.

"Thank you for giving my life and my legs back to me, Mara. I owe this moment to you."

"I lo...I have such kinning for you, Tristan."

"And I have such kinning for you. I want you to always be my friend."

"I will always be your friend." She blinked as if fighting tears.

The front door rattled as someone tried to open it.

Floppy snarled.

Tristan drew Mara away from view of the door's window behind a table then peeked toward the window. He caught a glimpse of cropped black hair, sad brown eyes, and a black uniform. "Damn. Cadaran."

The door shook as if someone were kicking it in. Tristan pulled Mara up, and they began to run toward the side door.

Chapter 19

Her heart and the wheeze of her breath so loud she could barely hear those pursuing her, Mara ran down the canyon bed toward the ship. The ground in front of her rolled and twisted like a fever hallucination, and all she wanted to do was fall to her knees and retch from gravity sickness, but there was Tristan and Floppy running behind her who wouldn't save themselves by leaving her to Cadaran, and there was the baby within her who must live free from the harem.

A high-pitched large animal's whistle rattled around the canyon walls.

She thought dispassionately of death by the local version of the tyrlin, whatever terrible shape it might assume, and kept running.

Tristan left his protective place behind her and ran at her side. "Kellen. Dolphin talk. Shark's behind us, but he's stopping it or slowing it down."

Lasers blasted behind them as shots were fired and returned.

Ahead, the canyon wall slanted gradually upward toward their hidden spaceship.

Mara's heart twisted at the thought of the open hillside's exposure, but she didn't slow her pace.

Above her, a figure raised up from behind a boulder, a large laser in her hand.

Mara faltered, and Tristan almost slammed into her back before she recognized Dorian, who fired toward those behind them. Mara plowed doggedly upward.

Kellen shouted, "Get down."

Tristan grabbed Mara's waist and dragged her to the ground. He pulled them both behind a boulder too small for one and shielded her body with his.

She peered toward the canyon bed.

Cadaran and three troopers darted from rock to rock toward them. Kellen returned their fire as he retreated. A trooper with a laser rifle on her back was scaling the other slope to a small ledge which would give her easy shots at them before they could reach the safety of their ship.

Tristan swore and fired at the trooper although she was too far away for the range of the pistol.

Mara prayed for a miracle to save them from certain death.

Lightning shot over her head from above and smashed into the other canyon wall. Rock exploded outward, careening down into the canyon in front of Cadaran and her troopers.

Through the dust blowing toward them, Mara could just see the sharpshooter rolling toward the ground. The fallen rock seemed to have completely blocked the canyon between them and Cadaran.

Mara whispered a shocked prayer of gratitude for the miracle.

Tristan yanked her up, and she forced herself to scramble upward again. He lifted and almost tossed her into the open hatch of the ship then leaped in behind her.

Staggering to the waste disposal unit near the control console, she pushed it open, fell to her knees, and heaved out the contents of her stomach.

Kellen and Dorian charged through the hatch, and Tristan slammed it closed as Kellen raced toward the ship's controls. The ship began to hum with engine noise.

"Thanks for the cover fire, Flop," Kellen said. "You saved our bacon, even if you did miss them." He laughed. "Flop says he didn't miss. He deliberately caused the avalanche because he didn't want to shoot Hallie." Kellen's voice softened. "I don't want to shoot Hallie either, Flop."

Mara rested her head on the edge of the disposal and thanked the Goddess for miracles like genius rab-cats who were precocious with human machines.

The engines revved. Kellen said, "Here we go, get settled. Seat restraints fastened."

Mara tried to stand, but she floundered, her legs refusing to work. Tristan swooped her up and settled in his chair. He fastened himself in and held her in his arms against take-off as she always held Floppy.

She glanced around for the rab-cat. Floppy sat cradled on Dorian's lap. His ears tilted jauntily as if he were very pleased with himself. Mara curled into Tristan's chest. Trying to ignore how deathly ill she felt and her fear of losing her baby, she closed her eyes and concentrated on the sound of Tristan's heart, his scent and heat, and the gentle stroke of his hand on her head.

TRISTAN sat on the edge of Mara's bed, her hand in his, and watched her drift into sleep.

Her face relaxed, the tension and fear disappearing, and he could see again the innocent pixie who'd leaned over him in the hospital and saved his life by the simple loving act of holding his hand and not letting it go through months of fighting death, terrible injuries, and an immoral government. He'd repaid that kindness by taking away her home and happiness, by giving her a remorseless and unstoppable enemy, and by deserting her emotionally when Dorian had reentered his life.

Sighing, he eased her hand onto her stomach then stood up. He motioned he was leaving to Floppy, who curled on the bed beside her. The rab-cat nodded then rested his head back on her leg.

Tristan walked into the ship's control cabin. Kellen leaned back in the captain's chair, a beer in his hand, his eyes on the scanner and the ominous blip of Cadaran's fighter. They'd only bought themselves a half day's head start with their nearly deadly fiasco on Scarpia.

"The bitch is gaining on us." Kellen glanced up at him. "How's Mara?"

"She finally fell asleep. Dorian assures me she and the baby are fine. She just had a bad case of gravity sickness. She's got a lot of courage to have kept going in the shape she was in. Where's Dorian?"

Kellen motioned toward the cabin area. "Speaking of a woman with guts...I sent her to bed." He grinned, his eyes twinkling with mischief. "Why don't you join Dory in bed. I don't need a baby sitter anymore, and I'll cover for you with Mara if she gets up."

Tristan sputtered.

"Go on! I've been walking the cabin at night from claustrophobia, but it's obvious enough what's been eating you. Go have a proper reunion with Dory."

Flushing, he didn't know how to explain he'd been thinking of Mara's bed, not Dorian's, or to admit the gut-wrenching shame he felt for such disloyalty to the woman he intended to marry.

"Don't be so concerned about what Mara thinks. She understands you're through with her. And I certainly understand your seducing her to save yourself. I'm not ashamed of doing that to Hallie. We're at war with the planet and its women. You're being damn decent to set her up on Earth." Kellen grinned. "I just might take a shot at her myself. I need to find a woman of such tenderness to help me get over the sexual cringes, and she fits the bill. She's as beautiful as a Tenly sunset, too."

"Stay away from her!"

"You don't want her, you have Dorian, and I don't intend to hurt

Mara. I might even marry her. What's the problem?"

Panic and anger welled up within Tristan, but he forced himself to unclench his fist. Kellen was playing some kind of game with him, and he wouldn't fall for it.

"I know Mara loves you, but—"

"What does she know about love? She'd never even seen a man before she met me. She hasn't even had a chance to know if I'm the right man."

Kellen shrugged. "A woman who'd risk her life and give up everything for a man must be in love. That's as pure a proof of true love as I've ever seen, and the way I always figured it love's a special living gift given to two people. If they're both willing to cherish it and work to keep it alive, it will stay alive. You might be her first male everything, but if you're willing to work very hard to keep that love alive, you'll be her only love despite the other men she meets. I mean if you actually loved her yourself. I know you don't. You were only using her."

Feeling as if he were blindly treading through mental and emotional quicksand, Tristan flushed again. "I wasn't..."

"Hell, it doesn't matter. We won't live to see Earth again with Cadaran catching up so fast." Kellen sagged. "I've been doing some thinking. It's time we turned and fought the bitch. We should land on the next habitable planet, and I'll go after Cadaran's ship. I should be able to dent them before they get me, and I'll give you and the ladies a head start."

"No. We both go if it comes to that."

"Listen—"

"I have a better idea." Both men jumped at Dorian's voice and turned. Dorian stood behind them. Looking like a little girl dressed for a slumber party, she wore a long white nightgown covered with a simple blue robe. Her long brown hair draped from her shoulder. She held out a data cube.

Tristan took it from her and motioned she be seated beside them.

Kellen grimaced as if in pain and glowered at her. "And what is this wonderful idea?"

Dorian lifted an eyebrow at his surly tone and settled into the chair by Tristan. "I didn't want to say anything until I was certain it was viable. According to the computations I just finished, it is."

"Dory?" Tristan examined the data cube.

"Put it in the computer. The file name is 'Tor.'"

Tristan did as she asked and accessed the file. An astral map of a small segment of space appeared on the screen. A small planet circling a distant star was highlighted in red. "This isn't too far away. What's the point?"

"When I was preparing for my journey to Arden, Tor Orion gave me this data cube. He said I should use it only if all my other options were gone. If everything were hopeless."

"That about describes now," Kellen muttered.

Dorian nodded. "Have you ever heard of Eagle's Haven?"

"It's a spacer myth," Tristan said. "A hidden planet base of smugglers."

"No," Kellen said. "Not a myth. I've heard too much for it to be completely made up."

"It exists." Dorian tapped the screen. "This is a map."

Kellen whistled. "And Tor gave you this? No smuggler in his right mind would pass out this information."

"Tor wanted me to succeed... for your sakes. He thinks a lot of you two."

"Feeling's mutual," Tristan said. "But this?"

"He said you rescued him from the labor camp on Black Tembu. This was the least he could do."

"And he saved our butts a few times in recompense," Kellen said.

"Dory, we've known each other too long. What aren't you saying?"

"All right. He has a crush on me. But it didn't lead anywhere. He knew our feelings for each other so he didn't push it."

"Damn decent," Tristan muttered dryly. "A man of impeccable taste."

Kellen scowled. "The only things Tor loves are his ship and his freedom."

"People change." Dorian shrugged. "Find the subfile 'planet,' Tris."

Tristan typed in the name. A planet with an atmosphere and clouds surrounded by a dense asteroid belt appeared on the screen.

"That is Eagle's Haven."

Tristan shook his head. "No one can get in through those asteroids, and the planet must be pitted with asteroid craters. You couldn't survive all the quakes and destruction when these big babies smash into the planet."

"Tor said that there is a route in. The planet itself is protected by a forcefield."

"That can't be right. We don't have that kind of technology."

"Whoever was there before humans found it did. The field's still in place."

"And the sentients?" Kellen asked.

"Tor didn't know. Rumor has it they are still on the planet. No one who's gone to look for them has ever come back."

Tristan stared at the computer screen and the orbiting asteroids. "It would take the devil's own skill to navigate through these rocks. Kell, think you can do it?"

Kellen flexed his hands. "Before Arden, probably. After all that crap they used on me...I don't know if my reflexes are that good anymore."

Dorian said, "Ask for the file 'navigate.' The route in is programmed and ready to go. All we do is put it in the navigation computer, and it'll fly us in."

"Tor did trust you to give you that," Tristan said.

Kellen tapped his fingers impatiently on the screen. "And once we get in. What then? The smugglers will see we're strangers and kill us."

"I wondered that myself," Dorian admitted. "Tor told me that Eagle's Haven is the private domain of Saxon Haloran, a deposed prince of the Dynamara."

Tristan glanced at Kellen who replied, "A small group of planets—Earth colonies outside the Colony Congress—ruled by a hereditary king. Very medieval in custom but not technology. Machiavellian in the political maneuverings of the nobles among themselves."

"Yes," Dorian agreed. "Haloran lost a power struggle and was forced to flee with his family and a few servants, his enemies hot on his tail. He found Eagle's Haven, and they can't get him there. He opened it up to the smugglers in return for goods and credits. The smugglers are welcome as long as they behave themselves. No fighting or liberties against the locals."

"So we'll be welcome?" Tristan asked.

"We might," Dorian replied. "Or we might have to prove ourselves. Tor gave me the means if we need it. Prince Saxon seems to owe him a big favor, and we're collecting on it."

Tristan studied the planet on the screen. "And we can make it to Eagle's Haven before Cadaran's ship catches us?"

"A few hours to spare if we change course now. A five-day journey. She won't be able to follow us in."

Kellen sipped his beer then glanced down as if surprised to find the can empty. "So we get there, and then what?"

"We wait until Cadaran gets tired of waiting for us and leaves," Dorian said.

"Or runs so low on fuel or supplies, she's forced to leave," Tristan added.

"I don't like it," Kellen said. "We might be trading one prison for another."

"It's the only chance we've got," Dorian said. "Or do you have a better idea?"

A MUFFLED knock rattled Mara's cabin door. She sat up in bed and pushed the control switch by her bed. The door opened. Light poured into the room.

Standing at the threshold, Kellen shifted uncomfortably on his feet. "Flop said you wanted to see me."

"Thank you for coming. Please come inside." She cut up the cabin's illumination then took the small computer she'd been working with off her lap and placed it on the bed beside her.

Kellen perched on the chair by her bed as if ready to escape if she moved toward him.

She smiled sadly to herself at the paranoia he couldn't control even with a woman he knew wouldn't touch him. She'd even turned him down when he'd offered her breeding before she'd known the horrible price he'd pay for the act.

When she handed him the remote control to the door, he studied it blankly. "I'd like the door closed, please. I'd prefer to keep our conversation private. You may open it if you feel uncomfortable."

He flushed. "I'm sorry. I can't help it. I know you wouldn't..."

"I'm sorry, too, Kellen. So sorry and mortally ashamed for what my people did to you."

The door closed, and he placed the remote control on the bed stand with a trembling hand. "How are you feeling?"

"Quite well. Rested after two days in bed."

"I'm glad. It's obvious how much your baby means to you."

"He matters more than anything else in the world." She didn't add that the child was all she had left.

Kellen brushed back his short black curls as if they were much longer. "Tris tell you about Eagle's Haven?"

"He explained our situation. I trust his judgment in getting us safely to Earth. I trust both your judgments."

Kellen nodded.

"I need a friend, Kellen. Someone I can ask advice of." She rubbed her damp palms against her coverlet.

"Tris or Dory?"

She chuckled mirthlessly.

"I guess not." A trace of humor flashed in Kellen's green eyes before he looked away. "Guess I'll have to do."

"You'll be a wonderful friend." She smiled sweetly at him. "First, I wanted to talk to you about Floppy. If something should happen to me, I know Tristan will see to him, see that he gets back to Arden and his people when it's safe."

"Nothing will happen to you."

"Even if it doesn't, there's still the question of Floppy's people. Will you be able to prove they're sentients?"

"Piece of cake." At her confused twist of head, he added, "It will be very easy. They have a complex language structure, oral history and literature, religion, games. The whole gamut of intellectual activity except for writing and mathematics which they don't need with their culture. Very like the dolphins and whales on Earth who have had sentient rights and its protections for three hundred years."

"That's what I want for the rab-cats. When Arden opens up to the outside, I don't want his people hurt or exploited."

"I'll see they aren't. I have some contacts in the Colony Congress from my work with the...," he made a noise halfway between a cough and sneeze, "who live in the Aldo system."

"Wonderful."

"Flop's people are protected by your government?" Kellen scowled as if thinking of the difference between the treatment of the rab-cats and men on the planet.

"They're not allowed as pets. Most of the protection is sentimental and practical. They're loved by the children. They're also excellent predators against the tiny animals which destroy our grain and vegetable crops so the farmers welcome their presence on their farms."

"Hallie told me." Kellen's hand moved toward the door control as if his horrible memories were intruding, then he forced his hand back into his lap.

"When things are more peaceful, and you've had time to sort out his vocabulary and syntax, I'd like you and Floppy to teach me his language."

"We'd be honored."

She took a deep and steadying breath. "I also wanted to ask your opinion about my life on Earth. The culture is so complex."

"Not so very complex. Earth is very accepting of differences. So many from other human cultures return there."

"Tristan said he'll see me settled on Earth."

"Only decent thing to do."

"Tristan is very decent." Her eyes narrowed as she fought a flash of fury. "I do not wish to be settled. I have no desire to be around to see Tristan and Dorian together. It would be too painful and humiliating." When amusement flickered in Kellen's rab-cat eyes, she added defensively, "I have a right to save my pride, don't I?"

"Every right in the world. I certainly wouldn't want to have a close-up view of some other guy having the happiness I wanted with the woman I loved."

Some sadness in his voice made her ask, "This happened to you?"

"Years ago. I fell in love with a happily married woman. I got the hell out of there before I caused any of us any more misery."

"I'm sorry."

Kellen shrugged. "We survive."

"We survive."

"So you want to get away from Tris. What about the baby?"

Angry heat flooded her face. "He called it 'your baby.' Can you imagine that? 'Your baby,' as if it were not his at all."

"Ho, ho, ho. So the angel of Arden has a temper."

"It's not funny. How dare he!" She bit her lips to calm herself. "Well, if he does not wish to claim our child, he does not deserve the right to share its life. I will not be 'settled' by him to assuage his conscience."

"What other choice do you have?"

"I intend to accept his family's hospitality until I regain control of the profits from my mother's energy converter. The credits should come to me on Earth, not to those monstrous rulers on Arden."

"You'll be a very rich woman. What will you do?"

"Did Tristan tell you about my father?"

"Randell the astronomer and explorer. I've read some of his papers. Excellent work."

She blushed with pleasure. "Thank you. I have researched his life. Both his father and mother are still alive in a place called London. He teaches astronomy, and she teaches quantum physics."

"Probably London University."

"Yes. I will seek my father's parents out. They are my blood and my child's blood. They are the only living family I have."

Kellen leaned back in his chair and frowned.

A prickle of uneasiness ran down her spine. "What's wrong with this plan?"

"Don't expect them to welcome you with open arms."

"Because of where I come from?"

"Partly."

"My father loved my mother, and my mother my father. They chose to breed with each other. I was conceived with as much love as any child from an Earth marriage."

"But the harem destroyed your father."

"That is not my sin."

"No." Kellen rubbed his chin.

"What is your true concern?"

"Did Tristan ever tell you about my childhood?"

"No."

"My parents were xeno-anthropologists."

"Like you."

"Yes. They loved me a great deal. I traveled with them and lived among whatever alien sentients they were learning to communicate with at the time."

"That sounds like an interesting childhood."

Smiling with old memories, Kellen nodded. "It was. When I was six, almost seven, we were on Vega II among the Glok." The name sounded like Kellen had cleared his throat. "Starsus plague hit the colonists, and the planet was closed off."

"Like Arden."

"Yes. My parents died."

"Oh, Kellen." She reached over to take his hand in comfort, but some inner warning forced her to withdraw her hand before she touched him and broke his relaxed trust in her. "What happened to you?"

"The human colony was in absolute chaos. They didn't have time for some dead strangers' child. The Glok took care of me." Kellen smiled fondly. "They were good people. A mile above all those so-called humane, superior humans."

"How long did you stay?"

"They found a cure for starsus after a year of deaths. But I didn't want to return to the humans. I was happy where I was. In my fifth year with the Glok, I came down with the plague, and they had no other choice but to return me to the humans to be cured. As soon as I was well, the locals shipped me back to Earth, kicking and screaming."

Mara chuckled. "I can imagine."

"I had a paternal grandfather who was still alive."

"He must have been so glad to see you."

"Hardly. He didn't give a damn about me."

"What is wrong with Earth?" She shuddered with horror. "What is the reason they cannot love their children?"

"It's not Earth. It's just humans. Some of us just aren't cut out for parenthood."

"Children are precious. I don't understand."

"I hope you never do. Arden loves its children because of the plague. The women who conceive do so after a great deal of expense and difficulty. Everywhere else conceiving a child is easy. Too easy."

"What happened to you after you returned to Earth?"

"My grandfather sent me to boarding schools then paid for college. I was to thank him for this largess by staying away from him. I did. He died when I was in graduate school. He left me enough money to pay for *The Helen*." Kellen shrugged. "I never knew family until I met Tristan in college, and he and his loving family more or less adopted me, and the six-year-old kid grieving inside me finally found peace."

Mara considered his story. "So you fear my father's parents might not want me and my baby."

"It's a possibility you should consider."

"Then the child will only be mine." She straightened. "I knew what I would risk when I chose to help Tristan. I knew what I would lose when I contacted Dorian and brought her to Arden. So be it. I would choose the same again and accept the same fate."

"You're one hell of a woman, Mara. Tris is a damn fool."

She grinned. "Yes, he is."

Kellen began to laugh, and she joined him. When their merriment ended, he stood. "You should rest. I enjoyed our talk. I'm happy to be your friend, angel."

"I am happy to be yours." They shared a warm smile, then Kellen turned toward the door. She opened it, and he walked out. She left the door slightly open so Floppy could return when he wished.

Tristan's raised voice filtered through the crack. He was shouting at Kellen. She strained to hear his words then scowled. He was furious that Kellen had seen her, had been in her room alone.

She slammed her fist against her cover. Tristan had not only cut her off from himself, he now seemed determined to destroy any chance for friendship she had.

Chapter 20

Sweat dripped down Tristan's back as he watched the huge asteroids whiz by the ship's viewing screen. He shifted his body instinctively in his flight chair to avoid a massive asteroid in front of them, his right hand miming the flight maneuver he would have used if he controlled *The Trojan Horse*. The ship veered around the asteroid under the navigation computer's control. He grimaced and forced his hand into his lap.

Kellen, his own hand poised over the ship's controls in case of computer error, watched the asteroids with the cool calm of a man who had nothing to lose with death.

His fingers clinching, Tristan scowled. He had a great deal to lose. He wanted to live to see his family again, raise his own family with Dorian, continue his black hole research, spend his nights in bed with...He staunched the image of Mara's face, damp and glowing with passion, and pictured Dorian, fully clothed, snuggling against him in front of a blazing fire.

Satisfied with the chaste sweetness of this image, he turned toward Dorian's flight chair. She slouched nonchalantly, her eyes on the viewing screen, but sweat beaded her face. Of any of them, she had the right to distrust computer navigation after losing David because of a computer glitch.

Beyond her, Mara sat with Floppy in her lap, her arms tight around him to protect him from the ship's rapid shifts in direction. Mara's eyes glistened with excitement, and Floppy leaned forward, his ears tilted rakishly. They acted as if they were on an amusement park ride. Both trusted too much in the computer's program and Kellen's skill. Neither had seen, as Tristan had, a ship explode when an asteroid breached its hull.

Kellen inhaled hard, drawing Tristan's gaze back to the screen. A pock-marked asteroid filled the screen as they rushed toward it. Kellen grabbed for the manual controls, but the ship tilted ninety degrees and whipped edgewise through a canyon and around the asteroid.

"Damn Tor and his show boating," Tristan muttered. If he

survived this mess, he was going to buy Tor a beer to thank him for his help then kill him for scaring the life out of them.

"Exit hole through the forcefield ahead," Kellen warned.

The ship righted itself, and they were into clear space. In the distance was Eagle's Haven, its blue atmosphere and clouds much like Earth's.

"The ship's computer just sent out a recognition code," Kellen said.

"Tor's," Dorian explained. "So we wouldn't get blasted out of the sky."

"Damn thoughty," Kellen said. "Where do we land?"

"That's in the program, too," Dorian said. "The private port near the Haloran home."

"Private?" Kellen lifted his eyebrows. "Tor must be in this prince's good graces."

"As I said, he owes Tor a big favor."

They all became silent as the ship slowed and began to enter the planet's atmosphere. Clouds filled the view screen, then the ship broke through. Below was a blur of green, the gray of mountains, and the blue of ocean. Gradually, the colors became a defined landscape—a small town with a large landing port. Beyond the town was a collection of buildings near a smaller port. The ship veered toward the smaller port and decreased speed. It hovered then gently settled onto the tarmac with a slight bump and cut off its engines.

Kellen unfastened his restraining belt and stood up. "Let's see what amenities this place has to offer."

"And if the natives are really friendly." Tristan came to his feet.

They gathered at the ship's door. Tristan checked to see if everyone was armed then opened the door. Fresh cool air blasted inward, followed by sunlight. The air smelled of rain, damp soil, and piny evergreens.

Tristan waited a moment to get his eyes adjusted to the brightness then stepped down. Kellen hopped down beside him and eyed the tarmac around them. A small hanger near them stood open, exposing the rear of a luxury yacht style spacecraft. Parked beyond were several deadly looking fighters with armaments more than capable of blasting *The Trojan Horse* into rubble. No one was in sight.

The ground was dappled with varying shadows, some moving slowly, others swiftly. For a moment, Tristan thought them cloud shadows, then he glanced up at the nearly clear sky. He winced at his own stupidity. The shadows were from the orbiting asteroids. Even though they couldn't been seen during the day, the sunlight passed through them, and their presence left shadows. At night they must glimmer like shooting stars.

"Seems friendly enough," Kellen said and turned toward the ship's hatch. Before Tristan could protest, he was helping Mara down to the tarmac with his hands around her waist. Tristan scowled but said nothing.

Mara smiled her thanks then glanced at Floppy who leaped down nimbly. Kellen walked away, leaving Dorian to scramble down.

Tristan cursed his inattention, but Dorian seemed unperturbed at his lack of gallantry. She landed with the grace Floppy had shown and examined the area around them. She pointed. "Company."

A small troop convey and a luxury land vehicle rolled toward them from the direction of the Haloran compound. They stopped ten yards way, and the doors of the troop convey thrust open. Eight men rushed out, their laser rifles pointed at them. Tristan remained still as did the others and waited for the brains behind these huge fighters to appear.

The land vehicle's front door opened, and a Zzanon in the same gray uniform as the soldiers got out. He studied them with his reptilian eyes, sunlight glistening on his green scales, then walked over and opened the rear door of the vehicle.

A human woman in her late fifties stepped out. Her graying hair was pinned back in an elegant coil which highlighted aristocratic cheekbones, a harsh nose, and assessing black eyes. She wore a long dove-gray dress of simple yet elegant style and fabric.

"Ma'am," Tristan greeted politely.

She raked them with a cool stare then studied their ship. "The ship is not Orion's, the passengers are not Orion, the ship's code was Orion's."

"We'll be happy to explain, ma'am."

The woman jerked her head toward the ship and ordered the Zzanon, "Search the ship for others."

The alien hissed agreement and walked toward the ship.

Kellen muttered something almost under his breath. Tristan caught Mara's name. He glanced toward her. Not heeding Kellen's warning, she stared at the Zzanon with child-like wonder.

Tristan winced, the lizard people hated to be stared at, but before he could get her attention, the Zzanon stopped in front of her. The snaky musk of his body hit Tristan whose hackles rose in instinctive revulsion.

The Zzanon hissed, displaying pointed teeth and fangs. "You look, warm-blooded one. You not like Zar? You fear Zar?"

Tensing, both Tristan and Kellen prepared to launch themselves at him before he put his poisonous fangs into her.

Blushing, Mara blinked with surprise. "I'm terribly sorry. I didn't mean to be rude. I've never seen one of your race before."

"Not like Zar?" The alien displayed more fang.

"You are a very beautiful people." She smiled with guileless sweetness.

The Zzanon writhed with pleasure, his fangs disappearing.

"Zar," the woman commanded. "The ship."

The alien walked past them and entered the ship.

Tristan let out the breath he'd been holding.

"The angel of Arden strikes again," Kellen muttered to Tristan.

Smiling politely at the woman, Tristan kept his face calm, but she said nothing, her own expression impassive.

After a long wait, the Zzanon stepped out of the ship and closed its hatch. "Empty. Only living supplies. Very specialized medical lab."

The woman lifted an eyebrow.

"I'm an immunologist," Dorian said.

"A healer?"

"Research, not practical healing. I can handle minor medical problems."

"You are not needed here."

Dorian opened her mouth for a snappy comeback, changed her mind, and closed it.

The woman motioned to them. "You will come with me."

Tristan glanced warily at the soldiers who kept their guns leveled then followed behind the woman to her land vehicle. Zar opened the rear door, and the four human prisoners slid into the back seat. Floppy, so far ignored by the woman and soldiers, hopped in and crawled over Kellen to Mara's lap where he sat down, his ears twitching with interest.

The door closed and locked, and their compartment sealed closed in front of them, effectively trapping them.

Making an involuntary noise of panic and closed his eyes, Kellen fought his claustrophobia. Seated between him and Dorian, Mara murmured something to him which made him chuckle, and he relaxed slightly.

Tristan tightened his fists. Mara and Kellen were developing a relationship, and he didn't like it a bit. There was too much of an opportunity for hurt for both of them.

"Well, so far, so good," Dorian said.

Kellen grunted unhappily. "They won't shoot us or feed us to the Zzanon until the Prince checks us out."

The woman slid into the front seat with the driver, and the vehicle began to move toward the compound. They remained silent through the drive. The vehicle rolled past a huge mansion of gray marble with immense columns in front. Two large wings extended from the main building.

Mara gasped with pleasure. "How lovely."

"Should see the winter palace. Bet it's really something," Kellen whispered wryly.

The vehicle turned the corner of the left wing and stopped in a small paved courtyard.

"Servant's entrance for us," Kellen said. "Tor must not have been that high in his Royal Highness' graces."

The vehicle's door opened. Beyond, their eight guards waited with drawn guns.

Tristan slid out, followed by the others. The woman stood beyond the guards. "You will surrender your weapons. No one armed has an audience with His Highness."

Tristan lifted his laser pistol with two fingers and offered it to the nearest guard. "Anything you say, ma'am."

When the guards had received their weapons, the woman motioned them to follow her. "If you carry other weapons, our detectors will discover them. You will die then." With that pronouncement, she led them toward a rear door of the palace. They hastened after her, their armed guard flanking them.

The door swung open. Tristan glanced as unobtrusively as he could at the lock—a magnetic power bolt on a door which despite its elegant wood appearance was reinforced by luxel. To get in would require an assault cannon, to escape would be impossible.

He'd better be able to talk the Prince into helping them, or they weren't getting out of here.

The guard inside the door snapped to attention as the woman neared. They entered a hallway with gleaming black stone floors. The walls were white with gold swirl patterns which lighted the passageway.

The door behind them closed with the finality of a prison door.

The guard contingent had been left outside with the Zzanon. The woman escorted them through a long winding series of hallways. They caught glimpses of the rooms along the halls. Most were simple yet richly furnished offices. They passed more of the gray uniformed soldiers who saluted the woman. Whoever she was, the men respected and feared her. As they went deeper into the palace, they began to pass civilians in the clothes of household staff. These people also saluted the woman, but not in the military style. They touched their foreheads with their palms and motioned outward and downward, bowing slightly.

The woman nodded absently to most, but her eyes never ceased their assessment of the surroundings and all who passed her.

They entered a large room of even greater elegance. Chairs sat near the walls and a gold chandelier glowed above them. A guard stood at parade rest in front of a massive closed door on the other side of the room. He snapped to attention.

The woman said, "He awaits us?"

"Yes, Seneschal." The guard opened the door.

The next room was even larger and more grand, the walls lined with tapestries. Another guard waited at another door.

The woman stopped and gazed at them like a mother taking stock of children before an important event. She frowned, as if not liking what she saw. "You have passed the weapons' test. You may see His Royal Highness. Behave with decorum."

Tristan raised an eyebrow with equal arrogance and stared at her as if the comment were beneath his dignity to recognize.

Her eyes widened as if she were surprised, then she motioned to the guard, who swung open the door. Beyond was an even larger room, more subtly lighted by glowing gold along the ceiling. The black floor was decorated with a family crest of gold—an eagle in full attack with a Latin verse beneath. Tristan translated, "Strike and be damned."

The man on the throne in the center of the room stood and examined them. He was tall and slender, perhaps in his early fifties. Only a trace of gray touched the temples of his dark brown hair. His hooded predator eyes and beak nose told Tristan where the planet had gotten its name. The Prince wore the mantle of power with the ease of an aristocrat born to command and be obeyed.

The woman bowed. "The occupants of the ship, Your Highness."

"Thank you, Seneschal." He turned to Tristan and the others. "And you are?"

Tristan bowed slightly. "Tristan Mallory of Earth. Full professor of astrophysics and astronomy at Triangle University." He added a few more titles, honors, and degrees for effect. He held out his hand to the others.

"Dorian Dalia of Earth, a doctor of medicine. Private research in immunology. Affiliated with John Hopkins University of Space Medicine."

"Mara Randell." Mara said the last name defiantly as if expecting someone to refuse her the right to her father's name. "Doctorate in astrophysics. Private research." She glanced down at the rab-cat sitting at her feet as if tempted to introduce him but wisely remained silent. Floppy was going to stay a long-earred larot if at all possible.

"Kellen Votrain. Xeno-anthropologist specializing in linguistics and exploration. Affiliated with Triangle University."

The prince sat down on his throne and tapped his lips with his finger as if amused. "My, what an educated group." He motioned toward the woman. "My seneschal, Hoshi. I am Saxon Haloran. Alas, only a masters degree in human galactic history. First Prince of Tara, First Cousin to the King of Dynamara, Lord of..." He waved his hand negligently. "I won't bore you with the list."

"Your Highness." Tristan waited politely for the questions to begin.

"How did you come by Orion's code and the route into my planet?"

"He gave it to me, Your Highness," Dorian said. "In case of dire emergency. He knew we could be trusted to keep his secrets, and yours, safe."

"That remains to be seen. You will explain further."

"Gladly, Your Highness," Tristan said. "Kellen and I were on the way to a science conference on Omikron Five. Our ship was attacked by slavers."

"Slavers!"

"Yes, sir. Certainly you've heard of all the ship disappearances near this quadrant. The work of slavers."

"Interesting. Continue."

"I was almost mortally wounded so they left me to die and took Kellen. Mara found me. We contacted Dorian on Earth, and she came to help us. We traced Kellen and rescued him, but now the slavers are on our tail. We had no choice but to use Eagle's Haven as refuge, or we would have been recaptured."

"A melodramatic little tale."

"It's the truth." Not the complete truth but the truth.

"And you expect from me?"

"Sanctuary until it's safe to leave."

"And you offer?"

Dorian said, "State of the art medical equipment from Earth. A complete immunology lab worth a small fortune on Earth. It's priceless out here."

The Prince shrugged as if the money meant nothing.

Dorian said, "Tor Orion told me to tell you that you owe him a debt beyond price. If you help us, he will consider that debt paid."

"Cheaply paid."

"Not to us, it isn't," Tristan said. "A life of freedom is beyond price."

Kellen whispered, "Amen," under his breath.

"I will consider your story. You will be my guests until I decide your fate." The prince glanced at the seneschal. "Make arrangements."

"Yes, Your Highness."

He turned back to Tristan and the others. "You will join me for the evening meal. My wife will be pleased to meet you. She sees so few people. This world does not often host people of such culture and education, especially women of refinement." He nodded politely at Dorian and Mara.

"We'd be delighted, Your Highness." Tristan bowed, and the audience was over.

CLUTCHING her bundle of clothes protectively against her breasts, Mara peeked out into the hallway from her quarter's doors. The long hall of the guest quarters was empty. She breathed a sigh of relief and crept into the hall. Tristan's rooms were across the hall, Kellen's to his left, and Dorian's to the left of hers.

Crossing the hall, she tapped on a door. A male voice said, "Come in."

She opened the door and slipped into the room, closing the door quickly behind her. Stopping, she looked around. These quarters were much like hers—a sitting room, and a bedroom and bath, but this one was decorated in dark wood furniture with ornate carvings and the walls had wood plaques.

Kellen walked out of the bedroom. He wore a simple black robe of some silken material and a towel draped his shoulders. His hair was wet, his legs bare. He started when he saw her. "Thought you were

Tris."

Mara glanced nervously at the door. "Is he expected?"

"No." Kellen examined the dresses draped over her arm and the carrying case in her hand.

"I did not mean to interrupt your shower."

"Just finished. A water shower was heaven. First I've had since..." He scowled. "Another lifetime."

She held out the dresses. "I need your advice. That Hoshi had a servant bring these. To wear while I'm here. I know so little about Earther fashion." She smiled wryly. "Even on Arden I knew little about fashion."

Chuckling, Kellen relaxed slightly as if no longer suspecting her reason for being there. "Need help picking out what to wear to our royal meal?"

"Please."

He walked over to her and took a dress from her arm. "Let's look and see what we've got." He held out the sparkling confection of gold and silver. "Hmmm. Nice. A party dress but less formal than what you want." Resting the dress on a chair, he studied the next dress with equal care. He explained what occasions it was suitable for.

After several minutes he had all eight dresses spread about the room on the furniture. Only three were suitable for that evening.

"Which one do you think?" she asked.

"Something elegant which will knock Tris' eyes out."

"I don't care what he thinks." As the words left her mouth, she knew she was lying. "I *shouldn't* care what he thinks."

"Keep holding that head up high, angel. Don't let his damn fool ideas ruin your spirit."

"I will not."

"Now to this." Kellen picked up a white gown of silken material with gold thread shot through the fabric. He held it up to Mara and squinted as if imaging her in it. "This one. Definitely."

"It's beautiful, but..." She blushed. "It shows so much of my..."

"You have lovely breasts, an absolutely splendid figure. This will only show a bit of cleavage. It's not at all indecent by Earth standards."

"We always wear pants and never show any...cleavage."

"That's because you haven't got men to dress for. Bring men into the equation, and comfort and decency get factored right out."

She examined the gown. "I can see that."

"Trust me. Now your hair." He studied her shoulder length hair which she'd tied neatly at the nape of her neck. "Pinned up, but with curls like so." He indicated ringlets around her face. "You'll look like an earthly angel."

"I can do that. My best friend was always fussing with her hair, and I saw her do that." Mara fought a stab of loneliness. "I miss Patta."

"Buck up, angel. You got shoes and underthings with these?"

She nodded.

"Good. I guess you're all set then."

"Only one thing." She held out the case. "This contains... I think it must be paint for the face. Like Lolly wore on Scarpia."

Kellen's mouth twitched as if he were fighting amusement. "The tavern madame, owner, you mean."

Mara nodded.

"You don't want to look like she did. Your makeup should be more subtle."

Mara sighed with relief and admitted shyly, "I don't know how to put this 'makeup' on."

TUGGING at the tight, itchy collar of his black formal tunic, Tristan stared at the women's doors.

Behind him, Kellen chuckled. "Many centuries have passed in human history, and we've yet to make something comfortable to wear at these functions."

Tristan glanced at the chronometer on his wrist. "Or make women be on time."

Mara's door opened. She half-turned into her room. "I'll tell you all about it when I get back, Floppy. Have a nice nap." She wore a long white gown laced with gold which clung with indecent zeal to the curves of her body. The low cut of the gown revealed the tops of her full breasts with just a hint of cleavage, and a short slit in the skirt allowed tantalizing glimpses of her calf. Her chestnut hair was swept away from her face which was framed by feathery curls. She was an ethereal fairy queen.

His loins aching, Tristan inhaled hard. He'd never seen her more beautiful and desirable. She seemed a different person from the child-woman he'd known on Arden.

She pulled the door closed and faced them.

Tristan forced his emotions back into control. He opened his mouth to compliment her, but Kellen said, "Perfect, angel. Absolutely perfect. You're gorgeous."

She smiled shyly at Kellen. "You really think so? The..." She motioned toward her face.

"Just right." Kellen grinned his approval.

Tristan fought a surge of jealousy. She hadn't even looked at him as if his opinion didn't matter to her.

Mara examined Kellen in his black formal outfit with the gold piping around the neck and down the sleeves. "You look dashing. That is the right word to use?"

Kellen bowed. "An excellent compliment."

Dorian joined them from her room. She wore a gown of bronze silk which floated down her like the petals of a flower. Her hair was braided with copper thread and pinned in a coronet on top of her head.

"How beautiful," Mara whispered.

"Stunning," Tristan said.

Dorian smiled happily.

Clearing his throat as if fighting some strong emotion, Kellen held out his arm to Mara. She stared at it. He said, "A gentleman offers his arm to the lady he's escorting."

"Oh." Mara placed her hand on his elbow. Kellen tucked her arm properly into place and began to walk down the hall.

Tristan scowled then offered his arm to Dorian. She absently took it, her own eyes on the pair in front of them. Kellen whispered something to Mara, who giggled.

"What are they up to?" Dorian wondered.

"It's called a relationship." Tristan could barely force the words out of his tight throat. Mara had never looked at him once.

"Good," Dorian said as if she were saying, "Good riddance to them both."

Perhaps he'd been foolish to believe he and Mara could remain friends after being lovers. The only thing left between them seemed to be a carefully controlled anger and avoidance on Mara's part and guilt and lingering jealousy on his. "I don't want them to be hurt."

"They're adults. They can take care of themselves."

"I hope they can."

A soldier waited for them at the entrance to the guest quarters. He bowed slightly then began to escort them through the palace.

Tristan struggled to put his mind back on their more pressing problem. If Prince Saxon didn't approve of them and their behavior, he could toss them back to Cadaran or shoot them himself. Their future depended on tonight.

SITTING back in his chair, Tristan sipped the last of his wine. Beside him, Prince Saxon had turned his attention to his meal with the same absorption he'd shown in his conversation with his dinner guests.

Taking advantage of the lull, Tristan studied the others at the magnificent dining table filled with crystal, gold plates and utensils. Dorian sat across from him, her own focus on her meal. Kellen sat to her left and to his was Mara who chatted with Haloran's wife, Princess Linnea, a dark willowy woman in her early thirties who had remarkably kind brown eyes. Perhaps the Prince had sensed Mara's discomfort in the social situation and had placed her beside the Princess.

Mara and the Princess had talked comfortably through the meal, primarily about children and pregnancy. Mara, apparently, hadn't mentioned her own intimate knowledge of the second subject. These people seemed remarkably old-fashioned about marriage and children, and Mara and his relationship wouldn't please them.

Tristan winced inwardly. He wasn't exactly comfortable about it either. He'd never dreamed of conceiving a child in anything but a permanent love relationship, but the circumstances had been against him. He tried never to think about Mara's child.

To the Princess' left was a blonde, blue-eyed beauty named Xera who was some kind of lady in waiting to the Princess. She had flirted with Tristan when introduced, but the bulk of the man between them had thwarted her since they'd sat down to their meal. Riordan Haloran had the dark predator face of his older brother, but he was more massive with wide shoulders and a heavier build. Xera seemed content to flirt with Riordan, who handled it with casual familiarity, and with Kellen, who sat across from her at the table.

Kellen was anything but casual. Her coy smiles and fluttering lids, which a year before, he'd have reacted to with male relish, made him squirm and look away from her. He'd rested his arm on Mara's shoulders and touched her hand with his, Mara hadn't resisted his touch, but Xera had ignored these signals that he and Mara were a couple. If anything, it made her more eager for the hunt.

Several times, white-faced, Kellen had turned to Mara, who'd somehow been able to calm him.

Riordan, in the mean time, flirted with Mara, who was blissfully unaware he was trying to get her sexual attention. He postured and preened with renewed effort, but Mara only glanced at him as if doubting his sanity.

Tristan had to stifle a laugh behind his napkin at the ridiculous clash of two cultures, blind to each other's body signals.

"Your Highness." Kellen bent past Dorian. "I understand that sentients live on this planet."

"I understand the same thing, Dr. Votrain, but I have never seen them." The prince smiled. "No one has. Not closely."

"Or lived to tell about it," Riordan added. "I want to take some men into the mountains and flush them out, but my brother won't let me."

"The mountain ghosts, that's what my people call these sentients, control the forcefield which holds back the asteroids. We do not wish to anger them by attacking them. They could drop the forcefield," the prince explained.

"They would be condemning themselves as well," Tristan said.

The prince shook his head. "They live within the mountains. We have found vast underground cities they've abandoned."

"So that's why you know so little about them," Dorian said.

"Tris believes the asteroids are fairly new, created when the moon exploded about two thousand years ago," Kellen said. "To survive the asteroid hits, this race must have moved underground until they discovered a means to hold these rocks back, and by then, they had no desire to live in the open."

"A fascinating theory," the prince said.

Riordan motioned with his hand as if brushing away unimportant matters. "What I want to know about is the firestone." He turned to Tristan. "Some old smuggler, when we first came here, wandered into the mountains. He came back mumbling about going into one of their caverns. He found a firestone in some sort of sculpture. He said the stone was as big as a man's head."

"That's impossible," Kellen said. "No one's ever found one bigger than a man's fist."

"It would be a planet's ransom," Dorian said.

"Or a king's price to let us return home," the prince said. "It would even turn my cousin's cold heart toward me."

"You wish to return to your home world?" Tristan asked.

"Unlike Milton's Satan, I would rather live as a lowly subject on Tara than rule in Hell." The prince motioned around him. "Despite the pleasant surroundings, this world lacks scope."

"And people," the princess added. "Our children deserve better than this exile."

"Exile is death." Mara's voice vibrated with such sadness that the others looked toward her.

The door to the dining room opened, and a woman swept in like a barbarian queen. She wore a black formal gown, her arms trimmed with black fur. A thick gold collar necklace encircled her neck.

Kellen inhaled hard and lurched back in his chair.

Tristan finally recognized Cadaran, and his heart lurched in his chest.

Her cold panther eyes settled on the fugitives, but she smiled warmly at the prince as if they were old friends. "How splendid, Your Highness, you've caught my fugitives for me."

Chapter 21

At Cadaran's words, the occupants at the table went dead still. Tristan fought a wave of sick horror. Kellen jerked backwards and started to stand, but Mara and Dorian grabbed his arms and forced him to remain seated.

Cadaran smiled with satisfaction at their reaction and swaggered forward.

"I wasn't aware, Your Highness," Tristan said coolly, "that a man of your stature dealt with slavers."

Haloran eyed Tristan as if he were speaking an unknown language.

"A slaver? Me? Hardly." Cadaran bowed slightly to the Prince. "These people are terrorists, Your Highness, who attacked my world and fled."

Tristan sneered. "And a dangerous group we are. We forced people to listen to science lectures. Mass boredom. It was horrible."

"Enough," the Prince ordered and stood.

"I apologize for disturbing your meal, Your Highness. Allow me to take my prisoners, and I'll not disturb you again."

"These people are my guests." The Prince spoke with a silkiness edged with steel.

"And I am a profitable partner in your world. A trusted partner of some years standing."

"Who would do well not to displease me."

Cadaran bowed in acknowledgement.

"May I remind you, Your Highness," Tristan said, "of your obligation to Tor Orion and his request concerning us."

Princess Linnea made a garbled noise of distress.

"This is disturbing my wife. We will discuss this situation tomorrow." Haloran turned to Riordan. "Escort Cadaran Hastings to her compound." He stood. "The rest of you are excused."

"THE prince sent word he would see us after two this afternoon." Tristan studied the formal garden he and Dorian walked through. The morning sun beat down around them, the ever present asteroid shadows dancing among the flowers and shrubs.

Dorian caught his hand in hers and squeezed. "What are we going to do if..."

His shoulders slumped, Tristan pondered the question. "Haloran's a gentleman of the old school. I think I can convince him to give you and Mara sanctuary."

"I'm not some simpering, helpless female."

Tristan chuckled. "Definitely not, but if he offers, you take sanctuary. If for no other reason than to survive to take Arden down when you get to Earth."

"You have a point. I'll bring the cavalry to your rescue."

Although he didn't believe he'd live to see that rescue, he nodded. "Take Mara to my parents. They'll take care of her and the child."

"I won't fail you, Tristan."

"You never have. I always believed you'd come to Arden. Until I found out you thought I was dead."

"I sensed you weren't dead. I'd have felt it." She smiled and tugged his hand. "Come on. Let's enjoy the pretty morning."

"But Kellen's..."

"He can wait a few minutes."

Dorian lead him toward a sheltered nook created by an arbor of violet climbing roses. Sitting down on the marble bench, she pulled him down beside her then nestled into him, her head on his shoulder. He wrapped his arms around her and kissed the top of her head. "You smell nice."

"What a romantic smooth talker you are."

"I love you, Dorian. I have since we were kids. I just didn't know the depth of my feelings until David..."

"I love you, Tristan." She lifted her face expectantly toward his. He closed his eyes and kissed her gently on the lips. Sighing, she sagged into him, her arms going around his neck.

Their lips mingled, tasting yet never quite opening. Finally, Tristan pulled away, his body stiff with an unease he couldn't quite understand.

Blushing, Dorian buried her face into his chest.

He stroked her head. "This new relationship will take a bit of getting used to."

"Mmm hmm."

"Well, I guess we'd better go find Kell and have a council of war."

Bolting to her feet, she said sarcastically, "Can't let him fret."

"What makes you two so hostile? Ever since Scarpia."

"I'm not hostile; he's hostile."

"Of course," Tristan said dryly. "Not hostile at all."

"He's a neurotic jerk. God knows he has a right to be, but...All I did was touch him to get his attention, and you'd think I raped him."

"I see," Tristan murmured, although he didn't.

"I'm glad someone does." Dorian tossed her braid off her shoulder with a shake of her head. "Let's go."

They walked silently through the garden until they reached an open lawn. Kellen sprawled on a sunny patch of grass, his arms under his head, and stared up at the cloudless sky. Floppy stretched out beside him like a mellow puddle of black fur.

Tristan chuckled. "Guess Flop was going into sun withdrawal, too."

"Yeah. The whole time I was in the windowless, airless little pink hellhole, I didn't know which was worse—the rape and torture or being trapped in that coffin away from the sun. At least the rape was over soon, the suffocation was eternal."

Dorian cleared her throat.

Kellen jumped and glowered. "Didn't know you were here."

"I brought her for a council of war," Tristan said. "The Prince has given us an audience at two."

"Maybe he wants us in one spot to give us to his 'partner.'"

"Tor believes in his honor," Dorian said. "He may side with us."

Sitting up, Kellen shrugged. "Miracles can happen."

"Where's Mara?" Tristan asked. "I thought she was out here with you and Flop."

"The Princess sent her a personal invitation to meet the little princesses and princes. She left a while ago."

"Maybe Linnea can help us," Dorian said.

"Mara mentioned that," Kellen said. "She was going to give it a shot. Maybe the Angel of Arden can pull off that miracle."

Tristan plopped down beside Floppy, who wiggled an ear in sleepy greeting before he closed his eyes again. Dorian settled next to them with more grace. "Kell and I stayed up half the night thinking of options. We may have a way to convince the prince to help us without having to tell him the truth about Arden."

"And if not, there's Plan B," Kellen said.

"What's that?" Dorian asked.

Stretching, Kellen said casually, "I kill myself before she can take me."

LINNEA'S baby boy nuzzled Mara's breast, his tiny hand loosening its grip on her finger, then drifted into sleep.

Mara slowed her rocking, her heart aching with tenderness for this babe and the one she held within, and smiled down at the infant.

Princess Linnea took the child from her arms then gently placed him in his crib. Mara stood, took one last look at the beautiful child with his inky black lashes and sweet face, then followed Linnea out of the nursery. They walked down the hall past the other children's rooms toward the public part of the palace.

"You will be an excellent mother," Linnea said.

"I pray I have the chance." Mara rested her hand protectively on her stomach. "If Cadaran takes us, she will put him into slavery then kill me as she will have killed Dorian, Kellen, and Tris..." Mara's voice broke.

"I will do my best for you, but I have no power over my husband's ruling decisions."

"What control does that evil woman hold over him?"

Linnea straightened arrogantly. "No one rules my prince."

Mara considered her impression of Haloran. "No, I don't think anyone could. But there must be a reason he deals with Cadaran."

As if no longer offended, Linnea relaxed slightly. "When first we came here, we had little. Hoshi found Cadaran elsewhere. With her contacts and wealth, we were able to establish ourselves with the smugglers."

"Mmmm. I wonder how she..." Mara thought of Kellen's last owner with her addiction to imported pleasure drugs and the lotus which had been brought to Arden and changed to its most evil form. "So that's how my world is filled with poison."

"I beg your pardon."

"No matter. This must be her distribution point for illegal pleasure drugs."

"We do not allow such filth here." Linnea raised her eyebrows haughtily. "My prince does not approve of them."

"Not allowing and preventing are two different things. Even for a prince of such worth and nobility. You are dealing with a clever smuggler, after all."

"My prince does not allow. It is not done."

Mara hoped she was right. "What do smugglers carry besides pleasure drugs?"

"Computers and agricultural items which have high tariffs on some worlds, and medicine. That is a major item."

"Why? Medicine is good."

"Tor Orion explained it to me thus. Some worlds have powerful rulers, many who believe themselves voices for God."

"Theocracies?"

"Yes, many are called so. These rulers often believe a woman should not have the right to choose when to have a child." Linnea shuddered delicately. "Some sickly women who should not have children or have too many children to provide for need birth control medicine. They seek it from black marketeers who buy it from smugglers."

"Mmmm." Mara tried to imagine not wanting to have a child.

"Other rulers will not allow certain healing drugs because they believe God must choose when a person dies, and they will not allow the healers to heal."

"That's appalling. The Goddess gave us wisdom and the desire to learn to help us fight disease and misery. Nothing would stop me from seeking medicine to help my child, not even some foolish leader."

Linnea made a garbled noise of distress and leaned against the hall wall.

"Princess?" Mara rested a hand on the other woman's shoulder.

"Forgive me. The pain and fear still cling, and when reminded..." Linnea brushed a shaking hand across her forehead. "We nearly lost our eldest boy to a rare disease found only in our royal line. We did not have the medicine to cure him."

Mara recalled the tall slender boy with his father's austere face and his mother's tender brown eyes. "How terrible for you. It must have been agony. What happened?"

"Tor risked himself. He went to Dynamara and stole it. If they'd discovered the medicine was for us, the King would have killed him horribly. Tor saved our son." Linnea sniffed and blinked tears.

"Well, thank the Goddess he brought it back. It saved your child's life, and the great favor owed might save my child's life. A double blessing from the Goddess for one act of kindness."

"I pray it is so for you."

Mara thought over what they'd discussed. "And so Cadaran is a business partner to your husband."

Linnea began to walk forward again. "I do not like her. She is not welcome in our private quarters. My prince does not dispute my wish that she not be our guest. She has her own compound beyond the town."

"She hates men and despises women who do not."

"She condescends to me, and her eyes when she is around my prince.... She says nothing, but her eyes..."

"Her eyes," Mara agreed.

"Zar, my husband's chief bodyguard, does not like her. He claims to be able to see heat and color from mammals. Cadaran's is black and blood red." Linnea chuckled. "He hisses and shows his fangs when he sees her. He believes her capable of murdering my prince."

"Quite capable. If she no longer needed him."

"Zar, however, likes you. Your aura is like sunlight and the green of plants."

"How kind of him." Mara beamed.

"I know someone else who is quite taken with you. Riordan thinks you a woman worthy of a princess' crown and a prince's bed."

Mara twisted her head quizzically. "He wishes to marry me?"

"His interest is stirred. Perhaps later. You do not speak of the baby's father."

"I came to his bed wishing no other man for the rest of my life." Mara struggled with her anger. "He chose another woman over me and our...*my* baby." She admitted, "I still love him. I wish no other man."

"It must be Tristan. You never looked at him last night."

"Yes. He will marry Dorian."

"He watched you at the dinner table. He could not force his eyes away from your beauty."

"He was afraid I would make some horrible social gaffe."

Linnea smiled knowingly. "Dorian and handsome Kellen with the wounded green eyes did not look at each other either. Yet they were always aware."

"You are mistaken, Princess. They do not like each other, and Kellen was so badly hurt when...He will probably never take a wife."

"If he is capable of mating, he will take the mate of his heart one day."

"I hope so, Princess. I pray to the Goddess it will be so. He is a very special friend."

Linnea stopped at the entrance to the main palace. "Fight for what you want, Mara. Fight for his love with all your love and pride."

"I don't know how. I knew nothing of men and women or love before I met him."

"Do any of us really know? Love is a mystery we must all solve but never do. Follow your heart and what it tells you, and you will not fail."

"I'll try." They hugged each other goodbye, then Mara departed through the door of the Prince's private quarters.

Mara's soldier escort awaited her at the door. She said, "I'd like to join the rest of my party in the garden."

The soldier nodded and led her through the palace to an outer door. He opened it and pointed. "That way, ma'am."

She smiled her thanks then began to stroll alone through the topiary shrubs and flowers toward the lawn where she'd left Kellen and Floppy. The sun caressed her face and shoulders as she walked.

"Mara."

At Tristan's voice, Mara paused and turned around. He walked toward her. "Is anything wrong?"

He stopped. "No, I was..." He stared at her dress, a pretty pink floral print which came to her knees, then his gaze trailed down her stocking clad legs to her shoes then back up to her hair which she'd curled and left free. "I was waiting for you. The others are ready for a council of war."

"Let's go then."

"You look beautiful. You should wear dresses more often."

Her heart raced, but she said calmly, "We do not wear dresses on Arden." She turned and began to walk toward the lawn.

"Can we talk?" He led her to a small arbor covered with violet climbing roses, and she settled on the marble bench.

"What do you wish to speak of?"

Sitting down beside her, he rubbed his palms on his hips. "Any luck with the Princess?"

"She is on our side, but the Prince will not be influenced by her on state decisions. Cadaran helped him set up his smuggling operation here."

"That doesn't sound good."

"The Prince does not know that she smuggles pleasure drugs and lotus and uses this as a distribution point. He does not approve of pleasure drugs."

"Hmmm. That's a thought."

"The Halorans, especially the Princess, don't like Cadaran or trust her."

"But they continue to deal with her."

Mara remained silent.

"I guess we're right not to tell the prince about Arden and our plans to destroy Cadaran's power."

"I have no more to tell you." Mara stood.

Catching her elbow, Tristan pulled her back down. "About Kellen."

Angry heat flushed her face. "Am I allowed no friendship? Do you wish to put me in a box where I can see no one and where no one will care for me?"

"I want you to have a happy life. Really. I want you to find a man who loves you." Tristan smiled tenderly. "No one deserves a happy life more, but...Kellen's so fragile emotionally, and you're on the rebound."

She twisted her head in question.

"A person who's been hurt in romance sometimes starts a new relationship before she's ready. Before she's come to terms with her loss. That new relationship can only cause pain."

"Kellen is my friend. As Patta is my friend. As you were my friend before we..."

"And you might hop into bed with him, too, and hurt yourself and him."

"I will never hurt Kellen, and I will not sleep with him. I am not," she paused, searching for an unfamiliar word, "promiscuous. I would never share my bed with any man unless I love him." She stood.

"What the hell do you know about love for any other man? You're so damn naive you don't know what flirting is. Prince Riordan flirted half the night with you and you never noticed."

Her eyes narrowed as she glared at him. "You lost all right to share my life the day you left my bed." She thought frantically for some Earth term to express her feelings. "Butt out, Tristan Mallory."

"Now see here." His fair face pink with emotion, he jumped to his feet. At the corner of his mouth was a smear of red, the same red as Dorian's lip paint. He had been kissing Dorian!

"Go back to your precious Dorian. You have a right to bully her." Mara spun and began to stomp away.

Grabbing her arm, he jerked her back around. "I haven't finished."

She caught his wrist. "I can break your hand, Earther. You with your puny low gravity bones. Let me go."

Inhaling hard from pain, he released her. "I only want what's best for you."

"It is my life, and you gave up all right to it and our baby. Go back to your Dorian." Her heart aching with longing for all she wanted but could never have from him, Mara glowered at him. "Go back to Dorian, Tristan. She is what you wish."

He opened his mouth.

Remembering Linnea's words about fighting for what she wanted, Mara grabbed Tristan's tunic and pulled him against her. She pressed her lips against his. He remained still a moment as if stunned then began to back away. She wrapped her arms around his neck and held him. With her lips and tongue she wooed him with all the knowledge he'd given her of passion.

His arms encircling her, his lips and tongue meshing with hers, he relaxed under the pressure of her body. She concentrating on his reaction, easing them both toward the ground. Tristan landed on the grass with her on top of him, their lips never parting. She ground her pelvis against his and rocked as if in lovemaking.

When he groaned, his staff hard and throbbing against her through their clothing, Mara disentangled his arms and pushed them above his head and held them there.

Freeing herself, she stood. He remained sprawled on the ground, his face flushed, his eyes glazed with passion and stunned surprise.

Smiling, she swept back her hair from her face. "Go back to Dorian,Tristan, and see if she can do that to you." Laughing wickedly, she left him. Let Dorian wonder about her lip paint on him now.

ONCE again, Tristan stood in the formal throne room before Prince Saxon Haloran. Behind him, he could sense the others in his party.

His face impassive, The Prince sat on his throne. "I have given your request for asylum a great deal of thought. I have also given consideration to Cadaran Hastings' request for your return to her world."

His own face carefully empty of emotion, Tristan asked, "And your decision?"

"I do not wish to offend my loyal partner, and yet, I must honor Tor Orion's request for your safety. Therefore, I grant you safe asylum on this planet, she cannot harm you here, but once you leave it, you will be without my protection. If either party breaks this imposed truce, they will feel my wrath."

Tristan relaxed slightly. It was better than he'd hoped. "Would you give us a head start off the planet?"

"That I cannot give."

"You trap us here. Her ship is faster and better armed."

Haloran lifted his eyebrows arrogantly. "I can offer no more."

"I have a proposition then, Your Highness. A means to give us a head start, and yet free you forever from any obligation or need to deal with Cadaran."

The Prince's hawk eyes hooded as he studied Tristan. "I do not wish her dead."

"I'm a scientist, not an assassin, Your Highness," Tristan replied evenly. "Are you aware that she deals in pleasure drugs and lotus?"

"I do not allow drug traffic on my world."

"Yet she supplies my world with these poisons," Mara said. "And with human slaves."

"I do not believe this."

"Believe," Kellen said evenly. "I was Cadaran's personal bed slave for months." His voice broke slightly. "She kept me injected with lotus to make me perform."

Tristan glanced back at Kellen, whose face was white with humiliation. Kellen clutched Mara's hand. Tristan turned back to the prince, whose own eyes were on Kellen.

Kellen said, "Would you like to know her sexual preferences, her scars, her fondness for pain—mine and her own?"

"Enough."

"After she grew bored with me, she sold me to a very wealthy woman who had a stronger taste for torture and kinky sex than Cadaran. She was also addicted to pleasure drugs. Supplied by Cadaran with the lotus to use on me."

Haloran wiped his palm fastidiously on his thigh. "These are grave charges."

"I will take a truth test, if you wish," Kellen said.

"Cadaran must use your world as her distribution point for those drugs," Tristan said. "I wouldn't be surprised if her slavers use this world, too."

"Do many young male smugglers disappear here?" Kellen asked.

"A few shanghaied by other smuggler ships." A flicker of worry darted across Haloran's face.

"She is an evil woman," Tristan said. "We offer you a chance to free yourself from her obligation and free yourself from this world."

"You have my full attention."

"The firestone as big as a man's head. We will find it for you in the sentients' underground city."

"I do not wish to anger the mountain ghosts."

"We're scientists, not hot-headed young soldiers. Kellen is a premier expert at first contacts. We will negotiate with them. They must be as eager to free themselves of humans as you are to leave. The firestone is a small price to pay for that."

"You would be a dangerous political opponent, Dr. Mallory."

Tristan allowed himself a brief smile. "Academic politics are far more vicious than any other."

Haloran laughed.

"Even if we cannot get you the firestone, we will have opened friendly contact with your planetary neighbors. A great plus for you. By allowing us to go, you do not break your promise of our asylum. If we succeed, you gain your own freedom; if we do not, you lose nothing."

"And you will gain?"

"Two weeks head start before you let Cadaran chase us. Her wrath will be nothing to you then."

"Hmmm." The Prince tapped his lips. "Very well. I will provide supplies and transport for your expedition."

"We ask your brother's help in gathering all the known information on the sentients and their cities. I get the impression he's already well versed on the subject."

"You are correct. Easily granted. Riordan will be most irritated not to be included in this expedition."

Tristan kept the relief of not having to deal with the arrogant soldier from his face. "I ask one more favor, Your Highness. We wish to leave Mara here in Princess Linnea's care."

"My wife is much taken with Dr. Randell. Your reason?"

"She is pregnant and prone to gravity sickness. Dorian believes the traveling conditions will be too severe." Tristan smiled and said dryly, "After a great deal of discussion, Mara agreed."

"Granted. She will be our guest."

"If we do not survive, I would be deeply grateful if you'd see she gets safely to Earth. Ask Tor to take her to my family."

The Prince nodded assent, and the interview was over.

CADARAN sprawled back in her leather chair and examined the woman sitting, straight-backed and regal, in the chair opposite her in

Cadaran's private study.

She glanced out the window to where Lt. Hallie was leading her troopers in exercises in the fenced-in compound. "You have news, Seneschal?"

"The Prince will not be moved in his decision to protect your fugitives."

"If they return to Earth, I'm destroyed. You and your precious prince will be destroyed as well."

"The Haloran is beyond your petty problems, d'Hasta."

"Is he now? Is he beyond missing all the profits my enterprises bring to this world?"

"He is above the minor details of our arrangement. It is I who must dirty my hands in commerce."

"Illegal drugs, slaves, and military weapons are a bit plebeian for His Royal Pureness." Cadaran smirked.

"He must have the wealth and prestige worthy of his greatness. I returned that to him with all the means at my disposal."

"And with all my means, I can take it away. You should remind him of that."

"You cannot touch my prince. His protection is complete."

"How complete is his protection of the fugitives?"

Hoshi raked her with arrogant black eyes. "They are beyond your reach in the palace."

"But outside the palace?"

Something of passion touched Hoshi's aristocratic face for a moment, and she clinched a hand. "They, all but the one called Mara Randell, go into the mountains to the sentients' cities in two days. They seek a firestone worthy of the High King. My prince wishes to negotiate his return to Tara with it."

Cadaran lifted her eyebrows in surprise. "I see. He wishes to leave this place and our obligation to each other."

Hoshi said nothing.

"And why do you share this information? You know I will stop them."

"I do not wish to return to Tara. This world has more scope for me. I will keep my prince here where he will live safely and remain a prince, not a commoner on Tara."

Cadaran fought a knowing smile. "So you are as moved by private greed as the rest of us. I thought you were unnaturally selfless."

"It is not wealth I seek."

"Power is the biggest turn-on, isn't it? Much better than sex. But you wouldn't know about that." Cadaran stroked her chin and thought. "I'll arrange an 'accident' for the others when they leave the palace, but Mara..."

"You may not enter the palace. I will not risk the Prince's security."

"Me? Me seek the Prince's life? Never."

"Zar will feed well the day you try, d'Hasta."

"Then you must lure Mara out."

"It can be done. I will attend to it. You must use some of your hirelings."

Cadaran nodded. "I regret not seeing to it personally. Having that sweet little scientist causing me such problems galls me. But I leave her in your capable hands. I will console myself with killing the others personally."

Chapter 22

Mara leaned her chin on her hand and stared at the computer screen. Sighing, she tried to make herself concentrate, but the biography of Albert Einstein which had enraptured her the day before was hopeless gibberish now.

Hopping up, she paced the length of the sitting room of her quarters then glanced at her wrist chronometer. Only three hours had passed since Tristan, Floppy, Kellen, and Dorian had left for the sentients' mountains. She forced herself to sit back down at the computer. At a minimum, they'd be gone a week. It wouldn't do her or her baby any good to worry so.

She should have gone with them. The hard traveling would have been infinitely easier than this waiting and worrying, and she'd tried to convince the others of that, but they wouldn't listen. Her only victory had been in convincing them that Floppy should go with them rather than staying to protect her. Protect her from what? Here in the Prince's private wing of the palace under Princess Linnea's kind eyes she was as safe as a child in her mother's arms. Floppy, with his mountain-born skills, was needed far more with the others.

Mara scrolled the biography's text forward in search of something to catch her attention.

Someone knocked discretely at the door.

"Enter." She straightened and glanced down at her pink tunic and pants. They were not stylish by the Princess' standards, but they would have to do.

A soldier she'd seen before stood hesitantly in the open door. "A message, ma'am."

Smiling, she took it, broke the gold Haloran seal, and opened the text. The words "accident," "Kellen," and "badly injured" leaped out at her. She glanced down at Riordan Haloran's signature then read the letter completely. Tristan and the others had been in a flitter accident outside Smugglers' Town. Kellen had been seriously hurt.

She wobbled to her feet. "Who brought this?"

"One of Prince Riordan's men, ma'am. He's waiting for you."

"I must go to them. My friends have been hurt." She bent and wrote a note to the Princess on the letter then gave it to the soldier. "Take me to my escort then give this to the Princess."

"Yes, ma'am."

Mara followed him through the private wing of the palace. Another soldier stood at parade rest outside the entrance to the main part of the palace.

"How are they?" Mara asked the new soldier. "What happened? How badly are they hurt?"

The huge man studied her with stolid blankness. "Had orders delivered with that message. Orders told me to take you to Smugglers' Town. Don't know nothing about any 'they's.'"

"Very good. Take me then." She glanced at the other soldier. "Please carry my note to the Princess." Not waiting for a nod of confirmation, she headed out the door with her escort in tow. "Come. I must get to my friends."

The ride to Smugglers' Town in the soldier's flitter was a blur of fear and horrible imaginings. Mara sat with her fists clinched and prayed for the others' safety.

The flitter passed over the outskirts of the small town with its narrow dirt streets and ramshackle buildings. Beyond, toward the center of the town, the buildings were more substantial, but here they were similar to the worst she'd seen on Scarpia.

"Is there a hospital here?"

The soldier snorted a laugh. "Got a doc. If he is a real doc. His Royal," the man paused as if fighting back a crude word, "Highness and his folks has a good 'un."

Mara nodded. The Princess' physician had examined her and concurred with Dorian that she and the baby were healthy. "Why are you taking me here then? I don't see a crash site."

"Orders is orders." He guided the flitter downward into one of the most narrow and filthy streets she'd seen then landed it with a careless thump.

The soldier released Mara's door latch, and she stepped out as it swung open. Straightening, she looked around for Prince Riordan. The flitter door began to close, and the soldier gunned the engine in preparation for lifting off.

Bending down, Mara shouted into the closing door, "Wait. Where is...?"

"Stay here. Someone'll come by."

She glanced uneasily at the dark alley beyond her. In the distance she could hear raucous, drunken male singing. "But..."

"Orders is orders." The door closed, and the flitter lifted, spraying her with dust, and vanished over the tops of the buildings.

Muttering a vulgarity Kellen was fond of, she glanced about. She'd best find as safe and inconspicuous a place as possible to wait until Prince Riordan or one of his men came for her. The street was lined with buildings which tilted with rotting precariousness into the street. Glass windows were covered with dirt or shattered. Doors and porches sagged. If anyone lived here anymore, she could see no evidence. The alley behind her was no better. Trash littered it, and the faint scent of urine wafted toward her.

Wriggling her nose, she decided the street was a better waiting spot. Struggling with an overwhelming sense of panic, she began to pace back and forth in front of the house she'd been left at. Kellen could be dying,the others horribly injured, and she had been dumped and forgotten in the foulest street in a criminal's paradise.

After several minutes, her unease increased. In the alley behind her, something crunched down on a metal can. She twisted toward the sound.

A big man in shabby civilian clothes stood and stared down with disgust at the beer can which had betrayed his presence.

Mara began to back away.

His smile was feral. "You ain't going nowhere, woman."

"I'm Prince Saxon's personal guest. If you touch me, he'll kill you."

"Where you're going, he'll never find you." The man pulled a knife and stalked toward her.

Spinning around, she began to run down the deserted street. Behind her, she could hear the slap of big feet in the dust. The steps moved closer.

With a burst of speed, she swerved into an adjoining street. Another man stepped in front of her. She slammed into him. His arms encircled her, trapping her against his chest. Screaming with terror, she broke free, her fingers going for his eyes, her knee for his groin.

He dodged the knee and swore.

Other hands grappled her from behind, and her hair was jerked back, forcing her chin up. She gasped with pain. Iron fingers clasped her hand behind her back as cold steel touched her throat.

The man she'd run into stared dispassionately down at her, the knife he held steady. "Got her, Eb?"

Her other arm was yanked behind her, metal encircled her wrists, and she heard the snap of closing restraining bracelets. Eb chuckled nastily. "Like a sheep to slaughter."

Afraid to wiggle against the blade, Mara said through clinched teeth, "I'm Prince Riordan's personal guest. If you hurt me, he'll kill you."

Eb grunted. "A pretty one, ain't she? Would bring a fine credit down at..."

"You want to risk *her* finding out." The man holding the knife shivered. " No thanks. We kill this one and hide the body."

"Please...Whatever you're being paid, the Prince will top it." Mara fought tears, unwilling to let them see her cry. "Please. I'm pregnant."

"Two for the price of one." Eb grabbed her cuffed wrists and dragged her backwards. "Let's do it and get out of here." Mara stumbled and fell to her knees.

The man in front of her lifted his knife and advanced toward her. She gazed pleadingly up at him. His face changing from blankness to stunned astonishment, he blinked and pitched forward.

She threw herself sideways, avoiding his body. A razor-edged throwing disk protruded from his back.

Something rustled beyond her, and a dark shape launched itself over her and pounced on the man behind her.

She was jerked upright and forward. Screaming, she fought the arms around her.

"Easy, Mara. It's Riordan," a male voice whispered against her ear.

Trembling, she leaned into the prince, who wrapped his arms around her waist and buried his face in her hair.

His fangs nearing Eb's throat, Zar pinned the struggling man to the ground.

"Don't, Zar," Riordan commanded harshly. "Let's hear what this one has to say."

Eb glowered, his eyes held by the lizard man's. "I ain't telling you nothing."

"Then you shall be Zar's lunch. His people prefer live prey."

"Nothing."

"He will paralyze you with his venom then eat you at his leisure. His people pride themselves on keeping their prey alive for a long period before it bleeds to death."

Zar smiled, displaying hideous fangs. “Yes. You will be a fine meal.”

Shuddering, Mara looked up beseechingly into Riordan’s dark, handsome face. Even Eb deserved better.

Riordan winked at her and barked, “Talk or be lunch.”

Eb squirmed as Zar neared his throat. “All right. All right.”

“Who hired you?”

“Hastings. Cadaran Hastings. Told us to finish the woman who would be left here. Hide her body where no one would ever find it.”

“She’s capable of doing her own killing. Why hire you?”

“She was heading into the mountains after some others.”

A woman’s voice said, “I knew it. Prince Riordan, it is as I suspected after I discovered the false message from you about an accident.” Hoshi, the Prince’s seneschal, advanced out of the shadows. “Cadaran Hastings intends to prevent Dr. Mallory’s party from reaching the firestone. She wishes to keep our Prince trapped here.” Hoshi smiled as if achieving a great victory. “Cadaran is worthy only of a quick death with no trial and the loss of all she holds here.”

Mara felt stupid from the last minutes of shocks and terrors. “Cadaran is going after Tristan? He and the others didn’t have a flitter crash?”

Riordan bent and released her restraining cuffs. “There was no accident. They should be reaching the mountains by now.”

Zar dragged Eb to his feet. “We must stop the Hastings before she destroys the golden one’s most precious.”

Mara blushed. “Most precious. Every one of them.”

Zar shoved Eb down the street toward other soldiers.

“Let’s go then,” Mara said.

“You will stay with the Princess,” Riordan ordered.

“Can you find Tristan immediately?”

“No, but I know their general location.”

“Well, I just happen to be a homing signal to one member of the party. If I come near them, they’ll find us. You have to take me.”

Riordan shook his head. “Who?”

“My adopted son Floppy.” Mara beamed more widely. They had no choice but to take her now.

Pleasure growing in his eyes, Riordan laughed. “We are alike in one thing. Neither likes to be left behind in a fine adventure. Let’s go.”

KELLEN shouldered his back pack and watched Dorian disappear into the nearby rocks and bushes to relieve herself. Floppy followed a discrete distance behind her on guard. The mountains around them looked safe enough, but predators, both human and animal, stalked them.

Tristan pulled his own pack out of the flitter and dropped it on the ground. He bent and retrieved his laser pistol and holster, then fastened them around his hips.

Glancing once again to make certain Dorian was out of sight, Kellen said with mock innocence, "I miss Mara already."

"You'll only hurt yourself and her if you push this romance." Tristan scowled at him.

"What about you? Will it hurt you?"

"Dorian and I..."

Kellen muttered a vulgarity and said dryly, "It's embarrassing the way you two can't keep your hands off each other."

Tristan flushed. "We aren't hormonal teenagers."

"You aren't hormonal anythings. I've seen more sex play between you and Elaine, and that's nonexistent."

His friend shifted uncomfortably. "With Mara around...We thought it best to wait until she..."

"It all comes back to Mara. I bet you had your hands all over her all the time."

"We were lovers. I've never denied that."

"Mara loves you."

"She snuggled up to you fast enough."

Kellen fought a smile. "We're only friends. Platonic friends. That's all it will ever be. She loves you."

"And I..." Tristan looked in the direction Dorian had gone.

"You are so insecure about Mara's feelings and the depth of your own for her you're tossing away your relationship for one with a woman you treat like Elaine. A nice safe relationship."

"I love Dorian."

"I love Elaine. She's the kid sister I always wanted."

"It's different."

"You're a damn fool, Tris."

"Butt out."

Kellen opened his mouth to prod some more, but Dorian pushed through the bushes and joined them. He lifted her pack and helped her slide it on. She nodded thanks, her brown eyes meeting his.

Pain scorched his loins, and he bit his lip. God, he wanted her, couldn't help but want her, even with the phantom lotus pain punishing him for that hunger. She definitely wasn't a sister to him.

"Let's get going." Tristan slammed the flitter door closed.

They began to walk down the mountain valley. Floppy loped on ahead, his ears upright with excitement. They trudged several miles through rough mountain terrain along a dried river bed. The mountains around them were pocked with entrances to the sentients' deserted underground cities. They'd decided, after studying Riordan's maps and notes, on an area near most of the mountain ghost sightings. Perhaps they'd find an entrance to an inhabited city.

Tristan paused to examine his map. "Our entrance should be around here." To their right was rocky canyon wall, to the left rocky wall with a bit of thorny evergreen shrubs.

Dorian shook her head. "I sure don't see one."

Floppy trotted to the shrubs and sniffed around them. He wiggled his ears. Kellen translated, "Flop smells moving air coming through the bushes. He's going to check it out." The rab-cat disappeared under the bushes. A minute later the evergreens shook violently and moved outward, exposing a cave entrance wide and tall enough for two humans to walk abreast. Floppy waved them forward with his ear.

"A hidden door!" Tristan said.

"Since the door's working and is hidden, there must be sentients down here," Kellen said, fighting to contain his excitement. "I think we've hit the jackpot."

"Or signed our death warrant if the natives are unfriendly," Tristan added.

"They've killed no one so far."

"Men have disappeared," Dorian protested.

"The dangers of the mountains and Cadaran's slavers probably explain them," Kellen said. "Hell, if the sentients have the technology to keep the asteroids up, they could have wiped out Haloran's people years ago."

Dorian shifted her pack on her shoulders. "I hope you're right. I'd as soon not be massacred by sents after coming this far."

Kellen unhooked his light from his belt and flicked it on. "I'll take the lead." The others followed him into the cave. The entrance was narrow for several hundred yards, the path smooth, then it opened up into a passageway at least twelve feet wide and ten feet high. As they left the cave's entrance, the door closed behind them. "It must be weight sensitive."

Ahead of them, Floppy wiggled his ears. "Cut off your lights," Kellen translated and flicked his off. Blackness surrounded them.

Tristan swore as the walls began to glow an eerie orange which lighted the section of tunnel they were in. By human standards, the glow was dim but offered enough illumination to show their way.

He touched the wall. "It's cool to the touch. Some kind of chemical reaction. Must be like the natural glow of the Earth firefly."

"Flop says it lights up when you near it," Kellen said. "Body heat activated?"

"Very sensitive if it is. It's lighted a good twenty feet ahead of us." Tristan pulled out his knife and scraped the wall then deposited the glowing powder into a piece of folded paper which he folded again and stuck in his pocket. "I'll get this analyzed when we get home."

"Always the optimist," Kellen muttered and walked on.

They traveled for miles, usually at a slight downgrade, through passages similar to what they'd first encountered. Kellen became slightly mesmerized by the glowing orange lighting and the sameness of the scenery.

When the wall glow turned green toward a crook in the passage, he stumbled to a halt. "What the..." He shook his head then advanced forward again. Floppy, who'd been scouting ahead, scooted around the corner and collided with his ankles.

He stumbled, and Tristan caught his shoulder before he collapsed on the rab-cat. Unhurt, Floppy wriggled his ears frantically. Kellen translated, "A big drop right ahead."

"Green must be a warning. Like red is in human culture." Tristan collected a sample of glowing green powder with his knife blade.

Kellen rubbed his bruised ankle. Floppy was solid muscle and bone for all his furry cuteness. "I'll keep that in mind." He edged forward with caution. Right past the corner, the passage floor ended sharply. He shone his light downward—a five-story natural drop to another passage.

Tristan played his light around their passage. "No indication of a means down."

"I guess it's ropes." Kellen slid off his pack and rustled among the contents. He pulled out his climbing gear.

Dorian moaned unhappily.

"She likes heights and climbing even less than I do," Tristan said.

"The acrophobic twins. Wonderful," Kellen muttered. "You can come down with me, Dorian. Tristan can bring Floppy."

Her face a sickly whitish green in the alien light, Dorian smiled gamely. Kellen outfitted her with a climbing belt then slipped his on while Tristan rigged the climbing rope to the rock face.

Kellen hooked her belt to the rope and helped her to the ledge. "I want you to go over. The belt won't let you fall."

"What about you?" Her voice was remarkably calm although she trembled. She had guts.

"I'll go down with you using my hands."

"You'll fall!"

"I'm a trained climber. Don't worry about me."

She slid over the edge and dangled, her nose against the face of the cliff. Kellen grabbed the rope and clambered down until his body covered hers. He spread his legs around hers then braced his feet against the cliff. His hands he brought around her waist then back to the rope. "I've got you. You won't fall."

"But you might." Flinching slightly as his lower body rubbed against her buttocks, she trembled with something that wasn't fear.

He forced himself to ignore his reaction to her closeness. "Okay, I'm going to hum 'The Blue Danube Waltz' and at every end line 'dum dum' we're going to descend a few steps."

"What do I do?"

"Just catch yourself with your hands and feet if we get too near the wall. I'll control the descent."

"Let's get this over with."

Kellen began the waltz, and they went downward, their bodies swaying together in a painful intimacy that was far more terrifying than any fall.

SIX of Prince Riordan's soldiers advanced down the mountain passageway ahead of Mara and the prince. Each held his laser pistol in case of ambush.

Mara rubbed her sweating forehead and kept pace with the men. Afraid of being left behind, she'd never admit she was weary after the last hours of travel through the subterranean passages. Somewhere ahead were her friends and probably Cadaran and her troopers ready to ambush them.

Zar, who appeared to possess some of the olfactory abilities of a hunting dog, was certain humans were ahead. He'd been able to trail them through the mountains from their flitter to the bush-hidden entrance to this cave, but he could not tell whether that scent was left by

Tristan's group or by Cadaran's troops. Or perhaps by both.

Biting her lips, Mara refused to dwell on all the disastrous possibilities for those she loved.

The glowing orange light flickered on Zar's scales as he trotted toward them from the tunnel ahead.

"Halt," Riordan said quietly, and the men opened ranks to let Zar through. He stepped in front of them and wriggled slightly with what Mara had learned to recognize as pleasure.

"Closer we get. Scent strong. Soon find golden one's most precious."

Mara smiled in reply. "They will come to us."

Riordan nodded. "We will take a break."

Wandering over to a large boulder, she plopped down. The passage had become rougher as they'd advanced through the mountain. Most of the passage appeared to be natural cavern now, widening and narrowing at odd intervals. The area they were in was a small cavern littered by boulders.

Yawning, she stretched.

Riordan settled cross-legged on the ground beside her with the elegant grace that defined his movements. He grinned. "Tara is a beautiful world. I'd love to show it to you."

"My world is beautiful, too. One day, if it becomes safe, you must come, and I'll—"

"You are most obtuse, Mara Randell."

Mara flushed. "Are you flirting with me? Tristan said you flirted at the dinner. I looked up the definition, but it did not go into detail. I must get Kellen to explain this flirting." She added, "On my world, we do not flirt."

Riordan sighed. "I wasn't flirting. I was asking if there might be a future between us."

"Oh!" Mara considered how she should answer then decided on the truth. "I love Tristan. I will always love Tristan. There will be no other man for me. Even if Tristan does not return that love."

"Linnea told me so, but..."

"One day you will find a woman worthy of your love who will return those feelings. You are a splendid man."

"Dr. Mallory is an idiot. Dorian is a striking beauty, but...You have eyes as tender as Linnea's. I would never care for a woman without those eyes."

Mara lowered her gaze shyly. "I'm deeply honored to be

compared to her. She's one of the most extraordinary..." A flicker of light by the rock caught her attention. She bent and picked up a clear crinkly wrapper. She studied it then sniffed. Mint and cinnamon wafted toward her.

Riordan bent. "What have you found?"

Mara held out the wrapper. "Do you have these here?"

"I've never seen one before."

"It wraps a special kind of candy on my home world...Cadaran's home world. It's a great favorite among my people."

"Would any of your..."

"Absolutely not. I packed everyone's..." She crushed the paper in her hand. "Cadaran and her troopers are ahead of us."

Riordan stood then helped Mara up with a hand. "Let's get moving, men. Our enemy is between us and the people we must save."

DORIAN stared in appalled horror at the passage in front of them. Once again, they'd found a deep drop off, but this time the eight-story step down didn't lead to a new passage. Instead, it was a great natural trough between them and the passage.

Kellen whistled. "Must be thirty feet across."

Tristan shook his head. "The mountain ghosts certainly don't want visitors, do they?"

"We turn around?" Dorian said hopefully.

"Kell?"

Kellen studied the cavern's roof and pointed. "We use the climbing gun to attach ropes there and swing across."

"Oh, no." Dorian tottered over to a nearby boulder and plopped down before her knees gave out. Closing her eyes, she shuddered as she imagined herself swinging over that deep canyon. It had taken every ounce of courage she'd had to go down that cliff, and this was ten times worse.

Touching her shoulder, Kellen said with surprising tenderness, "Don't worry. I'll get you across. All you have to do is hold onto me, close your eyes, and I'll do everything."

She smiled weakly. "I won't wimp out on you."

"That's my girl." He rested his hand on her head in a strangely gentle and possessive benediction, then scowled and walked back to the canyon.

With a puzzled frown, Tristan studied her, then his gaze trailed to Kellen then back to her. She smiled for his benefit then turned her back on the canyon and examined the enormous amphitheater of a cavern they'd just passed through. Rocks, boulders, and natural stalagmite and stalactite formations were jumbled about. The orange glow of the sentients' lighting gave them an eerie hellish cast.

She stood. Why was the orange still glowing in the back of the cavern when they'd passed through long ago? "Tristan." He walked over to her. "Look."

He drew his laser pistol then glanced around. "Where's Floppy?" He called out the rab-cat's name.

His high-gravity muscles exaggerating his cat leaps, Floppy bounced down the passage toward them.

"Mystery solved." Tristan holstered his pistol.

The cavern echoed with the whoosh of the climber's gun then a stone ping and crunch as the metal hook holding the rope fastened itself into the cavern roof. Kellen muttered, "Perfect."

Dorian winced. A second shot was fired.

Floppy slid to a stop in front of Kellen, who was tying off the other end of the two ropes to a small stalagmite, and began to wiggle his ears.

"You sure?" Kellen came over to Tristan and Dorian. "Mara's heading this way. Flop senses she's at least within a mile of here in the direction we came from."

"She snuck out and followed us!" Dorian said.

"No," Tristan replied. "That's not her style. She promised to stay so she'd stay."

Kellen nodded in agreement. "Something must be wrong to bring her after us."

"There's nothing to do but turn around," Tristan said, "and find out."

Floppy wiggled his ears in farewell then blasted back down the passage toward Mara like a furry rocket.

"We can go at a more reasonable pace." Tristan slung his pack over his shoulders.

A neutral expression carefully pasted on her face, Dorian replaced her pack. She couldn't dislike Mara. Who could dislike a woman with the kindness and courage to rescue Tristan and Kellen at the cost of her own life on Arden? But Mara always meant trouble, whatever Tristan and Kellen thought to the contrary.

They were almost out of the huge cavern when Floppy exploded toward them from out of the darkness. Panting, he waved his ears frantically.

"Cadaran's close behind us with ten troopers," Kellen translated. "Mara's not with them."

Tristan snapped his fingers. "That's it. Mara must be with Prince Riordan and his men. She came so Flop would sense her presence and warn us. Smart."

"I told you we should have brought a communications set," Dorian said.

Kellen shrugged. "Cadaran must have all the local frequencies bugged and jammed. I would in her situation."

"Do you want to run or fight?" Tristan said.

"Run," Dorian said.

Kellen shook his head. "Better to get them now when we can pick the time and place of ambush. We'll have them pinned between us and Haloran's men."

"Agreed." Tristan studied the great cavern. "Now, all we have to do is pick our spot."

THE sound of laser fire echoed down the passageway. Beside Mara, Prince Riordan swore. "We're too late. The fighting's started."

Mara's heart pounded with terror as she stared into the darkness beyond them. If anything should happen to Tristan, or Floppy, or Kellen, or even Tristan's beloved Dorian. Mara urged Riordan, "We must hurry."

"You stay behind me. I'll see you're protected."

"I can prot—" A small dark blur charged toward them.

Riordan aimed his laser pistol. Mara grabbed his hand. "No. Don't shoot."

Floppy ran to them and pounced upward into Mara's arms. She buried her face into the heaving rab-cat's fur and hugged him. Floppy butted his head gently against her neck.

"Oh, Floppy." She straightened. "Thank the Goddess you're safe. Are the others safe?"

Floppy nodded and pointed with his ears toward the sound of shooting.

"Riordan, this is my son Floppy."

Riordan bowed gravely in greeting. "Can you lead us around behind the enemy?"

Floppy nodded, caressed Mara's cheek with the tips of his ears, then hopped to the cave floor.

Riordan motioned to Zar, who came to them. "This is Zar. He will lead my men into battle. I will watch over Mara."

Nodding again, Floppy motioned with his ears for Zar to follow him.

The lizard man glanced at Mara as if in disbelief.

"He's a sentient from my world, Zar. I raised him after his mother was killed. He's very intelligent and has the hunting senses, speed, and agility to equal yours."

Zar hissed and wriggled with pleasure. "Golden one always surprises Zar. Zar go now. Save most precious." He disappeared down the passage after Floppy. The men trotted after them.

"We will follow at a more discrete distance," Riordan said, gazing longingly at his men.

"I'm sorry to spoil your male fun."

"An honorable warrior always guards the ladies first." Riordan smiled briefly. "Come."

Mara stayed close behind him as they entered an enormous cavern lit intermittently by glowing light.

Riordan's men seemed to be going to the left side of the cavern behind many of the boulders and stalagmites. Cadaran's troopers were in the front center of the cavern behind boulders. They fired upward to their right and left, the laser fire straight lightning in the dimness.

Riordan paused and studied the battlefield. "Excellent. Your party ambushed them from above with fire from two directions. They've pinned them to one spot. We'll just go in and mop up."

"Don't underestimate Cadaran. She's a vicious, smart fighter."

"So am I." He paused. "We shall go to the right away from the fire my men will draw. That will leave me in the position of finishing the enemy who will flee away from the fighting."

Her hand on the butt of her holstered laser pistol, Mara stayed close behind him. They reached the right wall and began to climb on their hands and knees a ridge that jutted from the wall. The ridge rose at a gentle incline toward one of her parties' firing positions.

Keeping her head low, Mara wished herself a small target. If Cadaran saw them, they would be easy shots. Directly below, Mara could hear the buzz of Cadaran's troops' weapons, then they were past.

"We need a safe firing place," Riordan whispered softly and kept crawling.

After several minutes, they reached the ledge above the defenders. Mara peered over the edge.

Tristan knelt behind a stalagmite and fired down at the troopers. Mara's heart gave a pained jolt of fear and recognition.

Sensing her gaze, Tristan spun, his laser aiming. He stopped, blinked, then waved to her to go back down. She shook her head and pointed toward Riordan. She mimed hiding.

Shaking his head in disgust, Tristan returned to his attack on Cadaran's forces.

They crawled upward to where the ridge lifted a lip of rock at its edge tall enough to offer protection. Riordan motioned she pass him and take cover. He slumped flat.

She crept over him and moved upward. The ridge ended abruptly. She gazed down into a great darkness. "Oh my!" Shuddering, she backed a few feet and crouched behind the lip of rock.

Riordan peered over the lip at the fighting. He lifted his pistol and began to fire.

The ridge shook as lasers fired back, and rocks splintered above them. Dust and gravel showered down on them. Mara covered her head with her arms.

"Damn, the rock's rotten," Riordan said. "We're sitting ducks if we move."

Mara grimaced. Prince Riordan was not the great fighter he believed himself. Tristan or Kellen wouldn't have done anything this stupid. "Stop shooting, and they'll ignore you."

Riordan eyed her with disbelief and fired downward.

Laser fire blasted around them. The ridge shook beneath them and began to crumble under Mara. She scrambled toward Riordan.

The ridge's end collapsed, and she slid toward the abyss, her fingers scratching for purchase. Riordan grabbed for her and missed, and she was falling downward. She heard Riordan's scream of horror, then Tristan's, and she fell into darkness.

Chapter 23

Tristan's scream of despair echoed through the cavern. Dorian shuddered as she watched Mara disappear silently into the darkness, her hands flailing in search of something to stop her.

All laser fire ceased as she fell.

Crouched beside Dorian, Kellen repeated the same violent curses over and over again and smashed his free hand against the boulder they hid behind. Tears glistened in his eyes.

Dorian bit her lips and blinked to fight her own desire to cry.

A stunned hush filled the cavern.

Kellen swore once more and began to shoot with cold anger. The enemy returned fire, but now they aimed for the stalactites which hung above them. Dorian gazed upward in frightened fascination. Were they as rotten as the ridge which had killed Mara?

Stone gravel powdered down from above, and a rumble filled the air. Fifty feet in front of them a stalactite bigger than a column of the Prince's palace crashed downward and smashed into a million boulder-sized pieces. Dust rushed toward them.

Dorian covered her eyes as it reached them. The monstrous crash echoed back and forth through the cavern. A laser shot, and another chunk of ceiling disintegrated in front of them. She sneezed as small gravel and dirt sprayed them.

Kellen tugged her sleeve. "Cadaran's troops have to keep changing position to hit the different formations above us, but Riordan's men are slowing that movement. Get your pack. We've got to get out of here before they can shoot again."

"Where?"

He jerked his head toward the canyon.

"We'll be in the line of fire," Dorian protested.

"Look." Kellen pointed toward the enemy.

She blinked with bleary disbelief. The fallen debris formed a wall between them and Cadaran. The enemy couldn't hit them but were still able to hit the stalactites above them. Soon they would be completely sealed in. Laser fire struck over their heads.

She grabbed her pack and ran toward the edge of the canyon with Kellen right behind her. A stalactite exploded above where they'd been.

Tristan waited for them at the ropes. His face was grim with a blank coldness she'd never seen before, and tear channels ran down his dirty cheeks. Brown with dust, Floppy sat beside him with his ears drooped flat against his skull.

Kellen touched Tristan's shoulder. "Go first with Floppy. I'll need help landing with Dory."

His expression never changing, Tristan nodded. He slid on his climber's belt then tucked Floppy into his pack and fastened it closed. Kellen helped him settle it on his shoulders.

Dorian buckled her own belt as she watched Tristan hook his belt to the rope. He tugged the connection tight, took one look at the distant other side, then jumped off the edge.

Terror crawled up Dorian's back as Tristan sailed through the air, the abyss beneath him. She tried not to think of Mara's lifeless, broken body beneath them; she tried not to think of her own journey across with Kellen.

Reaching the other side, Tristan released the rope. He fell a few feet and landed, stumbling. He straightened and turned to face them.

"Our turn next, Beautiful." Kellen patted Dorian's shoulder.

Lasers buzzed. Dust showered downward.

Kellen glanced up, swore, and shoved Dorian down, covering her with his body. The universe shook, and explosive noise surrounded them.

Finally, it was over. Dorian floundered beneath Kellen, but he didn't move off her. She wriggled from beneath him and stared. Chunks of stalactite were strewn everywhere around them. Kellen slumped prone, his back peppered with small rocks.

She brushed at the rocks then pulled her med-kit from her pack.

"Dory!" Tristan shouted.

She ran her scanner over Kellen's body. "No broken bones. Bad bruises. A concussion."

Kellen stirred. He lifted his head, his eyes red and barely focused. "Get out of here. Now." He motioned upward with his hand and winced.

A laser bolt exploded against the huge stalactite above them.

"Go! Leave me."

"Like hell." She shoved her med-kit back into her pack then reached down to Kellen, dragging them both to their feet. His body draped against her, she wiggled out of her climber's belt and fastened it around Kellen's waist.

"Go!" he pleaded.

"Shut up." She cinched the belt closed then searched for the rope that would carry them across.

"I can't..." He sagged.

She walked crab-like to the rope, pulling him along, grabbed the rope, and fastened it to Kellen's belt as she'd seen Tristan do.

Kellen muttered into her hair, "Thought you were afraid."

"Scared spitless. Shut up." Laser fire buzzed above them. Dust fell.

Dorian reached the edge of the canyon, wrapped her arms around Kellen, buried her face into his chest, and jumped. The stalactite above them crashed downward in an explosion of noise.

The world swayed dizzily, and she felt the abyss trying to draw her in, then strong arms caught them and pulled them to solid ground.

Tristan released Kellen's belt from the rope. "You can let him go now."

Dorian burrowed tighter into Kellen's nicely sweaty chest.

"Let him go, Dory."

She reached out and clasped Tristan's arm to assure herself she was on solid ground then let Kellen go. Tristan eased his body down. Kellen was unconscious again.

"Look." Tristan motioned toward the canyon.

Grabbing her med-kit, Dorian glanced back. Boulders covered where they'd been. One more second of delay, and she and Kellen would have been dead.

"At least they can't follow us now," Dorian said cheerfully. "It looks like a solid cave-in."

"And we can't go back the way we came. We must find another exit, or we're buried here." Tristan smashed his fist against his thigh. "I hope that fool Riordan and Cadaran kill each other." A flicker of emotion touched Tristan's face. "Bastard. He let Mara die."

Dorian sensed that if Tristan gave in to emotion, the grief would paralyze him, and they couldn't afford that luxury now. She tugged at his sleeve. "Your pack's wiggling. Let Floppy out."

Zombie-like, Tristan obeyed her. The rab-cat hopped out and shook himself then walked over and sniffed Kellen's body. He cocked his head in question.

"Unconscious," Dorian told the rab-cat. "Nothing seriously

wrong."

Floppy nodded, rubbed his cheek against Kellen's, then walked over to the edge of the canyon and gazed downward.

Dorian tugged Tristan's shirt again. "Help me with Kellen." They settled him comfortably and wrapped a blanket around him. She brought out her scanner and went to work.

Her gaze kept shifting from her scanner readings to Kellen's still, dirty face, impossibly handsome even now, to Tristan's shocked blankness,to Floppy who perched at the edge of the canyon near where Mara had fallen. Dorian feared that Tristan or the rab-cat might leap in after Mara.

Trying to stop the forming lump, Dorian cleared her throat.

The rab-cat stiffened and leaned forward.

"Floppy, no!" Dorian shouted.

He backed a step, shook his head, then leaned over again, his ears going forward. They wriggled as if he were thinking aloud, then he spun and charged to Tristan, who sat slumped. Floppy grabbed Tristan's shirt in his teeth and yanked as if trying to drag the human toward the canyon's edge.

"Stop it," Dorian said. "Let him alone."

The rab-cat batted Tristan's hand to get his attention.

Tristan looked up. Floppy tugged at him again. Tristan spoke in a faint voice. "We'll go down and bury her later. I can't...I just can't right now."

The rab-cat shook his head then kneaded Kellen's shoulder as if trying to wake him. The human didn't wiggle.

Dorian could feel the rab-cat's desperate need to communicate. She cleared her scanner, put it on record then placed it down on the floor. "Use this."

Floppy's green eyes met hers in relief, then he bent over the keyboard and began to tap at the keys with his paw.

When he finished, she read the message. "Mara not dead. Feel her." Dorian explained kindly, "A human couldn't survive a fall like that, Floppy. She has to be dead. You only feel what you wish to be true."

Shaking his head no, the rab-cat typed, "Mother die. Stop feeling her. Mara alive."

Tristan sat up. "Floppy's mother was killed when he was a kitten. Maybe he's right."

"An eight-story fall onto rough terrain. She was crushed, Tris."

He jumped to his feet as if he hadn't heard her. "I'm going down to look."

With a sigh, Dorian bent back over Kellen. Perhaps it would be better for both Tristan and Floppy to find Mara's body and know for sure.

FOR the first time since Mara had disappeared over the edge of the canyon, Tristan felt as if he were stepping out of the fog that enveloped him into cold unfeeling. Only his need to see Dorian, Kellen, and Floppy to safety had kept him moving. He fastened a rope clamp into the stone floor of the passageway and connected a rope to it. He yanked it to test it then slung his pack onto his back.

Floppy nudged his leg and motioned to himself with his ears.

"Let me look first. If... if you're wrong, I don't want you to have to..." He shuddered at the images in his mind. "Let me check first."

Dorian said, "Be careful. I need you, Tris. Kellen needs you, too. Don't take chances."

"I won't." Tristan clicked on the light which hung from his belt then began to climb down the rock face into the darkness. The air around him felt strangely spongy with the bouncy tension of a child's trampoline. He'd never felt anything like it. He journeyed downward, his circle of light tiny in the great darkness. After an eternity of hope for Mara and its opposite—resignation, he touched solid ground. Unhooking his light, he shone it around him. The floor was rocky and rough as if this had once been a subterranean river bottom. He turned left toward where Mara had fallen and began to trudge forward.

"Hello?" A tentative voice floated in the thick darkness.

His heart smashed into his ribs as he called out, "Mara?"

"Tristan?"

Stumbling among the rocks, he ran toward the voice. His light caught a faint shadow. As he neared it, the shadow became Mara standing there.

He threw his arms around her and pulled her into his chest, expecting her to vanish like the ghost she must be.

She embraced him fiercely and buried her face into his shoulder.

"Oh God, oh God, thank you. Thank you for this miracle," Tristan muttered into her filthy hair and began to cry.

Mara sobbed with relief against him, her fingers clutching his skin as if she feared he'd disappear.

When he could finally speak, he asked, "Are you hurt?"

"Skinned knees and hands from tripping in the darkness. You?" Her voice was harsh with exhaustion.

"Fine."

"Floppy, Kellen, Dorian?"

"All fine. Kellen got a mild knock on the head. How did you?"

"Riordan, Zar, others?"

"I don't know. A cave-in blocked them from us. What happened to you?"

"Fell fast at first then when passed canyon edge, slowed down. Floated like a feather to the floor."

His chuckle sounded near hysteria. "An antigravity unit."

"The mountain ghosts must use it as a bridge across these gaps in their passages. They just walk across the open spaces."

"But then why did you go downward?"

"We must weigh more than they do. It's set up for their weight." Mara laughed and rubbed her face into his shoulder. "Figured it out while I waited. Had little else good to think about down in this darkness. Thank the Goddess you heard me shouting. I thought I'd be left down here to starve."

"Didn't hear you. Heard nothing. Flop felt you from the edge of the canyon."

"The antigravity must dampened sound and everything else."

"Mmmm hmmm." He kissed the top of her head. "Let's get out of here." He led her to his rope. "Can you climb?"

"Watch." She grabbed the rope and struggled upward a few feet before sagging back. "Sorry."

"I'll climb up." He handed her an extra light from his pack and his climber's belt. "Put this on and hook yourself to the rope in a few minutes. I'll pull you up."

Nodding, Mara cut on the light.

Tristan began to climb. He struggled upward a few yards. It was like crawling through cold molasses. He released the rope and floated to the floor. "Damn. The antigravity's one way. It has us trapped."

DORIAN knelt by Tristan's rope and stared down into the darkness. He'd been gone for ages. What could be happening?

Floppy trotted back from his perch near where Mara had fallen. He cocked his head. "Not a thing," Dorian said. "Could you hear anything?"

The rab-cat shook his head no. The rope wiggled. Dorian caught it, but couldn't feel human weight on the other end. After several minutes, it wiggled again. Recalling that early divers used a rope to communicate with the surface, she began to pull at the rope.

It came up grudgingly, but she kept hauling. Tristan's notebook was attached to its end.

She and Floppy bent over it, and she read aloud, "Mara is unhurt. Sents use antigravity unit to cross canyon. It slowed her descent. Now antigravity holds us here. When Kellen able, drag Mara up. Will stay right here until then."

Dorian blinked tears and covered her mouth with her hands. "Oh, Floppy, you were right."

His eyes glistening, Floppy bounced up and down like a ball.

When the relieved euphoria faded, Dorian frowned. If the antigravity was so strong, she and Kellen alone wouldn't be able to haul Mara up, let alone Tristan. What could they do?

THE suffocating darkness seeped around Tristan's meager light as if wishing to kill it and the two humans it cheered. Tristan yawned and stared into the blackness. He leaned back against the canyon wall where they sat.

Mara stirred against his side and yawned into his shoulder. He caressed the top of her head. "Have a nice nap?"

"Lovely. Any news?"

"No."

"Hope Kellen is getting better."

"With his hard head, no problem."

She giggled sleepily into Tristan's chest.

"How are you feeling? Any twinges?"

"I am fine. The baby is fine, if you're interested."

"I care about the child, too. I find it difficult to talk about it. This isn't the way I'd planned to have my first child."

"Or the woman you wanted to have it with." Her voice was more sad than angry.

"I was happy to commit myself to you until Dory...It's hard to explain."

"You love her; you don't love me. Simple."

"Simple," Tristan added miserably. Simple when he considered all the years he'd known Dorian and the depth of their emotional relationship. Not so simple when he considered his sexual feelings for Mara and the strength of his emotions when he'd thought her dead.

Simple when he didn't think about the hollowness he felt at the possibility of not having Mara in his future. Simple.

DORIAN knelt by Kellen's sleeping form and daubed his lips with a dampened medical sponge. He jerked and opened his eyes, staring wildly about him.

She stroked his hair. "It's all right. You're safe, Kellen."

He drew away from her fingers. Frowning, she hastily withdrew her hand from him. "Sorry. How are you feeling?"

"Head aches. What?"

"You have a concussion. Rocks fell on you. Remember?"

"Yeah. Tris?"

Dorian opened her mouth to tell him the truth then changed her mind. He wasn't quite ready for the news which, though happy, would shoot up all his vital signs. "He's scouting ahead with Floppy."

Kellen studied her suspiciously. She picked up her scanner and began a fresh reading of his condition. When she finished, she gave him her best bed-side manner smile. "I imagine you're ready for something to eat."

"Starved."

Bending, she slid her arm under his shoulders and helped him sit up, then tucked her pack behind him. As she was releasing him, she felt his eyes burning her face. She glanced down. His gaze caught hers, sexual attraction flaring like a nova between them. She caught her breath as wanting flooded through her.

For an eternal instant, they stared into each other's eyes, then Kellen reached up, caught her behind her neck, and pulled her down to him. Their lips met.

He kissed her with a harsh urgency that had nothing of tenderness in it. She relaxed into him, her own passion answering that animal hunger. Her body exploded with the empty longing of two never-ending years.

His lips left hers, and he shoved her away.

Sitting up, she covered her lips with her hand in surprise at the intensity of her reaction.

Kellen said coldly, "That was what you wanted, wasn't it? You with your hands all over me. That's the best I can give you."

Anger burnt where hunger had been, and she replied with equal chilliness, "That was tenderness I was showing. But, perhaps, you've forgotten what that is. Or maybe you've never known." She glowered at him. "If you don't know the difference between tenderness and lust, love and sex, I pity you." Turning away, she peeled open a cup of vegetable soup. She lifted it and waited for the cup to heat the soup.

Kellen said quietly, "I know what love is. About four years ago, I went to a party with Tris, and I saw this tall, leggy beauty with gorgeous brown hair and eyes. Something peculiar happened inside. Instant lust I'd felt before, but not this strong. And my heart gave a peculiar twist like I'd never felt before. I met her, and my heart twisted harder at her tenderness, intelligence, and fire."

Dorian didn't turn despite her inclination to. "Love at first sight?"

"Something like that. But the funniest thing. She wasn't even aware of me. Not really. And I knew I had no hope of winning her because she could only see the husband she was so crazy in love with."

"That's sad."

"Yes, it was. So I went away, and when I came back to Earth, she was a widow and beginning to heal from the terrible grief, but she'd gotten it in her fool head that she was in love with a man who was like a brother to her, and so I..."

Dorian jerked with awareness and spun. "Kellen!"

"No, his name was Tristan, and he wasn't in love with her either so I dragged him off to a conference so they could both learn the error of their ways, and I could woo the gorgeous lady myself, but then my ship was....Well, you know the rest of the story."

"I'm stunned. I don't know what to say." She handed him the soup cup.

Kellen studied her over its rim then sipped. "Then don't say anything at all."

"I love Tristan."

"I do, too, but I don't want to marry him. You don't either. It'd be like marrying your brother."

"You're wrong."

"No, I'm not. I'm trained in body language. Body language and emotions are as much a language as what comes out of your mouth. You both act like—"

"You're wrong," she said weakly.

"No, I'm not." He shrugged and drank again. "Doesn't matter to me anymore. I can't offer a woman anything, that damn Arden and the lotus made sure of that, but you and Tris deserve better than a lustless marriage, and Tristan and Mara..." His voice trailed off, and he swore. "Not even a happy ending for the Angel of Arden."

Dorian took the half-empty cup from him and told him the truth about what Tristan had discovered in the canyon, then got up to let him have privacy to digest that shock.

Digesting her own shock, she walked down the passageway a bit. Floppy had gone on a scouting mission many hours before, and she was beginning to be worried. Far beyond, the walls began to glow orange, the brightness moving toward her with the swiftness of a rab-cat.

Floppy bounced down the passage toward her, skidded to a stop, motioned she follow, then retreated. Intrigued, she walked after him.

He finally came to a halt and watched her expectantly. Beside him was a creature four feet high, humanoid-shaped, and covered with grayish fur. It had a face like a chipmunk, but flatter, with twinkling black button eyes. It wore a long robe of shining fabric.

Dorian smiled. This cute creature would be a charming model for a child's stuffed toy. Then her heart leaped in her throat. Floppy had found one of the mountain ghosts. She raised her hand in greeting and wished Kellen with his first contact skills were here.

The mountain ghost, the supposedly horrifying creature of the smugglers' tales, raised his six-fingered hand in reply and chittered pleasantly.

Dorian laughed with relief. Rescue, it seemed, had come in the form of two sentients cuddly enough to be teddy bears.

HER hands rubbing against its pleasantly squishy surface, Dorian leaned back in her living fungus chair and studied the room. Its stone walls and floors were covered with a textured moss of varying and pleasing patterns, its slightly rounded ceiling glowed like a daffodil in spring sunlight. All the furnishings were made of growing fungus and mushrooms whose shapes and textures were created by genetic manipulation.

Tristan and Kellen sat together on a sofa. Facing them, also seated, were two sentients—a male and female, and an elderly human male called Shaw. Mara perched on a mushroom stool to Kellen's left with her attention divided between the social chitchat and Floppy, who chased after a ball on the floor with a toddler sentient.

Dorian stroked her temples. The last four days since they'd been rescued seemed like an Alice in Wonderland dream. The mountain ghosts...She shook her head. They called themselves a word which sounded like 'E' and a hiccup which Shaw said translated into 'Children of the Rock.' Dorian thought of them as the E. The E male had rescued

Tristan and Mara from the antigravity canyon and had arranged transportation into the E city where they'd discovered they weren't the first humans to meet these illusive beings.

Shaw, whether that was his first or last name he didn't say, had lived among the E for over ten years. One the first smugglers on Eagle's Haven, he'd wandered into an E city by accident, liked who and what he saw, and remained, leaving only to spy among the humans to discover their intentions about the peaceful E and to disperse frightening tales of the E among the humans.

His presence had speeded Kellen and Tristan's diplomatic negotiations with the E because he acted as both a representative of the sentients and as a translator. Kellen hadn't needed to learn the E language, but he obviously itched to know the people and their culture better.

Shaw translated the E female's chittered pleasantry to Mara about Floppy, who played with her child, then cleared his throat as if ready to get down to the business of this meeting between the humans and the E dignitaries who visited them.

His blue eyes shrewdly examining the other humans, Shaw fingered his white beard and spoke with a slight burr of a Scottish accent. "The Children of the Rock and I have talked long and well about you. Decided we have that you be decent folk, and we'll let you leave our city with our blessings."

Dorian straightened. She hadn't been aware they'd been prisoners. She'd never felt the least bit threatened or afraid of these charming chipmunk-faced humanoids. Tristan and Kellen showed no emotion but pleasure. They must have guessed.

Tristan bowed with the dignity of a head of state. "We thank you for your trust. We will honor your request for silence on all we have seen."

"Very good then." Shaw smiled. "The Children also will grant ye one of their large firestones." He chuckled. "You'll not be telling Haloran the stones are common down here?"

Kellen laughed. "And let that 'unique' stone lose its value to us and to Haloran's king? I don't think so."

"We will remain silent on this subject as well," Tristan promised. "These kind people don't wish to be trampled by human miners."

Shaw said, "The Children have no objection to sharing this planet with Haloran's people. They, after all, live underground in the mountains, and the humans live above in the flat lands, and Haloran has always left us in peace, but the Children do not wish to have the other humans remain with Haloran gone."

Tristan nodded. "He is the civilizing influence on the smugglers. Without him, they will fall into violence and anarchy."

"Exactly my feelings on the matter."

"We will stipulate all the humans exit as the price for the firestone," Tristan said. "Or Haloran must return the stone to you."

Shaw rubbed his hands. "Then we're all done then. Everything's all right and tight between us."

"We're done," Tristan agreed. "Do you wish to come with us? We can arrange for you to leave with the other humans."

"Nay, here I am and here I stay till I join my adopted peoples' ancestors in the rocks. I've seen enough of humans, and I dinna like what I saw much of the time. These folks talk of peace and kindness and actually live it."

Kellen said, "One day, may I come back? Just to learn?"

"You're welcome to come. You and other searchers of peace, knowledge, and understanding. The Children will welcome such visitors."

"Thank you." Kellen smiled, his eyes content and at rest as Dorian had never seen them.

In response, her heart twisted with a tenderness so great it hurt. She leaned back in her chair in stunned surprise. Somehow, somewhere, some time, she'd started to fall in love with Kellen Votrain. Wounded, vulnerable Kellen who could never return that love.

Chapter 24

Her eyes misting with tears, Mara hugged Princess Linnea and murmured, "I will miss you so much."

Linnea brushed her cheek with warm lips. "You must come visit me on Tara. As soon as your baby can travel."

Mara pulled away and swiped away tears. "I'd like that." Around her on the tarmac of Prince Saxon's private space port, Tristan, Dorian, and Kellen were saying goodbye to the prince. As if eager to leave, Floppy sat, waiting for them, in the hatchway of *The Trojan Horse.*

Mara walked over to Zar, who stood near the prince and Hoshi. She went up on her toes and kissed his scaly cheek. "Thank you. Floppy told me how you saved him from the rock slide and hurt your arm."

The lizard man wriggled with pleasure and patted his bandaged left arm. "Soon be better. For golden one and brave little smart cat is nothing." She smiled farewell and strode to Prince Riordan, who stood stiffly nearby as if aware he wasn't particularly welcome.

Holding out her hand to him, she said gently, "Goodbye, Prince Riordan."

Ignoring her hand, he blinked with surprise, his face still puffy and black from the punch Tristan had delivered the first time they'd seen each other after the cavern fight with Cadaran. Riordan had not returned the blow.

"I don't blame you for my fall. It was an accident." She lowered her hand.

Riordan's gaze shifted toward Tristan, Kellen, and his brother. "I blame myself as do others. Your death would have been from my own stupidity and unwillingness to miss the fighting."

"I'm just so relieved that none of your men were seriously hurt in the fighting." She offered her hand again. "Friends?"

He bowed and kissed her fingers. "Always."

"Love and wisdom don't come when we expect it, but they usually come if we are willing to change and grow," Mara said. "Or at least that's what a special woman with tender eyes told me today."

"If Linnea says it to be true, I have hope." Riordan released

Mara's hand.

She reached the others as Prince Saxon said, "I've determined that someone in my palace fed Cadaran the information about your quest into the mountains. So few knew about it." He glanced toward Hoshi, the Seneschal. "I've learned a great many surprising things since I've looked into my business affairs with Cadaran Hastings. A very many unpleasant things. And someone will pay."

"What have you heard about her location, Your Highness?" Kel-len asked.

"Hastings and her troops are still hiding somewhere on the pla-net. She had such a head start after trapping Riordan and his men in the tunnels that she could be anywhere."

Kellen nodded politely although the news was days old. "Then you haven't found her secret base where she's hidden her ship?"

"No, but if she tries to come after you, my men will blast her from the sky." The Prince motioned toward the wicked looking man-ned fighters near their ship.

"Very good, Your Highness," Tristan said. "This is farewell then. We wish you the best of luck in your negotiations with your king."

"We'll be home soon. You gave me an ample bribe to assure me of that. This planet will be empty of humans within a year, and I'll blast enough of the asteroids into different orbits so that none of the pi-lot programs will work. I will keep my end of the bargain with the mountain ghosts."

"Your honor was never in question, sir." Tristan bowed again, and Mara and the others boarded the ship. Mara waved goodbye then went into the control room and strapped herself down in her chair. Floppy hopped onto her lap.

Kellen started the ship engines. "Everyone in their seats?"

Mara wrapped her arms around Floppy. "Ready."

"We're all set. Let's get the hell out of here and go home." Tris-tan buckled himself down.

"Your word is my command." Kellen punched on their autopilot exit program and settled his hands over the ship's controls in case of emergency.

They soared upward, their view screen filled with clouds, then they were in space. The ring of asteroids loomed above them.

Blips appeared on the scanner screen. Kellen glanced down. "That's the prince's fighter squadron."

Mara's racing heart slowed, and she breathed deeply in relief.

They were safe now. In less than a month they would be on Earth, and she would start a new life without Tristan.

Her gaze drifted to him. He sat bolt upright, his eyes on the scanner and view screen. His hand in his lap wiggled as if he were men-tally guiding the ship around the asteroids surrounding them. Past him, Dorian gazed with pained fascination at the asteroids. Sweat glazed her face.

Mara stroked Floppy's head thoughtfully. Ever since they'd been rescued by the mountain people, everyone had been acting strangely. Both Tristan and Dorian were uncomfortable with each other and unhappy as if some emotional problems worried them. And Dorian absolutely fidgeted around Kellen and would hardly look at him or say a word to him. But she wasn't angry with him anymore. When Kellen wasn't fighting bouts of depression about his own blighted emotional future, he positively smirked with self-satisfaction as if he knew something the others didn't about themselves.

Floppy remained Floppy. His only change had been his tendency to stay closer to her since her near death, but already he was relaxing enough to spend more time with the others.

Mara, herself, was so filled with gratitude for her and her baby's lives being spared that she was almost resigned to living without Tristan. Her baby would be loved and have a wonderful, safe future, and she would take her comfort from the child's happiness. She would survive as her mother had—alone. At least her true love would be alive and happy somewhere.

Kellen swore violently.

Her eyes drawn back to the view screen, Mara gazed at the enormous pock-marked asteroid in front of them. Cadaran's ship rose like a malevolent spirit out of its biggest crater and fired at them.

Kellen grabbed at the controls, but *The Horse* jerked into a straight climb, slamming them into their seats. The energy bolts blasted past their ship, rocking it slightly.

"God bless Tor and his grandstanding," Tristan whispered. "I'll handle the weapons." Leaning forward, he began to finger the control panel in front of him.

Their ship shook as its energy bolts fired. Cadaran's ship dodged with a slight roll and swooped toward them like a bird after a bug.

A tiny asteroid exploded near their nose. Kellen swerved the ship to avoid the debris. "Prince's fighters coming up behind us."

Mara wondered if the fighters were after them, too. Ready for the kill, Cadaran's ship hung over them.

The Horse dove under an asteroid as the Prince's fighters fanned out above them and strafed Cadaran's ship.

"Hot damn," Kellen said. "I want a chunk of her hull myself."

"No!" Tristan's voice filled the control room. "No. Get us out of here. We don't have the weapons or shield for this, and we paid Haloran to stop her. We almost paid too high a price."

Mara colored, realizing he was referring to her.

"But..." Kellen protested.

"Now. They're giving us a head start if they can't stop her. Let's not waste it."

The struggle between his hatred of Cadaran and his common sense was visible on Kellen's face. He tightened his lips, his fingers moving on the controls. "One head start coming up."

THE head start hadn't been long enough, Kellen thought as he studied the scanner and the blip behind them. Cadaran would catch up with them in fifty-two hours.

He leaned back in his command chair. He was out of ideas to save them. Their only option seemed to be to run until caught and then destroy themselves and Cadaran with them.

That possibility no longer comforted him as it once had. He'd discovered he wanted to live again and rebuild. He'd known it since the Angel of Arden had smiled vulnerably at him and asked him to be her friend, and he'd rediscovered his own tenderness. He had known it since he'd seen the flame of something deeper and more beautiful than lust blossom in Dorian's eyes when she gazed at him, and his own reawakened heart had answered it. He had known it since Tristan's certainty of his feelings toward Dorian had been shaken to its roots by Mara's near death.

But how could they survive with Cadaran so close?

"Kell?" Tristan's voice made him jump.

Kellen spun around in his chair. "Thought you were going to bed. I can take this shift."

"I was but..." Tristan grinned crookedly. "I was still edgy so I decided to clean up our room some and found this." He held out a filthy, ripped pair of his pants. "It was under your bunk."

"So? Should I weep over its condition or apologize for kicking it under my bed?"

"Funeral services will be held later this evening." Tristan chuckled. “No. I wore these that day on Scarpia when Cadaran blew up the ICC tower.” He pulled out a sadly rumpled news story printout from its pocket. “I found this. I shoved it in my pocket in the ICC office and forgot it.”

“Oh, you’ve come to read me the comics.” Kellen clapped his hands like a child. “Goody.”

“Later, maybe. First, I want to tell you about this article.” He pointed at the paper. “There’s a brand new military outpost we can reach before Cadaran catches up with us. It’s on Groat about fifty-two hours from here, and Jack Wildonson has been assigned as commander.”

Kellen straightened. “Hot damn, I saved his butt on Abercrombie Two.”

“As well as the rest of his anatomy. Here’s my plan. Cadaran will be on our tail by the time we reach the planet so we’ll have hide our ship when we land and go it on foot so she won’t shoot us down. She’ll expect us to try to send another message on the ICC net. I’ll pretend to do that. Draw her away from you while you head toward Jack’s outpost. He’ll believe you, even with our outlandish story and without Geoffrey’s backing. You get him and his troops and come to my rescue.”

“And Mara and Dorian?”

“Safely in the ship. We’ll draw Cadaran away from it.”

“No.” They turned at Mara’s voice. She stood behind them, wearing a robe over her gown, her sleep-tousled hair falling over her shoulders. Floppy stood at her side.

“Mara, you should be in bed.” Tristan said.

She lifted her chin. “I was hungry, and I won’t sit in this ship while you risk your life.”

Kellen chided, “You have the baby to think of. You don’t need more gravity sickness or an injury.”

“I have the baby’s father to think of, too. Your plan won’t work. How can you find Tristan in time? Cadaran could kill him before you do. I’ll go with Tristan.”

“All you’ll be is another hostage to her,” Tristan said.

“No, I’ll be a homing device Cadaran can’t stop from sending. Floppy can go with Kellen as evidence he has been on Arden, then Floppy can lead the rescue to us before Cadaran has a chance to hurt either of us.”

“I don’t like this,” Tristan protested.

Her shoulders straightening, Mara stared belligerently into his eyes. "You don't have to like it, and you have no real choice. We all escape Arden, or we all die trying. That's the only way I'll accept it, and if Dorian loves you half as much as I do, it's the only way she'll accept it either."

KELLEN and Dorian ran through a forest on Groat toward the militar-y outpost. He glanced at Dorian who loped alongside, her braid tossing in the breeze. His heart and loins ached with love and lotus pain.

Puffing slightly, he slowed then stopped. "A quick break. Until Floppy comes back from scouting ahead."

She nodded tersely and leaned forward, resting her hands on her thighs. Sunlight and leaf shadows dappled the luscious curves of her body and long legs. "God, you're beautiful."

Color rushed into her cheeks.

He flushed, realizing he'd spoken his thoughts aloud. "You are. And as spirited and brave as a wild horse."

"Thank you."

"I wish..." All the might-have-beens that Arden had stolen from him filled his voice with wistfulness.

She studied his face. "I wish, too."

"You do?" His heart began to pound against his ribs.

"You were right. A brother. Exactly like a brother. Kissing Tris felt like incest." Flames of love and passion glowed in her eyes as she looked at him.

Kellen's jaw hurt from the broadness of his smile "I'm glad for you both."

"Are you sure?"

"Absolutely. He's realizing himself the difference between how he feels for you and Mara. I hope he figures that out completely before he loses his brave pixie, who gave up everything because she loves him so much."

"He's surprisingly insecure."

"Aren't we all about love."

A long minute passed, their gazes linked, before she spoke aloud again. "If...when we get out of this mess...I have a beautiful horse farm in the Shenandoah Valley, a huge airy house. A place for healing and being free. You're welcome to stay with me while you're recupera-ting."

"Recuperating being a polite name for therapy."

"There's no shame in seeking help."

"No, there isn't."

Her brown eyes speared him again straight through the heart. "There are no strings attached in the offer. I don't expect anything physically or emotionally in return."

"I don't have anything physically or emotionally to return any more. I may never again."

"I know, but we deserve a chance to at least try with each other."

He smiled at her. "Then I trust you enough to come."

"I'm glad. And honored."

A small black blur of fur bounded toward them. "There's Floppy. Let's get going. Another twenty minutes or so of running, and we'll reach the outpost."

CADARAN and her troopers were close; Mara could feel them.

Her hackles rising, she followed Tristan through the dense woods toward the tiny town near Groat's only space port.

The forest was still, even the massive green leaves in the hardwoods unmoving in the slight breeze. The tiny creatures and birds which hopped and chirped cheerfully through the limbs were silent now as if aware of approaching danger. Leaves crunched with obscene loudness under her feet as she hastened after Tristan. He walked faster as if sensing their pursuers.

The total greenness made her even more nervous. Where were the pink trees and shrubs of a proper forest?

Tristan stiffened, grabbed her wrist, and led her toward a large outcropping of rock. She could hear nothing, but Tristan had splendid warrior's instincts so she followed without protest.

He pulled her down into a tiny cul-de-sac among the rocks, and they hid by crouching. Mara closed her eyes and listened for Cadaran. His thigh rubbed against hers, and his heat and male scent twined around and through her. An ache starting at her heart and womb, she sighed.

Forcing her eyes open, she tried to concentrate on their danger, but all she could think of was Tristan's body joined with hers. It had been too long since they'd been one.

Tristan's blue eyes glowed as their gazes locked. She blushed, fearing he read her thoughts.

The metallic hiss of a communicator almost beside them.

The forest and their danger rushed back into Mara's awareness.

She scrunched down further into their tiny hiding place.

Cadaran spoke, "Yes?"

The communicator hissed again, then a tinny female voice said, "We have located the black-headed male and the Earth female."

"Have you engaged them yet?"

"Negative. We intend to ambush them at the rock quarry near the military outpost we sighted from the air. They are heading directly through that quarry."

"Very good. Take the man alive but kill the woman. We'll continue after the other pair and meet you back at the ship. Cadaran out."

Tristan turned a sick white, and his hand tightened into a fist in the dirt. Mara touched his shoulder in comfort then refocused her at-tention back on Cadaran.

Feet crunched through the leaves past them, then moved away from their hiding place.

He pulled Mara into his arms.

His lips brushed her ears as he whispered, "I must warn them. I can reach them before they arrive at the quarry. You'll only slow me down and risk the baby. Stay here in hiding until Floppy or I come back for you."

Mara nodded. Their role as bait had been a miserable failure. Tristan's choice was the only logical one. Her illogical heart twisted violently, knowing she risked losing him if he were caught. She kissed his cheek. "Don't worry about me. They won't hurt me because I'm pregnant. The baby makes my health sacrosanct by law and our deepest felt customs."

"Cadaran hasn't been stopped by any of your moral laws yet." He brushed a kiss on her forehead. "Take care, pixie, and don't do anything stupid for the baby's sake."

She nodded a promise.

Turning, he vanished out of their hiding place like fog in wind.

Blinking tears, she concentrated on the sounds around her and prayed to the Goddess for their safety.

He hadn't been gone a minute when a rubbing on the stone Mara crouched behind warned her. She grabbed her laser pistol but was smashed face down into the ground by a huge trooper. The gun spun out of her hand.

As she lunged for the pistol, the trooper cracked her across the shoulder with her fist. Mara slumped. She wanted to keep fighting, but an inner voice reminded her of the baby and the impossibility of winning against a trained soldier twice her weight.

The trooper yanked her upright. "Filthy traitor! This is for Veta."

Mara's arms shielded her belly as the other woman's fist smash-ed toward her stomach. "I'm pregnant."

The fist didn't connect. The trooper glared at her with hatred but helped her gently to her feet and nudged her out of the cul-de-sac.

Mara staggered forward until they reached Cadaran in a nearby small clearing. Hallie and two other troopers stood behind her. Mara's gaze met Hallie's in pleading request, then she turned her attention to Cadaran.

Her huge brown eyes glowing, her hands on her hips, Cadaran smiled like a tyrlin before killing and examined Mara. "Well done, Ada. So, daughter of Jorel, I've found you at last. No reputation, stu-pid princeling and his pathetic fighters, or fellow scientists to help you here."

Lifting her chin proudly, she met Cadaran's gaze. "I need none."

Cadaran chuckled. "So tell me. Where is that pretty blond bed slave?"

"He was mortally wounded on Eagle's Haven."

"I won't accept lies." Cadaran slashed her open hand toward Mara's face.

Mara flinched but didn't cringe.

Ada plucked the hand out of the air and held it.

Cadaran stared with absolute disbelief at her trooper.

Ada dropped her commander's hand with a servile nod of apology. "She's pregnant, sir."

Cadaran's eyebrows went up, and she clenched her hand as if she fought her desire to hit Mara despite Ada and the other troopers' presence. "So, another beautiful little boy for my harem. How splendid."

"Never."

"I don't lose." Cadaran glanced around. "Well, he couldn't have gotten far." She unclipped her communicator from her belt and flipped a switch. Her voice boomed out of the communicator and seemed to shake the silent forest. "Tristan Mallory, I have Mara. Surrender to me now, or I'll blow her head off. I'll kill her if you aren't here in five minutes."

"You won't shoot me. He knows you won't."

"He knows I will. With great pleasure." Cadaran smiled again, and Mara realized she would.

Mara's heart twisted. Tristan wouldn't come back. Especially not when he thought Cadaran wouldn't shoot her. Even if he did believe she would, he'd choose Dorian's life over Mara's because he loved Dorian. If Mara had the same terrible decision to make, she'd choose Tristan's life over Kellen's. She'd hate herself forever, but she'd choose Tristan as Tristan would choose Dorian.

Chapter 25

Cadaran's words echoed through the forest around Tristan as he ran toward the rock quarry. He jerked to a halt, heaving for air. Fear lanced through him like a laser. Mara!

Closing his eyes, he saw her falling downward into that abyss, her hands flailing for purchase. He remembered Cadaran's merciless eyes and imagined her casually blasting Mara.

Shuddering, he spun to run back. But Dorian! Cadaran had ordered her death, too.

His heart ripped inside him. Dorian or Mara?

He recalled Mara saying, "You love her; you don't love me. Simple."

"Oh, God!" He bent his head and pounded on his temples with his wrists. Which one? Dorian was as dear as Elaine was, but Mara...Sweet, loving Mara. Passionate, sexy Mara. Funny, brilliant Mara. Mara who made his heart sing and his blood boil. Mara, the woman he loved and couldn't bear to lose again. This time forever.

Mara! He jolted upright, his feelings clear for the first time in months. He loved Mara, only Mara. Eternally Mara. As she loved him.

Simple.

He began to run back to where he'd left her.

CADARAN yanked Mara against her, forcing her right arm behind her back, and poked a laser pistol into her temple.

Mara held herself erect and serene. Her gaze caught Hallie's again, and she remembered the trooper playing ball with Floppy in her garden. Hallie's face twisted with sadness and disgust, but she made no move to stop her commanding officer.

Minutes trickled like the runnels of cold sweat down Mara's back. A flying insect circled them then disappeared into the golden sunlight filtering through the trees.

Mara thought a prayer for everyone she loved and was leaving behind.

The troopers stirred restlessly. One whispered, "But she's

pregnant!"

Another muttered, "Only women have honor. He won't come."

Cadaran yawned. "Kneel. I don't want to spatter my uniform with your blood and brains."

Mara stared beseechingly at Hallie and the other troopers, but only lowered eyes met hers.

Cadaran twisted Mara's arm, forcing her downward. Kneeling, Mara closed her eyes tight. The cold muzzle of the laser pistol caressed her temple, and the other woman chuckled.

"No, wait!" At Tristan's shout, Mara's eyes shot open. Tristan stood at the edge of the clearing. His chest heaved as if he'd run hard.

Mara blinked tears of relief, of grief for what Tristan now faced, and selfish happiness that he'd chosen to come back for her. Gasping hard, Tristan smiled at her, his eyes ocean deep with love and tenderness.

Holding his hands above his head, he tossed his laser pistol to the ground in front of him. "Don't hurt her. I'm here."

Not lifting her weapon from Mara's head, Cadaran ordered the troopers, "Take him."

Her face as sick with relief as Mara's must be, Hallie circled Tristan and forced his arms behind his back. The manacles snapped closed.

Cadaran straightened and holstered her gun. "Let me see. The proper punishment for them. Ada, restrain her."

The burly trooper pulled Mara up and began to manacle her hands behind her back.

Tristan struggled against Hallie. "You promised you wouldn't hurt her if I came."

"And I won't. I'll take her back to Arden. After the baby's born, I'll give her to the harem school for the young men to practice their bed techniques on, and she'll give me many fine boys for the harem and girls to sell to childless women."

"You filthy bitch."

"Now you..." Cadaran smashed her fist into her open hand. "Hallie, fasten his arms over that limb. I intend to teach this slave some manners."

Hallie answered quietly, "No," and stepped from behind Tristan.

Cadaran shook her head in disbelief. "Insubordination from you, Lieutenant?"

"I won't allow you to abuse him. His honor and courage shame us all, especially a coward like me." Hallie raised her pistol to cover Cadaran and Ada. "I won't harm him or allow you to."

"You won't..." She motioned to the other troopers. "Take her."

The other two troopers lifted their laser pistols and aimed them at Cadaran.

Hallie didn't even glance at them. "I told those I trust the truth. They know what you are. We know about the plague no longer existing, and about the men being abused for your profit, and how you tell women their baby boys die of the plague and how you really steal them for the harem. We've seen too much evidence to deny the truth about it and you. We had a ship trial and found you guilty."

The troopers nodded.

Cadaran shrugged. "So? We all profit from a few lies. I've always shared my wealth and power with my troops. I've treated you well. I always will. And after all, we're only talking about men, not someone important. Let's just forget this happened, and I won't punish you."

"It won't be forgotten. Everyone on Arden knows the truth. Right before we left home, someone put irrefutable proof of your crimes on the communication channels. We intend to take you home to stand trial."

Ada grunted with stolid disbelief. "It's the truth?"

Cadaran laughed as if amused at her naive stupidity.

"The baby boys stolen and not dead?" Ada stepped away from Mara, reached into her holster with two fingers, and tossed her pistol at Hallie's feet. "My momma lost a boy when I was little. It almost killed her with grief."

All her years of power and command emanating from her, Cadaran seemed to grow taller. "Obey me, or I'll have you shot for the mutinous traitors you are."

The troopers shifted uneasily on their feet, but Hallie straightened. "You are the traitor. All Arden knows the truth about you, and will condemn you for it."

Tristan said, "If your most loyal troops damn you like this, no one else on Arden will support you either. Give up, Cadaran. You've lost."

"Never!" Worry flickered across Cadaran's smug face as if she realized her absolute power was crumbling.

Hallie released Tristan's manacles then handed him her gun. She pointed the manacle controls at Mara and said apologetically, "I wouldn't have let her shoot you." Mara's manacles slipped off her wrists and fell to the ground. With a nervous glance at Cadaran and

Hallie, Mara bent and scooped up Ada's laser pistol.

Cadaran drew her pistol and aimed at Hallie.

Tristan blasted the pistol out of Cadaran's hand.

"A man will never defeat me. Never!" Cadaran's face twisted with madness and hatred, her veneer of civilization vanishing, and she launched herself at Tristan.

He dodged her and smashed his elbow into her ribs. She fell. He holstered his gun. "I don't have to defeat you. You defeated yourself."

She screamed like a tyrlin and kicked at his legs. He jumped her moving feet then stepped back, his strength and courage an aura of dignity over him. "A man who isn't drugged and wired with a pain stimulator isn't so easy to beat. Especially a man trained in fighting by Kellen Votrain."

Nothing human remained of Cadaran as she leaped toward him, her nails and teeth seeking his throat.

Mara raised her gun, but Cadaran was too close to Tristan to risk a shot. Tristan punched her chin, and she crumbled face first onto the ground. Mara sagged with relief.

"She's all yours, Lt. Hallie. Take her home to trial."

Nodding, Hallie bent to pick up Tristan's manacles.

His smile as full of warmth as summer sun, he beamed at Mara and started toward her. Out of the corner of her eye, she saw Cadaran's hand reach for the laser pistol Tristan had dropped earlier. Before Mara could shout a warning the gun was pointed at Tristan's back.

A flash of black fur.

His ears down, his eyes blazing red, Floppy pounced on Cadaran's shoulders.

She collapsed, the gun falling out of her limp hand.

After a stunned moment, Mara gasped.

The rab-cat hopped off Cadaran's body.

Hallie knelt by Cadaran and felt for her pulse. "Live like a tyrlin, die like a tyrlin."

"A suitable epitaph." Tristan scooped up Floppy, then he was holding Mara, the purring rab-cat sandwiched between them. She clutched them both, her knees suddenly very shaky.

Armed men and women in blue uniforms charged toward them from all sides, and the unresisting Arden troopers were hustled away.

Puffing with exhaustion, Kellen and Dorian reached them. Kellen grinned and holstered his gun as he glanced at Cadaran's body. "Looks like we're too late."

Tristan laughed happily. "Just in time."

Mara found herself in a four person, one rab-cat hug as Kellen and Dorian wrapped their arms around them.

"We're free," Tristan whispered. "We're finally free."

"'Lord God Almighty, we're free at last.'" Kellen laughed.

"We thought her troops were going to capture and kill you," Mara said soberly.

"I captured them." Kellen pulled away.

Her hands on her hips, Dorian tossed her braid with a saucy flip of her head. "*We* captured them."

"Yes, *we* did." Kellen grinned jauntily.

Tristan breathed a great sigh of relief that belied his words. "I figured you could handle them without my help."

Kellen's rab-cat eyes met Tristan's in silent communication, then Kellen took Dorian's hand. He planted a big kiss on her lips. She enthusiastically kissed him back, her arms around his neck. "Come on, gorgeous. I want to introduce you properly to Jack Wildonson."

Dorian opened her mouth to protest then closed it and followed him with surprising docility.

Shocked, Mara watched them leave. Tristan caught her chin and turned her face toward him. His eyes drilled into hers, and she felt a shiver of cold and heat spread through her.

In her arms, Floppy squirmed to be let down. She brushed a kiss on his head. "Thank you, Floppy." She put him on the ground, and with a genial farewell wiggle of his ears, he trotted after Kellen and Dorian. "What in the world is going on?"

"This." Tristan led her away from the others. They stopped under an ancient tree, its limbs a canopy above them, and he drew her into his arms.

She sighed happily and rested her head on his shoulder, her arms around his waist. His heart pounded under her ear, and his essence filled her to completion. "We're finally free."

"Free to have a future together. If you still want me after the way I've acted."

"Toge..."

"Yes. I love you, Mara. I want to marry you and make love, baby astrophysicists, and black hole equations with you for the rest of my life."

"But Dorian—"

"Is like a sister to me, and I'm obviously like a brother to her.

She's never kissed *me* like that. It took me a long time to figure out, but I finally realized my true feelings a little while ago. I realized what a blind and insecure idiot I've been with you and that I should trust your love as I trust you. I do love Dorian, but it's the same way I love Elaine. It's not the way I've loved you from the moment I first saw you. I have no desire to do this with her." His lips nudged Mara's.

Her lips bumped playfully back, then they clung together, their lips meshing, their bodies melting into each other's. One of them quivered, then she felt his growing staff rubbing her thigh.

Groaning, he powdered kisses across her face.

She smiled coyly. "Do you wish to breed with me?"

"I want to, very, very much. Will you marry me, Mara?"

His eyes glowed with the brightness of Arden summer, and she saw within many more summers of love they would share together. "I still love you. I never stopped. Yes, Tristan, I want to, very, very much."

MARA shifted the baby in her arms so the baby and Floppy would both fit comfortably on her lap. Adam Randell Mallory gurgled and smiled as his rab-cat brother licked a kiss on his cheek.

Floppy's ears wiggled with delight.

Mara nodded. "Yes, he does look more like his father everyday. I didn't think it possible, but his eyes are getting bluer and his hair curlier."

In the chair beside hers, Tristan chuckled and leaned back. Sunlight sifted through the huge window above him and colored his hair a purer honey and their living room a glorious white. "Breeding will tell."

Kellen wrapped his arm around Dorian beside him on the couch, and she nestled against him. "My parents had blue and hazel eyes. I was kind of hoping Adam would have green eyes. That would keep all the busybodies wondering."

"Bite your tongue," Tristan said. "I've had enough lurid stories about us and public attention to last a lifetime. Oh, for the good old days of a scientist's obscurity."

"I don't think you've done badly. You are the acting delegate for Arden in the Earth Colony Congress."

"Co-delegate," Mara corrected.

Kellen bowed. "Forgive me, Your Excellency."

Floppy's ears wiggled.

"I'm corrected again by the rab-cat ambassador of Arden. You also are the acting human spokesmen for the rab-cats. I mustn't forget that. It's far more important a role than trying to protect the rights of ex-slavers."

Tristan shook his head. "You still can't put aside the hate even after Arden's women destroyed the harem and enfranchised the men."

"You weren't tortured while a whole world refused to help." Kellen looked away, and when he turned back toward them, his anger had eased. "I try to convince myself I should forgive, but I..."

Dorian squeezed his hand. "Our trip to Arden should help."

"That's the only reason I'm willing to help the women restructure their culture. My therapist doesn't think I can ever return Dorian's love as completely as I should until I put away the anger by helping to heal Arden." Kellen brushed a kiss on Dorian's lips. "And I want to return that special love more than anything else."

"First the bed, then a whole world." Dorian winked broadly.

"For you, gorgeous, whole galaxies." Kellen kissed her thoroughly.

As their lips parted, Dorian sighed happily. "Whole universes."

Kellen beamed. "Floppy and I are excited about becoming liaisons between his people and the humans. Hallie has made a small start with her rab-cats, but many more have yet to be contacted."

Floppy nodded vigorously.

Blinking tears, Mara caressed the rab-cat's head. "I'm going to miss you so much, but I understand why you must go home. I want you to find a wonderful mate so by the time Adam is old enough to accept heavy gravity, I can visit and meet her."

Floppy purred and twined his ears around her wrist.

Novia bustled into the room and held out a big white towel. "Time for Adam's bath. The Randells will be here soon."

Mara bounced the baby with her knee. "Bath, Adam, then Nana Randell?"

The baby gurgled.

"He can't wait." Mara regretfully let Novia take him. With a happy ear wiggle of farewell Floppy hopped down and followed Novia and the baby out of the room. Mara asked Dorian, "Would you like to help?"

"Oh, yes. It will be good practice for *later*." Dorian stood and tugged Kellen's hand. "Come on. You'll need practice, too."

"Where's *The Helen of Troy* when I need a quick escape?" Kellen trudged like a prisoner after Dorian, but as he reached the door to the hall, he grinned and winked. "All this, and she's as pretty as a Tenly sunset, too."

Tristan chuckled as they disappeared through the door. "I never thought I'd live to see him properly hooked and happy about it. Every planet he names will be after her from now on."

"Love is a wonderful thing."

"Yes, it is." Tristan growled, caught her wrist, and pulled her into his lap. "Come here, pixie."

Mara nestled against his chest. "I'm here, and you can't get rid of me."

"Who wants to?" He wrapped his arms around her waist and nuzzled her face. "I love you, Mara."

"I love you, Tristan. I always have, and I always will."

He nibbled a kiss in her hair. "When Kellen and I were on *The Helen*, I was very unhappy. I knew my life was empty, but I didn't know what was wrong. Then I made a silly wish on a yellow star, and all hell broke loose as we were attacked."

Mara twisted her head quizzically. "You wished to be attacked?"

"No." He traced the slope of her nose. "The star was your Trigellan, and it was the perfect star because it brought me exactly what I wished for—a very special pixie with a tender smile who'd fill all the empty spaces in my heart and life."

"Stars are magic. As real a magic as love and kinning. I'm glad that magic touched us."

"It's still touching us. It always will."

The End

Marilynn Byerly

Bestselling author Marilynn Byerly's writing passion is romantic adventure stories--past, present, and future. In her creations of swashbucklers, true love, and villains to vanquish, she also likes to add a dash of magic.

Her read life centers more sensibly around her family and pets. Her soulmate seems to be sitting out this reincarnation, but she enjoys spoiling her niece and nephews, reading, organic gardening, and surprising people with glints of the adventurer within.

Romantic Times, the bible of the romance industry, has called her an author to watch. *Affaire de Coeur* named her one of the five up-and-coming authors of 1998. Her paranormal romance, *Time After Time,* was voted one of the top 10 best ebooks in 1998 (Preditors & Editors Poll), and both the readers and reviewers of *Affaire de Coeur* named it one of the five best time-travel novels of 1998.

Printed in the United States
1412500001B/32

9 780759 901001